1/16.

Books should be returned or renewed by the last
date above. Renew by phone **03000 41 31 31** or
online *www.kent.gov.uk/libs*

_____

_____

SPECIAL MESSAGE TO READERS

THE ULVERSCROFT FOUNDATION
(registered UK charity number 264873)
was established in 1972 to provide funds for
research, diagnosis and treatment of eye diseases.
Examples of major projects funded by
the Ulverscroft Foundation are:-

- The Children's Eye Unit at Moorfields Eye Hospital, London
- The Ulverscroft Children's Eye Unit at Great Ormond Street Hospital for Sick Children
- Funding research into eye diseases and treatment at the Department of Ophthalmology, University of Leicester
- The Ulverscroft Vision Research Group, Institute of Child Health
- Twin operating theatres at the Western Ophthalmic Hospital, London
- The Chair of Ophthalmology at the Royal Australian College of Ophthalmologists

You can help further the work of the Foundation
by making a donation or leaving a legacy.
Every contribution is gratefully received. If you
would like to help support the Foundation or
require further information, please contact:

THE ULVERSCROFT FOUNDATION
The Green, Bradgate Road, Anstey
Leicester LE7 7FU, England
Tel: (0116) 236 4325

website: www.foundation.ulverscroft.com

Anne Perry is a *New York Times* bestselling author noted for her memorable characters, historical accuracy and exploration of social and ethical issues. Her two series, one featuring Inspector Thomas Pitt and one featuring Inspector William Monk, have been published in multiple languages. She has also published a successful series based around World War One and the Reavley family. Anne Perry was selected by *The Times* as one of the twentieth century's '100 Masters of Crime'. She now lives in Scotland.

DEATH ON BLACKHEATH

Greenwich, 1897: In the small area outside a
house on Shooters Hill, a macabre scene is
discovered. There has been a vicious fight,
and amid the bloodstains and broken glass
are torn locks of auburn hair. Thomas Pitt,
head of Special Branch, is called: this is the
home of Dudley Kynaston, an important
minister with access to some of the
government's most dangerous secrets, and
any inquiry must be handled with utmost
discretion. Although an auburn-haired maid
is missing from Kynaston's household, with
no body and no evidence there is little Pitt
can do. Until a corpse, mutilated beyond
recognition, is discovered a few weeks later
. . . As Pitt begins to investigate, what he
discovers could threaten not just Kynaston's
own family, but also his Queen and country.

ANNE PERRY

DEATH ON BLACKHEATH

Complete and Unabridged

CHARNWOOD
Leicester

First published in Great Britain in 2013 by
Headline Publishing Group
An Hachette UK Company
London

First Charnwood Edition
published 2016
by arrangement with
Headline Publishing Group
An Hachette UK Company
London

A catalogue record for this book is available
from the British Library.

ISBN 978–1–4448–2673–9

Published by
F. A. Thorpe (Publishing)
Anstey, Leicestershire

Set by Words & Graphics Ltd.
Anstey, Leicestershire
Printed and bound in Great Britain by
T. J. International Ltd., Padstow, Cornwall

This book is printed on acid-free paper

To Ileen Maisel

1

Pitt stood shivering on the steps leading up from the areaway to the pavement and looked down at the clumps of blood and hair at his feet. There was blood on the shards of glass as well, and some of it had already congealed. Splinters lay on the steps below and above. The January wind whined across the open stretch towards the gravel pits in the distance.

'And the maid is missing?' Pitt asked quietly.

'Yes, and sorry, sir,' the police sergeant said unhappily. His young face was set hard in the grey early morning light. 'Thought that seeing whose house it was, like, we should call you straight away.'

'You did the right thing,' Pitt assured him.

They were in Shooters Hill, a very pleasant residential area on the outskirts of London. It was not far from Greenwich, with the Naval College and the Royal Observatory from which the world took its time. The imposing house rising above them into the still, shadowed air was that of Dudley Kynaston, a senior government official deeply involved in matters of naval defence, a weapons expert of some kind. Violence so very close to his house was of concern to Special Branch, and thus to Pitt as its commander. It was a recent promotion for him and he was still uncomfortable with the extraordinary power it lent him. Perhaps he always would be. It was a responsibility that ultimately he could share with no one. His triumphs would be secret, but his disasters appallingly public.

Looking down at the grim evidence at his feet, he would gladly have changed places with the sergeant beside him. He had been an ordinary young policeman himself when he had been this man's age, twenty years ago. He had dealt with regular crimes then: theft, arson, occasionally murder — although not many with political implication, and nothing to do with terror and violence towards the state.

He straightened up. He dressed smartly now, if a little untidily, but even this new woollen coat could not dull the knife edge of the wind. He was cold to the bone. The chill was blowing up from the river a mile and a half away, not hard, but it had the steady bitterness of the damp. From this height he could see the low-lying stretches to the east shrouded in mist, and hear the mournful wail of foghorns.

'Did you say it was reported by the first servant to get up?' he asked. 'That must have been hours ago.' He glanced at the wan daylight.

'Yes, sir,' the sergeant replied. 'Scullery maid, slip of a thing, but sharp as a tack. Scared the poor child half out of her wits, all the blood and hair, but she kept her presence of mind.'

'She didn't run all the way to the police station in the dark?' Pitt asked incredulously. 'It must be a mile and a half at least, from here.'

'No, sir,' the sergeant responded with some satisfaction in his voice. 'Like I said, she's pretty

2

cool-headed, and all of about thirteen, I would guess. She went in and woke up the house-keeper, a sensible sort of woman. She has the use of the telephone, so after she'd checked that the blood and hair were real, not just from some animals fighting, she called the police station. If she hadn't, likely we'd still be on the way here.'

Pitt looked down at the blood, which could easily enough be human or animal. However, the strands of hair were long, auburn in the lantern light, and could only be human. He also thought that without the telephone to waken him at his home in Keppel Street on the other side of the river, he would have been having breakfast in his own warm kitchen now, unaware of any of this potential tragedy, and all the grief and complications that could arise from it.

He grunted agreement, but before he could add anything more he heard rapid footsteps along the pavement. The next moment Stoker appeared at the top of the areaway. He was the one man in Special Branch that Pitt had learned to trust. After the betrayals that had led up to Victor Narraway's dismissal, he trusted no one who had not earned it. Narraway had been innocent and, after desperate effort and cost, had been proved so. But that episode had still been the end of his career.

'Morning, sir,' Stoker said with only the slightest curiosity in his voice. He glanced down at the lantern and the patch of stone steps illuminated by it, then at Pitt. He was a lean man with a strong, intelligent face, although it was a bit too bony to be good-looking, and too dour for charm.

'One maid missing,' Pitt explained. He looked up at the sky, then back at Stoker. 'Make a note of exactly what you see. Draw it. Then pick up a few samples, in case we need them in evidence one day. Better hurry. If the rain comes it'll wash that whole lot away. I'm going in to speak to the household.'

'Yes, sir. Why us, sir? Missing maid — what's wrong with the locals doing it?' He gave the sergeant a nod, but the question was directed at Pitt.

'Householder is Dudley Kynaston — naval defence . . . ' Pitt replied.

Stoker swore under his breath.

Pitt smiled, glad not to have caught his exact words, although he probably agreed with them. He turned and knocked on the scullery door, then opened it — and walked past the stored vegetables into the kitchen. Immediately the warmth wrapped around him, along with the rich aromas of cooking. It was comfortable, everything in order. Polished copper pans hung from hooks, their sheen winking in the lights. Clean china was stacked on the dresser. Shelves were piled neatly with labelled spice jars. Strings of onions and dried herbs hung from the rafters.

'Good morning,' he said clearly, and three women turned from their tasks to look at him.

'Mornin', sir,' they replied almost in unison. The cook was a comfortably rounded woman, at the moment holding a large wooden spoon in her hand. A maid in starched and lace-trimmed

4

apron was setting out tea and toast ready to carry upstairs, and the scullery maid was peeling potatoes. She had dark, unruly hair and wide eyes. As soon as he saw her, Pitt knew that she was the one who had gone outside and found the blood and glass. The sleeves of her grey dress were rolled well above her elbows and her white apron was covered in smuts from relighting the stove.

The cook regarded Pitt apprehensively, unsure where to place him in the social scale. He wasn't a gentleman because he had come in through the back door, and he didn't have the natural arrogance of a man used to the attention of servants. On the other hand, he seemed very sure of himself in a different kind of way, and she could tell at a glance that his overcoat was of excellent quality. In the circumstances, he was probably a policeman of some sort, but he did not look like an ordinary sergeant.

Pitt gave her a brief smile. 'May I speak to your scullery maid, please? I would appreciate it if you could give me a quiet room where we will be without interruption. If you wish the housekeeper to be with her, that will be acceptable.' He phrased it as a request, but it was an order, and he held her eyes long enough to be certain that she knew that.

'Yes, sir,' she said, her voice catching as though her mouth were dry. 'Dora here can go with her.' She gestured at the startled parlour maid. 'I'll take that tray up to Mrs Kynaston. Maisie, you go with the policeman an' tell 'im what 'e needs to know. And you be civil, mind!'

'Yes, Cook,' Maisie said obediently, and led Pitt as far as the door. Then she turned to him, looking him up and down with bright, critical eyes. 'You look like you're froze to the bone. You want a cup o' tea . . . sir?'

Pitt smiled in spite of himself. 'Thank you, that would be very nice. Perhaps Dora would bring us a pot?'

Dora was strongly disapproving. She was a parlour maid, not someone to fetch and carry cups of tea to the likes of policemen and scullery maids, but she could not find the right words to say so.

Pitt's smile widened. 'Very helpful of you.' He acknowledged her departure from duty, then followed Maisie along the corridor to the housekeeper's sitting room. The housekeeper herself was no doubt about other duties necessitated by the alarming circumstances that had arisen this morning.

Pitt sat down in the armchair by the fire, which was newly lit and not yet warm. Maisie sat upright on the hard-backed chair opposite him.

'What time did you come down to the kitchen this morning?' Pitt started straight away.

' 'Alf-past five,' she replied without hesitation. 'I raked out the ashes an' took 'em out ter the ash can in the yard. That was when I found the . . . ' she gulped, ' . . . the blood . . . an' that.'

'About quarter to six?'

'Yeah . . . '

'It would be very dark then. How did you notice them? They weren't all that close to the

6

ash can,' he pointed out. 'Was there somebody else there, Maisie?'

She took a very deep breath, then let it out in a sigh. 'Opposite's boot boy, but 'e wouldn't never 'ave done anything like that. 'Sides, 'e likes Kitty . . . I mean she were nice to 'im. 'E . . . 'e comes from the country an' 'e misses 'is family, like.' Her dark eyes stared unwaveringly at Pitt.

'Who's Kitty?' he asked.

'Kitty Ryder,' she said as if he should have known. 'Mrs Kynaston's lady's maid wot's missing.'

'How do you know she's missing?' he asked curiously. He knew that ladies' maids seldom got up at half-past five.

' 'Cos she in't 'ere,' she replied reasonably, but he knew from the defiance in her face and her very slight sniff that she was perfectly aware of being evasive.

'You thought the hair on the steps looked like Kitty Ryder's?' he pressed.

'Yeah . . . some . . . '

A thought occurred to him, a chance to be seized before Dora came any moment with the tea, and, of course, remained as a chaperone.

'And you were afraid something had happened to Kitty?' he suggested.

'Yeah . . . I . . . ' She stopped. She looked into his face and knew that somewhere there was a trap in the question, but she did not look away.

He heard Dora's footsteps in the passage.

'So Kitty might quite likely be on the areaway steps in the middle of a winter night, and

7

possibly have a quarrel that could turn violent? A suitor you don't like?'

'A wot?'

'A young man?'

Dora came in through the door balancing a tray with a teapot, milk jug, sugar bowl and two cups and saucers. She placed it on the table and stood back a little, her face stiff with disapproval.

Pitt nodded his thanks but kept his eyes on Maisie. 'A young man,' he repeated. 'Kitty had a young man and she went out at night to meet him. That was why when you saw the blood and hair you immediately thought of her, and checked to see if she was home — and she wasn't. Is that right?'

Maisie stared at him with respect, and a new fear. She nodded silently.

'Thank you,' Pitt acknowledged. 'And did you find Kitty at all?' He asked that with a deep sense of impending sadness. He already knew the answer.

Maisie shook her head. 'She in't nowhere.'

'Would you like a cup of tea?' he asked.

She nodded, still not taking her eyes from his face.

'Dora, would you pour two cups of tea, please?' Pitt requested. 'I take mine with milk and no sugar. You'll know how Maisie likes hers. Then perhaps you would find either the housekeeper or the butler for me and have them come here.'

Dora glared at him, but did as she was told. She had been brought up to be very careful never to make trouble with the police, whatever sort they were.

★ ★ ★

An hour later Pitt had learned all that he could from the staff. He and Stoker made a complete record of the areaway with sketches and diagrams, then went together to the withdrawing room to speak first to Dudley Kynaston. If necessary they would also speak to his wife.

The room was spacious, as Pitt had expected. Surprisingly, it was also comfortable, as though it were arranged for their own pleasure, not for entertaining, or to impress. The carpets were mellow and well-worn, the leather of the chairs creased into lines of comfort, cushions placed for ease. Kynaston was standing in the middle of the floor, but there was a pile of papers on the sofa where he had apparently been sitting. He must have heard their feet on the parquet of the hall, and risen to his feet. Pitt wondered if that were out of good manners, or the instinctive desire not to be at a disadvantage.

Kynaston was a tall man, almost Pitt's own height. His face was handsome, regular-featured, with thick fair hair greying at the temples. He looked unhappy, but not more anxious than any decent man should be at the thought of possible violence.

Pitt introduced himself and Stoker.

'How do you do?' Kynaston replied courteously, but to Pitt, merely nodding towards Stoker. 'I don't know how I can help you. I

9

appreciate Special Branch's concern, but if my unfortunate maid is involved, then it is probably no more than an unusually vicious quarrel. Perhaps some young man had too much to drink and was reluctant to take 'no' for an answer. Unpleasant, but these things happen.' He was politely telling Pitt that he was wasting his time, and he did not have the air of a man making excuses.

'Is it usual for Miss Ryder to be about at this hour of the morning?' Pitt asked him.

Kynaston shook his head fractionally. 'No, that is most unusual. I can't explain it. She is normally a very reliable girl.'

Pitt felt more than heard Stoker fidget from one foot to the other behind him.

'You are sure she's not anywhere in the house?' Pitt asked.

'There's nowhere she can be.' Kynaston looked confused. 'She's never done this before. But, from what the butler tells me, the mess on the area steps indicates a rather nasty quarrel. It's all very unpleasant, and we shall have to let her go, but I hope she isn't seriously hurt. Beyond permitting you to search the house for yourself, and question anyone you please, I can't think of any way in which I can be of help.'

'Thank you, sir,' Pitt responded. 'Perhaps I could speak with Mrs Kynaston? I'm sure she will know more about the domestic servants. As you say, it is probably no more than a quarrel that became violent, and once we have found Kitty Ryder and assured ourselves that she is all right, then we can close the issue.'

Kynaston hesitated.

Pitt wondered if he were being protective of his wife, or afraid she might say something unintentionally indiscreet. It could be irrelevant to the hair and blood on the steps, possibly some other matter entirely, but one that he would still like to keep private. So many times Pitt had investigated one thing, only to uncover secrets of a completely different nature. Privacy, once intruded upon, was never entirely the same again. He felt a moment's pity for Kynaston, and he regretted that he could not afford to indulge it.

'Mr Kynaston?' he prompted.

'Yes . . . yes, of course,' Kynaston said with a sigh. He reached over and rang the bell by the side of the fireplace. It was answered by the butler, a sober man, his pleasant face marred by an anxious frown. 'Ah, Norton, would you please ask Mrs Kynaston to come to the withdrawing room?' Clearly he had no intention of allowing Pitt to speak with her alone.

Norton retreated again and they waited in silence until the door opened and a woman came into the room. She was of average height and at first of very unremarkable appearance. Her hair was thick, but an ordinary shade of brown. Her features were regular, her eyes neither grey nor blue. When Pitt thought about it afterwards, he could not remember what she wore.

'I'm sorry to disturb you, my dear,' Kynaston said quietly. 'But it seems that the local police have called in Special Branch about the blood and hair on the steps. At least until we know that

11

Kitty is not badly hurt, we must allow them to pursue the issue.'

'Good gracious!' she said with surprise. She looked straight at Pitt with sudden interest. 'Is the safety of the nation so little threatened that you have time to investigate the misbehaviour of a domestic servant?' Her voice was the one memorable feature about her. It was rich and soft. Pitt could not help thinking that if she sang she would do so beautifully, with the kind of timbre that made all the notes throaty and full of emotion.

Kynaston was clearly at a loss for words.

'We don't know that it was Miss Ryder's hair, ma'am,' Pitt replied for him. 'Or her blood.'

She was slightly taken aback. 'I believe the hair found was of a reddish brown, which Kitty's is. But I imagine that would be true of many people. Perhaps it has nothing to do with this house at all? It was found on the area steps, wasn't it? Anyone might have been there.'

Kynaston's face pinched momentarily. Then the instant he was aware of Pitt looking at him, he smoothed the expression away. 'Of course,' he agreed. 'Although we do not get troubled by passing strangers. We have few neighbours.' It was an unnecessary comment; the truth of it was obvious. They were surrounded by open country, a few trees, and the large gravel pits that were common between Blackheath village and Greenwich Park.

'Really, Dudley,' Rosalind Kynaston said patiently, 'people will always find a place! And this time of the year, the shelter of the areaway must be a great deal pleasanter than the open in the wind.'

Pitt allowed himself to smile. 'No doubt,' he conceded. 'But could one of the people have been Kitty Ryder, in this case?'

'I suppose so.' She gave the slightest shrug, barely a movement of her rather graceful shoulders. 'There's a young man she walks out with now and then. A carpenter or something of the sort.'

Kynaston looked startled. 'Does she? You never mentioned it!'

She regarded him with an expression that almost concealed her impatience. 'Of course I didn't. Why on earth would I? I hoped it would pass. He is not particularly appealing.'

Kynaston drew in his breath as if to say something, then let it out again, and waited for Pitt to speak.

'You don't care for the young man?' Pitt asked Mrs Kynaston. 'If she ended the acquaintance do you think he might have taken it badly?'

She considered for several moments before finally replying. 'Actually, I had not thought so. I believed he had an affection for her, but that he had no prospects. Also, to be frank, I thought Kitty had more sense than to choose the area steps in the middle of a winter night to tell him so.'

'She should have been safe enough just outside her own scullery door!' Kynaston protested. His expression darkened. 'Just how unsuitable was he?'

'He wasn't unsuitable, Dudley, he was just not

13

as well as she might have done for herself,' she explained. 'Kitty is a very handsome girl. She could have been a parlour maid in the city, if she'd wished to.'

'She didn't wish to?' Pitt was curious. What would keep a good-looking girl here in Shooters Hill if she could have been in one of the fashionable squares in London? 'Has she family locally?' he asked.

'No,' Rosalind assured him. 'She comes from Gloucestershire. I don't know why she didn't take her chance in the city. I'm sure she had offers.'

It might be irrelevant, but Pitt made a mental note to look further into the reason for Kitty's loyalty, if she did not very soon turn up alive and well.

'I suppose your advice didn't go down very well,' Kynaston observed, looking at his wife. 'I thought she had more sense.' He turned to Pitt. 'We appear to have wasted your time. I apologise. If there is anything at all to deal with, which there probably isn't, then it is a police matter. If Kitty doesn't turn up, or we have any reason to suppose she has been harmed, we'll report it.' He smiled and inclined his head a little, as if it were a dismissal.

Pitt hesitated, unwilling to let go of the matter quite so easily. Someone had been hurt on the areaway steps, possibly badly. Had it been a daughter of the house rather than a maid, no one would be dismissing it.

'Can you describe Miss Ryder for me, sir?' he asked, without moving.

14

Kynaston blinked.

'How tall is she?' Pitt elaborated. 'What build? What colouring?'

It was Rosalind Kynaston who replied. 'Taller than I am, at least a couple of inches, and very handsomely built.' She smiled with a dry, private amusement. 'She had excellent features, in fact were she a Society girl we'd say she was a beauty. She has a fair skin and thick, auburn hair with a wave in it.'

'I think you're being over-generous, my dear,' Kynaston said with a slight edge to his voice. 'She's a lady's maid who was being courted by a young man of very dubious background.' He turned to Pitt again. 'And as I'm sure you are aware, maids have a half-day off at the weekends, but stopping out in this manner is not acceptable — which, of course, is why she has done it on the sly. If you are still concerned, you might consider the possibility that she has eloped with him.'

Rosalind was saved from making a reply by the entry into the room of another woman. She was taller, in fact only two or three inches short of Kynaston's own height, and her hair was silver-blond. But it was her face that commanded attention, not by its beauty, which was questionable, but by the power of emotion in it, which was more arresting than mere regularity of feature. Her eyes were of a burning blue.

'Have you found the housemaid yet?' she asked, looking directly at Kynaston.

'Lady's maid,' Rosalind corrected her. 'No, we haven't.'

15

'Good morning, Ailsa,' Kynaston said, rather more gently than Pitt thought he would have, in the circumstances. 'Unfortunately not. This is Commander Pitt of Special Branch.'

Ailsa's delicate eyebrows rose. 'Special Branch?' she said incredulously. 'Dudley, you haven't called in Special Branch, have you? For heaven's sake, my dear, they have better things to do!' She turned to stare at Pitt with new curiosity. 'Don't you?' she challenged him.

'My sister-in-law, Mrs Bennett Kynaston,' Kynaston explained. Pitt saw a shadow of pain cross his face, dismissed instantly, but with an effort. He recalled that Bennett Kynaston had died roughly nine years earlier. Interesting that his widow had kept such close touch with the family, and clearly had not married again. She was certainly handsome enough to have had many opportunities.

'How do you do, Mrs Kynaston?' he replied to her. She was staring at him, her eyes wide, so he answered her question. 'A young woman is missing and there is blood, hair and broken glass on the area steps — enough to indicate the possibility at least of a very nasty fight. The local police called us because they are aware of Mr Kynaston's importance to both the navy and the Government, and how serious any threat to him might be. If it turns out to be no more than a very unpleasant lovers' quarrel, then we shall leave it to them to take what action is necessary. At the moment Miss Ryder appears to be missing.'

Ailsa shook her head. 'You need to replace her,

16

Rosalind. Whether she comes back or not, she is clearly no better than she should be, as they say.'

A look of anger crossed Rosalind's face, but so quickly Pitt was not absolutely certain he had seen it at all. Had he imagined it, because he knew how his own wife, Charlotte, would have felt about such high-handed instruction from anyone else — even her sister Emily, close as they were in affection?

Before Rosalind could frame a reply, Pitt intervened, speaking to Kynaston. 'We shall keep the case open until Kitty Ryder is found, or you have some news of her, whatever it may be,' he said. 'In the meantime, she appears not to have taken any of her belongings with her. The housekeeper told me even her nightgowns and hairbrush are still in her room. In light of that, we have to assume she did not plan to leave. If you discover anything of value missing from the house, please inform the local police. I would suggest that you be more than usually diligent in making certain that the doors are locked at night. You might inform your butler of the possibility of robbery . . . '

'I dare say that is what it is,' Kynaston agreed. 'Most unpleasant. She came to us with good references. But your advice is well placed, and I shall certainly take it. I am obliged to you.'

'I don't believe Kitty would be involved in robbing us,' Rosalind said with some heat, a slight flush on her pale cheeks.

'Of course you're reluctant to think so,' Ailsa said gently, moving a step closer to her sister-in-law. 'She was your personal maid, and you trusted her. One does! Usually one is right, but anyone can be misled, now and then. I understand she fell in with a very nasty type of young man, and we all know they can take people in — heaven knows, even in the best families, let alone a girl far from her home, working as a maid.'

The truth of the remark was unarguable, but Pitt saw in Rosalind's face disbelief and frustration that she could not defend her feelings.

'Quite.' Kynaston nodded at Ailsa, and then turned to his wife. 'Perhaps you could use Jane for a while. You like her, and she seems quite capable, until we get someone else to fill the place.'

'What about Kitty?' Rosalind said sharply. 'For heaven's sake, Dudley, she's only been gone a few hours! You're speaking as if she were dead and buried!'

'Even if she returns, my dear, she is obviously unreliable,' he said more gently. 'I think this is the best decision.' He turned to Pitt. 'Thank you again for your promptness, and your advice, Commander. We won't detain you any longer. Good day.'

'Good day, sir,' Pitt replied. 'Ma'am,' he acknowledged both women. Then he and Stoker left, going out through the front door into the deserted street. Rain was beginning to come across the open land of the heath.

'What do you make of that, sir?' Stoker asked curiously, turning up his coat collar as he

18

walked. His voice was light but when Pitt glanced at him he saw the doubt in his face. 'There was a lot of blood on that step,' Stoker went on. 'More than a scratch, I reckon. If someone hit that girl it was pretty hard. She must be daft to go willingly with anyone who'd use her like that.' Now the doubt had turned to anger.

'Perhaps she cut herself on the glass,' Pitt said thoughtfully. He pulled the brim of his hat down and his scarf tighter as the rain increased. He looked up at the sky. 'Good thing you made a sketch of it before this started. In twenty minutes there'll be nothing to see.'

'There was blood on the glass,' Stoker said. 'And the hair. Torn out by the roots, from the look of it. Kynaston may be important to the navy, but he's covering something up . . . sir.'

Pitt smiled. He knew Stoker's subtle and quite delicate insolence. It was not directed at him personally, but more at their political masters, whom he knew Pitt occasionally disliked as much as he did himself. He was still nervous that Pitt might yield to them, and not absolutely certain whether Pitt's predecessor in command had done so or not. But Victor Narraway was a very different kind of man, at least on the surface. He was a gentleman, beginning as a junior lieutenant in the army, then through university in law, and as devious as an eel. Stoker had never been comfortable with him, but his respect for him was boundless.

Pitt, on the other hand, was the son of a country gamekeeper, risen through the ranks of the regular Metropolitan Police. He had been promoted sideways into Special Branch, much against his will, when he had offended certain very powerful people and lost his job as Superintendent in Bow Street. Pitt might think he was subtle, but to Stoker he was as clear as the rising sun.

Pitt was aware of all this as he replied, 'I know that, Stoker. What I don't know is if it is something we should be concerned about.'

'Well, if there's something messy going on in that house, and a maid gets the bad end of it, we should care,' Stoker said with feeling. 'Perfect set-up for a spot of blackmail.' He left the rest of his thought implied.

'You think Dudley Kynaston was having an affair with his wife's maid, and knocked her around on his own kitchen steps in the middle of a winter night?' Pitt asked with a smile.

Stoker flushed faintly and stared straight ahead, avoiding Pitt's eyes. 'Put it like that, no, sir. If he's that crazy he wants putting in the madhouse, for everybody's sake, including his own.'

Pitt was going to add that it was probably just what it looked like, but he wasn't sure what it looked like. The maids had found nothing missing to account for the glass. There was too much blood for a graze, and actually there was no way of telling if it was even human, let alone if it was that of the missing maid — who seemingly had gone without even taking her hairbrush. And was it her hair, or only a similar colour?

Who knew the nature of a lovers' quarrel, if that is what it was?

'We'll have the local police keep an eye on it, and let us know if she comes back,' he said to Stoker. 'Or if she turns up anywhere else, for that matter.'

Stoker grunted, not satisfied, but accepting that there was nothing more they could do. They trudged through the rain silently, heads down, feet sloshing on the wet pavement.

★　★　★

Pitt arrived home at Keppel Street comparatively early, although at this time of the year it was already completely dark. The streetlamps gleamed like beacons through the rain, haloed in light for a brief space, darkness swirling between them.

Pitt went up the steps to his front door and was about to hunt through his always overstuffed pockets for his key when it opened in front of him, bathing him in the glow of the inside lights and the warmth of the parlour fire where the passage door was open.

'Evenin' sir,' Minnie Maude said with a smile. 'D'yer like a cup o' tea before dinner's ready? My, yer in't 'alf soaked!' She looked him up and down with sympathy. 'I reckon as it's rainin' stair rods out there.'

'Indeed it is,' he agreed, dripping steadily on to the hall floor as the front door closed behind him. He looked at her freckled face and her piled-up red-brown hair, and for a moment he imagined the missing maid from Kynaston's house and wondered where she was. Minnie Maude was handsome too, in her own way, tall and womanly; worldly-wise, domestically capable, and naïvely full of trust. He felt a tightness in his chest at the thought of her alone outside somewhere, perhaps hurt, cold to the bone, desperate for shelter. What on earth had happened to Kitty Ryder?

'Yer a'right, sir?' Minnie Maude's anxious voice intruded on his thoughts.

Pitt eased himself out of his wet coat and took off his sodden boots. He gave her his hat and scarf as well.

'Yes, thank you. And I will have a cup of tea. And I'll have something to eat. I can't remember what lunch was.'

'Yes, sir. 'Ow about a couple o' crumpets?' she offered. 'Wi' butter?'

He looked at her. She was about nineteen, four years older than his daughter, Jemima, who was far too rapidly growing into a woman. Thank God Jemima wouldn't be a servant living in somebody else's house with only strangers to turn to.

'Thank you,' he replied. 'Yes . . . bring them to me in the parlour, please.' He wanted to add something more, but there really wasn't anything to say that was appropriate.

★ ★ ★

After dinner, when Jemima and her younger brother, Daniel, had gone up to bed, he sat

22

beside the fire in his usual chair, opposite Charlotte, who had abandoned her embroidery for the evening and sat with her boots off and her feet up, hidden by her skirts. The light from the gas brackets on the walls was a golden colour, muted a little by the glass. It softened the lines of everything it touched: the familiar books on the shelves on either side, the few ornaments, each with its own associations in the memory. The long curtains across the French windows on to the garden were drawn against the cold. He could not imagine anywhere more comfortable.

'What is it?' Charlotte asked. 'You are making your mind up whether to tell me, so it can't be a secret.'

In the past, when he was still in the police, he had shared many of his cases with her. In fact, some of them she had known to involve crime before he did. She had been something of a detective herself. She was acutely observant of human nature, and alarmingly fearless in pursuing what she felt was justice.

Of course, now so much more was secret and he could not share with her nearly as much as he used to, although he still would were he able. He was often tempted, only the cost restrained him. A betrayal of trust would damage him in his own eyes, and in hers. The loss of his position would destroy his career, and therefore also his ability to look after his family. He had faced that once when he was dismissed from the police, without the hope of ever being reinstated. He had powerful enemies, among them, unfortunately, the Prince of Wales, who would be only too delighted if Pitt's entire career were called into question.

Charlotte was waiting for an answer. No secrets of state were involved. So far it was nothing but a rather unfortunate domestic incident.

'Evidence of a fight on the areaway steps of a house on Shooters Hill,' he replied. 'And a missing lady's maid. She was courting so it's possible she eloped.'

'I didn't think there were houses up on Shooters Hill,' she responded, frowning a little. 'If I mustn't know, then don't tell me, but what you've said so far doesn't make any sense.'

'I know it doesn't make any sense,' he agreed. 'Blood and hair on the steps, and broken glass . . . and a missing maid at a time of day when she should have been there, and always has been in the past.'

'Why you?' she said curiously. 'If there's a crime involved at all, isn't it for the local police?' Then her face lit with understanding. 'Oh . . . it's somebody important!'

'Yes. And you're quite right, if it's anything at all, it belongs to the local police. You said Jemima needs a new dress?'

She tucked her feet up a little higher. The coals settled in the fire with a shower of sparks.

'Yes, please . . . at least one.'

'At least?' He raised his eyebrows.

'She's going to the party at the Grovers' as well,' she explained. 'It's quite formal.'

'I thought she didn't want to go to that?' He was momentarily confused.

24

There was a slight shadow in Charlotte's face. 'She doesn't,' she agreed. 'But Mary Grover was very kind to her, and Jemima promised she would be there to help.'

Pitt remembered Jemima's argument on the subject, then he looked at Charlotte again. 'Don't you think . . . ?' he began.

'She doesn't want to go because the Hamiltons are having a party as well, and she wants to go to that instead, because she likes Robert Hamilton.'

'Then — '

'Thomas . . . she owes Mary Grover a debt of kindness. She will pay it. And don't tell me 'later'. 'Later' doesn't do.'

'I know,' he said quietly.

'I'm so glad.' Suddenly she smiled and it warmed her whole face with a melting gentleness. 'I don't want to fight both of you — at least not at once.'

'Good,' he said, relaxing also at last, although he did not doubt for a second that she would have, had he forced her into it.

2

Three weeks later, at the end of January, Pitt was at breakfast in the warmth of the kitchen when the telephone rang. It was a marvellous instrument and had been of great service to him, but there were times when he resented its presence. Quarter-past seven on a winter morning, before he had finished his toast, was one of them. Nevertheless he stood up and went out into the hall where the telephone sat on the small table, and picked it up. He knew no one would call him without good reason.

It was Stoker on the other end, his voice thick with emotion.

'They've found a body, sir.' He took a breath and Pitt could hear the sounds of footsteps and other voices around him. 'I'm at the Blackheath police station,' Stoker went on. 'It's a woman . . . young woman, far as we can tell . . . handsome build . . . ' He swallowed. 'Reddish hair . . . '

Pitt felt his own throat tighten and a wave of sadness pass over him. 'Where?' he asked, although the fact that Stoker was calling from Blackheath told him that it was not far from Shooters Hill.

'Gravel pit, sir,' Stoker replied. 'Shooters Hill Road, just beyond Kynaston's house.' He seemed about to add something, then changed his mind.

'I'll be there,' Pitt replied. He had no need to tell Stoker that it would take him at least half an hour. Keppel Street was little more than a mile from Lisson Grove, where his office was, but it was a long way west and north of the river from Blackheath, let alone from Shooters Hill.

He put the phone back in its cradle and turned to see Charlotte standing at the bottom of the stairs, waiting for him to tell her what it was. She would know from his face, even from the angle of his body, that it was bad news.

'A body,' he said quietly. 'Young woman found in one of the gravel pits on Shooters Hill.'

'I suppose you have to go . . . '

'Yes. Stoker's already there. That was him on the telephone. I suppose the local police called him.'

'Why?' she asked.

He smiled bleakly. 'Because the local police are very diligent — or because I have a strong idea that he's kept on checking on them in case they found Kitty Ryder's body. But I think the truth is most likely that they sense a bad case coming, and they'd very much like not to have to deal with it themselves.'

'Can they pass it to you, just like that?' she said dubiously.

'Since it's on Kynaston's doorstep, and might well be his maid, yes they can. If it is her, they'll have to give it to Special Branch anyway.'

She nodded slowly, sadness pinching her face. 'I'm sorry. Poor girl.' She did not ask why anyone would kill her or if Kitty might have done something, such as attempting blackmail, in order to bring it on herself. She had learned over their sixteen years of marriage how complicated tragedies could be. She was just as blazingly angry at injustice as she had been when they first met, but now very much slower to judge — most of the time.

He walked back to the warm kitchen and its smells of coal, bread and clean linen, to eat the last few mouthfuls of his toast, and drink his tea, if it wasn't cold. He hated cold tea. Then he would go out into the icy morning and find a hansom. By the time he got to the river it would be sunrise, and daylight when he got up the hill to the gravel pit.

Charlotte was ahead of him. She took his cup off the table and fetched a clean one from the Welsh dresser. 'You've time for it,' she stated firmly before he could get the words out to argue. She topped up the teapot from the kettle on the hob, waited a moment, then poured it.

Pitt thanked her and was drinking it gratefully — hot if a trifle weak — when Minnie Maude came in, carrying potatoes and a string of onions. Uffie, the small, shaggy orphan pup she had adopted a year ago was, as usual, practically treading on her skirts. He had begun by being denied the kitchen, but it had not worked. If Charlotte had had any sense, she would never have imagined it would!

Pitt smiled, then thought of Kynaston's kitchen and how different it would be there. 'I don't know when I'll be back,' he said quietly, and turned to leave.

Pitt reached the gravel pit, as he expected, just as the grey light spread over the waste where the earth had been dug and exploited. The wind from the east carried flecks of ice, stinging the exposed skin of his face and finding the vulnerable parts of his neck. In earlier days he would have worn a long woollen scarf, wound round and round to keep out the cold. Now he felt that would be a little scruffy and informal for his rank, and he had a silk one instead. It was difficult enough to impress people anyway. His predecessors had all been gentlemen from their birth, and in many cases senior officers in either the army or the navy, like Narraway, assuming the obedience of others quite naturally.

'Morning, sir.' Stoker walked towards him with an easy gait, his feet crunching on the frozen grass. He refused to huddle his body against the wind. 'She's over there.' He indicated a small group of men about fifty feet away, standing close together, coats whipping a little around their legs, hats jammed on their heads. The light of bull's-eye lanterns glowed with a false warmth, yellow in the gloom.

'Who found her?' Pitt asked curiously.

'The usual,' Stoker replied with a shadow of a smile. 'Man walking his dog.'

'What time, for heaven's sake?' Pitt demanded. 'Who the devil walks his dog up here at half-past five on a winter morning?'

Stoker lifted his shoulders slightly. 'Ferryman down on the Greenwich waterfront. Takes people

29

who cross the river to be there before seven. Sounds like a decent enough man.'

Pitt should have thought of that. He had come over the river by ferry himself, but barely looked at the man at the oars. He had dealt with murders most of his police career, and yet they still disturbed him. He had never seen the victim alive, but the accounts of her by the other staff at Kynaston's house had given her a reality, a vivid sense of laughter and friendship, even of dreams for the future.

'He reported it to the local police station, and they remembered your interest, so they sent for you,' Pitt said.

'Yes, sir. And they telephoned my local station, who sent a constable around for me.' Stoker looked uncomfortable, as if he were making some confession before it caught up with him anyway. 'I came up here first, before calling you, sir, in case it wasn't anything to do with us. Didn't want to get you out here for nothing.'

Pitt realised what he was doing — accounting for the fact that he was here first. He could have had his own local police call Pitt, and he had chosen not to.

'I see,' Pitt replied with a bleak smile, in this grey light, barely visible. 'Where did you find a telephone up here?'

Stoker bit his lip but he did not lower his eyes. 'I went to the Kynaston house, sir, just to make sure the maid had not returned and they had forgotten to tell us.'

Pitt nodded. 'Very prudent,' he said, almost without expression. Then he walked towards the

30

group of men, who were openly shivering now as the wind increased. There were three of them: a constable, a sergeant and the third whom Pitt took to be the police surgeon.

'Morning, sir,' the sergeant said smartly. 'Sorry to get you all the way up here so early, but I think this one might be yours.'

'We'll see.' Pitt refused to commit himself. He did not want the case any more than the sergeant did. Even if the body was Kitty Ryder's, her death probably had nothing whatever to do with Dudley Kynaston, but the danger of scandal was there, the pressure, the public interest, the possibility of injustice.

'Yes, sir,' the sergeant agreed, the relief not disappearing a whit from his face. He indicated the older man, who was shorter than Pitt and slightly built, his brown hair liberally sprinkled with grey. 'This is Dr Whistler,' he introduced him. He did not bother to explain who Pitt was. Presumably that had been done before he arrived.

Whistler inclined his head. 'Morning, Commander. Nasty one, I'm afraid.' There was a rough edge to his voice from perhaps more than the wretched morning, and an unmistakable pity in his face. He stepped back as he spoke, so Pitt could see behind him a rough cloth covering the body they had found.

Pitt took a deep breath of the air, cold and clean, then he bent to remove the cloth. In summer there would have been a smell, but the wind and the ice had kept it at bay. The body had been severely mutilated. Most of the face

31

was so damaged as to be unrecognisable: the nose split, the lips removed as if by a knife. The eyes themselves were gone, presumably taken by scavenging animals. Only the arch of the brow was left to give an idea of their shape. The flesh was stripped from the cheeks, but the jawbone and teeth were intact. One could only imagine how her smile might have been.

Pitt looked at the rest of her body. She was quite tall, almost Charlotte's height, and handsomely built, with a generous bosom, slender waist, long legs. Her clothes had protected most of her from the ravages of animals, and the normal decay had not yet reached the stage of disintegration. Pitt forced himself to look at her hair. It was wet and matted from exposure to the elements, but it was still possible to see that when one took the pins out it would fall at least half-way down her back, and that once dry it would be thick and of a deep chestnut colour.

Was it Kitty Ryder? Probably. They had said she was tall, handsomely built, and had beautiful hair, a shade of auburn like that found on the area steps, with the blood and glass.

He looked back at the surgeon. 'Did you find anything to indicate how she died?' he asked.

Whistler shook his head. 'Not for certain. I think there are some broken bones, but I'll have to get her back to the morgue to remove her clothes and look at her much more carefully. Nothing obvious. No bullets, no stab wounds that I can see. She wasn't strangled and there's no visible damage to the skull.'

'Anything to identify her?' Pitt asked a little sharply. He wanted it not to be Kitty Ryder. He would be very relieved if the body had no connection to the Kynaston house, except a reasonable proximity. More than that, he wanted it to be a woman he knew nothing about, even though they would still have to learn. Nobody should die alone and anonymously, as if they did not matter. He would just prefer it to be a regular police job.

'Possibly,' Whistler said, meeting Pitt's eyes. 'A very handsome gold fob watch. I looked at it carefully. Unusual and quite old, I think. Not hers, that's for sure. It's very definitely a man's.'

'Stolen?' Pitt asked unhappily.

'I should think so. Most likely recently, or she wouldn't be carrying it around with her.'

'Anything else?'

Whistler pursed his lips. 'A handkerchief with flowers and initials embroidered on it, and a key. Looks like the sort of thing that would open a cupboard. Too small to be a door key. Might be a desk, or even a drawer, although not many drawers have separate keys.' He looked across at the sergeant. 'I gave it all to him. I'm afraid that's it, for the meantime.'

Pitt looked back at the body again. 'Did animals do that to her, or was it deliberate?'

'It was deliberate,' Whistler replied. 'A knife rather than teeth. I'll know more about it when I look at her more closely, and not by the light of a bulls'-eye lantern when I'm freezing up here on the edge of a damn gravel pit at the crack of dawn. It looks like the bloody end of the world up here!'

Pitt nodded without answering. He turned to the sergeant, holding his hand out, palm up.

The sergeant gave him the small square of white embroidered cambric and a domestic key about an inch and three-quarters long, and the old and very lovely gold watch.

Pitt met his eyes, questioning.

'Don't know, sir. There's a few gentlemen as could have a watch like this. If someone picked his pocket he would have complained, depending where he was at the time, if you get my meaning?'

'I do,' Pitt answered.

'Or 'e could 'ave given it 'er, as payment for services,' the sergeant added.

Pitt gave him a bleak look. 'It's worth a year's salary for a lady's maid,' he said, looking again at the watch. 'What about the handkerchief?'

The sergeant shook his head. 'No ideas yet, sir. The initial on the handkerchief is an 'R'. Seeing as how Mrs Kynaston's name begins with an 'R', I thought I should leave that to you.'

'There are only twenty-six letters in the alphabet, Sergeant,' Pitt pointed out. 'There must be scores of names beginning with 'R'. If it had been Q, or X, that might have narrowed it down a bit. Even a Y, or Z.'

'That was exactly what I was thinking, Commander,' the sergeant replied. 'And I'm sure Mr Kynaston would have told me so, with some disfavour, if I had started out by asking if this was his wife's handkerchief.' Again he seemed about to add something more, and then changed his mind. Instead he turned to his own constable, standing a couple of yards away with his collar turned up and his back to the wind. 'I expect the commander'll want you to stay until his own man gets here — more than Mr Stoker, that is. So I'd better get back to the station.' He gave Pitt a bleak smile. 'That suit you, sir?'

'What happened to the man who found her?' Pitt asked, turning beside the sergeant and starting to walk back over the rutted ground towards the road.

'Got his statement, written and signed, then sent him on his way. Poor devil were a bit shaken up, but he's got his living to earn just the same,' the sergeant replied.

'Do you know him?' Pitt said a trifle sharply.

'Yes, sir. Zeb Smith.'

'But you know him?' Pitt repeated.

'Yes, sir.' The sergeant increased his pace. 'Zebediah Smith, Hyde Vale Cottages, about a mile or so over that way.' He pointed north, towards Greenwich port, and the river. 'Had a bit too much to drink a couple of times — must be a few years ago now. Then he got married and settled down.'

'Zebediah . . . ' Pitt murmured, more to himself than to the sergeant.

'Yes, sir. Religious mother. We know where to find him, if we need him again. Frankly, sir, ferrymen are good witnesses. Don't want to get the reputation for giving them a hard time for no reason.'

'Understood,' Pitt acknowledged. 'Did Mr Smith tell you anything useful? Does he walk up here often? When was the last time? Did he see anyone else up here this morning? Any sign of someone? A figure in the distance, footprints? There's enough mud and ice to show them. What about his dog? How did it react?'

The sergeant smiled, a tight, satisfied expression. 'Not a lot, sir. Except that he came up here yesterday morning as usual, and the body wasn't here then. Even if he hadn't seen it himself, his dog would. Good animal. Good ratter, apparently. Didn't see anyone else. I asked him that several times.' He stepped over a ridge of tussock grass and Pitt followed. 'Not a soul,' he went on. 'No footprints as make any sense. Looks like there's been an army up here, but not recently. Weather does that. No more to see a couple of hours ago than there is now.' He looked down at the ground with a slight curl of his lip. 'Useless,' he added, regarding the cracked, rutted earth, as they came closer to the road. Some of it was still frozen, more swimming in mud. 'Anything could have passed that way.'

Pitt was obliged to agree with him. 'And the dog?' he asked again.

'Didn't see anyone else,' the sergeant said. 'Didn't bark. Didn't want to chase anything. Just found the body, an' howled!'

Pitt had a sudden vision of the dog throwing its head back and letting out a long wail of despair as it came across sudden death in the grey fog before dawn, shivering and alone amid the dripping weed heads and the few shadowy, skeletal trees.

'Thank you, Sergeant. I'll keep you informed

36

as I may have to hand the case back to you.'

'Ah . . . yes . . . sir,' the sergeant said awkwardly.

Pitt smiled, although he felt very little humour. The last thing he wanted to do was disturb the Kynaston family again, but it had to be done some time. Perhaps it was not only the most efficient thing to do, but also the kindest not to leave the news, which would inevitably reach them, hanging over their heads like the sword of Damocles.

He came to the entrance to the pit, spoke briefly to the sergeant, then set out briskly to walk to the Kynaston house.

Because of the early hour of the morning, he went again to the back door. He did not want to be announced and ask permission to speak to the servants, with an explanation, and possibly an argument about the body in the gravel pit.

The areaway steps were scrubbed and clean, nothing worse on them now than a thin rime of ice, slick on top from the misty rain. He went down carefully, and knocked on the scullery door.

After several moments it was opened by Maisie, the little scullery maid. For a moment she was confused. He was obviously not a delivery man, and yet she was aware that she knew him.

'Good morning, Maisie,' he said quietly. 'Commander Pitt, Special Branch, you remember? May I come in?'

'Oh, yeah!' Her face lit with a smile. Then she recalled his original reason for coming, and suddenly she was terrified. 'Yer found Kitty, 'ave yer?' She wanted to add more, but the rest of her thoughts were clearly too hideous to speak aloud.

'I don't know,' he answered, still keeping his voice low so as not to attract the attention of the other servants in the kitchen a few yards away. 'You will hear very soon, probably from the first delivery boy of the day, that we've found a woman's body up in the gravel pits, not far from here. It's difficult to tell who she is.'

Maisie gulped but she did not reply.

He pulled the handkerchief and the key out of his pocket. 'Have you seen this handkerchief before, or one like it?'

She took it gingerly as if it were a live thing that might have bitten her. Very carefully she opened it out.

'It's pretty,' she said with a shiver. 'If she got one like this, mister, she's a lady. It's got summink stitched on it in the corner, 'ere . . . ' She held it out.

'Yes, it's a letter 'R'. I imagine it belonged to someone whose name begins with 'R'.'

'Kitty don't begin with an 'R',' she said with certainty. 'I can't read, but I know that much.'

'The thing is,' he said as casually as possible, 'it may not be her own handkerchief. As you said, ladies have ones like this. It may have been given to her by someone . . . '

The understanding in Maisie's face was immediate. 'You mean the woman wot you found could be Kitty, and someone give it 'er?'

'It's possible. If we could find out whose

38

handkerchief it is, then it might help us to know if this is Kitty, or not.'

'Did she drown in the pits?' Maisie asked. She was shaking now, as if they were standing outside in the wind and the ice.

'I don't know yet.' He had no choice but to be honest. Evasion would only make it worse. He showed her the key. 'Do you have any keys like this in the house?'

She frowned. 'Everybody does. What's it for?'

'Probably a cupboard, or a desk drawer.' He offered it to her.

She picked it up reluctantly, then walked over to one of the cupboards on the further side of the room. She tried it in the lock, and it would not fit. She tried a second, and a third with no success. On the fourth one it slipped in and after a little difficulty, it turned.

'There y'are,' she said, her face still white. 'We all got cupboards a bit like that. Don't mean nothing. Mister, can't you do summink ter know if it's our Kitty?'

She had made the point well. It was a very ordinary key that might fit some lock or other in any of a hundred houses in the area, or for that matter, out of it. It probably served more as a handle than a device of security.

'She was only discovered this morning,' he replied gently. 'We'll do all we can to find out who she is. A few more questions and we may be able to say at least whether it is Kitty or not. If it isn't, then we need to know who she is. And you should go on believing that Kitty is somewhere alive and well, but perhaps too embarrassed to tell you why she ran off without saying goodbye to anyone.'

Maisie took a deep breath and let it out shakily. 'Yeah . . . yeah, I will. Can I get yer a cup o' tea? It's fair perishin' out there. Colder than a — ' She stopped abruptly.

'Witch's tit,' he finished for her. He was perfectly familiar with the expression.

She blushed hotly, but she did not deny that that was what had been in her mind. 'I didn't say it,' she murmured.

'Perhaps I shouldn't have,' he apologised. 'I beg your pardon.'

'S'all right!' Then she gave him a dazzling smile. 'I'll get yer a cup o' tea, and tell Mr Norton as yer 'ere.' And before he could protest she whisked away around the corner into the kitchen.

★　★　★

Fifteen minutes later, and after a good hot cup of tea, Pitt was in the butler's pantry with a grim-faced Norton. It was quite a large room, painted cream and brown, and around the walls glass-fronted cupboards for the china and crystal in daily use. There were wooden horses for drying glass and tea cloths, a table for pressing cloths or ironing and folding newspapers. There were also all the usual keys, funnels, corkscrews, and — as was customary in most houses — a picture of the Queen.

'Yes, sir, Mrs Kynaston has handkerchiefs similar to this,' Norton agreed. 'But I cannot say that this one is hers. She does occasionally give such things away, if she has new ones, or it is no longer . . . serviceable. Such as if it is frayed, or stained in some way. They do not last indefinitely.' He looked at it again. 'It is difficult to say, in this condition, what state it would be if washed and ironed.'

'Yes, it is,' Pitt agreed. 'But the monogram is clearly an 'R'.'

'Many ladies' names begin with an 'R'.' Norton pulled his lips tight. 'As for the key, it is a very simple thing. I dare say half the houses in London have something it would open. I'm afraid we can be of no assistance to you.'

'I have no wish that the poor woman in the gravel pit should be Miss Ryder,' Pitt said with feeling. 'But I am obliged to do all I can to find out who she was. She deserves a burial, and her family deserve to know what happened to her.' He stood up from the stool where he had been sitting. 'I preferred to come myself, since that was very much a possibility, rather than send a sergeant to disturb you at this hour.'

Norton stood also. 'I apologise, sir. I was ungenerous,' he said a little awkwardly. 'It was a kindness that you came yourself. I hope you find out who the poor creature is. Apart from the handkerchief, and the fact that the gravel pit is not far away, is there anything that made you think it was Kitty Ryder?'

'She was the height and build you described, and she had thick auburn hair,' Pitt replied. 'It is unusual colouring.'

Norton was momentarily stunned. 'Oh dear.

Oh — I'm very sorry. I . . . this is absurd. Whoever she is she deserves our pity. Just for a moment the thought of someone we know made it so much more . . . real.' He cleared his throat. 'I shall inform Mrs Kynaston of your call, sir, and your consideration. May I show you out?'

★ ★ ★

It took Pitt some time to find Zebediah Smith at his home, and confirm with him what the sergeant had told him. He was not surprised to learn nothing new. His real purpose was to satisfy his own mind that Zebediah was as straightforward as he seemed. The man was still visibly shaken when he told Pitt how he had set out for his usual walk, and in the darkness the keen nose of his dog had scented something different and gone to find it. Then it sat and howled until Smith had come up to it himself, and — in the light of his lantern — seen the pathetic corpse.

He shook his head. 'Who'd do that to a woman?' he said miserably. 'What kind of a . . . I suppose I gotta call 'im a man, although 'e ain't human. 'Ceptin' animals don't kill their own for nothing.'

'There'll be a reason, Mr Smith,' Pitt replied. 'It's my job to find it — when we discover who she is.'

Zebediah looked up and met Pitt's eyes. 'Ain't no reason to do that to anyone, sir, an' I don't care 'oo you are — government, police nor nothin' — you find 'im, an' when you do, God 'elp yer what you do to 'im.'

Pitt did not argue. He was satisfied that Zebediah was telling the exact truth, and also that since he walked the same paths every morning, the body could not have been there twenty-four hours earlier.

★ ★ ★

By mid-afternoon Pitt was in the morgue with Dr Whistler. There was no place he disliked more. Outside the wind had risen considerably. Gusting rain blew hard and cold one moment, then the next, in sheltered places, simply dripped with surprising power to soak through even the best coats. Now and then there were brief blue patches in the sky, bright, and then gone again.

Inside the morgue it seemed to be always winter. The windows were high, perhaps to conceal from the passing world what happened there. The cold was necessary to preserve the bodies as they were wheeled from one room to another for examination. Those stored for any length of time were kept in ice chambers, the chill of which permeated everything. The smell was mostly antiseptic, but it was impossible to forget what it was there to mask.

Whistler's office, where he saw Pitt, was warm and — had it been anywhere else — would have been quite pleasant. Whistler himself was dressed in a grey suit and there was no outward sign of his grisly occupation, except a faint aroma of some chemical.

'I'm not going to be very helpful,' he said as

soon as Pitt had taken a seat in one of the well-padded but still uncomfortable chairs. They seemed to have been constructed to oblige one to sit unnaturally upright.

'Even the omission of something might be useful,' Pitt said hopefully.

Whistler shrugged. 'She's been dead at least two weeks, but I imagine you had worked that out for yourself, from the state of her, poor creature. It is as I said: that abomination was done to her face by a clean, very sharp knife.'

Pitt said nothing.

'I can tell you she was moved after she was dead,' Whistler went on. 'But you must have concluded that too. If she'd been lying there for a couple of weeks someone else would have found her before now. Apart from other people who walk their dogs on the paths across the old gravel pits, there's Mr Smith himself.'

'As you said,' Pitt observed drily. 'Not much help so far. I've spoken to Mr Smith. I agree, she wasn't there yesterday. If she's been dead a couple of weeks, where was she all that time? Do you know that? Or can you at least make an educated guess?'

'Somewhere cold, or the deterioration would be worse than it is,' Whistler answered.

'Brilliant.' Pitt was now openly sarcastic. 'At this time of the year, that narrows it down to anywhere in England except somebody's house who has decent fires in all the main rooms. Even then it could be someone's outhouse.'

'Not quite.' Whistler pursed his lips. 'She was pretty clean, apart from a smear or two of mud and bits of gravel and sand caught up in her clothes. And that could be from where she was lying. Wherever she was kept for the time in between death and being put in the gravel pit, it was clean. And although she's badly mutilated, when I looked more closely, that appears to have been done recently, after the flesh had begun to decay. I suppose that could be useful?' He shrugged. 'It more or less rules out anywhere outside.'

'More than that.' Pitt sat forward a little. 'If you're quite sure about that: no rats? Absolutely no rats?'

Whistler took his point. There were rats almost everywhere, in cities or the country, in the sewers, in the streets and gutters, in people's houses, even cellars, potting sheds, and out-houses of every kind. One did not see them so often, but any food left lying, certainly any dead and rotting body, they would have found.

'Yes.' Whistler nodded, his eyes meeting Pitt's squarely for the first time. 'You may safely conclude that wherever she was, it was cold and clean, and sufficiently well sealed that neither flies nor rats could get in. Of course there are no flies at this time of year, but there are always beetles of some sort. Narrows it down quite a lot.'

'Any idea how she got there?' Pitt pursued.

'Impossible to tell. The body's too badly damaged and too far deteriorated to find any marks of ropes, or whether she lay on slats, or boards, or anything else. You've got a nasty one . . . '

45

Pitt looked at him coldly. 'That also I had worked out for myself.'

'I'll let you know if I find out anything more,' Whistler said with a faint smile.

'Please do.' Pitt rose to his feet. 'For example, how old she was, any distinguishing marks that might help identify her, what state of health she was in, any healed injuries, old scars, birthmarks? Particularly, I would like to know what killed her.'

Whistler nodded. 'Believe me, Commander, I very much want you to find out who, and then exact everything from him the law allows, in some attempt at payment for it.'

Pitt looked at him more closely, and for an instant saw, behind the defences of anger and a quiet belligerence, the sense of helplessness and pity for the agony of a stranger now beyond his help. Whistler was embarrassed by his own grief, and hid it behind a bitter professional detachment. Pitt wondered how often he had to do this sort of thing, and why he had chosen it instead of a practice with the living.

'Thank you,' Pitt said gravely. 'If I learn anything that might be useful to you I'll see that you are informed.'

Outside again he walked quickly. The air was cold and had the sting of sleet in it; its odour was the sourness of soot and smoke, the smell of horse dung and swift-running gutters, impersonal, ordinary, but he breathed it in with relief.

Questions were teeming in his mind. Who was she? Was it Kitty Ryder, or someone else who happened quite by chance to resemble her, at

46

least superficially? How had she died? And where? Had she remained where she was killed, or been moved first somewhere safer, and then last night taken to the gravel pit? Why? What had necessitated that?

If he knew where she had been, would that tell him also who she was? And therefore quite possibly who had killed her, how and why?

As he came to the first major street corner he saw the newspapers for sale. The black headlines were already up — 'Mutilated corpse found on Shooters Hill! Who is she? Police are keeping silent!'

They were like hounds on the scent of blood. Inevitable, even necessary, but he flinched at it all the same.

But then without Zebediah Smith's dog they would not have found the poor woman before there was far less of her left — less chance of identifying her, less chance of finding out what happened to her and who was responsible.

He hoped profoundly that it was not Kitty Ryder — but he knew it probably was.

3

It was well after five by the time Pitt was again in the Kynaston house, this time standing in the morning room opposite Kynaston himself. It was dark outside by this hour, but the fire had probably been lit all day and the room was warm. In other circumstances he might have appreciated the elegance of the furniture, the books on the many shelves, even the paintings. They were a curious choice, most of them snow scenes, clearly not anywhere in Britain by the scale and magnificence of the mountains. There was a soaring beauty to them, and yet a detail as if the artist were familiar with them. He wondered why Kynaston had chosen them, but today he was too preoccupied to give them more than a glance.

Kynaston was waiting for him to speak. He stood in the middle of the thick Turkish carpet, his face tense and puzzled.

'I expect you have heard already,' Pitt began. 'There has been a body found early today, before dawn, at the gravel pit to the east of here. It's that of a young woman, but it is so damaged that it is not possible to make an immediate identification. I am very sorry, but we cannot say if it is Kitty Ryder or not — at least not yet.'

Kynaston was very pale, but he kept his composure, even if it was with difficulty. 'I take it from the way you phrase it that it could be. Do you believe that it is?'

'I think it is probable, yes,' Pitt admitted, then instantly wondered if perhaps he should have been more cautious.

Kynaston took a deep breath. 'If she is unrecognisable, poor creature, why do you believe it may be Kitty?'

Pitt had seen people fight the inevitable before. It was the natural instinct to deny tragedy as long as possible. He had done it himself, but had always had to give in in the end.

'She is the same general height and build as Kitty,' he replied quietly. 'Her hair is auburn.' He saw Kynaston's body tense even more and the muscles along his jaw tighten. 'And she had in her pocket a lace-edged handkerchief with the letter 'R' embroidered on it,' he continued. 'Your butler says Mrs Kynaston has some like it, and that she occasionally gives away old ones.'

There was a long moment's silence; then Kynaston straightened his shoulders a little. 'I see. It does seem . . . probable. Nevertheless we shall not leap to conclusions. I would be obliged if you did not tell the rest of the household that it is Kitty . . . until there is no doubt left. Then we shall have to deal with it. My butler and housekeeper are both excellent people. They will help the more emotionally affected of the staff.'

Pitt took the gold watch out of his pocket and saw Kynaston's eyes widen and the colour drain from his face. 'This was found on the body also,' he said very quietly. 'I see you recognise it.' It was not a question.

'It . . . it's mine.' Kynaston's voice was a

croak, as if his mouth and lips were dry. 'It was taken out of my pocket a couple of weeks ago. Somewhere on the street — damn pickpockets! The fob and chain were taken too. Kitty didn't take it — if that's what you're thinking!'

Pitt nodded. 'I see. I'm afraid it happens. Now, I would like to speak to both your wife and your sister-in-law, if that is possible. I appreciate that they too will be distressed, but either of them may have knowledge that would help us.'

'I doubt it.' Kynaston's mouth pulled down in a gesture of distaste. 'I think you would learn more from the other maids . . . if anything is known at all. Girls talk to each other, not to their mistresses. You surely don't imagine Kitty would have spoken to my wife about her . . . romance . . . if we could use that word for such a liaison.'

'I was not thinking of confidences so much as your wife's observations of Kitty,' Pitt answered. 'My own wife is a very good judge of character. I imagine Mrs Kynaston is also. Women see things in other women, whatever their social station. And no woman who runs a house well is ignorant of the character of her maids.'

Kynaston sighed. 'Yes, of course you are right. I wished to spare her this distress, but perhaps it is not possible.'

Pitt smiled a trifle bleakly, knowing in his mind exactly how Charlotte would have reacted had he tried to conceal such a thing from her. 'If you would be good enough to ask her to give me half an hour or so of her time . . . '

'What about the other maids?' Kynaston did

not move. 'Or the housekeeper? Female staff are her concern.'

'I will have Sergeant Stoker speak to them, when he is finished with the scene of the . . . discovery, and with the local police.'

'I see,' Kynaston said thoughtfully. 'I see.' Still he hesitated.

This time Pitt did not help him. He had long learned that silence can betray people as much as words, sometimes in the subtlest of ways.

'I . . . ' Kynaston cleared his throat. ' . . . I would like to be present when you speak to her. My wife is . . . is easily distressed. If indeed it is Kitty, she will take it extremely hard.'

Pitt did not want Kynaston there, but he had no excuse to deny him at this point. Had it been Charlotte, at the time when Gracie Phipps had been with them, she would have been distraught at the idea of her having been hurt at all, let alone beaten to death. For that matter, so would Pitt himself. Even their new maid, Minnie Maude Mudway, had found a large place in their affections already.

'Of course,' he agreed. 'I shall be as discreet as possible.' He was about to explain further, and realised he was being gentler than was wise. If the body was that of Kitty Ryder, then a great deal of pain, possibly even of embarrassment, was inevitable.

Kynaston excused himself and returned twenty minutes later with not only Rosalind Kynaston, but his sister-in-law, Ailsa, as well. Both of them were immaculately dressed as if ready for an evening outing.

51

Rosalind wore a beautifully tailored costume of dark blue. It was a cold colour for winter, but with pale lace at the throat it became her well enough. There was a dignity in her manner, though she was gaunt and when she met Pitt's eyes her hand instinctively reached out to clasp on to something. Kynaston offered his arm, and she ignored it.

Beside her, Ailsa, taller and so very much fairer, looked magnificent in soft greys. Pitt could not have said exactly how, but he recognised the latest cut in sweeping skirt, now short enough not to touch the ground and get wet. The whole costume needed only a fur hat to be perfect, and no doubt she had such a thing. She took Rosalind's arm, without asking her permission, and guided her to the large, soft sofa, easing them both into it, side by side. She stared at Pitt with sharp blame in her blue eyes.

Kynaston remained standing, as though he felt that to sit down would somehow relax his guard.

'We do not yet know what happened to Kitty, Mr Pitt,' Ailsa said a little brusquely. 'My sister-in-law told you that we would inform you if we did.'

'Yes, Mrs Kynaston, I know that,' Pitt replied. The woman irritated him and he had to remind himself that although she certainly did not look it, she was probably afraid, more for her sister-in-law than for her own sake. The thought flickered through his mind that she might be more aware of the domestic realities than the younger and apparently more delicate Rosalind. He had a sudden cold vision of Kynaston's possible affair with a handsome maid: quarrels, embarrassment, even an attempt at blackmail, a flare of temper out of control.

Was that what he saw in Ailsa's vivid eyes, and the fear of everything that exposure would bring? To whom? Scandal to Kynaston? Or disillusion to Rosalind? But he was days ahead of himself, and quite probably mistaken.

Ailsa was waiting, somewhat impatiently.

'I am sorry to inform you that we have discovered the body of a young woman up at the gravel pit to the west of here,' Pitt told her. 'We do not know who she is, but we would like to assure ourselves, and you, that it is not Kitty Ryder.' Out of the corner of his vision he saw Kynaston relax a little. It was no more than a slight change in his stance, as if he breathed more easily.

Ailsa gave the ghost of a smile. Rosalind did not stop staring straight at Pitt.

'Why don't you find out who she is, and then you would have no need to disturb my sister-in-law?' Ailsa said with an edge of criticism in her voice. She did not like Pitt and she had no intention of concealing the fact. It might not have any meaning in this case, or with Kitty Ryder, but he wondered why. Rosalind did not seem to have any such feelings. But perhaps she was too numb to feel anything. Did she usually need Ailsa to protect her?

If the body were that of Kitty Ryder, Pitt suspected that there was going to be a difficult mass of emotions to untangle, many of them irrelevant. Everyone had secrets, old wounds that still bled, people they loved or hated, sometimes both.

'You would have heard of it within a day or two at the outside,' Pitt assured her. 'And if we have not eliminated the possibility that it is anyone from your house, it will be far more distressing.'

'For goodness' sake why don't you know now?' Ailsa demanded. 'She was a perfectly recognisable young woman. Get the butler, or someone, to go and look at her. Isn't that your job? Why on earth are you here bothering us?'

Rosalind put her hand on her sister-in-law's sleeve. 'Ailsa, give him a chance to tell us. I dare say he has his reasons.'

Pitt avoided the answer, aware of Kynaston's eyes on him and a sharp, almost electric tension in the air.

He looked at Rosalind. 'Mrs Kynaston, I imagine that, like most ladies, you have a number of handkerchiefs, some of them embroidered with your initials?'

'Yes, several,' she replied with a frown.

'Why on earth does that matter?' Ailsa snapped.

Kynaston opened his mouth to reprove her, and changed his mind. He looked even tenser than before.

Pitt took the handkerchief from the corpse out of his pocket and passed it across to Rosalind.

She took it, damp in her fingers, and dropped it instantly, her face white.

Ailsa picked it up and examined it. Then she looked up at Pitt. 'It's a fairly ordinary

54

lace-edged handkerchief, made of cambric. I have half a dozen like it myself.'

'That one has an 'R' embroidered on it,' Pitt pointed out. 'Does yours not have an 'A'?'

'Naturally. There are thousands like these. If she was not the kind of person to own one herself, she could have stolen it from someone.'

'Did Kitty Ryder steal it from you, Mrs Kynaston?' Pitt asked Rosalind.

Rosalind gave the slightest shrug: a delicate gesture but unmistakable. She had no idea. Taking it between her fingertip and thumb, she passed it back to Pitt.

'Is that all?' Kynaston asked.

Pitt replaced the handkerchief in his pocket. 'No. She also had a small key, the sort that might open a cupboard or a drawer.'

No one responded. They sat stiff and waiting, not glancing at each other.

'It fits one of the cupboards in your laundry room,' Pitt added.

Ailsa raised her delicate eyebrows slightly. 'Only one? Or did you not try the rest? In my house such a key would have fitted all of them.'

Rosalind drew in her breath as if to speak, and then changed her mind.

Was it anger in Ailsa, or fear? Or simply defence of someone she saw as more vulnerable than herself? Pitt replied to her levelly, politely. 'I am aware that there are only a limited number of types of keys, especially of that very simple sort. I have cupboards in my own house, and I have found that all the doors in one piece of furniture can be opened by the same key. This one opened one set of doors, but nothing in your kitchen, or pantry, for example.'

Ailsa did not flinch. 'Are you concluding from this ... evidence ... that the unfortunate woman in the gravel pit is Kitty Ryder?'

'No, Mrs Kynaston. I am hoping there is some way of proving that she is not.' It was perfectly honest: he would very much rather she were someone about whom he knew nothing, whose friends or relatives he would meet only when there was no hope left of her being alive. It was easier, he admitted to himself. You went prepared. Probably it would be a case for the local police, not Special Branch at all.

Kynaston cleared his throat, but when he spoke his voice was still hoarse.

'Do you wish me to look at this poor woman and see if I recognise her?'

'No, sir,' Pitt said gently. 'If you will permit me to take your butler, Norton, he will know her better and be in a position to tell us, if it is possible, whether this is Kitty Ryder, or not.'

'Yes ... yes, of course,' Kynaston agreed, breathing out slowly. 'I'll tell him immediately.' He seemed about to add something, but glancing first at Ailsa, then at Rosalind, instead he said goodbye to Pitt with a brief nod, and turned to go and seek Norton.

'That is all we can do for you, Mr Pitt.' Ailsa did not rise to her feet, but her dismissal was clear.

'Thank you for your consideration,' Rosalind added quietly.

Pitt and Norton travelled to the morgue by hansom cab. Norton sat bolt upright, his hands clenched in his lap, knuckles white. Neither of them spoke. There was no sound except the clatter of the horse's feet and the hiss of the wheels on the wet road, then the occasional splash as they passed through a deeper puddle.

Pitt let the silence remain. Norton could have felt anything for the girl he was perhaps going to identify, from indifference, possibly irritation, dislike, through respect even to affection. Or the clearly intense emotion he suffered now could be quite impersonal, simply a dread of death. Anybody's death was a reminder that it was the one unavoidable reality in all life.

Perhaps he had lost someone else young: a mother, a sister, even a daughter. It happened to many people. Pitt was lucky it had not happened to him — at least not yet. Please God — never!

Or it might be that Norton feared that if it were Kitty, then her murder had some connection with the Kynaston house and someone who lived in it, either family or staff.

And there was the other possibility also, as there was in every household, that close and intrusive police investigation would expose all kinds of other secrets, weaknesses, the petty deceits that keep lives whole, and private. Everyone needed some illusions; they were the clothes that kept them from emotional naked-ness. It was sometimes more than a kindness not to see too much; it was a decency, a safety to oneself as well as to others.

It was Pitt's duty to watch this man as he looked at the body, read all his emotions, however private or, for that matter, however irrelevant. He could not find justice or protection for the innocent without the truth. But he still felt intrusive.

It was also his duty to interrogate him now, while he was emotionally raw and at his most vulnerable.

'Did Kitty often go out with the young carpenter?' he began. 'That was very lenient of Mrs Kynaston to allow her to. Or did she do it without asking?'

Norton stiffened. 'Certainly not. She was allowed her half-day off, and she went out with him sometimes, just for the afternoon. A walk in the park, or out to tea. She was always home by six. At least . . . nearly always,' he amended.

'Did you approve of him?' Pitt asked, now watching his face for the feeling behind the words.

Norton's shoulders tightened — he stared straight ahead. 'He was pleasant enough.'

'Had he a temper?'

'Not that I observed.'

'Would you have employed him, if he had a domestic ability you could use?'

Norton thought for a moment. 'Yes,' he said at last. 'I think I would.' A faint smile crossed his face and vanished. Pitt could not read it.

They reached the morgue and alighted. Pitt paid the driver then led the way inside. He stayed close to Norton because he was afraid the man might faint. He looked white, and a little awkward, as though he were not certain of his balance.

As always, the place smelled of carbolic and death. Pitt was not certain which was the worse. Antiseptic always made him think of corpses anyway, and then of loss, and pain. He hurried without meaning to, and then had to wait for Norton to catch up when he reached the end of the passage and the door to the cold room that they wanted.

The attendant seemed to disappear into the grey walls, the sheet that had fully concealed the corpse in his hands. Now it was covered only as much as decency required. She looked even more broken and alone than she had lying sprawled out in the gravel pit on the freezing grass.

Norton gasped and choked on his own breath. Pitt took his arm to support him if he should faint.

There was no sound but an irregular dripping somewhere. Norton took a step closer and looked down at the body, the blotched and rotted flesh coming away from the bone, the hollow eye sockets, the ravaged face. The auburn hair was thick and tangled now, but it was still possible to see where clumps of it had been torn out.

Norton backed away at last, staggering a little, uncertain of his footing although the floor was even. Pitt still kept hold of him.

'I don't know,' Norton said hoarsely. 'I can't say. God help her, whoever she is.' He began to shake as though suddenly the cold had reached him.

'I didn't expect you would,' Pitt assured him. 'But you might have been able to say that it was not her. Perhaps the hair was wrong, or the height . . . '

'No,' Norton gulped. 'No . . . the hair looks right. She . . . she had beautiful hair. Perhaps it was a little darker than that . . . but it looked . . . messy. She was always very careful of her hair.' He stopped abruptly, unable to control his voice.

Pitt allowed him to walk away and go out of the room into the cold, tiled passage, then along to the door to the outside and the steady drenching rain that held nothing worse than physical discomfort. They still did not know if the woman from the gravel pit was Kitty Ryder, or some other poor creature whose name and life they might never learn.

★   ★   ★

The next morning Stoker finished all the enquiries he could make locally, and on leaving the police station in Blackheath he walked up the rise towards Shooters Hill. He was careful to keep his footing on the ice. Pitt had said little yet as to how they would approach the staff in the Kynaston house regarding Kitty Ryder. Stoker was surprised how much he still wanted to find her alive.

Without realising it he had increased his pace, and he had to steady himself. The footpath was

60

treacherous. Perhaps someone could tell him a detail, a fact that would prove that the woman they had found in the gravel pit was not her, could not be, from some quirk or other: a birthmark, the shape of her hands, a particular pattern in the way her hair grew — anything. Maybe there was something the butler, Norton, had been too emotionally overwrought to notice.

It was all ridiculous. He knew that. One woman's life was as important, as unique as another. He knew nothing about Mrs Kynaston's maid, except what Pitt had told him. If he had met her he might have found her just as ordinary, as trivial, as the most unattractive person he knew. To allow his imagination to become involved was bad detection. He knew that too. Facts. Deal with the facts only. Allow them to take you wherever they lead.

He reached the areaway steps where he had first found the blood and broken glass. There was nothing there now. They had been swept clean, apart from a few iced-over puddles where endless feet coming and going had worn a dip in the stone.

He knocked on the door and after a few moments it was opened by Maisie. She looked at him blankly for a moment, then lit up with a smile when she recognised him.

'Yer come ter tell us yer found Kitty, an' the body in't 'er at all?' she said immediately. Then she screwed up her eyes and looked at him more closely. Her voice caught in her throat. 'It in't 'er — is it?'

She was only a child and suddenly Stoker, in

61

his mid-thirties, felt very old.

'I don't think so.' He meant it to sound gentler, but he was not used to softening the truth.

Her face crumpled. 'Wot d'yer mean, yer don't think so! Is it 'er or not?'

He resisted the temptation to lie, but only with difficulty. 'We don't think it's her,' he replied. 'We just need to be sure. I have to ask all of you some more questions about her.'

She did not move aside. 'Din't Mr Norton go ter look at 'er?'

'She's in a bad way. It didn't help a lot,' he replied. 'Can I come in? It's cold out here, and you're letting it all in with the door open.'

'S'pose so,' she said grudgingly, stepping back at last and allowing him to go past her into the scullery.

'Thank you.' He closed the door firmly behind him. The sudden warmth made him sneeze and he blew his nose to clear it. Then he smelled the onions and herbs hanging on the racks.

Maisie bit her lip to stop it trembling. 'I s'pose yer want a cup o' tea, an' all?' Without waiting for his answer, she led him into the kitchen where the cook was busy preparing dinner, rolling pastry ready to put on top of the fruit pie on the counter.

'You got those carrots prepared then, Maisie?' she said sharply before she noticed Stoker following. 'You back?' She looked at him with disfavour. 'We only just got rid o' yer gaffer. 'E bin 'ere 'alf o' yesterday upsetting everyone. Wot is it now?'

Stoker knew how irritated people were when interrupted in their work, and least likely to tell you what you needed to know. He wanted them to be at ease, not merely answering what he asked, but filling in the details, the colour he could not deliberately seek.

'I don't want to interrupt you,' he said, filling his tone with respect. 'I'd just like you to tell me a little more about Kitty.'

Cook looked up from her pastry, the wooden rolling pin still in both hands. 'Why? She ran off with that miserable young man of 'ers, didn't she?' Her face crumpled up with anger. 'Stupid girl. She could 'a done a lot better for 'erself. Come ter that, she couldn't 'ardly 'a done worse!' She sniffed hard and resumed her smoothing and easing the shape of the pie crust.

Stoker heard the emotion in her voice, and saw it in the angry tightness of her shoulders and the way she hid her face from him. She had cared about Kitty and she was frightened for her. Anger was easier, and less painful. He knew from relatives in service, old friends he seldom saw, that few household servants had family they were still in touch with. If they stayed for any length of time the other servants became family to them, full of the same loyalties, squabbles, rivalries and intimate knowledge. Kitty might have been the closest this woman, bent over her pastry, would have to a daughter of her own.

Stoker wanted to be gentle, and it was almost impossible.

'Probably she did,' he agreed. 'But we didn't find her, so we've got no proof of it. Got to know

63

who this woman is in the gravel pit. I'd like to know for sure it's not her.'

She looked up at him, her eyes filled with tears. 'Yer saying as that 'orrible . . . fool . . . did that to 'er?'

'No, ma'am, I'm saying I'd like to prove it's got nothing to do with this house at all, and keep the police away from having to trouble you.'

She sniffed and searched for a handkerchief in her apron pocket. When she had found it and had blown her nose, she gave him her full attention. 'Well, what do you want to know about Kitty? She might 'a been a fool about men, goin' an' picking the stupidest great lummox she could find.' She glared at him, daring him to argue.

'How did she meet him?' Stoker asked.

'Came an' did a carpentry job 'ere,' she answered. 'Kept coming back even after it were finished, just to see 'er.'

'Was she frightened of him?' He tried to keep the sudden anger out of his own voice, and his face.

'Not 'er! Ask me, she were sorry for 'im,' she responded. 'More fool 'er! 'E played on it. 'Oo wouldn't?'

'She was gentle?' he said with some surprise. The idea he had in his mind was of a strong woman, handsome and sure of herself. But the cook might know of a vulnerable side to her that her mistress didn't.

The cook laughed and shook her head. 'Yer just like all men, aren't yer! Think because a woman's 'andsome, an' got a mind of 'er own,

64

that she can't be 'urt, can't cry 'erself ter sleep when no one sees 'er, like anyone else. She were worth ten of 'im, any day, an' 'e knew it.' She was obliged to blow her nose again, hiding the tears on her face.

'Did that make him angry with her?' Stoker asked.

'Didn't think so.' She glared at him. 'You tellin' me I'm wrong?'

He did not answer. He needed to know more: for example, if it was indeed Kitty lying in the morgue, how had she come by the gold watch that had been stolen from Dudley Kynaston?

'Who else did she know?' he asked. 'Anyone who gave her expensive presents?'

'No she didn't!' the cook snapped back at him. 'If she were a fool like that, you think she'd 'a bin a lady's maid?' There was contempt in her voice, and she was too hurt to try to govern it. He was only a policeman of sorts and she had done nothing wrong to fear him. 'If you mean to stay in a quality house like this, you don't never let your greed get the better o' you,' she said witheringly. 'You're thinking just because she got soft over a young man what wasn't worth it, that she were stupid all the time? Well, she weren't. If she'd 'a been born in the right family, and learned 'ow ter be'ave 'erself like a lady, she could 'a married the best an' never 'ad ter work a day in 'er life. Yer take wot life gives yer, an' get on with it. You too, an' all!'

Stoker smiled, something he did not often do on duty. Most of his work was grim — and, more often than not, he did it alone. Perhaps he was too sober? He would have liked Kitty Ryder, if he had known her.

'You are quite right,' he conceded. 'So apart from her choice in admirer, she was wise in her friends.'

'I'm not sayin' as she didn't 'ave some daft ideas,' the cook said more amiably. 'An' some dreams as wouldn't never 'appen. Course she did. Wot girl don't? An' she could fight 'er corner if she'd a mind to. But not like some, she could own up if she were wrong . . . sometimes, any 'ow.'

'Thank you, you've been very helpful. I'd like to speak to the rest of the staff, if you please.' He did not expect them to add much, but it was possible some of those nearer Kitty's age might know other things, details he could use. He had spoken to them before, but this was different. Now there was the matter of the gold watch. The handkerchief might be Rosalind's, and possibly given to Kitty. The watch was unquestionably Kynaston's, and stolen from him, but seemingly by a pickpocket in the street. It was essential that they prove beyond any reasonable doubt that the woman in the gravel pit was someone else. That was his job, in order to protect Dudley Kynaston. Then the presence of the watch would be a coincidence — probably!

★ ★ ★

Late that same afternoon Pitt received a message that he should report to the Home Office at his

66

very earliest convenience. Perhaps seven o'clock that evening would be a good idea.

He read the note at quarter past six, but knew that he had no choice but to make it convenient. So after changing his wet jacket and his muddy boots, he took a hansom. Shortly after ten past seven, he entered a pleasant room with portraits of Home Secretaries of the past, some of their faces from every child's history books, pompous and unsmiling.

Pitt glanced at the newspapers on the table near the fireplace. The headlines caught his eye. 'Mutilated Corpse in Gravel Pit still Unidentified'. And underneath it: 'Police Say Nothing!' Pitt deliberately looked away.

He waited for a further twenty minutes before being greeted by a well-groomed young gentleman who came in and closed the door behind him.

'So sorry to keep you waiting, Commander Pitt,' he said with a slight smile, as though well-mannered in spite of his own importance.

Pitt thought of several terse replies, and then how he could not afford to make them.

'I was late, Mr Rogers,' he said equally politely. 'I could not come here covered in mud.'

Rogers' fair eyebrows rose. 'Mud?'

'It is raining outside,' Pitt said, as if perhaps Rogers had not noticed.

Rogers glanced down at Pitt's immaculate polished boots, and then up at his face.

'We found a body in a gravel pit at Shooters Hill before dawn yesterday,' Pitt explained. 'I had occasion to go back there.'

'Yes . . . yes. About that . . . ' Rogers cleared his throat. 'Extremely distasteful, of course. Have you identified her yet?'

'No. There is a possibility that it is the missing maid from Dudley Kynaston's house, but the butler was unable to confirm or deny the body is her.'

'Really?' The young man's eyes widened. 'I find that hard to believe. Is the man lying, do you suppose? I assume he did look? He didn't . . . evade it, turn away? Faint?'

'She has been dead for some time, and is badly mutilated,' Pitt told him. 'Apart from her very serious facial injuries, the flesh is beginning to decay. I can go into detail, if you wish, but I imagine you would prefer that I didn't. Her eyes are missing, but her hair is unusual.'

'Yes, I see,' the man said hastily. 'That makes it difficult . . . I appreciate the . . . ' He stopped. 'However, the important thing is that you cannot say for certain that it is Kynaston's maid, correct?'

'Correct,' Pitt agreed.

The young man relaxed the stiff line of his shoulders. His voice, when he spoke, was suddenly softer. 'Excellent. Then it will not be difficult for you to leave the matter to the local police. She is probably some prostitute who was unfortunate in her choice of customer. Sad and extremely ugly, but not a Special Branch matter, and certainly nothing to do with Kynaston. The Home Secretary asked me to convey to you his appreciation of your discretion in stepping in so quickly, just in case the local police were clumsy and caused any degree of embarrassment to the Kynaston family, and therefore to the Government. We have enemies who would seek to profit from even the slightest appearance of an . . . unfortunate association.' He inclined his head slightly. It was dismissal.

Pitt wanted to argue, to point out that the issue was not finished yet, and it was too soon to assume it settled. But he had been dealing with crimes and investigation all his adult life. He understood both gossip and authority. He had learned how to use them, not always successfully. Reason agreed with the young man, instinct spoke against him. It had not been phrased so, but he knew this was an order. It was part of his new position that he should not require anything blunter.

'Of course,' he said quietly. 'Good evening.'

The young man smiled. 'Good evening, sir.'

Pitt was later home than he had wished to be, and he found that the rest of the family had already eaten dinner. Charlotte, however, had waited for him. She offered him the choice of the kitchen or the dining-room table, and he chose the kitchen. It was warmer, both literally and in the sense that it was the room at the heart of his family's life. Their closest friends had sat around this table in anxiety, working on desperate challenges, in grief when they seemed beaten, and in celebration when victory was grasped.

Now he ate hot beef stew with vegetables, lots of onions, and dumplings.

The discovery of the woman's body in the

69

gravel pit was in no way secret, reported, as it had been, in the newspapers. Of course the usual speculations had accompanied the few known facts.

'Is it the missing maid?' Charlotte asked, leaving her own portion of stew untouched.

'I wish I knew,' he replied when he had swallowed his mouthful.

'Are they going to admit it, if it is?' She looked at him directly, demanding his attention.

He smiled in spite of himself. He should have known she would say that, or something like it. She had learned to curb her tongue over the years, but never her thoughts, and never with him.

'Not if they can help it,' he replied.

'Will you go along with that?' she persisted. 'I suppose you'll have to. Is Kynaston really so important? Thomas, for heaven's sake, do be careful.'

He heard the sudden gravity in her voice and realised she was genuinely afraid for him. She had been proud when he was promoted, and never for an instant doubted he was able to fill Narraway's position. Furthermore, until now she had concealed almost completely her understanding of the danger of it. Or was it that he had never told her the worst? There were whole areas he could not speak of, not as he had in the past when he was merely a policeman.

'My dear, it is simply a missing maid,' he said gently. 'It seems she ran off with a rather unpleasant young man who had been courting her. If it is her body in the gravel pit, it is a tragedy. But regardless of who it is, it is a young woman dead. The fact that she used to be Mrs Kynaston's maid — if it is her — draws attention to him it would be better to avoid, no more.'

She waited for a moment, then relaxed and smiled. 'I saw Emily today.' Emily was her younger sister, now married to Jack Radley, for some time a Member of Parliament. 'She knows Rosalind Kynaston slightly. She says she's very quiet and frankly rather boring.'

Pitt took another mouthful before he replied. 'Emily is easily bored. How is she?' He had not seen Emily since Christmas, now six weeks ago. Once she and Charlotte had helped in some of his more colourful cases, particularly those involving the wealthy and socially prominent, where they had access, while he, as a policeman, was sent round to the servants' entrance. It felt like a long time ago now. Emily's first husband had had both wealth and title, and had died tragically. For a short and desperate time in her life, Emily had been suspected of his murder. That, too, was well in the past.

Charlotte shrugged very slightly. 'You know how it is in winter.'

He waited, expecting her to add something. Instead, she stood up, went to the stove, lifted a treacle pudding out of its steaming pan and turned it out, upside down on to a large plate, watching with satisfaction as the rich, melted golden syrup ran down its sides. She knew it was one of his favourites. There was nothing more satisfying at the end of a long, cold, wet day. He

71

found himself smiling in anticipation, even though he was quite aware that she had deliberately evaded his question about Emily, which had to mean that there was something wrong.

4

It was two more days before Pitt heard from the police at Shooters Hill — or to be more precise, from the police surgeon, Dr Whistler. He received a short note, sealed in an envelope and delivered by a messenger who did not wait for an answer.

Pitt read it a second time.

Dear Commander Pitt,

I have further examined the body of the woman found in the gravel pit on Shooters Hill. I have learned a number of facts, not previously visible, which change the situation quite fundamentally. It is my duty to report these to Special Branch so you may act as you believe appropriate in the interests both of the state, and of justice.

I shall be in my office in the morgue for the rest of the day, and at your service.

Yours sincerely,
George Whistler, MD

Pitt obeyed the summons immediately. His first thought was that Whistler had found some way of being certain that the body was indeed Kitty Ryder, and her death was murder, and connected to the Kynaston house.

There was nothing to keep him at Lisson Grove. The matters in hand were all routine and very capably handled by others. He informed the appropriate people where he was going. Fifteen minutes later he was in a hansom on the long, traffic-clogged journey first to the river, across Westminster Bridge, then eastwards to Greenwich and the morgue. He was cold and uncomfortable in the hansom. He had several miles to cover, and the ice on the roads made the journey even slower than usual.

Finally he stood in Whistler's office. His coat was on the stand by the door and the warmth slowly seeping back into him, thawing out his hands and allowing his tense shoulders to ease a little.

Whistler had lost the slightly aggressive air he had had earlier. In fact he looked distinctly unhappy, as if he did not know how to begin.

'Well?' Pitt prompted him.

Whistler was also standing, but closer to the fire. He pushed his hands hard into his trouser pockets. 'Rather a lot of things, I'm afraid,' he replied. 'On more detailed examination of the body, it became apparent that she had died considerably earlier than I had thought from the degree of decay . . . '

Pitt was confused. 'Don't you tell the time a person has been dead from the degree of decay?'

'Will you let me finish?' Whistler snapped, his temper fraying at the first touch.

Pitt realised with a jolt that the man was more than merely annoyed with himself for having to alter his diagnosis. Something was disturbing him more deeply, even brushing him with a kind of dread.

Whistler cleared his throat. 'Bitterly cold temperatures, below freezing, can delay the process greatly, even put it off altogether, if they persist without break. This is why people keep ice houses for meat storage.' He hesitated, but Pitt did not interrupt again.

'This body was kept at or below freezing for some time, and the decay was slight. But she was not kept at the place where we found her. In fact she was not in the open at all, or scavenging animals would have got to her — at the very least, insects would have. Therefore she was in a very cold and completely enclosed place. Do you follow me so far?'

'You mean such as in somebody's ice house?' Pitt prompted.

'Precisely. We already know from witnesses that she was not where we found her, because it is close to a public footpath, used very infrequently, particularly at this time of year, but all the same, still used, and by people with dogs. I had assumed she had been placed there during that night — moved from wherever she was killed perhaps a day or two before, even a week.' Whistler was watching Pitt closely. 'It seemed to make sense that possibly someone killed her, in an unplanned attack, and then had to consider how to dispose of her body. It took him a few days to find a way of getting her up to the gravel pit unseen, and considering the circumstances, without anyone else's assistance.'

'A reasonable assumption,' Pitt agreed. 'No longer tenable?'

Whistler grunted and let his breath out

between his teeth. 'I examined the body very closely for the cause of death. While doing so I realised that the decay was much further advanced than I had supposed from the exterior. She had been kept somewhere extremely cold and . . . ' he took a deep breath before continuing, ' . . . and she had been cleaned up quite a lot after the injuries that caused her death . . . '

'What?'

Whistler glared at him. 'You heard me correctly, Commander. Someone made an attempt to clean her up, then instead of disposing of her, kept her body somewhere very cold, but thoroughly sealed so no scavengers found her. Therefore it was not in an ordinary outhouse, even in this weather. Most of the damage we saw, particularly to her face, was indeed done with a very sharp blade of some sort, including the removal of the eyes . . . and the lips. It was not animal depredation occurring during the one night she lay exposed in the gravel pit. And don't waste your time asking me for an explanation. I can only tell you the facts. Understanding them is your business, thank God!'

'And the cause of death?' Pitt felt cold again, in spite of the bright fire.

'Extreme violence,' Whistler replied. 'Blows hard enough to break her bones, specifically her shoulder blade, four ribs, the humerus in her left arm, and her pelvis in three places. But that was some time before the mutilations to her face. That is my point!' He glared at Pitt, his outrage aching for any other answer. 'Ten days at the absolute minimum.'

Pitt was appalled. It was one of the most savage beatings he could imagine. Whoever did it must have been completely insane. No wonder Whistler looked so wretched. If she were a prostitute it was no ordinary quarrel she had fallen victim to, it was an attack by a raving madman. If he could do that once, how long would it be before he did it again?

Suddenly the room seemed not warm and comfortably protected from the elements. It was more like a suffocating, airless imprisonment from the clean, driving sleet outside, and he longed to escape into it.

'What with?' he asked, his voice wavering a little. 'What did he use?'

'Honestly?' Whistler shook his head. 'This side of a lunatic asylum, I would say he ran her down with a coach and four. Hard to tell after the passage of time, and I'd say it's been three weeks or so by now. Some of the injuries could have been caused by horses' hoofs or carriage wheels. Considerable impact, from several directions and it could have happened all at once, like horses panicking.'

A momentary fury welled up inside Pitt. The man could have told him that in the first place. Hideous accidents happened. The damage and the pain were the same, but the horror was nothing like that of imagining a homicidal human being doing such a thing deliberately. He longed to actually hit Whistler, which was childish and he was ashamed of himself.

Nevertheless it was true. He clenched his fists and kept his voice level, even if it was tight and grated between his teeth.

'Are you saying that this woman's death could have been a traffic accident, and not a crime at all, Dr Whistler?'

'It could have been any number of things!' Whistler's answer rose to all but a shout. 'But if it was a traffic accident, why in God's name was it not reported to the police?' He waved his arms wide, only just missing the bookcase. 'Where the devil was she for two or three weeks? Why put her out in one of the Shooters Hill gravel pits for the foxes and badgers to eat her and maul her about, and that poor soul walking his dog to find?' He drew in a deep breath. 'And why the terrible mutilations so long afterwards? To tear her face, so she was unrecognisable?'

This time it was Pitt who was silent.

Whistler gave a shuddering sigh and fought to regain control of himself. He looked slightly embarrassed by his emotion and avoided meeting Pitt's eyes. Perhaps he thought himself unprofessional, but Pitt liked him the more for it.

'Anything further about who she was?' Pitt asked at last. 'Something not obliterated by this . . . lunatic?'

'Probably in good health, as far as I could tell at this stage,' Whistler answered. 'No apparent disease. Organs all fine, apart from beginning to decay. If you find whoever did this to her, I hope you hang him! If you don't, don't come back to me for any help!' His glare swivelled to Pitt, then away again. There was a faint flush in his cheeks. 'She was probably a domestic servant. Little things, you know? Good teeth. Well-nourished. Clean nails, good hands, but several small scars from burning, the sort you see on a woman who does a lot of ironing. Difficult things not to burn yourself with now and again, flat irons. Especially if you're ironing something fiddly, like lace, or gathered sleeves, delicate collars, that kind of thing.'

'A lady's maid . . . ' Pitt said the inevitable.

'Yes . . . or a laundry maid of a more general sort. Children's clothes are fiddly too.'

'So you still have no idea whether it is Kitty Ryder or not?'

'No, I haven't. Sorry. But she wasn't a lady. Ladies don't do their own ironing. And she wasn't a prostitute — much too clean and healthy for that. She must have been in her mid- to late twenties. On the streets, by that age she'd have looked a lot worse. A servant, or a young married woman, taking in laundry. Not likely. Everyone around here has their own servants for that sort of thing. And she'd had no children. With the injuries and the rot I don't know if she was still a virgin.'

'Thank you,' Pitt said grimly, as a matter of courtesy; it was the last thing he actually meant. He did not want the case, and he knew that Whistler would rather not have found the evidence, or have had to tell him about it. It was all inevitable now: the slow, sad unravelling of whoever's tragedy it was. 'Have you told the local police?' he added, almost as an afterthought.

A bitter amusement flashed in Whistler's eyes. 'Yes.' He did not add their reaction, but Pitt could guess it. They would be delighted it was a problem they would have to give up to Special Branch, just in case it should end up involving Dudley Kynaston.

Pitt took his damp overcoat and hat off the coat rack and put them on. He said goodbye to Whistler and went out into the passage, and then the cold street again. He could have got a hansom here and ridden all the way back to Lisson Grove, but he preferred to walk down to the river and sit in a ferry on the choppy grey water, alone with the wind and the rain, and think what he was going to do next, and how he was going to do it. He could get a cab on the far side.

There were too many questions unanswered. If this were the body of Kitty Ryder, had it also been her blood and hair on the steps of the Kynaston house? Was it a quarrel, but she had still eventually gone willingly? Or had she been taken by force? Why would her suitor have done such a thing? If he had killed her there, it had been an extraordinarily violent quarrel to conduct so close to an inhabited house. Why had no one heard anything? In fact, why had she not screamed, and brought the whole household out?

Why had he not left her there and escaped as fast as he could? She was a big woman for someone to have carried anywhere. If he had run off into the night, leaving her dead in the alleyway, he had an excellent chance of never being found. London was a large city to lose yourself in, and there was the whole of the countryside beyond that! Or, if you were desperate enough, ships sailed every day from the Pool of London for every part of the world.

Pitt looked across the rough water at them now: masts jostling against the sky in the distance; steamers heavier, and more solid; barges and lighters threading between them. A man could lose himself here in a day, never mind three weeks. None of this made sense. What was he missing?

The silent ferryman at the oars and the rhythmic slap of the water on the sides of the boat helped him to concentrate.

Where had she been from the time she left Kynaston's house until she was placed in the gravel pit? Was she killed straight away, or later? Why put her in the gravel pit anyway? Why not bury her? That made no sense. It was almost as if someone had intended her to be found.

The longer he considered it, the uglier and more senseless it appeared. He still hoped it was not Kitty at all, but he knew he must proceed as if it were.

★   ★   ★

At Lisson Grove, Stoker would have heard that Pitt had been summoned by Whistler, and must have been watching for Pitt to return. Within ten minutes he appeared in Pitt's office. He closed the door behind him and stood expectantly, waiting to be told.

Pitt did so, briefly.

81

Stoker listened in silence. His strong, bony face was unreadable, except for the increased pallor. He looked down at the floor, his shoulders hunched a little, hands in his pockets.

'No choice, have we?' he stated. 'This doesn't make any sense. There's a major part of it we don't know anything about.' He looked up, his blue-grey eyes brilliant. 'Maybe it has nothing to do with the young man she was courting, sir. It could all be in the Kynaston household. According to what I learned about her from the other servants, she was smart, and didn't miss much. A lady's maid gets to know a lot of things, that's why they stay in places a long time. You can't afford to let them go, 'specially not to a position with anyone in your own circle.'

'What are you suggesting?' Pitt faced the inevitable. 'That she was blackmailing someone in the house, and they refused to pay? Or that they killed her simply because she knew?'

Stoker winced. 'Either one, sir. Maybe she knew what they'd do and she tried to run away, an' that's where they caught her?'

'And she didn't cry out?'

'Couldn't you kill a woman without letting her scream, sir? I could.'

Pitt imagined it: Kitty terrified because she knew what she had seen, or heard, running out of the house, even in the dark in the winter. She would have gone through the dimly lit kitchen and scullery to the back door, struggling with the bolts on the doors, flinging them open and going outside into the bitter air, scrambling up the steps. Had she known her killer was only yards behind her? Or had he come silently, his footsteps masked in her ears by her own pounding heart? There had been a brief, terrible fight on the steps, a blow — fatal sooner than the killer had realised. He had gone on pounding, beating, until the hysteria had died down inside him and he had seen what he had done.

Then what?

He had moved the body quickly. Where to? A cellar? Somewhere bitterly cold, until he could move it again. And some mischance had delayed that.

Pitt looked at Stoker's face and saw a trace of the same thought in his eyes.

'Most likely Kynaston,' Stoker said aloud. 'We'd better find out.'

There was no argument to be made, only careful plans, and perhaps something of Dudley Kynaston himself to be learned before they began. 'Yes . . . ' Pitt agreed. 'I'll start with Kynaston tomorrow. You start with Kitty Ryder.'

★   ★   ★

Stoker did not wait until the morning. He had already learned all he could about Kitty Ryder from where she had lived and worked.

He and Pitt had naturally checked with police all over the area to see if there had been similar attacks, and found nothing.

Stoker himself had spoken to the institutions that kept the criminally insane. No one had escaped. There was no record of such mutilations anywhere else.

No matter where else they looked, they were turned back to Kitty herself, and her connections with the Kynaston house.

Stoker lived alone in rented rooms. He had no family in this part of London. In fact there were only himself and his sister Gwen left anyway, and she lived in King's Langley, a short train journey away. Their two brothers had died in childhood, and a sister in giving birth to her own child. His work filled his life. He realised how much, with an awareness of suddenly being anonymous as he walked along the wet pavement from the island of light beneath one streetlamp through the mist and shadows to the island beneath the next.

Other people seemed to be moving more rapidly, heads bent, as if hurrying towards some purpose. Were they eager for what was ahead of them? Or only weary of what was behind?

Stoker had begun in the navy as a boy, and the hard life on a ship had taught him the worth of discipline. One might argue with men, trick or deceive them, even bribe them, but no one argued with the sea. The bones of those who had tried littered the ocean's floor. He had learned both obedience and command, at least to a moderate level, and had expected his life to follow that path.

Then an incident while in port had involved investigation by Special Branch, and he had been recruited by Victor Narraway, at that time its commander. It was a different life; more interesting; in its own way more demanding, certainly of his imagination and intelligence. He found to his surprise that he had a considerable skill for it.

Then Narraway had been forced out. It was only Pitt who had been loyal to Narraway and eventually saved his reputation, perhaps his life, but not his position. Pitt had inherited that himself, much to his embarrassment and dismay. He did not wish to profit from Narraway's loss. Nor did he, frankly, think that he had the necessary skills or experience to succeed.

Of course he had not said so to Stoker, possibly not to anyone at all. But Stoker was a good judge of men, and he saw it in a dozen tiny details. Less so now, perhaps, after a year, but still there, to one who had recognised them before.

Stoker liked Pitt. There was an innate decency in him it was impossible to disregard. However, occasionally he worried that some quality in Pitt would stay his hand when he should strike. The position he now held demanded ruthlessness, and therefore an ability to live with mistakes, to forgive himself and move on, not allowing the memory of them to debilitate him.

And yet even with that realisation, he did not want Pitt to change. It saddened him that perhaps that was inevitable. He might even be driven to take a lead in that himself one day.

Kitty Ryder troubled him also. He had never even met the woman or seen a likeness of her. He pictured her in his mind: something like his sister Gwen, who had thick, soft hair and a quick smile, nice teeth, one a little crooked.

Even though he did not see her more than

perhaps once a month, the closeness between them was always in his mind. Gwen would have been a good lady's maid, if she had not married young and started a family. She was lucky; her husband was a decent man, even if he was away at sea too much of the time.

He came to the pub where he ate frequently and went inside to the noise and the warmth. He ordered a steak and kidney pie, but even while he ate, his mind was on Kitty Ryder. What had she been like? What made her laugh, or cry? Why had she apparently loved a man that everyone else thought was unworthy of her? Why did any woman love a man?

Here he was, sitting alone in the pub, angry over the fate of a woman he had never met and who was probably nothing like Gwen at all!

He paid for his ale, and walked out into the cold, wet night. She was the victim, at the very least, of a hideous mutilation and abandonment. He was a detective, he should find out about her. He took a hansom back up to the Shooters Hill area and went into the café near the Pig and Whistle on Silver Street. He was not naturally convivial but it was part of his job to mix with people, start casual conversations and ask questions without seeming to.

It was growing late and he was all but ready to give up when the waiter, refilling his tankard, mentioned Kitty.

''Aven't seen 'er lately,' he said with a shrug. 'Pity. We'd music sometimes. She used ter sing real sweet. Don't like them 'igh, tinkly sort o' voices, but 'ers were low and gentle. No edge to it, if yer know what I mean? Not as she couldn't carry a jolly good tune, an' make us laugh, an' all.'

'She came in here often?' Stoker tried to keep the eagerness out of his face, avoiding looking at the man's eyes.

'Yer know 'er, then?' the waiter asked curiously.

'No.' Stoker forced himself to drink some of the fresh cider before he went on. 'Friend o' mine liked her quite a lot. He hasn't seen her in a month or so either. Maybe she got a new place . . . ' He let the suggestion hang in the air.

'More fool 'er,' the waiter said drily. 'Got a good position, it don't do to change it. She never spoke like she meant ter. But then she kept 'er own counsel, that one. Never talked loose, like.' He shook his head. ' 'Er and 'er ships . . . real dreamer, she was. 'Ope she landed on 'er feet.' He turned to the room. 'Drink up, gents. I ain't stayin' open all night.'

'Ships?' Stoker said quietly. 'What kind of ships?'

The waiter grinned. 'Paper ones, mate. Pictures of all kinds o' ships: big ones, little ones, foreign ones what sail out east, like up an' down the Nile. She kept 'em an' stuck 'em in a book. Learned all about 'em, she did. Could tell yer where they went an' 'oo sailed 'em. Will yer be wantin' another pint, then?'

'No, thank you,' Stoker declined, but he pulled a sixpence out of his pocket and put it on the table. 'But here's for the last one, and have one yourself.'

The waiter snatched it up instantly and smiled. 'Thank you, sir. You're a gent.'

Stoker went outside into the rising wind, walking down towards the river to catch a ferry across. He would have a better chance of finding a cab on the other side for the long ride home.

By the time he reached the north bank and climbed the steep stairs up to the road the night was clear. The moon lit the water so he could see the real ships riding on the tide, dark hulls on the silver, black spars against a paler sky.

* * *

Pitt was at the Kynaston house on Shooters Hill by half-past eight the next morning. Any later and he might have missed Kynaston himself, and Rosalind would almost certainly refuse to see him without her husband present.

This time, at Pitt's request they met in Kynaston's study. Pitt had no time alone in the room, which he would have preferred. However, even as they spoke he looked more closely at what he was able to see without obviously staring.

Kynaston sat behind his desk. It was a large, comfortable piece of furniture with a patina of age, and suitably untidy. The sand tray, sealing wax, pens and inkwells were easily to hand, not set straight since last used. The books on the shelf behind were there for reference, not ornament. The sizes were odd, the subjects aligned rather than the appearance. There were several paintings on the walls, some of ships, or seascapes, one of a striking snowscape with trees, and mountains of some height in the distance, like the ones pictured in the morning room.

Certainly it was not a depiction of any part of Britain.

Kynaston saw Pitt looking at it.

'Beautiful,' Pitt said quickly, racing in his memory to find some comment from his earlier days in the police when he had dealt with theft, frequently of works of art. 'The clarity of the light is extraordinary.'

Kynaston looked at him with a spark of sudden interest. 'It is, isn't it!' he agreed. 'You get it in the far north, almost luminous like that.'

Pitt frowned. 'But it's not Scotland, surely? The scale is more than artistic licence . . . '

Kynaston smiled. 'Oh, no, it's pretty accurate. It's Sweden. I've been there, very briefly. My brother, Bennett, bought that one. He . . . ' A shadow of pain crossed his face as if the sharpness of loss suddenly revisited him. He took a breath and started again. 'He spent some time there, and grew to love the landscape, especially the light. As you observed, it is quite individual.' A pleasure came back into his voice, the timbre completely different. 'He always used to say that great art is distinguished by a universality, some passion in it that speaks to all kinds of people; combined with something unique to the artist that makes it totally personal, the sensitivity of one man, an individual eye.' He stopped as if memory filled him and the present time and place were forgotten.

Pitt waited, not because he expected to deduce anything of value either from what Kynaston had said, or the way in which he had said it, but because to have interrupted with some trivial comment would have broken the possibility of any understanding between them.

Instead he let his eye wander a little towards the other pictures in the room. The pride of place above the mantelpiece was taken by a head and shoulders portrait of a man of about thirty, bearing so strong a resemblance to Kynaston that for a moment Pitt thought that it was he, and the artist was taking too much of a liberty, perhaps for dramatic effect. Kynaston was striking-looking, but this man was handsome, an idealised version with thicker hair and bolder eyes, a face of almost visionary intensity, and dark-eyed, where Kynaston's eyes were blue.

Kynaston followed his gaze.

'That's Bennett,' he said quietly. 'He died a few years ago. But I expect you know that.'

'Yes,' Pitt answered quietly. 'I'm sorry.' He knew nothing of the circumstances, except that they were sudden and tragic, a man of great promise dying on what seemed like the eve of achievement. It had been an illness of some sort. There was no suggestion of scandal.

Kynaston's face looked bruised, as if the grief were still raw. He made an effort to dismiss it and regain his composure. He raised his eyes and looked squarely at Pitt. 'But I presume you are here over this wretched body in the gravel pit — again. There is absolutely nothing I can tell you, except that we are missing no more servants.' He sighed.

Pitt decided bluntness was the only course open to him. Tact would allow Kynaston to dismiss him.

'We know a little more about her now,' he replied with a slight smile, as if they were discussing something trivial and not particularly unpleasant. 'She had no signs of disease, or of life on the streets in any manner. In fact, she was well fed and well cared for, very clean apart from the surface dirt of having lain in the gravel pit. She did have slight burns on her hands, as many maids do who have occasion to do a lot of ironing. Such burns are distinct from those of a cook or a scullery maid.'

Kynaston paled. 'Are you saying it was Kitty? How could it be? She was only just found!'

'Indeed,' Pitt nodded. 'But the police surgeon says that she actually died at least two or three weeks earlier, and was kept in a cold place, sufficiently sealed that no animals or insects could get to her. This is all information I imagine you would prefer Mrs Kynaston did not have to know . . . '

'Good God, man! What on earth are you suggesting?' Kynaston was now ashen. He searched for words and was unable to find any.

'That it is possible that the body is Kitty Ryder's, and that her disappearance, most probably her murder, is a very ugly issue. Your work for the Government is sensitive. There are those who disapprove of it. This is not going to be dealt with quietly and discreetly,' Pitt replied, 'unless we can prove almost immediately that her death had nothing whatever to do with her employment or residence in this house. I know of no way of doing that, beyond damaging speculation, except to find out exactly what really did happen — and possibly, that the woman in the gravel pit is not Kitty at all. To do that, I need to know all that I can about her: not in polite whispers, but openly and provably, the less attractive as well as the good.'

Kynaston looked as if he had been struck and was still absorbing the pain, unable to respond.

'Why . . . ' he stammered. 'Why in God's name would anyone kill the poor girl and leave her body in the gravel pit . . . weeks after she was — ' He stopped.

'I don't know,' Pitt responded. 'Obviously there are many things we do not know, and we need to learn them as soon and as completely as possible. Stoker will do all he can to learn about Kitty and to follow up on the young man she was courting, in the possibility that she is alive and well, or if not, that it was he who killed her, or someone she met after she left here . . . '

'And you?' Kynaston asked hoarsely.

'I shall do what I can here, on the much worse assumption that the body is hers, and that she was killed because of her associations here.' He met Kynaston's eyes and saw the fear in them. 'I'm sorry,' he added. 'But the scrutiny is bound to be close — and unpleasant. The only defence is to be prepared.'

Kynaston leaned back in his chair slowly and let out his breath. 'All right. What is it you wish to know? I hope you will have the decency to

keep my wife out of this as much as possible.'
That was a statement, almost an order.

'As much as possible, of course,' Pitt agreed, thinking how different Rosalind Kynaston was from Charlotte. Charlotte would resent being kept out of it, protected from reality, as she would see it. And she would unquestionably think the murder of a servant in her house to be her business.

'Murders have motive,' Pitt said. 'And usually some event that caused them to happen at the time and place in which they did. I would like to see your diary, and that of Mrs Kynaston, for the two or three weeks before Kitty disappeared, please, sir.'

'Neither my wife nor her engagements can have any effect on — ' Kynaston began.

Pitt raised his eyebrows very slightly. 'You think Miss Ryder's death may have more to do with your life than with your wife's?' he said with some surprise.

'I don't think it has anything to do with this house at all!' Kynaston snapped. 'It is you who are supposing it.'

'No, sir, I am supposing that the police and the newspapers will take a close, and possibly prurient interest in all events in this house, and we need to be able to answer every question, preferably with corroboration, even with proof, before they are allowed to do that in print.'

Kynaston flushed. He picked up a leather-bound book from the desk near his elbow and passed it across to Pitt.

'Thank you.' Pitt took it and rose to his feet.

'If you can give me a place where I can read it, or take any notes that are necessary, I'll return it to you before I leave. Perhaps you would be kind enough to lend me Mrs Kynaston's diary as well, then I can accomplish this exercise all at the same time?'

Kynaston's face tightened. 'I can't see how it can help anything, but I suppose you know what you're doing.' He did not sound as if he believed it. 'My appointments are quite public.'

Pitt thanked him without adding anything.

Norton offered him a small, rather chilly room, which appeared from its furnishings to be a sitting room for summer use, facing on to the garden, and without a fireplace. Pitt thanked him as if he had not noticed the cold.

He read through both the diaries, making notes. He was looking not for Kynaston's social engagements so much as where they were the same as Rosalind's and where they were not, and for any discrepancies. He found a few, but they were easily explained as carelessness, even misreading of Kynaston's own handwriting, the mistaking of a 5 for an 8, a date or an address wrongly copied down.

He smiled as he read Rosalind's more casual accounts of invitations, and side notes as to what to wear, and why. She was apparently aware that Kynaston was making excuses about certain functions he chose to avoid.

There were also notes in the back of his diary as to purchases, gifts and invitations. Kynaston had a weakness for good brandy and cigars, membership of clubs Pitt knew were extremely

94

expensive, first-night tickets for the best theatres and operas, several appointments with a very good tailor indeed. He was a man who cared about his appearance, and was not loath to indulge his tastes.

There were a few errors and one or two omissions, but it seemed natural for the unedited diaries of a man with very human foibles. Had all details been exact, it would have raised Pitt's suspicions.

Thoroughly chilled, but determined not to show it, he returned the diaries to Norton and took his leave.

Outside he walked briskly to get warm again, and while irritated that he had found nothing of value, he could not help a certain liking for Dudley Kynaston, and a feeling that perhaps Rosalind was a more interesting woman than her rather colourless appearance suggested.

5

Two mornings later, and well into February, Pitt was at his desk reading reports regarding a case in Edinburgh when Stoker knocked. Almost before Pitt had replied, he came in and closed the door behind him. His face was grim and flushed from the sting of the wind in the street.

'Have you seen the billboards this morning, sir?' he asked without preamble.

Pitt felt the warmth of the room fade. 'No, I came by hansom. I wanted to be early and deal with this business in Edinburgh. Why?' He named his worst fear. 'They haven't identified the body as Kitty Ryder, have they?'

'No, sir.' Stoker never exaggerated the suspense, which was a quality about him that Pitt valued. 'But apparently one of the Members of Parliament raised rather a lot of questions about the body we've got, and asked what are we doing to ascertain if it is her or not.'

Pitt was stunned. 'In Parliament?' he said incredulously. 'Have they nothing better to do?' A flicker of expression crossed Stoker's face and disappeared too rapidly to be readable.

' "Can the Prime Minister assure us that everything possible is being done to protect not only the safety but the reputation of Mr Dudley Kynaston, a naval inventor of great importance to the safety and welfare of this country?" ' he quoted. 'That sort of thing, then others asking

96

about his family's safety, and so on.' His eyes met Pitt's squarely; there was no hostility in them, only questions.

Pitt put away the papers to do with the case in Edinburgh. He swore fiercely, and without apology.

'Exactly my opinion, sir,' Stoker agreed. There might or might not have been amusement in his eyes.

'Who was it who was asking these . . . questions?' Pitt enquired. 'Doesn't the idiot realise that by asking them in Parliament, where they will be reported by the press, he is making Kynaston's vulnerability all the greater? Sometimes I wonder who the devil elects these people! Don't they ever look at them first?'

'That's rather the trouble, sir,' Stoker said grimly.

'Elections?'

Again the smile touched Stoker's lips, then vanished. 'No, sir, that's a separate problem altogether. The MP in the case was Somerset Carlisle, who is really rather good.'

Pitt drew in his breath to respond, and let it out again in a sigh. He would not have described Somerset Carlisle as 'rather good'. He was brilliant, eccentric, and personally loyal, even when at great cost to himself. He was also unpredictable, unreasonable and beyond anyone's control, as far as Pitt knew. Even Lady Vespasia Cumming-Gould herself, whose friend he had been for years, seemed to exercise very little influence over him.

Stoker was still waiting, but his face reflected

his awareness of at least some of the ghosts he was awakening. Pitt hoped fervently that it was not all of them. The whole issue of the supposed resurrectionists should remain well covered over — in fact, completely buried. The long-ago episode in his career involved Somerset Carlisle and corpses that would not remain buried. Stoker did not know of it, or the nature of the detection and scandal it had caused. Pitt would very much rather it remained that way. But if Carlisle were willing to have Pitt, or anyone else, open it up again, then this must be of overpowering importance to him.

'Perhaps I had better go and see Lady Vespasia.' Pitt stood up and moved towards the coat stand in the corner of the room. 'It's a bit late to get ahead of this, but I'd like to be as close behind as possible.'

'Are you sure you want to be out of the office when they send for you, sir?' This time Stoker's face was unreadable.

'I'm damn sure I'd like to be miles away,' Pitt said fervently. 'But I'll be within reach — if Lady Vespasia is at home. If I'm sent for, leave me a message there and I'll go straight to Whitehall.'

Stoker looked dubious.

'I want to know what's going on!' Pitt told him, taking his coat off the stand and putting it on as he went out of the door.

* * *

Vespasia was still at breakfast but her maid was used to Pitt turning up without announcement, and frequently at inconvenient times. She simply tightened her lips a little, and requested the maid to bring fresh tea.

In her youth Vespasia Cumming-Gould had been accepted by many to be the most beautiful woman of her generation. As far as Pitt was concerned, she still was, because for him beauty was a quality of the mind and the heart as much as of physical perfection. Her hair was silver and her face now reflected decades of passion, grief and laughter, and a courage that had seen her through triumph and loss of many different kinds.

'Good morning, Thomas,' she said with some surprise. 'You look tired and exasperated. Sit down and have some tea, and tell me what has happened. Would you like something to eat as well? Toast, perhaps? I have a new and most excellent marmalade. It is so pungent I can feel it right through my head.'

'It sounds like exactly what I need,' he accepted, pulling out the chair at the opposite side of the table from her and sitting down. He had always liked this yellow breakfast room where she often took all her meals when dining alone, or with only one guest. It felt as if the sun always shone here, regardless of the weather beyond.

The maid returned with the second cup and saucer, and Vespasia requested more toast.

'Now tell me what has occurred,' Vespasia said as soon as they were alone again.

He had never hesitated to tell her the truth, even when perhaps it was indiscreet, and never had she betrayed his trust. She knew many people's secrets, and the fact that she had not relayed them to him only increased his certainty of her judgement. Briefly, between mouthfuls of toast, and the marmalade that was as good as she had claimed, he told her about the missing maid, and the body in the gravel pit on Shooters Hill.

'I see,' she said at last. 'It is a dilemma, but I do not yet understand why you think I can be of help. You are far better able to pursue it than I.'

'I am expecting a telephone call here, any moment, and I apologise for requesting it be forwarded to me without asking your permission . . .'

'Thomas! Please reach the point of this visit before that happens!'

'It will be from someone in the Prime Minister's office asking me what I know, and what I am doing about it,' he explained.

Her silver eyebrows arched even higher. 'You told the Prime Minister about it? For heaven's sake, Thomas, why?'

He swallowed the last of his toast. 'No, I didn't! That is exactly the point. He knows because there were questions in the House, yesterday evening.'

'Oh dear . . .' In her mouth the words were extraordinarily expressive, even catastrophic.

'Asked by Somerset Carlisle,' he finished.

'Oh dear,' she said again, a little more slowly. 'Now I see why you have come to me. I'm afraid I have no idea how he came to know of the affair, or why he should raise it in the House.' She looked worried. 'I assume you are involved because the body may be that of this poor maid of Dudley Kynaston's? Tragic as it is, it would not concern Special Branch otherwise, would it?'

'No, it wouldn't. And I still have considerable hope that it is not Kitty Ryder — '

'But you fear that it is?' she interrupted him. 'And that either her death involves the Kynaston household, or it will be made to look as if it does? Why? To ruin Kynaston personally, or to embarrass the Government?' She refilled his cup from the pewter teapot.

'I don't know,' he replied. 'But if it is to embarrass the Government it seems rather a poor effort. It's tragic and sordid, if the poor girl was killed because of some romantic involvement, either with one of the male servants, or with Kynaston himself . . . '

'Don't be so delicate, Thomas,' Vespasia said briskly. 'If it has anything at all to do with the household, it will be with Kynaston himself, or at the very least there will be the suggestion that it is. Frankly it sounds most unlikely to me, and I do not believe that Somerset Carlisle is naïve enough to become involved in such a thing. Certainly not in order to embarrass the Government!'

'That was my conclusion.' He sipped the tea. It was hot and fragrant. 'Therefore it is something else, but why is he asking questions in the House, instead of coming to me? If it is of any legitimate concern to him anyway.'

'I have no idea,' she replied, passing him more toast. 'But I shall certainly do what I can to find out.'

'Thank you,' he accepted. He was just about to eat it when there was a knock on the door. The maid came in quietly.

'Excuse me, my lady, but there is a message on the telephone for Commander Pitt.'

'What is it?' Vespasia asked.

The maid turned to Pitt. 'The Prime Minister requires that you go to Downing Street immediately, sir, where a government official is waiting to speak to you.'

Vespasia sighed. 'You had better take my carriage, Thomas. Send it back when you reach there. There is no convenient place for it to wait for you, and I believe I have some errands to run myself. Goodbye, my dear, and good luck.'

'Thank you,' Pitt said grimly, putting the cup down again and rising to his feet. He finished the toast as he went out into the hall.

★　★　★

He had only fifteen minutes to wait in one of the outer rooms in the Prime Minister's offices before he was escorted into a larger and much warmer room to face one of the Prime Minister's assistants, a well-upholstered man whose look of ease belied his nature. It must have been well cultivated.

'Morning, Pitt. Edom Talbot,' he introduced himself. He was a burly man with a very ordinary face, except for remarkably penetrating eyes; it was impossible to tell if they were grey or brown. He was a man it might be easy to underestimate, but probably most unwise so to do. He did not invite Pitt to be seated, although there were two comfortable leather chairs near the fire, which was already burning up well.

'Good morning, Mr Talbot,' Pitt replied, trying not to sound wary.

Talbot wasted no time with niceties. 'We've got a few nasty questions we don't know how to answer. Can't afford to be caught on the wrong foot again.' He looked critically at Pitt. 'I suppose we could say the fellow who asked them did us a kind of back-handed favour, though. Brought it to our attention, and we won't be caught out this time.' He stared at Pitt almost unblinkingly. 'Expect the answers from you, sir. Or if not, then a damned good explanation that'll do in the meantime.'

'Yes, sir.' Pitt returned his steady gaze. 'What were the questions?'

Talbot looked bland. 'Good,' he said with almost no tone in his voice. 'Look at the press with that blankness. Know nothing.' Then suddenly all the muscles in his neck and shoulders tightened and his mouth went into a thin, flat line. 'But don't damned well try it on me, sir!'

Pitt felt his temper flame, but he controlled himself as if nothing had changed. He did not ask again for the questions but waited for Talbot to continue.

'You've got your nerve, I'll say that for you,' Talbot observed. 'Or else you're too damned stupid to understand the issue. I suppose, God help me, I'll find out which soon enough. Who is the woman whose body was found in the gravel pit on Shooters Hill? What happened to her, and how did she get there? What the hell has all this got to do with Dudley Kynaston? Or anyone else in his house? And when are you going to get this damn great mess sorted out? And most importantly, how are you going to keep the lid on it until you do? And if you can't do the job, then tell me, and we'll get Narraway back, damn his hide!'

With an effort, because he knew he must be careful, Pitt began at the beginning. 'We do not know whose the body is.' He measured his words and kept his voice unnaturally calm. 'It is too far decomposed to be easily recognisable, beyond the fact that she was probably a lady's maid, or a laundress of sorts.'

'How do you know that?' Talbot interrupted, his eyebrows raised.

'Burn marks on her hands, such as you get in the use of a flat iron,' Pitt said with satisfaction.

'I see. Go on! How do you propose to find out who she is, then?'

'By eliminating the possibility that it is Kitty Ryder, Mrs Kynaston's maid,' Pitt replied. 'I presume that's all you really want?'

Talbot grunted, but it was vaguely a sound of appreciation.

'What happened to her is harder to ascertain,' Pitt continued. 'How she got there is not known, and may never be. Certainly she did not walk to the place where she was found. She seems to have been dead for some time before she was put there. Probably she was kept somewhere extremely cold. I dislike the thought of it, but it

104

might be the time to examine Mr Kynaston's cold rooms, ice house and so on, rather more thoroughly.' He was satisfied with the look of extreme distaste in Talbot's face.

'As to what it has to do with Dudley Kynaston,' Pitt said. 'I am hoping that we can prove that it had nothing to do with him. And if the body is not that of Kitty Ryder, then there is no connection to him at all.'

'If it's as badly decomposed as you say, how the devil do you presume to prove that it is not her?' Talbot asked, his eyebrows raised so high his forehead was ridged like a ploughed field.

'By finding her somewhere else, alive and well,' Pitt told him.

Talbot considered the reply for several moments.

Pitt waited. He had learned the value of silence, requiring the other person to speak first.

'That would be the best possible outcome,' Talbot said finally. 'And the sooner the better. In your opinion, how likely is it that such will be the case?'

Pitt did not need to weigh that before answering. 'Unlikely,' he said grimly. 'We may have to settle for identifying the body as someone else, for which we need luck as well as skill.'

Talbot nodded. He had expected as much. 'Then what we need from you is that you find out, beyond reasonable doubt, preferably beyond any doubt at all, who this unfortunate woman is and how she met her death. If it has to do with Kynaston then prove it, but do nothing further.

Report back to me before you act. Is that understood?'

'I can't order the police — ' Pitt began.

'That is precisely why Special Branch will deal with the case!' Talbot snapped. 'Tell them whatever you want! Spies, secret documents, whatever serves the purpose, but keep them out of it.'

'We'll be a lot longer finding Kitty Ryder alive without police help,' Pitt pointed out, with a sharpness to his own voice.

Talbot gave him a long, cold stare. 'Be realistic, man! The woman is dead. Identify her, or prove the body is someone else's. And either prove Kynaston's guilt, or his lack of connection to the whole affair. Report to me. If this woman is not his maid, then find out if this apparent connection to him is bad luck, or someone taking advantage of a miserable coincidence. Or worse than that, a deliberate ploy to implicate him. And if it is that, then we need to know by whom.'

'And why?' Pitt added with a touch of sarcasm.

'I can work that out for myself,' Talbot said tartly. 'Report to me any significant progress that you make, and do so discreetly. I need all details. Do not stop until you have them.'

'Exactly what is Kynaston doing that is so important?' Pitt asked.

'You do not need to know that,' Talbot answered immediately, his eyes hard and angry.

'I'm head of Special Branch!' Pitt snapped, his temper rising at the annoyance, and even more the stupidity, of ordering him to search for answers and then keeping him half blind. 'If you want me to do my job, then tell me what I need to know.'

'You need to know what your instructions are,' Talbot retorted. 'If this is a piece of dramatic stupidity, we will deal with it accordingly. Thank you for coming so soon. Good day.'

Pitt did not move. He opened his eyes very wide. 'Stupidity?' he repeated the word as if it were meaningless. 'Someone beat a young woman to death, concealed her body for three weeks, mutilated her face until it was unrecognisable, then dumped her in a gravel pit for wild animals to destroy. If that is regarded by Her Majesty's Government as stupid, what does one have to do to be regarded as criminal?'

Talbot paled, but he did not flinch. 'You have your instructions, Commander Pitt. Find the truth, sooner rather than later, and report it to me. Dispensing justice is not your job.'

'I wish that were true,' Pitt said bitterly. 'Too often it is exactly my job. There is no time, and no discreet or legal way of doing it and allowing me to walk away and keep my conscience clear. Or perhaps that is something you were not aware of?'

Talbot's face was white, mouth pinched at the corners. 'Kynaston is of great importance to the Government, and his work is both secret and sensitive. It may even be the key to our survival in any future war. That is sufficient information for you. It is also highly confidential. If your staff don't obey you without asking questions, then you have not the command of them that you should have. Now stop arguing the issue and making excuses. Do your job. Again, Commander Pitt, good day to you.'

'Good day, Mr Talbot,' Pitt replied with some satisfaction, even if it lasted no longer than it took him to reach the street. Regardless of what Talbot said, he needed all the information he could gather regarding Dudley Kynaston's value to the Government, not only to find out what Kitty Ryder might have learned that made her dangerous, but who else might profit from Kynaston's downfall, for any reason. And if he were actually innocent, then who had engineered his appearance of guilt? There was only one man to ask, and that was Victor Narraway. He would prefer to consult him without others, particularly Talbot, knowing he had done so.

Narraway, like himself, was one of the few people who owned a telephone in his own home. Since his forced retirement from the leadership of Special Branch, he had been elevated to the House of Lords, but that was more of a sop to his reputation than any opportunity to be of use. Previously he would not have been at home at this hour, but now there was a reasonable chance he would not have gone to the House of Lords, or to one of his clubs for luncheon. Such things grew stale quite quickly to a man of Narraway's intelligence. Also, since he had no part in political affairs, he felt sidelined, no more of interest to those who used to hold him in awe. He had never said as much, but Pitt had heard it in his silences.

As it turned out, Pitt had to wait about half an hour for Narraway to return from a brief walk. Considering the weather, Pitt imagined he had gone at all only as a matter of discipline. Narraway had begun his career in the Indian Army, and the virtues of abstinence and hard, strict self-mastery had never entirely left him.

Narraway's manservant offered Pitt a late luncheon, which he accepted gratefully, realising that he was actually quite hungry. He was just finishing an excellent slice of hot apple pie, served with cream, when he heard the sound of the front door closing, then Narraway's voice in the hall.

Narraway came into the sitting room, having removed his overcoat. His thick hair was flattened a little where his hat had been, and his lean, dark face coloured by the cold.

He glanced at the plate where the apple pie had been, and which now held only Pitt's folded spoon and fork.

'You came for more than luncheon, I presume?' he said with a slight lift of curiosity. He walked towards the fire, which was burning strongly where the manservant had added fresh coals. He stood in front of it from habit, holding his hands out to catch the heat.

'Luncheon seemed like a good idea,' Pitt replied with a tight smile. 'Since I spent my own luncheon time being hauled over the coals in Downing Street by a rather officious man by the name of Talbot.'

Narraway straightened up, forgetting the fire. He stared at Pitt with interest. 'I imagine you are at liberty to tell me what about, or you would not have come here? And it is both urgent and discreet, or you would have suggested luncheon at some restaurant. Please don't disappoint me . . . ' He said it lightly, but Pitt caught the flash of emotion in it, the sincerity there, and then concealed again.

'It seems a shame not to have you deduce what it's about,' Pitt said drily, in part to cover the fact that he had caught the moment's vulnerability.

Narraway sat down in the chair opposite and crossed his legs elegantly, hitching the knee of his trousers not to spoil the line. 'Have you got time to wait for that?' he asked, his eyes bright with amusement.

Pitt smiled back. 'No, I haven't. Did you read about the young woman's body found in the gravel pit on Shooters Hill?'

'Of course. Why? Ah! I see.' He sat forward again. 'Is that what Somerset Carlisle was referring to in his questions to the House yesterday? I saw that headline on the sandwich boards as I passed. I admit I didn't make the connection. Why the hell would Carlisle think a dead woman on Shooters Hill was anything to do with Kynaston, or might endanger him and his family? What danger? Who was the woman? What had she to do with him?'

'Probably nothing,' Pitt replied. 'But his wife's maid is missing, and she answers the description.'

'Bit thin, isn't it? Wouldn't half the young women in Greenwich or Blackheath answer it?'

Narraway was looking at him steadily, waiting for the missing facts that made sense of it.

'Taller than average, handsomely built and with thick auburn hair?' Pitt asked. 'Gone missing in the last three weeks? No, they wouldn't. And the gravel pit is only a short walk from Kynaston's house.'

Narraway nodded. It was so slight a movement it was barely visible. 'I see. Are we supposing Kynaston was having an affair with this maid? Or that she learned something about either Mr or Mrs Kynaston so potentially damaging that Kynaston killed her? Seems a little drastic, and honestly pretty unlikely. But I suppose those are the ones that catch us out.'

'Why does Carlisle care?' Pitt countered. 'Has he changed so much that he'd go after a man simply to make a point? What point could be worth that to him? And why Kynaston? We have far more vulnerable members of the Government than that! I could name half a dozen whose private lives would be open to question — if that were his purpose.'

Narraway's mouth twisted in a wry smile, his black eyes bright. 'Only half a dozen. For God's sake, Pitt, where are your eyes?'

'All right, a couple of dozen,' Pitt conceded. 'Why Kynaston?'

'Opportunity,' Narraway answered. 'He was the one near whose house the corpse turned up?' He pulled his mouth into a thin line. 'I'm slipping. That isn't a reason to raise the subject publicly. The real question is what for? What does he want?' He thought in silence for a few moments before looking up at Pitt again. 'Kynaston works for the War Office. But that's extremely vague. I think we need to know a lot more precisely than that. If he's open to blackmail because of some idiotic domestic affair, seemingly gone very badly wrong, then we should know about it. At least you should,' he corrected himself. 'And you need to know a lot more about Kynaston professionally.'

'Don't you know? I asked Talbot, and was told fairly tersely to mind my own business.'

'Good,' Narraway responded. 'Then there's something there. You'll get the door shut in your face. I've got a few favours I can call in . . . '

'Or threats you can hold over people,' Pitt said a little bitterly. 'I'm beginning to learn the power of this job.'

'That's the favour,' Narraway answered. 'I won't carry out the threat. Lesson, Pitt — never carry out a threat unless you absolutely have to. Once it's done, you've no more power with it.'

'If I never do it, why would anyone believe that I would?' Pitt asked reasonably.

'Oh, you'll have to, once or twice,' Narraway assured him, a shadow passing over his eyes as if memory darkened them for a moment. 'Just put it off as long as you can. I hated doing it — you'll hate it even more.'

Pitt remembered a large party, a house full of laughter and music, and a scene where a man lay on a tiled floor, blood pooling out from the shot with which Pitt had killed him.

'I know,' he said almost under his breath.

Narraway looked at him with a moment's

intense compassion, then that too vanished.

'I'll see what I can find out about Dudley Kynaston,' he promised. 'Might take a couple of days. Keep on trying to identify your corpse. You might be lucky and find out it's not your missing maid, but don't count on it.'

Pitt stood up. 'I'm not,' he said quietly. 'I'm preparing for the next round.'

★ ★ ★

It came exactly as Pitt had expected. Nothing further had been learned about the identity of the woman in the gravel pit, nor had Stoker been more fortunate in finding any trace of Kitty Ryder. Narraway telephoned Pitt and invited him to call by just after dark. He would have invited him to dinner, but he knew Pitt's desire to be at home with his family. If he envied him that, he disguised it so well Pitt had seen no more than perhaps a glimpse of it.

He offered Pitt a brandy, something that Pitt very seldom accepted, though he did on this occasion. He was tired and cold. He needed the fire inside as well as burning in the hearth.

Narraway got to the point immediately.

'Kynaston is cleverer than he looks, and — at least professionally — a lot more imaginative. He works on the design of submarines for the navy, and now particularly on submarine weapons, which is a field of its own: obviously different from weapons fired above the water.'

'Submarines?' Pitt realised the yawning gap in his knowledge. He frowned, not wanting to make

113

a fool of himself. 'You mean like in Jules Verne's *Twenty Thousand Leagues under the Sea?*'

Narraway shrugged. 'Not quite that clever yet, but definitely the naval warfare of the future, and not so far ahead either. The French were the first to launch a submarine not relying on human power for propulsion — *Plongeur*, back in '63, then improved on in '67. Fellow called Narcis Monturiol built a boat forty-six feet long, could dive down nearly a hundred feet and stay down for two hours.'

Pitt was fascinated.

'The Peruvians, of all people, built a really good submarine during their war with Chile in '79. Then the Poles had one about the same time.'

'Didn't we do anything?' Pitt interrupted with chagrin.

'I'm getting to it. Our clergyman and inventor George Garrett got together with a Swedish industrialist Thorsten Nordenfelt and made a whole series, one of which they sold to the Greeks. In '87 they improved it and added torpedo tubes for firing underwater explosive missiles. That one, sold to the Ottoman Navy, was the first to fire a torpedo while submerged.' He closed his eyes and for a moment his jaw tightened. 'One can only begin to imagine the possibilities of that on an island like ours, whose survival depends on our navy guarding not only our trade routes but our shores themselves: in fact, our existence.'

Pitt's imagination was already there, racing and yet cold with fear.

'The Spanish are working on it too,' Narraway went on. 'And the French have an all-electrical-powered one. It will be only two or three years before they're common.'

'I see,' Pitt said quietly. Indeed he did, all too terribly clearly. Britain was an island. Without their sea lanes the British could be starved to death in weeks. The importance of submarine weapons could hardly be exaggerated — which is why they had to value people like Dudley Kynaston, and be prepared to go to great lengths to protect him.

'I can't see why Talbot wouldn't tell me that,' Pitt said, both puzzled and angry.

'Neither can I,' Narraway agreed. 'I can only suppose that he thought you had been told.' Then he hesitated. 'Except that I imagine if so you would have gone on to ask a lot more questions, and the answers to those might be rather more . . . delicate.' Narraway was tense, sitting back in his chair as if casually, but Pitt saw the strain in the fabric of his jacket as his shoulders hunched very slightly.

Pitt could not leave it unasked. 'Technically delicate, or personally?'

'Personally, of course,' Narraway said with a wry twist to his lips. 'Technically is probably irrelevant, and would require a great deal more study than you have time for in order to understand. Are you aware that Dudley had a brother, Bennett, a couple or so years younger than he?'

'Yes. There's a picture of him in Kynaston's study, behind his desk.' Pitt could see it as clearly

115

as if it were before him now, even the eyes, the contours of the face. 'Odd place to put it, except that it's the best wall space, and the best light,' he added. 'And he will see it every time he comes into the room. Strong resemblance to Dudley, but even better-looking. But he's been dead for several years. What could he have to do with Kitty Ryder, or whoever this woman was?'

'Probably nothing,' Narraway agreed. 'But there was a scandal concerning him several years ago. I haven't been able to uncover it, which means they took very great care indeed to hide everything, or disguise it as something else. I haven't even been able to learn if Dudley is aware of it himself. Apparently at least some elements of it happened abroad. Again, I don't know where. The only thing I gathered from both sources I tried is that Bennett was not to blame for it. Of course that may, or may not be true.'

'At the time of his death?' Pitt asked.

'No, some years before.'

'Which would mean it was at least a decade ago, or longer,' Pitt concluded. 'Kitty Ryder would have been a child.'

'Relevant only to Dudley Kynaston's sensitivities,' Narraway pointed out. 'And therefore his immediate reaction to conceal things that perhaps other people would not, even if he were completely innocent. He and Bennett were very close, as you have deduced from the portrait in the study.'

Pitt thought about it for a few moments. It would account for Dudley Kynaston's behaviour, the unease Pitt had sensed, even the tiny errors of omission in his diaries.

'Yes,' he said with a degree of relief. Perhaps Kitty Ryder was likeable, but unwise, and she had eloped with the young man the household staff so disapproved of, and the woman in the gravel pit could turn out to be unrelated to the Kynaston house.

Narraway saw the sudden ease in his face. 'Protect Kynaston as long as you can,' he said quietly. 'We need a navy as strong as possible. There's a hell of a lot of unrest in the world. Africa is stirring against us, especially in the south. The old order is changing. The century is almost worn out, and the Queen with it. She's tired and lonely and growing weaker. In Europe they're looking for change, reform. We may think we are isolated, but it's a delusion we can't afford. The English Channel is not very wide. A strong swimmer can make it, let alone a fleet of ships. We need to have the best navy in the world.'

Pitt stared at him. None of what Narraway had said was unknown to him but put together as he had just done, it was a darker picture than he had allowed himself to see.

He did not answer. Narraway knew he understood.

6

Charlotte had not seen her sister Emily for several weeks, and not spent much time alone with her when they could talk to each other in more than formalities since before Christmas. She decided to write a letter to Emily asking if she would like to take luncheon and, if the weather permitted, to walk in Kew Gardens. Even if it were cold, the massive glasshouses filled with tropical plants would be warm, and a pleasant change from sitting inside.

Emily wrote back immediately, agreeing that it would be an excellent idea. She had married extremely well, just before Charlotte had married Pitt. Emily had gained a title and a very large fortune, if not a commensurate happiness. Tragically, George had been killed in circumstances to which they never referred. Emily found herself first a suspect in his death, then a very wealthy widow with a son, in whose name both the title and the inheritance were vested.

Later she had fallen in love, wildly and quite irresponsibly (so she told herself) with the handsome and charming Jack Radley. He had no profession and no inheritance at all. Everyone else had agreed with her that it would be a disaster, and in their first few years together Jack had done little but enjoy himself, and be excellent company. Then the ambition had seized him to do something of value, and he had fought very hard to win a seat in Parliament. Emily had been enormously proud of him, as indeed had Charlotte. He had more than justified their belief in him.

Young Edward's inheritance allowed Emily to live extremely well, without using up what would rightfully be his when he reached majority. This was a little while in the future because he was roughly the same age as Jemima, who was now fifteen.

Emily kept a carriage for her personal use, and it was in that that she came to pick up Charlotte for their luncheon.

She came into the house in Keppel Street, barely glancing at its hallway, so much smaller than her own. Nor did she look at the stairs, which went straight up to the first-floor landing, not in the sweeping arc of those at Ashworth House, never mind those at their country seat, which could accommodate twenty guests without inconvenience.

Charlotte was still in the kitchen, giving Minnie Maude last-minute instructions for dinner, and warning her not to let Uffie steal the sausages, which he was presently creeping towards, imagining no one would notice him.

'See that Daniel and Jemima have no more than hot soup when they come in from school,' Charlotte added, picking up the little dog and putting him back in his basket. 'And that they go straight upstairs to do whatever homework is assigned them.'

'Yes, ma'am,' Minnie Maude agreed, giving

Uffie a stern look. He thumped his tail happily in reply.

Emily was looking extraordinarily dashing, wearing the very latest fashion in capes. It was double-breasted, with two rows of large fancy buttons down the front. It was very becoming and from the way she walked it was apparent that she knew it. The whole outfit was a mixture of blues and greens, an up-to-the-minute daring combination, frowned upon only a year ago. Her hat was positively rakish. She was younger than Charlotte, only just approaching forty, and had always been slender. Her fair hair had a deep wave to it, the finer tendrils curling delicately. With her porcelain skin and wide blue eyes she had a refinement approaching beauty, and she never failed to make the best of it.

Charlotte felt a little drab beside her, even though her skirt had the latest cut, with five pieces making the fullness fall very gracefully to the back. But it was an ordinary terracotta in colour. She would have added a cape, but she had little spare income to spend on memorable clothes she could not afford to be seen in next year, and the year after, and probably after that too.

She hugged Emily quickly and stood back to admire her. 'That's wonderful,' she said sincerely. 'You manage to make winter look as if it is fun.'

Emily smiled suddenly, lighting her face, and only then did Charlotte realise that the moment before Emily had looked tired. She made no remark on it. The last thing any woman wanted to hear was that she did not look fresh. It was almost as bad as ill, and approaching the worst of all — old.

Charlotte reached for her hat, a rich brown ordinary felt one. It was nothing like as beautiful as Emily's, but it did suit her richer colouring, and she knew it.

They had an excellent luncheon. As always, it was Emily's gift. They had become so used to that over the years that they ceased to argue about it, even though since Pitt's promotion Charlotte's means were considerably improved. Still they were not in the same sphere as Emily's.

They spoke of family matters, how their children were faring. Besides Emily's son, Edward, she had a younger daughter, Evangeline. Children changed so rapidly there was always something to report.

They also spoke of their mother, Caroline Fielding, who had scandalised everyone by remarrying after their father's death — and to an actor, of all things! Not only that, but he was very considerably younger than she was. Life had changed radically for her. She had a whole new set of occupations and issues to engage her mind and her emotions, and to worry about. She was happier than she had imagined possible.

'And Grandmama?' Charlotte said finally, over dessert. It was a subject she would have preferred to ignore, but it hovered between them unsaid, but with such weight that eventually she surrendered.

Emily smiled in spite of herself. 'Nearly as appalling, as always,' she said cheerfully.

'Complaining about everything, although I think it is merely habit, and her heart is no longer in it. I caught her actually being nice to the scullery maid last week. I swear she'll live to be a hundred.'

'Isn't she there already?' Charlotte asked waspishly.

Emily's eyebrows shot up. 'For goodness' sake, do you think I asked her? But if you did, then please tell me the answer. I have to have some hope to cling on to!'

'What if she's only ninety?'

'Then say nothing,' Emily responded instantly. 'I couldn't bear it — not another ten years.'

Charlotte looked down at the folded napkin and the empty plate. 'It could be twenty . . . '

Emily said a word she would later deny ever having used, and they both laughed.

They rose from the table and had the carriage sent for, and agreed that a walk in Kew Gardens would be just what they would most enjoy.

The air was cold and bright, but with no wind at all it was very pleasant. Scores of other people seemed to have had the same idea.

'I suppose you don't get the opportunity to help Thomas with cases any more,' Emily remarked, as they passed several very handsome trees. Neither of them bothered to read the plaques in front saying what they were, and which were their countries of origin. 'All too secret,' she added, referring back to Pitt's cases.

'Not much,' Charlotte agreed. She heard the wistfulness in Emily's voice. She even felt a little of it herself. Looking back, some of their adventures, which had been dangerous or even tragic at the time, now were softened by memory and only the better parts remained.

'But you have to know something about them,' Emily insisted. 'Don't you?'

Charlotte glanced sideways at her, just for a moment, and saw a hunger in her, almost a need. Then it vanished, and as they passed a couple of well-dressed women she smiled at them charmingly, full of confidence. The old Emily was there again, beautiful, funny, intensely alive, brave enough for anything.

'It's all very . . . shapeless,' Charlotte relented and answered the question. 'Thomas was called in because they found the body of a woman in a gravel pit up on Shooters Hill. For a little while they were afraid it might be Dudley Kynaston's missing maid . . . '

Emily stopped abruptly. 'Dudley Kynaston? Really?'

Charlotte had a sharp stab of misgiving. Perhaps she was breaking a confidence to have told Emily so much?

'It's confidential!' she said urgently. 'It could cause an awful scandal, quite unjustifiably, if people started to speculate. You mustn't repeat it! Emily . . . I'm serious . . . '

'Of course!' Emily agreed smoothly, beginning to walk again. 'But I know something already. Jack said Somerset Carlisle was asking questions in the House about Kynaston's safety.'

'Somerset Carlisle?' Now Charlotte was intrigued, and touched with a cold finger of fear. She had not forgotten about Carlisle and the resurrectionists either. 'What else did Jack say?' she asked, attempting to keep the urgency out of her voice.

Emily's mouth tightened and she gave an elegant shrug of her slender shoulders, but it was a tiny movement, as if her muscles were tight. 'Not very much. I asked him because I know Rosalind Kynaston a little, and I suppose it would really be her maid, not his. But Jack didn't answer me.'

'Oh.' It was a meaningless response, except to acknowledge that she had heard. Had she also understood? Was this one answer that closed Emily out, perhaps because Jack did not know anything more, or what he did know was in confidence? Or had he just not been listening closely enough to realise that Emily wanted an answer?

They walked for a few moments without speaking again. They passed exotic trees, palms whose structure was utterly unlike the oaks and elms they were used to, or the soaring, smooth-limbed beeches. On the ground there were ferns, almost like green feathers a Cavalier might wear on his hat, but far larger. Emily buried her hands in her muff, and Charlotte wished that she had one.

'What is Rosalind Kynaston like?' Charlotte said to break the silence before it grew too deep to disregard.

Emily gave a tiny smile. 'Ordinary enough, I suppose. We spoke little about anything in particular. She's older than I am. Her children are all married. She doesn't see them very often.

124

Army, or something, I think.'

'There are hundreds of other things to talk about!' Charlotte protested.

'Gossip,' Emily said tartly. 'Have you any idea how boring that is? Half of it is complete rubbish. People make it up in order to have something to say. Who on earth cares anyway?'

It was mid-afternoon and the days were lengthening again. The sky was clear and the lowering light shone brightly and a little harshly on their faces. For the first time Charlotte noticed the very fine lines in Emily's once-perfect skin. Actually they were the marks of laughter, emotion, thought. They were not unkind. They even gave her face more character, but they were lines none the less. She did not for a second doubt that Emily had also seen them. Of course they were there in Charlotte's face too — more of them, a little deeper — but she did not mind. Did she?

Pitt was a little older than she, and time had touched him with a brush of grey at the temples. She liked it. She was beginning to find youth less interesting, even callow at times. Experience lent depth, compassion, a sharper value to the good things. Time tested one's courage, softened the heart.

But did Emily see it that way? Jack Radley was remarkably handsome, and her own age. Men matured nicely. To some people, women simply got older.

As if reading her thoughts and taking them further, Emily spoke again.

'Do you suppose that Kynaston was having an

125

affair with the maid, and got her with child, or something? Then he had to get rid of her?' she asked.

'That's a bit extreme, isn't it?' Charlotte said with surprise. 'She far more likely ran off with her young man.'

'To a gravel pit, in the middle of winter?' Emily said with an edge of sarcasm. 'Have you lost your imagination? Or do you think I have? Or is this your way of telling me you can't discuss it with me?'

Charlotte heard the hurt in her voice beneath the surface irritation. She wanted to turn and study Emily's face more closely, but she knew that in doing that she would make an issue of something that was too delicate to force.

'We don't know that it was her body in the gravel pit,' she said instead. 'If it wasn't, and we accuse a government scientist of what amounts to murder, we are hardly guarding the safety of the state. In fact,' she added, 'we are doing the enemy's work for them.'

Emily stopped, her eyes wide. 'Now that is a really interesting thought.'

Charlotte's heart sank. Unquestionably she had said too much now. How could she get out of it? She had never been able to fool Emily; they knew each other far too well. Emily, the youngest of the three sisters, had always been the prettiest, possibly a little spoiled, and forever trying to catch up. Socially and financially, it was many years since she had overtaken Charlotte. The memory of their elder sister, Sarah, murdered in the terrible affair of the Hangman of Cater

126

Street, was one Charlotte seldom touched. There was a pain of grief still left, and also regret over the stupid quarrels, and a nameless guilt that she was dead while Emily and Charlotte were alive, and happy. There was too much darkness in it, the kind of thick, heavy shadow that eats the light.

'That's all it is!' she said, more sharply than she had intended. 'A thought.'

Emily smiled, a sparkle in her eyes.

'Anyway, the person who's drawing attention to it is Somerset Carlisle, and he's hardly an enemy of the country. Nor is he stupid enough not to understand what he's doing.'

'Maybe we could find out?' Emily suggested.

Charlotte had no quick answer. She was trying to extricate herself from the difficulty she had created by raising the subject at all. She shivered very visibly. 'Could we do it walking again? I'm freezing standing here.'

'You don't want to.' Emily started to move, actually quite quickly, making conversation difficult. 'Stop tiptoeing around me, Charlotte. You're as bad as Jack.'

Charlotte stopped again, colder than she had been even the moment before. What was this about? No more involvement in detection? Being bored and losing interest in gossip and pointless parties just to fill the day, serving no larger purpose? Or was it really about Jack? Certainly it had little if anything to do with Dudley Kynaston or the body in the gravel pit.

Emily was still walking away, though she had slowed down. Charlotte hurried to catch up with her. There was no point in being subtle now; in fact it might only make things worse.

'Do you really know Rosalind Kynaston?' she asked a little breathlessly. She wanted desperately to help, and yet the slightest clumsiness would close off the opportunity, perhaps for a long time. She knew even as she was doing it that it might be dangerous, and Pitt would not approve, but she knew also that what she had thought was temper on Emily's part was really pain.

They had known each other all the life they could clearly remember. Sharing was woven through all childhood. It was nothing to do with toys, lessons, dresses, books; it was memory. As little children they had run hand in hand. As girls they had shared secrets and laughter, quick squabbles. As young women there had been adventures, hope, falling in love, and heartbreak. Now, probably more than half-way through life, there would also be disillusion, coming to terms with other kinds of pain, inequalities that would always be there.

Emily shook her head. 'Not very well, but that could be mended. In fact, it will have to be, if Jack takes a position with Dudley Kynaston. He's likely to be offered it. It must be a promotion.' And yet there was no lift in her voice, no excitement.

Charlotte hesitated, then decided honesty was the only safe choice. 'But you don't like it? Or is it just this messy maid business that worries you?'

Emily kept her eyes forward. 'I don't know

why you say that . . . '

'Shall I explain it?' Charlotte asked. 'Or would you rather talk about something else?'

Emily pulled her mouth into a grimace. 'I'm not as sure as he is that it would really be upward. I think it's rather more sideways. Honestly . . . ' She gave a little sigh and looked away again. 'Promotion carries some burdens as well. He could be away more . . . a lot more.'

'Oh . . . ' Charlotte immediately wondered whether Emily was going to miss him, or if she were more worried about what he might do far from home, and perhaps if he would miss her as much. As far as Charlotte knew, Jack had not been unfaithful to Emily, even in thought, but before marriage he had certainly been widely experienced, and had not hidden the fact. The novel thought of being completely faithful to one woman was part of the new adventure of marrying. So also, of course, was the equally novel experience of being financially far more than comfortable, with at least two very fine homes of his own, instead living most of the year as a guest in someone else's house, there because he was charming, entertaining and always agreeable, but never secure.

He was a Member of Parliament commanding considerable respect from his peers, and being offered advancement entirely on his own merit. Emily had begun as the privileged one; now Jack made his own way. Charlotte realised with surprise that that was a bit like herself and Pitt, except that all she had possessed at the beginning was an excellent upbringing and the entrée to certain circles in Society, no money at all. The change that Pitt's promotions had brought delighted her, especially the respect he was now accorded by those who had previously condescended to him. The only disappointment was the inability to take part in his cases, no excitement, no detection. With a jolt of surprise she realised that she too had become a trifle bored. She was definitely affected with a feeling that she was repeating the same tasks over and over, and perhaps they were not really either as useful, or as interesting as she had imagined.

Emily had waited as long as she was going to. 'What do you mean?' she demanded.

'I know what you mean about promotion,' Charlotte answered. 'It brings more money, and more responsibility, but not necessarily more satisfaction. And certainly not more fun.' Then afraid she had given away too much about herself, she hastened on. 'What does Jack say?'

Emily gave a slight shrug. 'Not a great deal. In fact, not enough. He says he wants the promotion, but it isn't the exact truth.' She glanced at Charlotte, then away again, and kept on walking. Their surroundings were like some other-worldly forest, hard winter sunlight reflecting back off the glass-domed ceiling while groups of strangers walked under extraordinarily shaped trees and trailing vines, pretending they had not seen each other so they did not break the spell of being in another world.

'The trouble is,' Emily went on, 'I don't know which part of it is the lie, or what it's for. Is it self-protecting, so if he doesn't get the promotion he can tell me he really doesn't mind? Or does he want the position for some reason he doesn't want me to know?'

Or possibly he just did not consult Emily any more, not as he used to, but that was not a thought that Charlotte wanted to speak aloud. On the other hand, maybe he wanted the job very much, and he was afraid Emily's advice would be negative.

'Do you know much about it?' Charlotte asked.

'The position? Not a lot. After the last disaster, none of which was Jack's fault, I don't know whether to encourage him or not, and he isn't telling me enough for me to make an intelligent comment anyway. I . . . I don't know whether he doesn't trust me, or if he doesn't care what I think . . . ' Now the misery was so heavy in her voice she seemed on the brink of tears.

Charlotte said the only thing she could.

'Then we must find out. It is better to find out the worst and deal with it than to spoil something that wasn't actually the worst at all, by fearing and being filled with an unjust suspicion.' She looked at Emily's face. 'I know that's very easy to say, and you think I've never experienced it.'

'You haven't!' Emily said sharply. 'Thomas would no more look at another woman than grow wings and fly in the air! If you dare patronise me, so help me, I'll push you and your best dress into that pile of wet soil over there — and you'll never get the smell out as long as you live!'

'An excellent solution to all problems,' Charlotte said disgustedly. 'Push it into the manure. It'll make us all feel so much better — for about five minutes . . . '

'Ten!' Emily snapped. Then in spite of herself she began to laugh, even though the tears running down her face were not really those of amusement.

Charlotte put her arms around her and hugged her briefly, then stepped back. 'We had better get started,' she said in a businesslike way. 'We must get to know Dudley and Rosalind Kynaston, and the possibility of Jack being offered a position with Kynaston is the perfect excuse.'

Emily put her shoulders back and lifted her chin a little. 'I shall begin immediately. I'm freezing standing here. I thought tropical jungles were supposed to be warm! Let's go home and have some tea by the fire, and hot crumpets soaked with butter.'

'An excellent idea,' Charlotte agreed. 'Then I shall have to have a whole wardrobe of new dresses, a size larger.'

'You could give me that one,' Emily regarded it with pleasure. 'I could have it taken in to fit me!'

Charlotte pretended to slap her, and tripped over a piece of fallen branch, only just righting herself before she overbalanced. This time Emily really laughed, a swift, bubbling sound full of delight.

'How kind!' Charlotte said under her breath, then couldn't help laughing as well.

★ ★ ★

The arrangement was fulfilled three days later
when Charlotte and Pitt met Emily and Jack at
the theatre. There had been no further progress
either in finding Kitty Ryder alive, or in
identifying the body on Shooters Hill. Other
news had overtaken the issues raised in
Parliament by Somerset Carlisle's questions.
However, it was only a matter of time before
they would need to be addressed more urgently.
Pitt had not deluded himself that the case was
over, and Charlotte was quite aware of the
tension in him above that of the usual concerns
of his position.

It was the opening night of a new play, and
therefore something of an occasion. Emily had
been both fortunate and clever to obtain four
tickets. Formal dress was required, which Pitt
hated. On the other hand, he enjoyed seeing
Charlotte wear a really beautiful gown of warm
coral and russet tones with even a touch of hot
scarlet in the brocade. It was brand new; the
skirt was perfectly flat at the front and around
the hips, not a line possible for everyone. It
widened like a bell at the bottom, so cleverly was
it cut. It was unadorned; the beauty of the fabric
said everything.

Glancing at herself in the looking-glass for a
final time, Charlotte had to admit that even
without expensive jewellery she looked striking.
She could not afford such things and did not
wish Pitt to be extravagant in giving them to her.
She wore no necklace at all. This was rather a

daring decision, but it only drew attention to her still smooth jawline, her slender throat and the warmth of her natural colouring. Her thick, dark chestnut hair was coiled upon her head and there was a slight flush in her cheeks. Her pearl and coral earrings were perfect.

Pitt did not say anything, but the admiration in his eyes was more than sufficient. Even Jemima was impressed, although she was reluctant to say so.

'That's a nice gown, Mama,' she muttered as Charlotte reached the top of the stairs. 'Better than the green one.'

'Thank you,' Charlotte accepted the compliment. 'I prefer it myself.'

Pitt bit his lip to hide a smile.

'You look very handsome, Papa,' Jemima added, this time more wholeheartedly.

Pitt did not imagine for a moment that he was handsome — distinguished at best — but in his daughter's eyes he was, and that was of far more importance. He gave her a quick hug, and then followed Charlotte down to the waiting carriage, which had been hired for the occasion.

It was a gusty evening with an edge to the wind, but at least it was dry.

They arrived in good time, but the theatre foyer was already quite crowded. From the moment they came up the steps into the arc of the glittering lights, Pitt saw people he knew, albeit professionally rather than socially. He was absorbed into nods of acknowledgement, brief words of greeting, a smile here or there. They were his acquaintances, not Charlotte's, which was a radical change from the early years of their marriage when she had known everyone and he had been there only because of her. She found herself smiling, walking with her head a little higher. She was proud of him . . . actually, very proud.

She was the first of them to see Jack. She was struck again by how handsome he was. The few extra years had given him maturity, a sense of something more than simple good looks. The sharp light was unkind in showing more than one might see in the gas or candlelight of a withdrawing room, but the few lines around his mouth and at the corners of his eyes gave him character, and knowledge of emotion rather than a blank page on which little was yet written.

Emily was a step or two away, speaking to someone else. Her fair hair gleamed, almost like an ornament in itself, making her diamond earrings unnecessary. She was wearing a gown of pink lilac threaded with silver and stitched with tiny pearls. It was gorgeous in itself, and of course had the perfect new skirt, but it did not flatter her as a cooler shade would have done. Also it was going to clash with Charlotte's gown about as much as it was possible for two colours to detract from each other. Perhaps they should have consulted together first? But Charlotte had little choice, and Emily had a room full of gowns. The fashion rage at the moment was turquoise, and it would have been perfect for her!

Too late now. The only option was to carry it off with bravado. She walked over towards Emily, smiling as if delighted to see her.

Emily turned from her conversation to see Charlotte almost beside her, and a moment later they kissed cheeks lightly.

Jack turned also and the appreciation in his eyes as he saw Charlotte was unmistakable. The evening was already off to a shaky start.

General polite greetings and trivial conversation continued for another few minutes until Jack seemed effortlessly to have guided them towards a couple who were striking-looking — at least the man was. He was tall with a mane of thick fair hair and strong features. The woman was more ordinary, but beautifully dressed. Her face was gentle, but there was no fire in it, no passion. Her gown, on the other hand, was stitched — one might say encrusted — with turquoises and tiny beads of crystal, and of course the new, five-piece cut of skirt, totally flat around the hips and yet sweeping towards the full, bell-like bottom, and more beads just above the hem.

The man's eyes mirrored Jack's appreciation of Charlotte, then as he turned to Pitt, the light faded from them and he paled visibly.

'May I present my brother and sister-in-law, Mr and Mrs Thomas Pitt,' Jack said courteously. 'Mr and Mrs Dudley Kynaston . . . '

Kynaston swallowed. 'Commander Pitt I have met. How do you do, Mrs Pitt?' He bowed very slightly to Charlotte.

'How do you do, Mr Kynaston?' she responded, trying to keep the sudden flame of interest out of her expression. 'Mrs Kynaston.'

136

She was fascinated. Neither of them was what she had expected. Her mind raced for something harmless to say. She must engage them in conversation of some sort. 'I believe the play is quite controversial,' she began. 'I hope that is true, and not just a fiction to spark our interest.'

Rosalind looked surprised. 'You like controversy?'

'I like to be asked a question to which I don't have the answer,' Charlotte replied. 'One that makes me think, look at things I think I am familiar with, and then see them from another view.'

'I think you will find some of these views might make you quite angry, and confused,' Kynaston said gently, glancing at his wife before turning to Charlotte.

'Angry, I can well believe,' Pitt said with a discerning smile. 'Confused, I think less likely.'

Kynaston was startled, but he did his best to hide it.

Jack stepped in to bridge a rather embarrassed silence. He looked at Kynaston. 'Have you seen reviews of the play, sir?' he asked with interest.

'Hotly varying opinions,' Kynaston answered. 'Which I suppose is why they are sold out this evening. Everyone wishes to make up their own minds.'

'Or accept such an excellent excuse for a glamorous evening,' Emily suggested. 'I can see all sorts of interesting people here.'

'Indeed.' Rosalind smiled back at her. For a moment her face had a surprising vitality, as if a different person had looked out through her rather ordinary eyes. 'I think that is the main reason for most of them coming.'

Emily laughed and looked across an open space at a woman in a gown of outrageous green. 'And an excuse to wear something one could not possibly wear except in a theatre! It will probably still glow when the lights go down.'

Rosalind stifled a laugh, but already she was looking at Emily as an ally.

A few moments later they were joined by a grim-faced man and a tall woman with flaxen fair hair that gleamed like polished silk, a porcelain fair skin, and amazing blue eyes. She led the way and joined the group as if she were quite naturally a part of it. The man stopped a yard or so away, and Charlotte felt Pitt stiffen beside her.

The woman smiled. She had perfect teeth.

'Commander Pitt. What a pleasant surprise to see you here.' Her eyes slid to Charlotte, obliging Pitt to introduce her.

'Mrs Ailsa Kynaston,' Pitt said a little awkwardly.

For an instant Charlotte wondered if Pitt had made a mistake, using her Christian name; then she remembered that Bennett Kynaston was dead. She was Dudley's widowed sister-in-law. She acknowledged her with interest, and turned to the man now moving forward. He also seemed to know Pitt, but inclined his head to Charlotte politely. 'Edom Talbot, ma'am,' he said, introducing himself.

'How do you do, Mr Talbot?' she replied, meeting his hard, steady eyes. She wondered

138

how Pitt knew him, and whether it was as an ally or an antagonist. Something in his manner suggested the latter.

The conversation continued, mostly consisting of meaningless polite observations, the sort of thing one says to new acquaintances. Charlotte took part as much as was necessary, but mostly she studied Rosalind and Ailsa Kynaston. Ailsa must have been a widow for some time. She was striking to look at and clearly self-composed and intelligent. She could easily have married again, had she wished to. Had she loved Bennett Kynaston too much ever to consider such a thing?

But then, if anything happened to Pitt . . . Even the thought of it chilled her and caught the breath in her throat. Charlotte could not imagine marrying anyone else. She felt a sort of sympathy for the woman standing only a couple of yards from her, and with no idea that Charlotte had more than glanced at her when they were introduced. At what price did she exercise such courage? Looking at her now as the rest of them discussed what was rumoured of the play, she could see a tension in the other woman's body, in the ruler-straight way she held her back and the proud tilt of her head.

' . . . Mrs Pitt?'

Suddenly she realised that Talbot had been speaking to her, and she had no idea what he had said. If she replied foolishly it would reflect on Pitt. Honesty was the only course open to her.

'I beg your pardon.' She smiled at him as

charmingly as she could, although she did not feel it in the least. 'I was daydreaming and I did not hear you. I'm so sorry.' She made herself meet his eyes warmly, as if she liked him.

He was flattered; she could see it in the sudden ease in his face. 'The theatre is the place for dreams,' he replied. 'I was asking if you agree with your sister's opinion of the leading actress's last performance.'

'As Lady Macbeth,' Emily put in helpfully.

Charlotte remembered reading a critic's response to it and hesitated, wondering if she could get away with quoting them. She would look such a fool, so much too eager to impress, if she were caught. 'I read it was rather too melodramatic,' she replied. 'But I didn't see it.'

'Because of what the critic said?' Talbot asked curiously.

'Actually that would have made me more inclined to look for myself,' she replied without hesitation. Then she remembered what Emily had said of the performance. 'And Emily did tell me a few other performances were . . . ' She shrugged slightly, not willing to repeat the negative opinion.

'And of course you believed her?' Talbot said with a smile.

'I had a sister too,' Ailsa said quietly, her voice tight with a strain she could not disguise. 'But she was younger than I. I would still have taken her word for anything . . . '

Charlotte saw Emily's face and the shock of realisation in it. Jack was startled, then embarrassed. Clearly he had no idea what to say.

140

It was Pitt who broke the silence. 'Unfortunately my wife lost her elder sister many years ago. It is a memory we don't go back to, because it was very painful circumstances.'

'My sister also,' Ailsa said, looking at him with interest, almost challenge. 'Forgive me for having raised the subject. It was clumsy of me. Perhaps we should go into the theatre and find our seats.'

★ ★ ★

The following day Charlotte put off a dressmaker's appointment and went instead to visit her great-aunt Vespasia or, to be more accurate, Emily's late husband's great-aunt. She could think of no one in the world she liked better, or trusted more. February was still winter, in spite of the slightly lengthening afternoons, and they sat in front of the fire while rain beat against the windows out on to the garden. Charlotte put her feet as close to the fender as she could in the hope of drying out her boots and the hem of her skirt.

Vespasia poured the tea and offered the plate of wafer-thin egg and cress sandwiches. 'So you did not enjoy your visit to the theatre,' she observed, after Charlotte had mentioned it.

Charlotte had long since abandoned prevarication with Vespasia. In fact, she was more honest with her than with anyone else. She felt none of the emotional restrictions that she had with her mother, or with Emily. Even with Pitt she was sometimes a little more careful.

'No,' she said, accepting the tea and trying to

141

judge how soon she could sip it and let its warmth slide down inside her. Certainly she would burn herself with it now. 'The conversation lurched from the edge of one precipice to the edge of another, and finally, for Emily, toppled over into the abyss.'

'It sounds disastrous,' Vespasia responded. 'Perhaps you had better tell me the nature of this abyss?'

'That she isn't funny or wise or beautiful any more. And, more specifically, that Jack is no longer in love with her. I suppose it is the sort of thing we all have nightmares about some time or other.'

Vespasia looked very serious. She did not even pick up her cup. 'Possibly,' she replied. 'But usually we do not tell other people, because it comes more like a realisation that it is dusk, not a sudden nightfall. Has something happened to Emily?'

'I don't think so. But she is restless — bored, I think. We used to be involved in so much, not always as exciting or pleasant as it seemed, looking back on it now. I know that, and I think Emily does too. But being a good Society wife, and an attentive mother to children who need you less and less, hardly exercises the imagination. And it is certainly not exciting . . . ' She saw the understanding in Vespasia's expression and stopped. 'I think at the heart of it she is very aware that she will soon be forty, and a part of life is slipping out of her grasp,' she added.

'And Jack?' Vespasia enquired.

'Jack is as handsome as ever, in fact I think more so. A few added years suit him. He is not so . . . shallow.'

'Ooh!' Vespasia gave a tiny wince, so small as to be almost invisible.

Charlotte blushed. 'I'm sorry . . . '

'Don't be.' Vespasia picked up her cup at last and took a sip, then offered Charlotte the sandwiches again before taking one herself. 'Which particular precipice did you fall over yesterday evening?'

'Someone assumed that Emily was my older sister.'

'Oh dear.' Vespasia sipped her tea again. 'Sibling rivalry is a snake you can never quite kill. I'm afraid Emily has been used to being a step ahead for rather too long. She is finding it hard to adjust to being a step behind.'

'She isn't behind!' Charlotte said instantly.

Vespasia merely smiled.

'Well . . . she needs something to do, I mean something that matters,' Charlotte tried again. 'The way we used to when we could help with Thomas's cases, before they were secret.'

'Be careful,' Vespasia warned.

Charlotte thought of denying that the affair of Kynaston and the missing maid was in her mind, but she had never deliberately lied to Vespasia, and their friendship was too precious to begin now, even to defend Emily.

'I will be,' she said instead. It was half-way to the truth.

'I mean it, my dear.' Vespasia's voice was very grave again. 'I know Thomas is inclined to believe that Dudley Kynaston is not unfortunately involved with this missing maid, and possibly even that the body in the gravel pit was not hers. He may be right. That does not mean that Kynaston has nothing to hide. Be very careful what you do . . . and perhaps even more careful what you arrange for Emily to do. Her mind is filled with her own misgivings: her fear of boredom, and thus of becoming boring herself. Her beauty, to which she has been accustomed, is beginning to lose its bloom. She will have to learn to rely on character and charm, style, even wit. It is not an easy adjustment to make.' She smiled with deep affection. 'Especially when your older sister has never relied on her looks and has already learned wit and charm, and now at the age when other women are fading, she is coming into bloom. Be gentle with her, by all means, but do not be indulgent. None of us can afford the errors that come with carelessness, or desperation.'

Charlotte said nothing, but she thought about it very deeply as she took the last sip of her tea. Regardless of Vespasia's advice, and the wisdom she knew it held, she was going to involve Emily, she had to.

7

Stoker stood in front of Pitt's desk, his face bleak, and oddly bruised-looking.

'How did you find it?' Pitt asked, looking at the sodden wet tangle of felt and ribbon on his desk. It was barely recognisable as a hat. It was impossible to tell what colour it had been, except from the tiny flash of red on what was left of a feather.

'Anonymous tip-off, sir,' Stoker said quietly. 'Tried to trace who it came from, but no luck so far. Just a note in with the post.'

'What did it say, exactly?' Pitt asked. He was pursuing it as a matter of course. He did not seriously think it would prove of any value.

'Just that the sender had been out walking in the early morning and sat down on a frozen log, then seen this odd-looking mass of what looked like fabric. He poked it with a stick, and then realised that it was a hat. He knew there'd been a body found up near there, and wondered if it might have any connection.'

'Those words?' Pitt said curiously.

'No, I'm elaborating a bit.' Stoker grimaced. 'Word for word, it was more like 'Was sitting on a log up the gravel pit where that woman got found. Thought this might have something to do with it, like maybe it was hers.''

'What kind of paper?' Pitt asked. 'Pen or pencil? What was the writing like?'

Stoker's mouth pulled tight. 'Ordinary, cheap paper, written in pencil, but no real attempt to disguise the hand. Bit of a scrawl, but perfectly legible.'

'And the spelling?' Pitt asked.

'Right spelling,' Stoker replied. 'But there was nothing difficult in it. Simple words.'

Pitt looked at what was left of the hat, and then up at Stoker. He did not need to ask the question, but he did anyway.

'Why do you think it's Kitty Ryder's?'

Stoker answered as if his throat were tight and he had to force the words out. 'The red feather, sir. I got to know one of the barmaids at the Pig and Whistle who was a friend of Kitty's . . . Apparently they had tea together on their days off. Kitty really wanted a hat like that and she saved up to buy it. It was the red feather that mattered, because it was unexpected. In a way it didn't fit in with the rest of it, and it made people look, and smile. At least that's what Violet said — Violet Blane, the barmaid.'

'I see. Thank you.'

Stoker did not move. 'We'll have to go back to Kynaston, sir.'

'I know that,' Pitt agreed. 'Before I do that I want to go over all the statements he's made and everything we know about him. I want the inconsistencies, anything with which I can prove he's lying. So far all we have is that Kitty worked for him, and that the woman in the gravel pit had his watch, which he says a pickpocket took, which his wife confirms. Which means nothing. We've searched the house and found nothing.

None of the servants know anything of use. We've been over the cellars and the ice house and found no trace of Kitty, or anything at all out of order. And the servants were in and out of there all the time anyway.'

'Yes, sir,' Stoker said flatly. 'I've got notes as to what Violet said and if you compare it with Mrs Kynaston's diaries, and then his, I think you'll find a few places where it doesn't match.'

Pitt did not answer, but opened one of the drawers beside the desk and took out his notes from the Kynaston diaries, then held out his hand for Stoker's notebook.

'Why didn't we find the hat when we looked before?' he asked.

'Probably too intent on the body,' Stoker replied. 'It was thirty feet away. If you didn't see the red feather you wouldn't have seen the rest. It looks like leaves on mud.'

That was true. It had been found now only by chance.

'Thank you. I'll look at all the notes again, then I'll go and see Kynaston this evening. He won't be there at this time of day.'

* * *

Even so, Pitt was a little early. He disliked having to harass the man again. He personally liked him, therefore he determined to finish this business tonight and get it over with. He did not want to give Kynaston the chance to come home, change and then go out to dinner somewhere. After meeting Kynaston and his wife and sister-in-law at the theatre this was even more unpleasant.

He stood uneasily in Kynaston's morning room, staring at one bookshelf after another, unable to concentrate on the titles. Occasionally he paced back and forth. He had actually been invited by Mrs Kynaston to wait in the withdrawing room, but he felt guilty about accepting it when his purpose was far from social.

He had been there less than half an hour when he heard Kynaston come in through the front door, and within minutes he was in the morning room, smiling.

Pitt's heart sank and he felt his throat tighten. He walked forward from the fireplace.

'Good evening, Mr Kynaston. I'm sorry to intrude on your time, but I have further questions I need to ask you.'

Kynaston indicated the chair near the fire, and when Pitt sat down, he took the other one himself. He looked slightly puzzled, but not yet alarmed.

'Has there been some further development?' he enquired.

'I'm afraid there has. We discovered a hat at the gravel pit, near where the body was found.' He watched Kynaston's face as he spoke. 'It's in a state that makes it impossible to identify, but it is an unusual shape, as much as we can make out, and quite clearly it still has a small red feather tucked in the ribbon where the crown meets the brim. It is distinctive, and one of Kitty's friends we have spoken to says that she

148

had exactly such a hat with a red feather, and saved up until she could buy it.'

Kynaston blanched but he did not avoid Pitt's eyes. 'Then it was Kitty . . . ' he said very quietly. 'Perhaps it was foolish, but I was still hoping that it wasn't. I'm so sorry.' He took a deep, rather shaky breath. 'Will you be looking for the young man she was walking out with? I believe he was a somewhat itinerant carpenter. He went where the work was a lot of the time.' There was an edge to his voice, but it was not anger, and — as far as Pitt could judge — it was not fear either. Was he really so sure of himself, and his own safety?

'Of course,' Pitt agreed. 'We haven't searched diligently enough yet. Admittedly I think we are guilty of also hoping that the body was not hers.'

'But now . . . ?' Kynaston's mouth pinched at the ugliness of the thought, and with something that appeared to be pity.

'His name is Harry Dobson,' Pitt replied. 'And yes, we will ask the police further afield to co-operate with us in finding him. So far we've looked only locally.'

'If he's any sense he'll have gone away as far as possible,' Kynaston observed with a grimace. 'Liverpool, or Glasgow, somewhere with a lot of people where he can get lost. Although I suppose it's not hard to lose yourself in London, if you're desperate enough. Even ship out . . . go to sea. He's able-bodied.'

'That's possible too,' Pitt admitted.

'Thank you for telling me.' Kynaston gave a bleak half-smile. 'I will inform my wife, and the staff. They'll be upset, but I imagine they will be half-expecting it.' He leaned forward as if to rise to his feet.

'I'm sorry, sir,' Pitt said quickly. 'But that is not all.'

Kynaston looked taken aback, but he relaxed into the chair again, waiting for Pitt to explain.

Pitt drew in his breath and held Kynaston's gaze. 'It is not just a matter of finding this wretched young man and charging him, which is a police matter. I'm Special Branch, and my concern is the safety of the state . . . '

Kynaston was now very pale and his hands were clenched on the arms of his chair, knuckles white.

' . . . And therefore exonerating you,' Pitt continued. 'And anyone else in this house. Unfortunately questions have been asked in the House of Commons as to your part in this, and your personal safety. I have to be able to assure the Prime Minister that he has no cause for concern.'

Kynaston blinked and there was a long silence as the seconds ticked by on the clock on the mantel. 'I see,' he said at last.

'I've checked over all the questions I asked you previously,' Pitt replied. He knew already that he was going to turn up something private and painful. It was there in Kynaston's face and in the stiff angles of his shoulders. He would like to have stopped it now. Possibly it had nothing to do with Kitty Ryder's death, but then it might have everything to do with it. He could not afford to believe anyone without proof. It had gone too far and was too serious for that.

'I have nothing to add,' Kynaston told him.

'You have a few errors to correct, Mr Kynaston,' Pitt answered. 'And a few omissions to fill in rather more fully. And before you do, sir, I would prefer to tell you in advance rather than embarrass you afterwards, that I shall be checking with other people, because this matter is too serious to allow what can be merely unintentional misstatements of fact.' He let hang in the air between them the awareness that they could also be deliberate lies, even damning ones.

Kynaston did not answer. It had gone beyond the point of pretence that he was not deeply uncomfortable.

Pitt could have asked him the questions one by one, and tripped him in the lies — or if they were, the errors — but he loathed doing so. This had to be lethal, but it could be quick.

'Your diary states that you went to dinner with Mr Blanchard on the evening of 14 December . . . ' Pitt began.

Kynaston moved very slightly in his chair. 'If I had the date wrong, is it really important?' he said reasonably.

'Yes, sir, because you left the house dressed for dinner, and according to our enquiries, you did not see Mr Blanchard. Where did you go?'

'Certainly not anywhere with my wife's maid!' Kynaston said sharply. 'Perhaps the dinner was cancelled. I don't remember. Has Special Branch really got nothing better to do than this?'

Pitt did not answer his question. 'And just over a week later, on 22 December, again you have

151

Mr Blanchard's name in your diary, and again you did not see him,' he went on.

Kynaston sat absolutely motionless in the chair, unnaturally so. 'I have no idea where I went,' he replied. 'But it was probably an engagement to do with a society I belong to, and couldn't possibly have anything less to do with my wife's maid.' He swallowed, his throat jerking. 'For God's sake, do you do this to everybody? Read their diaries and cross-question them as to whom they dined with? Is this what we pay you for?' There was a faint flush of colour in his cheeks.

'If it has nothing to do with Kitty Ryder's death, then it will go no further,' Pitt said, perhaps rashly. He felt grubby pursuing something that was clearly private, and embarrassing. Were it not, Kynaston would not be still evading an answer.

'Of course it has nothing to do with it!' Kynaston snapped, leaning forward suddenly. 'If anyone killed her, then it was this wretched young man she walked out with. Isn't that obvious, even to a fool?' He looked away. 'I apologise, but really, all this probing into my life is unnecessary and completely irrelevant.'

'I hope so,' Pitt said sincerely. He felt vaguely soiled that he had to pursue this to the bitter end. 'There are a few errors in your diaries, which is to be expected. We all get hours or dates wrong from time to time, or forget to note something at all, even do so illegibly. It is only the occasions when you left home, dressed for dinner, and consistently did not go where you stated that I am asking you about. There are at least a dozen of them in the last two months.'

Kynaston's face was now dark with colour.

'And I will not tell you, sir!' His voice wobbled a bit. 'Except that it had nothing whatever to do with Kitty Ryder. For God's sake, man! Do you think I am dining out in full evening dress with a lady's maid?' He managed to sound incredulous, even though his voice cracked a little.

'I think you are going somewhere that you feel the need to lie about,' Pitt answered. 'The obvious conclusion is that it is with a woman, but that is not the only possibility. I would prefer to think that rather than anything else you feel the need to keep secret from your family, and from the police, and Special Branch.'

Kynaston blushed scarlet. He caught Pitt's implication immediately. Pitt regretted it, but the man had left him no choice. He waited.

'I dined with a lady,' Kynaston said in little more than a whisper. 'I shall not tell you who it was, except that it was certainly not Kitty Ryder . . . or anyone else's . . . servant.'

Pitt recognised that that was the truth, and also that Kynaston did not intend to reveal who it was. The question in Pitt's mind was whether Kitty Ryder might have known of it, and asked for some kind of favour not to tell her mistress. There was no purpose in asking Kynaston. He had already implicitly denied it.

Pitt stood up. 'Thank you, sir. I'm sorry I had to pursue such a thing, but a woman is dead — violently — and her body dumped in a gravel pit for wild animals to eat!'

Kynaston winced.

'That is more important than anyone's sensibilities as to privacy for their indiscretions,' Pitt concluded.

Kynaston stood up also, but he said nothing more except to wish Pitt a good evening, icily, and as a matter of form.

Outside in the cold, damp night, the wind was blowing clouds across the stars and streetlamps dotted occasionally here and there. Pitt was glad to walk briskly for some considerable distance. He was likely to find a hansom easily to take him all the way back across the river to Keppel Street.

What should he tell Talbot? That Kynaston was having an affair, but with some woman he could dine with in full formal clothes? Certainly not a servant of any kind. Someone else's wife? That was the obvious conclusion, although perhaps not the only one.

Had Rosalind Kynaston any idea?

Possibly she had. It was then conceivable that she did not mind, as long as he was meticulously discreet. Pitt knew of marriages where such agreements were made.

It did not answer the question as to whether the bright and observant Kitty Ryder had been aware of it. If so, then it had to have been deduction. There was no way in which she could be in an appropriate place to have observed such a thing.

Deduced from what? What could she have seen or heard . . . or overheard? A conversation on the telephone, perhaps? A letter left open? A coachman's gossip?

Was she really so quick, so very acute a judge? Was Kynaston so desperate, and so callous as to beat a maid to death for her knowledge of his affair? He was embarrassed that Pitt had deduced it, but Pitt had seen no rage in him, not the slightest suggestion of violence of any sort, physical or political. He had not threatened Pitt's job or his position.

Was it necessary to report this to Edom Talbot?

He had reached the main road and found a hansom. He was sitting in it bowling along at a good speed by the time he reached the conclusion that it was, but he was still undecided exactly what he would say.

★   ★   ★

He was still collecting his evidence next day when a message came to his office requiring him to report immediately to Downing Street. It had to be Talbot, but how could he know what Pitt had learned the previous evening already? Surely that was impossible? Unless Kynaston had gone there ahead of Pitt, in order to — what? Complain? Deny the charge? Confess privately to Talbot who his mistress was, instead of to a mere policeman? Did he have far more influence in Government than Pitt had imagined?

Pitt had no choice but to obey. He put the papers in a small case so that, if Talbot demanded it, he could prove his assertion. Then

155

he went out into the street to catch a hansom.

He sat all the way through the traffic, turning over in his mind how much he would tell Talbot. He would be finished if he were caught in a lie, but he might get away with an omission.

Why was he even thinking of concealing the truth from Talbot?

Because he did not believe that Kynaston had murdered Kitty Ryder to keep the secret of an affair. It was too extreme for a man who appeared to be neither violent nor particularly arrogant. Nothing Pitt had learned of him suggested either. And he had learned a considerable amount. Kynaston was proud of his family heritage. He had mourned the loss of his brother, Bennett, deeply; in fact the grief was still there in him, masked beneath the surface. To all outward appearances he had been a good father and a dutiful husband, if not a passionate one.

Certainly he liked a few luxuries in his dress and in his dining, but even with his favourite wines — of which there were several — Stoker had found no one who had seen him seriously inebriated, and never in any circumstances aggressive.

His passion and imagination seem to have gone into his work. Thomas Pitt knew that only from the high esteem in which he was held by the senior naval officers who were involved with his inventions. Pitt had not heard this from them himself. It had been passed on to him by the appropriate authorities. Could that be an omission he needed to rectify? Underwater ships firing explosive missiles, invisible from the surface, might well be the warfare of the future. Britain was behind in the race, and — as an island — peculiarly vulnerable. She had no land borders with any other country across which to import food, raw materials, munitions, or any kind of help.

He arrived at Downing Street unusually nervous. The palms of his hands were sweating even in the cold, and he took his gloves off. Better to be dry, if numb.

He walked to the step and was let in almost immediately. There was always a policeman on duty and he was recognised without having to state his name.

Inside, he was shown immediately to the room in which he had met Talbot before. Talbot was waiting for him, pacing the floor. He swung around angrily as soon as Pitt came in and started to speak before the footman had closed the door, leaving them alone.

'What the devil are you playing at?' Talbot demanded. 'I would prefer to think you're incompetent rather than deliberately attempting to deceive Her Majesty's Government. Did you not understand my distinct command that you report to me — here — any further development in the Kynaston case? What is it in that which is unclear to you?' His cheeks were red, his nose pinched at the nostrils and his jaw tight. He glared at Pitt as if his fury were slipping out of his control.

'I was checking some of the evidence before I reported it to you,' Pitt replied. Damn! That sounded so feeble, so obviously an excuse, and yet it was the truth. 'I wished to — ' he began again.

'You wished to evade the issue!' Talbot said furiously. 'What about this bloody hat you found in the gravel pit?'

'It's not bloody,' Pitt corrected him.

'God damn it, man! Don't you dare tell me when to swear and when not to! Who the hell do you think you are, you jumped-up — '

'There is no blood on the hat . . . sir,' Pitt said between his teeth.

Talbot stared at him. 'What the hell are you talking about?'

'There was no blood on the hat,' Pitt repeated.

'That is totally irrelevant. Was it the maid's hat or not?' Talbot said slowly between his teeth, as if Pitt were simple.

'I don't know,' Pitt replied. 'But that is also irrelevant to Kynaston, unless we can prove that he had some illicit relationship with her, or that she knew of something else he was doing about which she threatened him.'

'And you have done! The man is having an affair! But you did not think it necessary to report that fact to me, as I commanded you to?' Talbot said grimly. 'I wonder if you would care to explain that? I rather think we are back to the beginning again.' His voice grated, full of ragged edges. 'Are you so arrogant that you think you can take decisions on this matter without reference to your superiors, or have you some reason of your own for protecting Kynaston from the truth? Just how well do you know him? You force me to ask.'

Pitt felt the heat rise up his face. Any answer he could give was going to sound like an excuse. And yet if he had come to Talbot earlier, before he was certain of Kynaston's affair, he would have been equally to blame for maligning an important man in the Government's plans for naval defence, not to mention the moral and civil wrong of false accusation. It would have brought Special Branch into disrepute and made its future work harder. It might even have earned Pitt's own removal from leadership.

A sudden horrible thought flashed into his mind that this was the purpose of Talbot's rage. This was an excellent platform on which to build the means of getting rid of Pitt altogether. He drew in his breath to frame some kind of a reply just as the door opened and Somerset Carlisle came in, closing it quietly behind him. He was older than when they had first met, but the remarkable arched brows and the quirky humour were still there in his face. It was only the deepening of the lines that changed him, made one aware that it was over a decade later.

'Ah! Pitt,' he said cheerfully. 'Delighted to find you here.'

'You are interrupting a private conversation — ' Talbot snarled at him.

'Yes, of course I am,' Carlisle cut across the rest of his remark. 'Just wanted to tell Pitt that I found the piece of information he was looking for.' He smiled at Pitt, gazing straight into his eyes. 'You were quite right, of course. The hat was no more Kitty Ryder's than it was mine!

159

Some damn fool was wanting to distract attention from his own rather stupid mistakes . . . drinks locally now and then, so he knew about the poor woman's disappearance, and the body you found in the gravel pit, of course.'

Talbot tried to interrupt but Carlisle carried on without taking the slightest notice of him.

'Knew she'd had a hat like that, poor girl, and bought one the same. Put a red feather in it.' He smiled even more widely and reached his hand into his pocket. He pulled out a rather crumpled piece of paper. 'Got the receipt. You'll see it's dated for the day before your informant found it.'

'Just all by pure coincidence?' Talbot said sarcastically.

'Hardly,' Carlisle replied with exaggerated patience. 'He was the one who found it!'

Talbot was standing motionless, his face filled with bafflement and even further mounting anger.

Carlisle was still smiling, as if the atmosphere in the room were one of co-operation, not open enmity.

'Policeman's job to be sceptical,' he went on, now looking at Pitt. 'Good thing you were. Made a highly embarrassing mistake if you'd reported to Downing Street that the body was Kitty's on evidence discovered by the man who put it there. Looked a bit of a fool. Not good for the reputation of Special Branch.' He shook his head. 'No doubt some journalist would have got hold of it and put it all over the front pages. Somehow or other they find these things.' He

160

shrugged. 'And then, of course, they put all kinds of other bits of fact — and imagined fact — together and come up with accusations. Too late to apologise when you've ruined a man.'

Pitt had recovered from his amazement, although he had no idea how Carlisle had known he was here, or become involved in the matter at all.

'Exactly,' he agreed aloud.

Talbot was still fighting the issue, his body stiff, his face pale.

'What unbelievable good fortune that you happened to be aware of all this . . . eccentric behaviour, Mr Carlisle,' he said sarcastically. 'I suppose we should be grateful some extraordinary chance took you to . . . what?' His voice became even more grating. 'How was it you learned that this particularly irresponsible man knew of Ryder's passion for a hat with a red feather, and also exactly where her body was found, and that he should purchase such a hat, plus feather, of course, and place it there? Such a piece of good fortune seems . . . beyond belief.' He pronounced the words slowly, giving every syllable emphasis.

Carlisle merely smiled a little more widely.

Pitt's heart was racing, but he dared not intervene. He had no explanation either.

'And of course that you should also, purely by chance, of course, know exactly where Commander Pitt was,' Talbot went on. 'And race here just in time to rescue him from having to give me some explanation as to why I had to hear of the whole apparent farce from someone else, and

161

demand he explain to me why he had not reported to me, as I had instructed him. I suppose you have answers for all that also?'

Carlisle spread his hands in an elegant gesture, rather like another shrug of his shoulders.

'The man who bought the hat is a constituent of mine,' he said calmly. 'He's been in trouble a few times for trying to draw attention to himself.'

'Kitty Ryder's desire for a hat with a red feather was hot in the newspapers,' Talbot said icily. 'And your constituency is miles from Shooters Hill.'

Carlisle laughed. 'For heaven's sake, man! People move around. He's a hound for scandal. He went and drank at the Pig and Whistle. He asked questions, listened to gossip. And as to finding Pitt here, when I put the pieces together I called his office and was told he's been sent for to come here. Not exactly the work of a genius.' His eyes were bright, his arched eyebrows even higher. 'Anyway, I'm delighted if I've saved you embarrassment — not to mention poor Kynaston.' He turned to Pitt. 'If your business here is finished, I'll walk to Whitehall with you.'

'Yes . . . thank you,' Pitt agreed quickly, then turned to Talbot. 'I shall keep you informed of anything I learn that is relevant to Mr Kynaston, especially should we find out the identity of the woman in the gravel pit. Good morning, sir.' And without waiting for Talbot to answer or give him leave to go, he turned and followed Carlisle out of the door, through the hallway and into the street.

They walked several paces along the quiet

162

pavement, past the usual police presence, since Downing Street was the home not only of the Prime Minister, but also of the Chancellor of the Exchequer.

'Was any of that true?' Pitt asked quietly as they turned into Whitehall.

Carlisle's expression barely changed. 'Close enough,' he replied.

'Close enough for what?' Pitt demanded, still uneasy.

'To pass muster, should Talbot choose to have it investigated,' Carlisle replied. 'Don't ask anything further, because you don't want to know, and I certainly don't want to tell you.'

'Does the hat have anything to do with Kitty Ryder?'

'Nothing at all, except that she did want one. Or, at least, she did want a red feather of some sort. It is entirely true that that was not her hat.'

Pitt let his breath out slowly. 'I'm extremely grateful.'

'You should be,' Carlisle agreed pleasantly. 'Don't cross Talbot; he's a nasty bastard. Doesn't mean Kynaston's innocent, of course. Just can't hang a man on a manufactured piece of evidence. And . . . and I wouldn't like to see you replaced by someone a lot worse. Good luck! Watch your back!' And with that he turned and walked in the opposite direction towards Westminster Bridge, leaving Pitt to go east, and down to the river.

It was only as he was nearing the riverbank and could hear the slurping of the incoming tide that Pitt allowed the wave of relief to run through him with a sudden warmth. He realised how close he had come to giving Talbot a reason to dismiss him. Of course he knew that many people did not find him a suitable person to follow Victor Narraway, who was undoubtedly a gentleman.

Pitt himself was the son of a disgraced gamekeeper, transported to Australia for theft when Pitt was a boy. He could scarcely remember him, only the shock and the indignation, his protest of innocence that was disregarded, then his mother's grief. She and Pitt had been allowed to remain in the large country estate; indeed, Pitt had been educated with the son of the house, to encourage the boy. It would not do for a servant's son to outdo the heir, and it was felt this might prevent such a thing. Although looking back on it now, Pitt thought that that had been an excuse to mask a kindness that was always intended.

Still, it was hardly a background to equal Narraway's, or one that a man such as Talbot — and to be honest, many others — would be happy with. He must remember that, and not let anger or complacency lead him into error again. Carlisle had rescued him this time, and Pitt was just beginning to appreciate now just how much. He had been gracious enough to make light of it, as if it were in his own interest, rather than in Pitt's, but that was a courteous fiction.

That there was also an antipathy between Carlisle and Talbot was clear, and Pitt would be wise to remember that and avoid being caught in the middle. Nevertheless his step was light as he made his way to the ferry.

★ ★ ★

Stoker sat at the kitchen table at his sister's house. He quite often came here on his days off. King's Langley was an ancient and very pleasant village in Hertfordshire beyond the outskirts of London, about an hour's journey on the train. Gwen was the only family he had left, and quite apart from that, he really liked her. All his best memories were somehow attached to her. She was two years older than he and had looked after him in the earliest times he could recall. It was she, more than the schoolteacher, who had taught him to read. She was the one who encouraged him to join the navy, and to whom he had recounted his adventures, enlarging the good and mostly skipping over the bad. Perhaps that was why he remembered the good so clearly, trying to share it with her, seeing her eyes widen, her holding her breath as she waited for the next turn in his stories.

It was also Gwen who had travelled miles by train, spending the little money she had, to come and visit him in hospital when he was injured. And of course it was Gwen who told him off when she thought he was wrong. She who had brought him the news of their mother's death, and she who nagged him about putting flowers on the grave, saving for the future, and even occasionally about getting married.

Now she was cooking dinner for her husband

and children when they came home. He watched her with pleasure because the kitchen was warm and smelled of baking pastry and clean sheets drying on the airing rail above them. There were strings of onions hanging in the corner and a small dresser with plates on it, and two copper pans, the pride of her possessions. The shine and the colour of them were too good to spoil with over-use.

He must get her something else pretty some time. It was too long since he had last done so. Her husband was a hard worker, most of the year at sea, as Stoker himself had been. But money had a long way to go to support a wife, and four children who grew out of their clothes and were always hungry.

Stoker was full of thoughts of Kitty Ryder, and relief that the hat with the red feather was not hers. He had not realised until Pitt told him about Talbot, and Carlisle's rescue of the situation, that he had been sad at her death. It was ridiculous! He had never even seen the woman!

Gwen was looking at him.

'What's the matter, Davey?' she asked. 'You've got a face on you like a burst boot! You said the hat wasn't hers. She could still be alive.'

He looked up. 'I know. But if she is, why doesn't she come forward and say so? Everybody in London knows we're trying to identify the body in the gravel pit, and that there's speculation it's her. And don't tell me she can't read! I know she can.'

'Are you staying to dinner? You're welcome,

you know? You're always welcome,' she assured him.

He smiled at her, quite unaware how it lit his face. 'I know. And no, I'm not. I've got to be on duty tomorrow.' That was not strictly the truth; he chose to be. But he had also made a good assessment of the meat in the stew and how if he accepted a portion, someone else would go without — almost certainly Gwen herself.

'They work you too hard,' she criticised.

'We've been over that,' he reminded her. 'I like the work, Gwen. It matters. I don't tell you much about it because it's secret. But Special Branch keeps us all safe, if we do it right.'

'What about this new guv'nor, Pitt?' she asked. 'Does he work as hard as you do? Or does he go back to a nice big house somewhere with servants to look after him and parties to go to?'

Stoker laughed. 'Pitt? He's not a gentleman, Gwen. He's an ordinary man, like anyone. Worked his way up. He's got a decent home, on Keppel Street, but no mansion. You'd like his wife. I don't know her well, but she's not all that different from you.' He looked around the room quickly. 'Kitchen's bigger than this one, but like it; smells of clean laundry and bread as well.'

She looked at him and smiled back. 'So why the face? And you might be Special Branch, an' all that, but you never could fool me, and you can't now, so don't waste both our time trying it.'

'Where is she?' he said simply.

'In love with the man she ran off with?' she

suggested, reaching out to pour him another cup of tea.

He raised his eyebrows. 'It's been over four weeks since she disappeared. No one's that much in love.'

She shook her head. 'You know, Davey, sometimes I worry about you. Have you ever been really in love? You haven't, have you? When you are, you can't see anything else, believe me. You walk into a hole in the road, because your head's in the air and your eyes full of dreams. Would you like some cake?'

'Yes, and no, not so that I fall into holes in the road,' he answered.

She stood up, still looking at him. 'You've got your head screwed on all right, so tight it's a wonder you can fasten your shirt collar.' She opened the pantry cupboard and took out the cake, cutting a really large wedge for him and putting it on a plate.

'Thank you,' he accepted, taking a bite of it immediately. 'That isn't the answer, Gwen,' he said with his mouth full. 'She knew something, and that's why she ran away. And the only thing that'd be safe for her is if she came out from wherever she's hiding and told people. Then there'd be no point in hurting her, it would only prove she was right.'

'For heaven's sake, use your common sense!' she said exasperatedly. 'Who's going to believe a lady's maid over a lord, or his wife?'

'He's not a lord, he's an inventor of some sort, working on experiments with new undersea weapons.'

168

'Under the sea?' she said incredulously. 'To kill what? The fish?'

'Ships,' he said succinctly. 'Hole them under the waterline, where they'll sink.'

'Oh.' She paled. 'And you're saying he isn't a gentleman either?'

'No! He's a gentleman, and he's got money and influence. And I suppose you're right, she'd have to have proof, and maybe she doesn't. I've got to find her, Gwen. I've got to prove what happened to her, I just don't know where else to try!'

She looked at him as if he were five again, and she were seven. 'What do you know about her?' she said patiently.

He described what he knew of her appearance. 'And she came from the country,' he added. 'Somewhere in the west. The local police looked to see if she'd gone home, and she hasn't.'

'Well, she wouldn't, if she were hiding, would she!' Gwen said, shaking her head. 'But she might go somewhere like it.'

'We thought of that. We can't find a trace of her at all.' He heard the note of panic in his voice and deliberately lowered it. 'She was very handsome to look at, easy to notice. And she was quick, and sometimes funny, so the other staff said, and her friends at the local pub. They were all surprised she took up with Harry Dobson. Said he wasn't anywhere good enough for her.'

'Nobody ever is,' she said with a sudden wide smile. 'But we love you anyway!'

She was teasing him and he relaxed a little, taking several more bites of the cake. She was a good cook, and the taste of it carried him back in memory to being home on leave from the sea, and sitting in another kitchen, before she moved out here to King's Langley. Everything had been different there — sparser, poorer, much smaller, back door opening into a small, grubby yard — all except the cake. She never stinted with cake.

'She liked the sea,' he went on. 'Used to carve little boats, real little tiny ones, out of soft wood. What kind of a man would kill her just because she couldn't help seeing that he was having an affair? And he was. Pitt caught him in lies and he had to admit it. But Pitt doesn't think Kynaston killed her. I think he's off on another world sometimes.'

Gwen frowned. 'It doesn't make sense,' she agreed. 'Who's she going to tell?'

'His wife,' he replied.

'Oh, for goodness' sake!' she said impatiently. 'Do you think she doesn't know? What's she going to do about it? Nothing now — except pretend she didn't see. It's not a crime, just a betrayal. And nobody else will want to know, I can promise you that. It could upset all sorts of applecarts to be admitting to that kind of thing . . . unless . . . ' She stopped.

'Unless what?' He put the last of the cake into his mouth.

'Unless it's with someone that really matters?' she answered thoughtfully. 'Someone whose husband would throw her out. That could happen, and then she'd be ruined. That's . . . possible . . . I suppose.'

'How do you know about things like that?' he said curiously.

'For goodness' sake!' she repeated exasperatedly. 'I was a laundress before I got married! I didn't live all my life inside a box with the lid on, Davey!' She stood up again. 'You'd better go and catch your train, before it gets late and you're out half the night. And don't leave it so long next time.' She came around the table and hugged him. He felt the warmth of her body, the softness of her hair, and how strong her arms were when she clung on to him. For a moment he hugged her hard in return, then put on his coat again and went out of the door into the yard and up the steps without looking back at the lights, or to see her standing there watching him.

★ ★ ★

While Stoker was in the train rattling through the darkening countryside back to London, Pitt was in the chair beside the fire in Vespasia's sitting room with its warm, pale colours. He was so comfortable it was an effort to keep awake. The fire was burning low, its embers glowing, the light reflecting in the facets of the small crystal vase in which were a few delicate snowdrops. He was startled at how richly their perfume filled the room. There were faint sounds of footsteps in the hall, and now and then the patter of rain on the window. It was only the urgency of the matter weighing on his mind that prevented him from relaxing.

' . . . Suspiciously, at the very last moment,' he

finished, describing the events of his rescue by Somerset Carlisle.

'And the very best moment,' she added drily. 'That sounds exactly like Somerset, although unusually fortunate, even for him. I see that troubles you . . . '

'I've been thinking about it,' Pitt admitted. 'Carlisle was the one who had asked the question in the House, making the whole issue far more public than it had been before. And yet he not only rescued me from Talbot, he rescued Kynaston, for the time being, from a situation that at the very best would have been embarrassing. At worst it would have brought him into suspicion of having killed and mutilated Kitty and put her body in the gravel pit. Why?'

'Somerset is a good man,' Vespasia said quietly, her mouth curving in a sweet smile, 'if, as you say, a trifle eccentric now and then.'

'That is a magnificent understatement,' he observed.

She smiled very slightly. 'I only overstate things when I am so angry I have lost my vocabulary,' she answered.

He raised his eyebrows. 'I don't believe you ever lose your vocabulary. I have seen a fluency from you that would stop a horse in full gallop, or freeze a duchess at twenty paces.'

'You flatter me,' she protested, but through laughter. 'I would like to think that his principle purpose was to make a fool of Edom Talbot, a man he loathes, but I appreciate that that could be no more than an agreeable side effect.' The amusement in her face died completely. 'But you

172

say that Dudley Kynaston is unquestionably having an affair, and that you think it is possible that Kitty, being bright, observant, and no doubt bored, may have been aware of this? You are certain, I presume?'

'The evidence is there, and he did not deny it,' Pitt said unhappily. 'I just don't believe he would kill his wife's maid because she had deduced that he was lying about where he had been. Either that is not the case at all, and is merely incidental, or there is something far more important that I'm missing. And where did she learn it? Why won't she come forward now, or at least send some kind of a message that she's alive? Maisie said she could read and write!'

'Who is Maisie?'

'The scullery maid.' Pitt remembered Maisie's eager face. 'Kitty was her . . . example. She not only liked her, she admired her. Maisie means to learn to read.'

'Just how ambitious was Kitty?' Vespasia asked doubtfully. 'Sufficient to improve herself, but not so rash as to exert a little unwelcome pressure? Are you sure, Thomas?'

'What could it gain her to attempt blackmail on Kynaston? Not a lot more than dismissal, and possibly a police charge. And she can't have been stupid enough to imagine anything else. The magistrates would not be very kind to her. They can't be seen to allow servants to gather information about their masters, and then use it that way.' He smiled ruefully and almost without bitterness.

'Of course not,' she agreed, her face reflecting

an unaccustomed sadness. 'It would be the end of the world, as most of us know it. And yet it will certainly happen, inch by inch. Nothing is more inevitable than change, for better and for worse. Perhaps it is the approaching close of the century, but it is a very mixed prospect. Events seem to be moving faster and faster.'

He looked at her face. It was still beautiful, still full of passion and vitality, but he also knew there was a fragility in it, a power to be hurt that he had not appreciated before. Her century was ending and she could not know what lay ahead.

Could Pitt say anything that would comfort Vespasia? Or would it be clumsy, and in reality make her more fragile?

He changed the subject completely. 'Do you trust Somerset Carlisle?'

She gave an abrupt little laugh, light and full of generous amusement.

'My dear! What a question. That depends very much upon what we are talking about. To be honest, yes, I do. To be generous and risk anything at all for what he believes? Unquestionably. To have values the same as mine, and to behave responsibly? Not in the slightest.'

'I owed him a lot today,' Pitt answered. 'I think Edom Talbot would be delighted to see the back of me from Special Branch. I am not the sort of man he judges suitable for the position, neither intellectually nor socially, especially the latter.'

'I have no doubt of it,' she agreed. 'For all that he is not quite a gentleman himself, he intends to become one. And yes, you owe Somerset a considerable debt. Now if you do not mind, my

174

dear, I have plans for this evening, and I need to get ready.'

'Of course.' He rose to his feet immediately. 'Thank you for your advice, as always.' He leaned forward and kissed her very lightly on the cheek, then felt instantly embarrassed for the familiarity of it. He could not remember having had the tenacity to do it before.

8

When Pitt left, Vespasia turned to the telephone and found herself curiously nervous. Beneath the muslin ruffles of her cuff, her hand was trembling a little. She steadied it and picked it up. When the operator asked whom she wanted, she gave her Victor Narraway's number.

It rang three times, and she was about to change her mind when he answered, giving simply his name.

She cleared her throat.

'Good evening, Victor. I hope I am not troubling you?'

'I am not certain how to answer that and be both courteous and truthful,' he said with a degree of amusement that she could discern, even in a voice distorted by the machine.

'It is serious enough, I think, that you may dispense with courtesy,' she replied. 'And not all of the truth may be necessary . . . '

He laughed. 'You always trouble me, but I should be bored without it,' he said. 'What is it that is so serious? I presume I may help? Or at least that there is that possibility?'

She was relieved, but also nervous, which was extremely unusual for her. She was accustomed to being in control of any social situation.

'Will you dine with me, and I can explain to you the situation I believe I am observing?'

'I should be delighted,' he said immediately.

'May I suggest a place where we may eat well, but not fashionably, and therefore be able to discuss without interruption whatever it is that troubles you?'

'I think that would do very nicely,' she accepted. 'I shall dress accordingly.'

'You will still cause a stir.' The idea seemed to please him. 'You cannot help it, and I should regret it bitterly if you tried.'

For once she could think of no suitable answer, except to say that she would see him in just over an hour.

In spite of what she had said about dressing quite ordinarily for dinner, she did not do so. Indeed, she took great care, choosing a gown of a dark blue-grey so soft that in the shadow it looked almost indigo. The line of the neck and the sweep of the skirt were both very flattering, and cut in the fashion of the moment. Deliberately she wore no jewellery, except very small diamond drop earrings. Her shining silver hair was ornament enough.

In the carriage as it made its way through the windy darkness of the streets, she was deep in thought, turning over and over in her mind the things that Pitt had told her.

There was a major part missing, in the sense of it. Now in the flickering light and shadow of the carriage interior, she could no longer deny it. She was almost certain who it was that had made it appear that Dudley Kynaston was deeply involved in the disappearance, probably even the murder of Kitty Ryder.

The thought was painful for a number of

reasons. She did not regard Kynaston as a friend. She had met him perhaps half a dozen times, but she did know of his importance to the navy, even if not any of the details of his particular skills. Remembering his face, his voice, his pleasant but slightly detached manner, she found it hard to imagine any circumstances in which he would feel a sufficiently violent and totally uncontrolled emotion that he would sink to such an act. And why, for heaven's sake? What could possibly be gained by it?

If his marriage were precious to him, would he have carried on a dalliance with a maid, however handsome she was? Even if his wife were too ill to offer him the usual comfort, or of a chill disposition and refused him, most men had more sense than to take their pleasure within their own households — if being discovered would be disastrous. However, such a thing would usually be regarded as shabby, but not ruinous. One could dismiss a maid easily enough. All it required was an accusation of petty theft, or even unseemly conduct. Many maids had found themselves on the street for less, and without a 'character' with which to gain another position.

The carriage slowed as traffic became more congested. It happened frequently but now it annoyed her because she was anxious to speak with Narraway.

It seemed far more likely that Kitty Ryder had been too clever and too observant for her own good. Even so, had she been reckless enough to try blackmail? What Pitt had said suggested that she was intelligent. A wise girl would have affected to know nothing, and expected in due course possibly to be rewarded for her loyalty and discretion — as she no doubt would have been.

According to Pitt, Kynaston had admitted having an affair, but with a woman of at least his own social class. But his wife's lady's maid was not in a position to know, surely?

Would it ruin the woman if it became public? Depending upon whose wife it was, that was indeed possible, if unlikely. Vespasia could think of a few candidates.

And of course there was the far more serious alternative: that the woman in question was the wife of someone who could ruin Kynaston's career and thwart any ambitions he might have for higher office. No reason would ever be given. Some might guess, but that would not save Kynaston.

It was still a stretch of coincidence and imagination to connect it with the disappearance and probable death of Rosalind Kynaston's maid.

The traffic cleared, and once again they were rattling through the early evening darkness. Vespasia could not shake the conviction that there was some other crucial part of the picture that she had not seen, something completely different that would change it entirely. It must be something that would explain why Somerset Carlisle, her friend for so many years, had asked questions in the House of Commons as to Dudley Kynaston's safety, with regard to the apparent dramatic and brutal murder of one of his servants.

And now it appeared that Somerset had also most fortunately rescued Pitt from a profound embarrassment, and even fatal damage to his career, when facing Edom Talbot in Downing Street. His appearance, so perfectly timed, was explainable. If he had called Pitt's office, as he had claimed, his staff would know where he was, because he would not have left without telling them. As for the other information, Somerset was a Member of Parliament, therefore anything known to the House of Commons might well be known to him, even if it were not said openly where the public might hear.

But there were other matters, like his apparently close following of the case of Kitty's disappearance. Then there was the coincidence that a member of his constituency, which was many miles from Shooters Hill, should follow the case even more closely, and a drink at the Pig and Whistle, an hour's journey from his home, in order to learn that Kitty had wanted a hat with a red feather in it. Then, according to Somerset, he had gone to a third area and bought just such a hat. He had also known where to place it, once again in Shooters Hill, in the right spot to have been missed by the police in their search around where the body was found, and yet still close enough that it was easy to believe it was hers.

And then there was the coincidence that someone found it, when only the red feather was noticeable in the surrounding mud and tussocks of dead grass.

No simple event in itself was unbelievable, just all of it together, particularly when coupled with the long history she knew of Somerset Carlisle. He had been willing to help Pitt, at her request, using his considerable influence in Parliament, even at times when it was embarrassing or inconvenient to himself. That had been true ever since Pitt had investigated the bizarre affair of the decently buried corpses which kept reappearing around Resurrection Row.

Of course Pitt had learned the truth, but he had chosen to ignore Carlisle's part in it. He understood his motives, and had not denied even agreeing with them.

What could Dudley Kynaston have done drastic enough to warrant this? Whatever her character, which might make it more understandable, betrayal of a wife was ugly, but hardly unique. Certainly it was not motive to stir Somerset to such dangerous and macabre action.

Or was Vespasia wrong in suspecting Somerset's involvement at all? She would very much like to think that it was the latter.

She arrived at the restaurant. It was one of Narraway's favourites, small and elegant with windows that overlooked the river.

Narraway was already waiting for her, as she had expected. He was always fifteen minutes early, just to avoid any possibility of her having to wait for him. He rose to his feet and came towards her, his face lit with pleasure. He was still as lean and straight as when she had first met him, although his thick, black hair had more grey in it than even a year ago. He was a little taller than she, but she was tall for a woman, and carried every inch of her height as if she balanced a crown on her head.

He took both her hands, lightly, and kissed her on the cheek. Then he stepped back and regarded her with his usual intensity, as if he could read not her thoughts but her emotions.

'Is it this miserable business of Pitt's?' he asked quietly as they were escorted to their table.

'You know me too well,' she replied. 'Or have I been reduced to the periphery of social life where I can have no other anxieties?' She said it with a smile. She intended to keep the conversation light. Oddly, she found herself nervous, not willing to trespass on to emotional ground.

'I know you well enough to be perfectly aware that there are issues in society that might interest you, or annoy you,' he answered. 'But your heart is engaged only where you care. Which suggests your family . . . even if slightly extended.' There was a flicker of something in his face that she could not identify, except as a kind of sadness, there and then gone again. Narraway had never married, and he had no family left. She had never thought it appropriate, or even kind, to enquire further. That there had been lovers come and then gone again, she knew perfectly well. It was not something one discussed.

They had been seated and ordered their meal before she answered his question.

'Thomas is in something of a cleft stick,' she said, sipping her wine, which had been brought just before the hors d'oeuvres. 'The evidence

182

seems to indicate that Dudley Kynaston is involved in this poor servant's death, and yet they have no definite proof that the body is hers, even though they cannot find her alive. Kynaston admits to having an affair, but with someone of his own social rank, and Pitt does not believe he would kill anyone to conceal that.'

'And you?' Narraway asked, watching her reaction.

'It seems a little . . . excessive,' she replied. 'And I agree, I had not thought Kynaston a man of such . . . '

'Stupidity?'

'I was going to say 'passion'.'

'Sometimes people have far more passion than they appear to,' he said quietly, his eyes on her face, tracing the outlines of it as if to make it indelible in his mind. 'Everyone else thinks them cerebral and a trifle cold because they keep their feelings hidden.'

She looked back at him. She wanted to press for his precise meaning, and was afraid to. It would leave her exposed as caring too much for the answer.

'Do you think Kynaston is one of them?' she asked, taking another sip of the wine. 'I find I know less about him than I thought. I remember his brother, Bennett. He died young . . . well under forty. He had great promise, so it was particularly upsetting. Dudley took it very hard.'

'I remember,' Narraway said thoughtfully. 'But that was several years ago — eight or nine, I think. They were very close, I believe.'

They were interrupted by the arrival of the

main course of a delicate white fish, dense-fleshed and tender. It was dessert before that particular conversation resumed. In the meantime they spoke of the kind of art, theatre, music they both enjoyed, and laughed at current political jokes.

'You did not ask to see me as an excuse to dine,' Narraway said at last, the gravity back in his face. '*I* might have done, but *you* have never needed to prevaricate.' He was smiling very slightly as he said it, but his concern was real and it would be a rebuff to pretend she did not hear it.

'I can though,' she admitted. 'I think there are strong currents beneath the surface of this. I feel them, but I don't know what they are. In fact, the more details I discover, the less can I make, sense of it. It seems an absurd mixture of trivia and tragedy.'

He watched her without interrupting. His eyes looked almost black in the candlelight from the chandeliers.

'A maid running off with a suitor is very inconvenient, but it happens quite often,' she continued. 'I think I have lost at least three that way, perhaps four, if you count a scullery maid. But a woman beaten to death and her body left in a public but deserted place, to be scavenged by animals, is both grotesque and tragic.'

He nodded. 'And they appear to be connected. I presume Pitt was called in because the missing maid worked for a man of great importance to the navy, and thus to the safety of the country. What else?'

'Kynaston, by his own admission, is having an affair, which is grubby, but far from unique . . . '

'By his own admission?' Narraway interrupted.

'Yes. When Thomas taxed him with it, he did not try to evade it.'

'Which does not mean it is necessarily true,' he pointed out.

She was startled, and about to argue when she suddenly realised what he meant. 'Oh! You think it is something worse? That an affair would be preferable to the truth?'

He gave a small, slight smile. 'I don't know, only that we should not assume anything for which we have no proof.'

'Of course not. You are quite right,' she agreed. 'So that is another strange contrast, an admitted affair, which may conceal something worse, or at least something he has a greater desire to keep secret. Victor, what do you know of this man Talbot? Why does he so desire to be rid of Thomas? Is it something as simple as prejudice because Thomas has no family background or military experience? That too is grubby, and completely irrelevant, but it is not uncommon, and it is certainly not a crime. Or is there something of which he is afraid?'

'He has the Government's confidence,' Narraway said thoughtfully. 'But the Government has no experience of criminal deviousness as opposed to moral or political.' He sighed. 'You may be right, Talbot dines at the right clubs and Pitt doesn't. He will never be one of them; you have to be born to it, and of course go to the right schools.'

'Pitt is better as he is, right schools and clubs or not,' she said sharply. Then she felt the colour hot in her cheeks as she saw the laughter in his face.

He leaned forward across the table. 'I know that, my dear. I am as aware of Pitt's worth as you are, professionally even more so. And in my own way, I am also fond of him.'

She looked down, avoiding his eyes. 'I apologise. Of course you are. I did not mean to doubt you. This conflict has me . . . wrong-footed.'

He touched her hand where it lay on the table, gently, and only for a moment.

'How charmingly you understate it. You make confusion about violence and murder sound like a missed step in a dance. I fear we shall run out of music before we reach that point. May I say what I think is really troubling you?'

'Could I prevent you?' she asked. Her voice was soft, but the words were a trifle defensive.

'Certainly,' he replied. 'Just tell me that you are not yet ready to trust me with it — or perhaps that you do not wish to.'

'Victor, I'm sorry. I am behaving with a discourtesy you do not deserve. I am evading the issue because I am afraid of it.'

'I know,' he said so quietly she barely heard him above the murmur of conversation around them. 'It is Somerset Carlisle, isn't it?' he continued.

'Yes . . . '

'Would Pitt have let it go had Carlisle not

asked the question about Kynaston in the House?'

'I think so. That made it impossible,' she agreed.

'And what are you afraid of — exactly?' he pressed.

She must now either answer him honestly, or deliberately refuse to.

He moved very slightly back again, no more than an inch, but she saw the shadow in his eyes. It was a moment of decision about far more than the admission as to what she feared regarding Carlisle: it was a moving closer, or apart, between Narraway and herself.

It seemed to stretch endlessly, isolated as if it were unreal, an island in time. She was afraid because where it led to might be painful. The chance to prevaricate was slipping out of her hands.

He moved back an inch further.

'I am afraid that Somerset might have engineered the whole thing,' she said huskily. I don't mean that he killed anyone,' she amended. 'I can't believe that any cause, however intense, would make him do that . . . ' She took a deep breath. 'But I think he may have used the police finding that tragic corpse; the continued disappearance of Kitty Ryder; the whole absurd episode of the hat with the red feather, which could have been hers and wasn't; and the man who supposedly put it there, and found it, and so opened up the whole case again.'

'And then blew it apart, and rescued Pitt?' he asked curiously, but the shadow had gone from

187

his face and his eyes were grave, and gentle. 'For heaven's sake, why?'

'That is what troubles me,' she confessed. 'It is the mountain that is filling the sky, too big to see its boundaries, and yet too far away to touch. He is manoeuvring Pitt, Victor. That is what I am afraid of. And I have no idea why, so I can't help.'

'Have you warned him?' he asked.

'Thomas? Of what? He can remember Resurrection Row, and the bodies all over the place, not to mention various other . . . irregularities since.'

His eyebrows shot up. 'Irregularities! What a wonderful term for them! Yes, my dear, Somerset Carlisle has an art for irregularities that amounts to genius. What injustices does he care about enough to do this?'

'I don't know: murder, betrayal, corruption at the highest level, treason?' The moment she said that last word she wished she had not. 'Or perhaps some personal debt of honour. He wouldn't tell me, and place me in the position of having to betray his trust in order to stop him.'

'But he would use Pitt, who showed him such unwise compassion before?'

'Maybe that's why Somerset rescued him from Talbot?' she suggested.

'You are being too idealistic,' Narraway replied sadly. 'He is perfectly prepared to use Pitt because he needs him, but I wish we knew for what purpose.' He looked at her steadily and this time she did not look away. It was an admission of something, a difference in the relationship

188

between them and she was not as afraid of it as she had expected to be. In fact she felt a relaxing of tension inside herself, almost a warmth.

'We are going to do something about it, aren't we?' he asked.

'Oh, yes,' she answered. 'I think we have to.'

Again his fingers touched hers across the table, just tip to tip. 'Then you must begin,' he told her, 'with Carlisle. I shall find out a great deal more about Mr Talbot.'

She smiled. 'Indeed.'

★ ★ ★

The following morning over breakfast Vespasia returned her mind to the question of Kynaston and his involvement in Pitt's case. She was concerned primarily for Pitt, because she was troubled by a fear that there was some element in it far more dangerous than a simple illicit affair. However, she had no idea yet what it was, except that it was ugly enough to provoke a particularly grotesque murder.

Which was why it also troubled her that Jack Radley had apparently been offered a position working more closely with Kynaston. She had grown fond of Jack for himself, but she would care about him regardless because he was married to Emily, and Emily's first marriage had been to Lord George Ashworth, who had been her nephew. The close affection had remained after George's death. Indeed, she now felt the same kind of bond with Charlotte also, perhaps even closer. They were in some ways more alike in nature.

If Kynaston were guilty in any way of Kitty Ryder's death, then the stain of it would extend to those close to him professionally. And because of this suspicion, she could not rid herself of the fear that this ugly affair was more than a personal matter. Somerset Carlisle might deplore the betrayal of an affair, but she believed he would not appoint himself to any kind of judgement regarding it. He was too wise to imagine such things were one-sided.

Was to suspect Carlisle in this the inevitable result of common sense, or was it an unfair prejudice, a leap to conclusions based on the past?

She was not hungry. The crisp toast sat uneaten in the rack, all except for one piece taken with her boiled egg. Only the hot, fragrant tea appealed to her. This morning she must see Somerset Carlisle and ask him exactly how he was involved, and oblige him either to tell her the truth or to lie to her. If for some reason, even a good one, he lied, then that would open a chasm between them, perhaps narrow, but a division nevertheless, and something that could never again be completely closed. It would break a thread of trust that had been there for years, delicate and strong, like silk, throughout all kinds of fortune, good and bad.

She had not appreciated before quite how precious that was to her. She had scores of acquaintances, but they had not known the people Vespasia had wept for. They had not lain awake at night, cold with dread because they knew what had actually transpired, and the terror that had not come to pass. For them it was not life, it was the pages of history.

Not that Carlisle was her age — he wasn't — but he had a fire, an idealism, for which he was willing to risk his own comfort, even his life. She admired him for that, and she was obliged to admit she liked him deeply. She did not yet wish to know exactly how he was involved in Dudley Kynaston's life, or what he knew about Kitty Ryder.

If she faced it with any degree of honesty, she was not yet prepared to deal with that knowledge. So long as she did not ask, she had left herself room to believe as she wished. Once she knew, she would be obliged to speak to Pitt and tell him all she was aware of and for which there was proof.

And yet, of course, if she did not, then she was responsible for what occurred out of his innocence.

Was Pitt naïve? No, that was not the word, he was simply not as subtle and devious of mind as she was — or Carlisle.

Even the tea ceased to appeal to her. She rose from the table and walked out of the yellow dining room and across the hall to the stairs. It was too early yet to see Carlisle. First she would address the problem of Emily's unhappiness.

★ ★ ★

Emily was delighted she had come, and welcomed her into the magnificent hallway with its marble floor and sweeping double staircases. Emily was so pleased, Vespasia immediately felt guilty that she had come for a very specific purpose. If Emily had any suspicion of that, she gave no sign of it at all.

'It's lovely to see you,' she said warmly. She looked well, if a little pale. 'I get so tired of snatching a word or two at some function, and having to be polite to everyone else. Although that play was fun, wasn't it? I enjoyed watching the audience almost as much as the stage.'

She led the way into a garden room, which was light and airy, even in this wintry February where brief bars of sunlight shone between bands of cloud. The fire was burning and the air was warm. If one closed one's eyes it was possible to believe in the illusion of summer. Vespasia was flattered that the shades so closely resembled those she had chosen for her own sitting room, which also faced on to the garden. They were subtle and yet there was depth to them, and nothing seemed chill or bleached of life.

'Indeed, so did I,' she agreed, sitting in one of the chairs by the fire and, when she was comfortable, Emily took the other. She was facing the light and Vespasia noted a tightness in her skin. It was perhaps due to nothing more than the usual effects of winter when one went outside less often, and riding in the park was hardly a pleasure. There was no grey in Emily's fair hair, but there were tiny lines in her delicate skin and a shadow in her eyes.

'Did you come for any special reason?' Emily

asked. She was a little more direct than her usual manner. After her encounters with Charlotte, was she afraid that there might be?

'No, but if there is something you wish to speak of then I am always happy to hear.' Vespasia practised the sort of evasion she had perfected over the years, both in society and within family. There were so many things one approached only in circles.

Emily smiled and relaxed a little. 'Loads of gossip,' she answered lightly. 'Did you hear that wonderful story from America in the newspaper?'

Vespasia hesitated for a moment, uncertain if there were something behind Emily's remark. 'I hope you are about to tell me,' she answered.

'You haven't?' Emily said happily. 'That's marvellous. It's absolutely gruesome. Her name was Elva Zona Heaster. Her death was ruled natural, but her mother claimed that her ghost came back and said her husband had broken her neck.' Emily smiled and her eyes were dancing. 'And to demonstrate, the ghost turned its head right around as she was describing her death, and walked away forwards, but with her head on backwards, still talking to her mother!'

Vespasia stared at her, incredulous.

'In a little town in West Virginia,' Emily continued. 'Honestly! That's more interesting than that Margery Arbuthnott is about to marry Reginald Whately, which is probably totally predictable.' Suddenly there was a flat note in her voice as the laughter vanished.

Vespasia affected not to have noticed. 'It seems

to be a very repetitive cycle,' she agreed. 'And unless you know them well, it is not interesting. I used to find it easier to pretend I cared than I do now. It seems to me there are so many things more important.'

'What is important, Aunt Vespasia?' Emily said with a slight shrug. It was an elegant gesture, very feminine, and yet there was a thread of hurt through it, something deeper than the words.

'Anything that concerns those you love, my dear,' Vespasia answered. 'But that is not for social conversation. We often do not tell people what matters to us. It is not always easy to say it even to those we know well, because we care what they think of us.'

Emily's eyes widened with momentary disbelief.

'Do you think I am too old to feel pain?' Vespasia asked, aware that she was risking far too much in admitting it, and yet knowing there was no other way to reach whatever it was that coiled so tightly inside Emily, crushing the woman she used to be.

Emily blushed scarlet. 'No, of course I don't!'

'Yes, you do,' Vespasia said gently. 'Or else you would not be so embarrassed that I have observed it. I assure you, pain does not lessen just because you have known it before. It is new each time, and cuts just as sharply.'

'What would hurt or frighten you?' Emily's voice was husky now. 'You are beautiful, wealthy, admired by everyone, even those who envy you. You are safe. No one can take from you all the wonderful things you have done. See some people's faces when you walk into a room. Everyone looks. No one ever thinks of ignoring you.' She took a deep breath and let it out slowly. 'You cannot lose who you are . . . '

'Is that what frightens you, losing who you are?' Vespasia looked at her carefully, searching her eyes. 'What frightens me is no one else knowing who I am — not what I look like, or what I said that might have interested or amused them, but what I feel like inside.' She gave a rueful little sigh. It was not the time for mock modesty. 'It has always been pleasant to be beautiful; it is certainly not a gift one should be ungrateful for.' She moved perhaps an inch. 'But love concerns the beauty that is within — and the pain, the mistakes, the dreams, the things that make you laugh, and cry. It is about how you deal with failure and own your mistakes. It is about tenderness and the courage to admit your own need, to be grateful for passion and generosity of soul. That has nothing to do with whether your nose is straight or your complexion without blemish.'

Emily stared at her, tears welling up in her eyes.

'I don't know whether Jack still loves me or not,' she whispered. 'He doesn't talk to me any more, not about things that matter. He used to ask my opinion. It's . . . it's as if I've already said everything he wants to hear, and I'm not interesting now. I look in the mirror and I see a woman who's tired . . . and boring.' She stopped abruptly, her silence begging for a reply.

Vespasia could not answer her immediately

and in the way she wanted. But this was too deep an unhappiness to allow a quick remedy.

'Are you bored, Emily?' she asked. 'There comes a time when Society is not enough, no matter how much you cannot afford to offend it. I remember very vividly when I arrived at that point the first time.' That was absolutely true. She had been younger than Emily, and bored stiff with being ornamental but completely unnecessary. It was a time she preferred not to think of. She had children she loved, but their daily needs were cared for largely by servants. Her husband was not unkind — he had never been that — simply without the fire in his soul or the flight of imagination she hungered for. But none of that did she intend to tell Emily, or anyone else.

Emily's eyes were wide, the tears forgotten. 'I can't imagine you bored. You are always so . . . so engaged in things. You are not just being . . . kind to me . . . are you?'

'I think you mean 'patronising', don't you?' Vespasia asked frankly.

'Yes, I suppose so, but I didn't mean to say it,' Emily admitted, then gave a small, very reluctant smile.

'I'm sure you didn't,' Vespasia smiled back. 'And no, I am not being either kind or, I hope, patronising. Do you imagine you are the only woman who finds mere comfort insufficient? Of course it is, when you don't have it. But one can become accustomed to it very quickly. Perhaps a little downfall would be helpful? Not of the physical kind, but of the emotional sort? One can

196

very quickly learn the value of something when you fear losing it. We take the light for granted, until it goes out. You are used to turning on the tap and getting water. You have forgotten what it is like to have to go to the well with a bucket.'

Emily's eyebrows rose. 'Do you think going to the well would make me feel better?'

'Not at all. But if you did so a few times, turning on the tap certainly would. But I mentioned it only as an example. Tell me, is Jack going to work for Dudley Kynaston, do you know?'

'No, I don't know! That is one of the many things he has not discussed with me.' There was a moment's conflict in Emily's face; then she made a decision. 'I would like to tell you to ask Charlotte. She seems to know everything, but that would only cut off my nose to spite my face, as they say. Somerset Carlisle was asking questions about Kynaston in the House. Is there really something wrong?' Now her concern was sharp and very visible.

Vespasia knew exactly what she was afraid of. It was not so long ago that Jack had looked for another promotion from a remarkable man, in high office, and who had favoured him. That man had proved to be a traitor, and Jack was fortunate to have escaped with his own reputation intact. Was history going to repeat itself? It was not an unreasonable fear.

'I dare say Jack is as concerned as you are,' Vespasia said. 'He will feel that he has let you down if he makes another error of judgement. And yet Kynaston may be totally guiltless in the disappearance of this unfortunate maid. She may simply have gone off with a young man and be living happily somewhere well outside London.' She sighed. 'Or, of course, she may have made a most unfortunate choice of lover, and it was indeed her body in the gravel pit, and she would have been perfectly safe had she stayed at the Kynaston house. Maybe Jack is trying to postpone his decision until Thomas has proved the matter one way or the other.'

'That would be pretty difficult,' Emily pointed out. 'It's going to be obvious what he's doing, and why. He would be letting the whole world know that he thinks Kynaston might be guilty.'

'Quite so,' Vespasia agreed. 'And that is enough to embarrass him, and make him wish he could be more decisive. I would lie awake at night were I to be faced with such a decision.'

'Then why doesn't he ask me?' Emily demanded.

'Possibly because he is stubborn, and proud. And also perhaps because he does not wish to burden you with the choice, because if it should turn out badly he will take the blame himself.'

'Do you think so?' There was a lift of hope in Emily's voice.

'Expect the best,' Vespasia advised. 'Then you will not be filled with guilt if you receive it. In the meantime, for heaven's sake find yourself something in which to be interested. You fear being boring because you are bored with yourself. And I do not mean that you should play at being detective! That would be dangerous, and highly undignified.'

'What do you want me to do? Go and visit the poor?' Emily's face was filled with horror.

'I don't think the poor deserve that,' Vespasia said drily.

'Some of the poor are very nice!' Emily protested. 'Just because . . . oh! Yes. I see.'

'Exactly my point, my dear,' Vespasia replied. 'They do not deserve to be patronised either. Do something useful.'

'Yes, Great-aunt Vespasia,' Emily said meekly.

Vespasia looked at her with alarm. 'You intend to find out about Kynaston! Don't you?'

'Yes, Great-aunt Vespasia. But I shall be very careful, I promise you.'

'Well, if you must meddle, find out about his wife. And if you say 'yes, Great-aunt Vespasia' again I shall . . . think of something suitable to control your impudence.'

Emily leaned forward and kissed her gently. 'Bed without any supper,' she said with a smile. 'Cold rice pudding in the nursery? I hate it cold.'

'I dare say you are well acquainted with it!' Vespasia observed, but she could not keep either the affection or the amusement out of her voice.

9

Emily's resolve remained strong for at least two days. It crumbled only when she faced Jack across the breakfast table on the third morning. He sat studying a folded copy of *The Times*. At least he did not hold it open so that he was entirely hidden behind it, as she had seen her father do on more than one occasion.

'Has something now occurred?' she asked, trying not to sound either plaintive or sarcastic, which was not easy as she felt a little of each.

'The world situation is worrying,' he replied, without lowering the newspaper.

'Is it not always?' she asked.

'I pulled the court circular for you.' He indicated a couple of sheets he had folded and placed on her side of the table. '*The Times* doesn't do fashion.'

She felt her temper flare up like fire in dry wood.

'Thank you, but I already know exactly what is fashionable, and probably possess it, and frankly I couldn't be less interested in the appointments for the day of numerous royal grandchildren and their families. I have no intention of attending any of them.' She sounded waspish, and she knew it. It embarrassed her because it displayed her vulnerability, and yet she did not seem to be able to help it. 'I am much more interested in politics,' she added.

There was a minute or two's silence, then he folded the paper and put it down. 'Perhaps I should get you a copy of Hansard,' he suggested, referring to the written report of what had transpired in Parliament.

'If you can't remember what happened, then I suppose I shall be reduced to that,' she responded, this time not even attempting to be polite.

Jack remained impassive, if a little pale. 'I can remember exactly what happened,' he said levelly. 'I just don't remember anything of the remotest interest. But I was not there all day. Is there something about which you have a particular concern?'

She felt the tears prickle her eyes, which was ridiculous. Grown women, approaching forty, did not weep at the breakfast table, no matter how alone or unnecessary they felt. The only way to stop it was to replace hurt with anger — carefully controlled.

'You didn't think that I might from time to time wonder about Dudley Kynaston and the disappearing maid, not to mention the mutilated corpse within a quarter of a mile of his home on Shooters Hill? Of course, if you have declined the offer of a position with him then it is no longer my husband's future at stake, not to mention my own, it is simply a matter of speculation, much as any other particularly grotesque murder might be.'

Jack was very pale now, and a tiny muscle was ticking on the right side of his face.

Emily swallowed the lump in her throat.

Perhaps she had gone too far?

'I am quite aware of the public speculation on the subject,' he said gravely. 'I am also aware that neither the police nor Special Branch has identified the corpse as being that of Kitty Ryder. Somerset Carlisle, who is as irresponsible as a man can be, has used his Parliamentary privilege to suggest that the body is Kitty Ryder, and that her death is connected to her service in Kynaston's house, but there is no proof of it, or even any evidence.'

'People won't care about that!' she said hotly.

'I care!' His voice was hard, angry in a way she had not ever seen before, and it chilled her deeply. This was not the man who had wooed her, adored her, held her in his arms as if he would never let her go. This was someone she barely knew.

Loneliness drowned her, sweeping her off her balance like a riptide.

'I've learned better,' he said grimly, measuring each word. 'I'm surprised you haven't. When George was killed . . . murdered . . . many people thought it was you who had done it. Do you remember that? Do you remember how afraid you were? How you felt everyone was against you, and you couldn't find any way to prove your innocence?'

Her mouth was dry. She tried to swallow and couldn't. 'Yes,' she whispered. Now, suddenly, she could remember it hideously well.

He looked at her very steadily across the table. 'And what would you think of me if I assumed Dudley Kynaston was guilty of having murdered his wife's maid, brutally, breaking the bones in her body and mutilating her face, when we don't even know that she's dead? Would you admire me for that? Even if I did it so that I wouldn't be stained by association should it turn out to be true?'

She took a very deep breath and let it out in a sigh.

'I would not admire you,' she said quite honestly. Then continuing in the same vein: 'But I would have appreciated your talking it over with me, so I understood what you were doing, and why. I don't know how to interpret silence.'

He looked startled, as if it required a moment or two of thought before he understood. 'Don't you?' he said at length. 'I thought you understood that . . . I told you . . . '

'No, you didn't!' She shook her head. 'I don't know what you're thinking, and I don't know what you're going to do.'

'I don't know myself,' he said reasonably. 'I really can't believe Dudley would have an affair with a maid . . . ' He stopped, looking at the lopsided, rueful smile on her face. 'Not that he's so righteous, Emily! I know perfectly well that plenty of men do! I just don't think Dudley Kynaston's taste runs to maids! Even handsome ones!' He was very slightly flushed. She saw it in his face, and the way his eyes almost avoided hers, and then didn't.

'You know who it is, don't you?' she said with conviction.

'Who what is?'

'Jack! Don't play games with me! You know

he's having an affair. You know who with! Which is why you don't think it is with the maid . . . '

He was on his feet, and she stood up too. 'Why on earth don't you tell Thomas? You could save Kynaston . . . practically from ruin! Thomas isn't going to make it public. He'll keep it just as secret as you do, if it . . . oh!' She stared at him, looking into his beautiful, long-lashed eyes, still feeling the beat of her heart shaking her. 'It's worse than the maid! Could it really be? Like whom? Someone he can't ever be seen with . . . ' Her imagination raced.

'Emily, stop it!' he said firmly. 'I said I didn't think maids were his taste, that's all. I don't know the man that well, and I certainly don't have his confidence in romantic affairs! Or even merely lustful ones. I very much want to work with him, but I don't know if it will be possible. I'd rather err on the side of thinking too well of him than of assuming his guilt before there's even proof of a crime he might be involved in. Wouldn't you?'

She did not answer. She wanted him safe, and she wanted him to talk to her. Above all she wanted him to love her the way he had before he became a Member of Parliament. But to say so would be appallingly childish, embarrassingly so. She blushed hot at the idea he might even guess that that was what she meant.

'I imagine I might,' she agreed. 'But there's something in your voice that makes me think you don't trust him, for all your generous words. I dare say you are right, and he wouldn't have an affair with a maid, or even take advantage of her in something less emotional than an affair. But there is something wrong, you just don't know yet whether it is something you should take notice of or not.'

He looked disconcerted for a long moment, then he smiled, with the same warm, easy charm she knew right from the beginning. She should stop telling herself she was not still in love with him. She knew better than to believe such a lie anyway.

'You have a gift for putting things horribly plainly,' he said with a degree of approval. 'You would never be a success in Parliament. I don't know how you do it in Society. I wouldn't dare!'

'You have to smile when you say things people don't want to hear,' she replied. 'Then they think you don't really mean it. Or at worst, they aren't sure that you do. And it's quite different for me anyway; nobody needs to care very much what I think. They can always discount it, if they want to. Except, of course, if I tell them they look marvellous and are up-to-the-minute in fashion. Then, naturally, I am talking perfect sense, and my opinion is infallible.'

He looked at her for a moment, not sure himself how much to believe. Then he shook his head, kissed her briefly but softly on the cheek, and left the room.

It was better than it might have been, not yet a disaster, but it was still very much too close to the brink. She must do something, and not with Charlotte this time. Regardless of who did what, Charlotte always got the credit.

Emily was ideally placed to spend an

afternoon with Rosalind Kynaston. She looked through the newspaper Jack had discarded and found a suitable event, and another for tomorrow, and the day after. Then she used her telephone to call Rosalind and invite her to an exhibition of French Impressionist paintings, and then perhaps afternoon tea. Very deliberately she did not invite Ailsa.

She was happily surprised when Rosalind replied that she had no engagements that afternoon that could not be put off, even though it meant that Emily was not nearly as well prepared as she would like to be as to exactly how she would conduct herself to gain the best advantage she could. She knew perfectly well that she wanted to acquire some information that would assist Pitt, and therefore Jack, in determining what had happened to Kitty Ryder, and who had caused it. She would very much like the perpetrator not to be anyone in the Kynaston house.

She took great care dressing. The pink had been a disaster. Simply for the memory, apart from anything else, she would not wear it again. In fact, she might well avoid all warm, light colours! She had sufficient means to choose anything she wished. With her fair hair and pale skin, especially after the winter, something delicate and cool was the obvious choice. How had she been so foolish as to do otherwise? Desperation is never a good judge!

She chose a very pale teal, half-way between blue and green, with a white silk fichu at the neck. She regarded herself critically in the glass, and was satisfied. She must now forget the whole dress issue and concentrate on what she would say.

★ ★ ★

They met on the steps of the gallery, Rosalind arriving only moments after Emily. They greeted each other warmly and went inside. It was a very pleasant day, but the wind still had a March bite to it.

'I apologise for such inconsiderate haste,' Emily said as they reached the entrance hall. 'I just had a sudden urge to go somewhere simply for the sake of it, not to be correct and have to make conversation.'

'I was delighted,' Rosalind said with feeling. She glanced at Emily very directly. 'We shall play truant from obligation for a whole afternoon.' She did not add anything about her sister-in-law, but somehow it hung in the air between them. The very absence of her name was an observance in itself.

Emily knew she must not be too direct too soon. She smiled as they walked towards the first gallery.

'I have always liked Impressionist paintings. They seem to have a freedom of the mind. Even if you don't like the work itself, it offers you a dozen different ways to see it and interpret it. Something that is strictly representational forces on you its reality straight away.'

'I never thought of that,' Rosalind said with very evident pleasure. 'Perhaps we could stay here all afternoon?' She did not add how much the idea appealed to her; it was clear in her face.

The first room was taken up almost entirely with paintings of trees, light on leaves, shadows on grass, and impressions of movement in the wind. Emily was happy to gaze at them for their own beauty for quite some time, and allow Rosalind to do the same, although she did glance several times at her face and study the expression in it. Rosalind was clearly troubled. Emily had been right in her observation that the subtle nature of the art allowed a great deal of one's own interpretation, the dark as well as the light. It had been an emotionally dangerous place to come. So much feeling could be laid bare. And yet with time brief, and perhaps the stark reality of betrayal waiting, still the best one. But one mistake of too much candour too soon could destroy it all, like smashing a mirror, so that you would never know what it had reflected.

She moved up to join Rosalind in front of a pencil drawing of windblown trees.

'Doesn't it make you wonder what was going on in the mind of the artist?' she said quietly. 'There is so much strain in those branches. Some of them look close to breaking.'

'I suppose everyone has their own wind, and their own darkness,' Rosalind said quietly. 'Perhaps that is what real art is. Any good journeyman can capture the individual and reproduce what the eye sees. A genius can capture the universal in what everyone feels ... or perhaps not everyone, but people of a thousand different sorts.'

There would never be a clearer opportunity. It was almost as if Rosalind were seeking an opening to speak.

'You are right,' Emily agreed quietly so that anyone else entering the room would not chance to overhear her. 'This drawing looks as if the branches are all hugging each other in the darkness, afraid of the violence outside.'

'I see the violence inside, and the darkness beyond,' Rosalind said with a tiny, tense little smile. 'And I see them huddling, but not together except by chance.'

Emily affected not to have noticed anything raw or painful in her words, but her heart was hammering in her chest. 'What about the picture over there?' She indicated one also of branches, but utterly different in mood. The inner knots unravelled, and one smiled simply to look at it. 'To me it is the complete opposite, and yet the subject is the same.'

'The light,' Rosalind said without hesitation. 'In that one the wind is warm, and they are dancing in it. All the leaves flutter, like frills, or skirts.'

'Dancers,' Emily said thoughtfully. 'That's right — absolutely. It is very difficult for someone else to tell how your partner is holding you, lightly, supportively, or so tightly you are bruised and you know you cannot escape. I wonder if someone has painted real dancers that way. Or would it be too obvious? It would be something to attempt, wouldn't it? If you were a painter?'

'Perhaps that is what group portraiture is

about,' Rosalind suggested.

Emily laughed. 'Not if you want another commission!'

Rosalind spread her hands in a tiny little gesture of submission. 'Of course,' she agreed. 'You must paint people the way they wish to be seen. But would any great artist do that, except to earn enough to live on?'

'Can anyone afford not to make accommodations?' Emily asked in return.

It was a moment or two before Rosalind replied. By then they had moved to the next room where most of the paintings were seascapes, or views of lakes and rivers.

'I like the sea pictures better,' Rosalind observed. 'The open horizon.' She hesitated a moment. 'That one is beautiful and terrible — the loneliness in it, even despair. It looks like a gravel pit, deserted and filled in with water.'

Emily said nothing, waiting.

'I'm sure you must have heard that my lady's maid is missing,' Rosalind went on, looking at the painting, not at Emily. 'And that there was a body found in the gravel pits near us. We don't know yet whether it is Kitty, or not.'

'Yes,' Emily agreed. 'It must be dreadful for you . . . I can't imagine.' She could imagine very well, but it was not the time to be speaking about herself, or the tragedies of her own past.

'The worst part is the suspicion,' Rosalind went on. 'I can't help hoping she is alive and well somewhere, for everyone's sake. But she wasn't an irresponsible person at all. Everyone is suggesting that she ran off with the young man

210

she was courting, but I don't believe it. I can't. She liked him, but she wasn't in love. Ailsa says she was, but I know better. Either she's dead, or she ran away for a reason that seemed real to her.' For a moment Rosalind's face looked as utterly bleak as the painted gravel pit on the wall.

Emily felt she must say something, not only because she could not let the opportunity slip out of her grasp, but out of ordinary kindness.

'Are you sure you are not letting your fondness for her make you overlook her faults?' she asked gently. 'Wouldn't you rather think she was flighty and on rare occasions selfish, rather than dead? After all, who could she be so afraid of that she would run off into the night without a word?' Dare she take it any further? If she did, it must be now! She hesitated only a moment. 'Wouldn't you have sensed it? A look in her face, a clumsiness perhaps, an inattention to detail? It is very hard to conceal fear great enough to make you run off alone into a winter night! It was January then, wasn't it? I don't really like to go out in January even wrapped up and in a carriage, and knowing I will come back to my own bed.'

Rosalind turned a little and stared at her, hollow-eyed. 'Neither do I,' she said in a little above a whisper. 'But I have been safe, physically safe, all my life. I'm not a servant, and I don't know anything that could be dangerous.'

'What could she know?' Emily seized the chance offered her. 'It would have to have been something she couldn't tell you . . .'

'That is what frightens me,' Rosalind replied,

her voice now so strained it was barely recognisable. 'There is nothing about me that is even interesting, let alone threatening to anyone. It must be about my husband, or my sister-in-law.' She took in a deep breath and let it out. 'Or Bennett. He's been dead nearly nine years, and yet it is as if he still lived in the house somewhere just out of sight. No one ever forgets him.'

Emily thought for only a moment. 'You mean Ailsa still loves him too much to consider marrying again?'

Rosalind did not answer immediately. She appeared to give the matter thought. 'I'm not sure,' she said at length. 'She does accept various social invitations from other men, but they seem to cool after a while. So yes, perhaps you are right. That is what she tells Dudley, anyway. But Dudley loved Bennett profoundly. Even for brothers, they were very close.' She smiled, and there was a deep warmth to it. 'That is one of the nicest qualities about Dudley: he is totally loyal and, if he judges at all, then he is kindly. He was always protective of the young, and of course Bennett was younger than he. I remember Dudley with our sons. He was patient, no matter how exasperating they were at times . . . and they were. In fact, he was gentler than I . . . I am ashamed to admit.'

'And your daughters?' Emily said with interest.

Rosalind shrugged. 'Oh, he was always patient with the girls, and with me. And with Ailsa, for that matter. Women don't tempt him to be otherwise. I'm not certain if that is because he doesn't expect so much of us . . . ?'

'Some men just *are* patient,' Emily agreed. She thought momentarily of Jack with Evangeline. She could twist him around her little finger, and he did not even bother to deny it.

She looked at Rosalind, deciding what line next to pursue, intensely aware of the distress in her. 'Ailsa seems to be strong-willed enough not to need a great deal of protection,' she observed. 'Am I jumping to too quick a judgement?'

'No, not at all,' Rosalind said instantly. 'I . . . ' She shook her head. 'No, I am at fault. I should not judge either. To me Ailsa seems immensely strong, but she was torn apart by Bennett's death. It was just that with her it seemed on the outside to be anger, even rage that fate had taken from her the one man she loved. I . . . ' She shook her head again. 'I never loved in that kind of way. Perhaps because I have children? I don't know. If Dudley died I would miss him terribly. I expect every day I would be aware of the emptiness, all the things he said, did, cared about . . . everything. I would weep inside, as he still does for Bennett, I know. But I don't believe I would rage at fate.'

Emily thought how she would feel if Jack were to die. Alone . . . as if she would be alone for the rest of her life. If she knew beyond doubt that he really had left her, either openly, physically, or just by being emotionally absent, then she would rage! Her anger might be beyond control, at times, but it would be a defence against tears. She knew that almost as if it had actually happened. It would be as if the sweet wine of life had turned to vinegar. The thought was cold and real inside her.

'What was he like . . . Bennett?' she asked.

Rosalind gave a little laugh. 'Like this picture, with the sunlight in the trees,' she answered. 'Do you think we should move on? Are we stopping other people from studying this one?' She glanced around to see if anyone were waiting, but no one else was in the room except a couple of men staring at a different picture over on the opposite wall.

'Probably,' Emily agreed. 'We'll see what's in the next room.'

It turned out to be landscapes in various moods, all of them profoundly beautiful in their own way. With so much passion around them it was easier to be honest than it might have been in a more conventional place with the politeness one was accustomed to, and the usual pretences of good manners.

'What was Bennett like?' Rosalind repeated Emily's question. 'When I think back on it, I didn't see him nearly as often as one would think, from the impression he made on me. He was very like Dudley in some ways: his interests, his mannerisms, his sense of humour. But he was quicker, more certain of himself. He had boundless dreams and he had few doubts that one day he would achieve at least most of them. In a way that's why it was so difficult to realise he was dead. It all happened very quickly. One day he was ill, and in a week he was gone. We couldn't grasp it — especially not Dudley. After all that had — ' She stopped.

Emily waited. They were standing near a broad, sweeping landscape with huge skies: the left side was filled with blue distance, the right a driving storm coming in rapidly, darkening everything, heavy with threat.

'We thought the worst was past,' Rosalind said simply, as if everyone would know what she meant.

Perhaps it was indelicate, but Emily could not now leave it.

'He had been ill before?' she asked.

'Bennett was in Sweden,' Rosalind said after a moment or two. 'Many years ago now. Before he ever met Ailsa. I don't know what happened. Dudley was frantic. I've never seen him so desperate. He received a message and dropped everything. He went to Sweden the very next day and I didn't hear from him for weeks. When he returned he brought Bennett with him, and they never told me what happened. Bennett looked ashen, and thin. He stayed with us. Dudley wouldn't let him out of his sight.'

Two gentlemen walked past them talking earnestly.

'He used to have nightmares,' Rosalind continued when they were out of earshot. 'I heard him crying out in the night. Dudley never told me what it was, and gradually it passed. Bennett regained his strength and went back to his work. A year or two after that he met Ailsa and shortly after they were married.'

'Then the illness returned?' Emily said with a heavy sense of tragedy herself. 'But this time it was too swift, and there was nothing they could do to help him?'

'I suppose so,' Rosalind answered, looking suddenly away from the painting and at Emily. 'But that was all long before Kitty came to us, and there was definitely nothing about it that was anything except tragic. I . . . I wish I could do something to help! Dudley has had more than enough pain.'

Emily looked at the racing clouds in the painting and the heavy shadow they cast on the land. She shivered involuntarily.

'That sounds self-pitying, doesn't it!' Rosalind said, annoyed with herself. 'We have a beautiful home. Dudley's work is terribly important and he is extremely good at it. We have money and position, and healthy sons and daughters, and here am I with the arrogance to speak of pain.'

'Not knowing is painful,' Emily said with sincerity. 'No matter how much you love, if you are afraid of losing it all, then the icy edge of that storm is upon you already.'

Rosalind smiled and there were tears in her eyes. She put her hand on Emily's arm in a quick gesture, then withdrew it again.

'Would you care for afternoon tea? I know it is a little early, but I should like to take you to a small place I know will be open, and is quite delightful.'

'An excellent idea,' Emily agreed.

★   ★   ★

All the way home in her carriage afterwards Emily thought over everything that Rosalind had said, and even more what she had left unsaid. Over tea they had spoken of many things, mostly totally trivial, often even funny. Rosalind was well informed about a number of subjects. She spoke with enthusiasm about music, and some knowledge of various pianists. She was interested in the history of glass, going back to ancient Egypt and forward to present day Venice and the glass features in Murano. Emily began to hope with some energy that Jack would find himself working for Dudley Kynaston. She would enjoy a further friendship with his wife.

A friendship with his sister-in-law did not even occur to her until she realised how seldom Rosalind had mentioned Ailsa. In fact, it had been only twice, and then only to say that they had gone together to some event that had been Ailsa's idea. Apart from that, they had had an interesting and entertaining afternoon without thought of her at all.

And yet Ailsa had appeared on other occasions to be so large a part of the Kynastons' life. Was it actually only a kindness, including her because she appeared to have no other family?

Thinking back on the few occasions Emily had been in the company of both women, she remembered it as if Ailsa had somehow been in charge, like the elder sister, although she was probably several years younger. But there had been little actual warmth between them.

Was that of any importance at all? Possibly not. Nevertheless Emily determined to learn as much more about Ailsa Kynaston as she was able to, preferably when not in Rosalind's company. Among many other things she had learned about Rosalind was that she was far wiser and more observant than she affected to be. It might be more than a little foolish to underestimate her.

Creating the opportunity to observe Ailsa was now the challenge. If Ailsa were indeed at the heart of the problem — the murder of Kitty Ryder — then it might be dangerous to be seen to enquire about her. The thought did not deter Emily, but she must plan it with care. She would find out Ailsa's interests, what plays she liked, what exhibitions, who were in her circle of friends that Emily herself might also know.

* * *

As it turned out, fate played directly into Emily's hands. Three days later she changed her earlier decision to decline, and instead accompanied Jack to a formal party with several other people in Government. Previously she said she would not go, afraid that she would appear clinging and a trifle possessive. Now her purpose regarding Ailsa changed everything. She was determined to support Jack not just tacitly, but positively, and oblige him to be aware of her and happy that she was present.

She dressed carefully in her favourite shade: palish green, more delicate than the earliest leaves, and known as 'waters of the Nile', but in the far more sophisticated French '*eau-de-Nil*'. It was the softest silk, floating when she moved, and the sheen of it caught the light. Naturally it was the latest cut: soft at the shoulder and neck, smooth and slender at the hip. Pearls might have been more appropriate considering the name of the colour, but she wore diamonds. She wanted the fire and the sparkle.

She was satisfied as she swept down the stairs towards Jack, who was waiting for her at the bottom, that she had achieved the result she wished. He said nothing, but his eyes widened and he gave a little sigh of satisfaction. So far, she was succeeding.

The effect of her entrance at the party was also gratifying. However, it took only a few minutes to realise that she certainly had no monopoly on beauty or attention. Moments later Ailsa Kynaston arrived, sufficiently late to be sure of everyone being aware of her, but not enough to be discourteous.

She was dressed in cream and gold. It was a daring combination for a woman of such pale colouring, but she carried it superbly, with a confidence that challenged anyone to find fault with her.

However, what took Emily's attention was the fact that she was on the arm of Edom Talbot, whom she knew to be one of the men closest to the Prime Minister, even though he held no specific government position. But Emily knew from Charlotte that Talbot had taken a dislike to Pitt, and made his investigation of the Kynaston affair more difficult than it needed to have been. Or perhaps it was not Talbot's intention, rather his necessity, because of the sensitivity of

Kynaston's position with the navy.

Looking at him very carefully now, Emily saw a man striking in appearance because of his height and casual strength. He carried himself as if he had tested and proved his physical superiority many times. There was a kind of unspoken arrogance in his posture, slightly intimidating.

Did Ailsa find that pleasing? To Emily it seemed slightly ill-bred. A gentleman did not ever intentionally make others feel uncomfortable, and to threaten, however tacitly, would do that.

Some women found dangerous men attractive. Emily considered their taste, conversely, to be a sign of some kind of inner weakness. And weakness was dangerous. It was those aware of their own disadvantage who attacked.

Someone spoke to her and she made a light and meaningless reply, smiling with the charm she had always known how to use.

Jack said something to her that she did not hear. She was busy watching Edom Talbot and Ailsa Kynaston, studying the way they moved together, who spoke and who listened, how often they met each other's eyes, or smiled. Who was leading?

At first it seemed to be Talbot. He knew more people, and introduced them to her. She was gracious, but not eager. Nothing in their conversation was so very interesting. He clearly admired her striking appearance, but then so did at least half the men in the room, and the women both envied and resented it.

Emily had not been paying attention to her own duties. She gave Jack a dazzling smile and joined in the conversation.

It was over half an hour before she could watch Ailsa and Talbot again. Now she was leaning towards him, smiling. Then she spoke to someone else, the moment after back to Talbot. He did not take his eyes from her, almost as if he could not. She was flirting with him, but so subtly only Emily, an expert at such things herself, was aware of it. Others walked by, made some passing observation, smiled, laughed, and moved on.

Talbot put his hand on Ailsa's arm, high, near the shoulder, as if to pull her a little closer to him. It was an oddly proprietorial gesture, almost intimate. Her face was turned away from him as she had been speaking momentarily to someone else. Emily saw the flash of more than distaste, it was almost hatred. Then deliberately she allowed herself to be drawn towards him before finding an excuse to move in a different direction.

Was she holding back through the memory of Bennett, the lost husband she could never forget? Or something else entirely? Perhaps something she knew of Dudley Kynaston and the adopted family whose loyalty to her she was repaying with a kind of protection now?

But protection from what? Could it be the same knowledge that Kitty Ryder had run away from? Or was killed for?

Perhaps Emily had been completely wrong in her estimation of Ailsa. That was something she had to find out. She must force herself to know her better, in spite of her instinctive dislike of her. Emily knew scores of people, perhaps hundreds. At least two or three of them must know Ailsa. She would begin looking for the best way forward tomorrow.

10

'You bring 'er back 'ere by 'alf-past five, you 'ear me, young man? I don't care 'oo you are, special police or not,' the cook said fiercely, staring at Stoker as if he were an errant bootboy.

Stoker smiled, but Maisie got the answer in before he could speak.

'Yes, Cook. Mr Stoker's a Special Branch policeman. 'E wouldn't never do nothing wrong.' She lifted her chin up even higher and met Cook's eyes directly, something she would not normally dare to do. But today she was in her best dress, the only one that she never used for work. The footman had polished her boots for her until the cat could see its face reflected in them. Mrs Kynaston's new lady's maid had put her hair up so that it was tidy, even at the back where she couldn't see it herself. She was going out to tea with Mr Stoker, to be asked some important questions, so important they couldn't be asked where other people might overhear them.

Stoker became serious again. 'We shall have tea, and then I shall bring her back,' he promised.

Cook gave Maisie a stern warning. 'You be'ave, Maisie. Don't you go gettin' ideas above yourself or givin' no cheek, you understand? And if you go repeating gossip what's none o' your business, you'll find yourself out on the street with no place. You watch your tongue, and that imagination o' yours.'

'Yes, Cook. I won't say nothin' at all but the truth.' Then, without waiting for the Cook to add anything more, she turned and walked away, her chin high, her back as straight as if she had been carrying books on her head.

Suddenly Stoker wished he had had a daughter. An old love of his had wanted to marry and settle down. She had been pretty, with dark eyes like this odd little scullery maid's. Stoker had been frightened by the idea of such responsibility. He had hesitated too long. By the time he had come back from the voyage Mary had found someone else. It had hurt for a long time.

He caught up with Maisie and they walked together, he being careful not to outpace her. They went down Shooters Hill Road towards Blackheath until they came to the tea shop, where he had already reserved a table for them.

'This yours, then?' she asked as he pulled out the chair and she sat down, more than a little self-consciously arranging her skirts.

'For now it is,' he told her. 'Would you like tea? And some cakes?'

She was too impressed to speak as the waitress stood ready to take their order. She had never been waited on before, or called 'Miss'.

'Tea for two, and your best cakes, please,' Stoker requested. He was loath to admit it, but he was enjoying himself. But time was short, and he had a lot to ask her. He could not afford to wait until they began tea.

'We found a hat up at the gravel pit we thought was Kitty's,' he began. 'But then we learned that it wasn't. Some stupid man put it there on purpose, just to get himself noticed.'

Maisie frowned. 'That's wicked. 'E just wanted ter make us all scared and sad, so's 'e'd be talked about? Is 'e daft, or summink?'

'I'd say so. But we found the receipt for the hat, and for the red feather, so we know it wasn't hers.'

Her eyes were bright. 'So mebbe she in't dead, then?'

'I'm going to believe she isn't,' he said firmly.

'But some poor cow is, eh?' She bit her lip. 'An' yer still gotter find out 'oo she is, an' 'oo done that to 'er?'

'If it isn't Kitty, and isn't anything to do with the Kynaston household, then it's the police's job to find out,' he replied.

''Cos you're special, right?'

He drew in breath to explain it a little less self-importantly but, seeing her bright face, changed his mind.

'Something like that,' he agreed awkwardly. 'But I still want to find Kitty, and prove she's alive.'

She put her head a little to one side. 'Ter save Mr Kynaston?'

He found himself slightly uncomfortable. Her eyes were bright, almost black, and both quick and innocent at the same time. He hesitated as to how he should answer her. He needed information from her, and yet she was second-guessing him. If she caught him in any

225

deception at all he would lose her trust, and therefore her honesty. He would also find that painful. He was getting soft.

'Mostly,' he agreed. 'But I'd like to find Kitty just to know she's all right as well.'

The tea came, with a whole plate full of little cakes and pastries. Maisie looked at them, then up at Stoker, then back at the plate.

'Which one would you like?' he asked.

'The chocolate one,' she said instantly, then blushed. ''Course, if you like it, the one with the pink sugar on it'd be all right.'

He made a note not to take the one with the pink icing, which he rather liked the look of too.

'I'll take the apple tart,' he assured her. 'You begin with the chocolate.' He considered asking her if she would pour the tea, then changed his mind. He did ask her how she liked hers, and then poured for each of them.

She ate the chocolate cake slowly, savouring each mouthful.

'To find Kitty, I need to know more about her,' he began. 'I know a few things. She could sing really nicely. She liked the sea, and ships, and used to collect pictures of ships from all over the world — with different kinds of sails.'

Maisie nodded with her mouth full. As soon as she had swallowed she answered. 'Real clever with 'er 'ands, she was. Course, bein' a lady's maid an' all, she could sew real well, even mend lace when it got tore.' Her eyes filled with tears. 'Please find 'er, mister. Tell us she's all right . . . I mean . . . alive, an' well . . . '

'I will,' he promised, and knew even as he was

saying it how rash he was being.

Maisie sniffed. 'P'raps she just went off wi' that great dollop, 'Arry. D'yer think?' She looked at the last piece of the chocolate cake on the plate. 'But why couldn't she 'ave told us? Why don't she even write a letter, nor nothing?'

'Are you sure she can write?' he asked.

'Yeah! She used ter write lists an' things. She were teachin' me.' She looked again at the last piece of her cake.

'Why don't you finish that, and then take the pink one?' he suggested. 'I'm going to have that one with the raisins.'

She looked at him to make sure he meant it, then did as he said, taking a delicate sip of her tea in between.

He hid his smile. Perhaps he was going about this the wrong way. Maybe he should be looking not for where Kitty would go, but for where Harry Dobson would choose.

'What was he like, this . . . dollop?' he asked.

Maisie giggled at his use of her word. ''E were all right. Crazy about Kitty, 'e were. Thought as the sun shone out of 'er eyes. An' I s'pose that's worth something, in't it? She just smiled at 'im, an' 'e were made.'

'But he wouldn't suit you?' he concluded. 'Why not?'

She looked down at the pink-iced cake, a little embarrassed. 'I in't never goin' ter be pretty like 'er, but I want ter better meself, all the same. I'd want someone wi' a bit o' fire, like; someone as wouldn't let me run rings around 'im.' She stopped, ashamed of her words. It was too self-revealing to say what she meant to somebody who didn't know her — or any man at all, for that matter.

'You might have to work hard to find someone you couldn't run rings around Maisie,' Stoker warned. 'But I heard that Kitty was ambitious too. Was that wrong?'

Maisie sighed. 'I s'pose when yer fall in love yer kind o' lose yer wits. Least that's wot they say.' She bit into the pink cake, then looked at it. 'This 'as got cream in it, all squashy and sweet.'

'Don't you like it?' he said quickly. 'You don't have to eat it. Choose another . . .'

She looked up at him. 'Oh, I like it. It's a bit like bein' in love, though, in't it? I s'pose yer don't know it's goin' ter 'appen until yer already bit into it, eh?'

'Maisie, you are so clever sometimes you worry me. All these cakes are for us, so take as many as you like. Tell me more about Harry Dobson, and if you really think she liked him enough to have gone off with him . . . without telling anyone. She must have had a reason for that. What might it be?' He drank some of his tea and added a little more, to keep it hot. Then he took another cake, because he was sure she would not take another until after he had. He had seen her count them, and she was going to be scrupulously fair.

'Do you think he would have made her go secretly?' he asked.

She shook her head. 'No! 'E wouldn't 'a made Kitty do nothin' as she didn't want. I reckon she must 'a bin . . . ' She hunched her shoulder a

228

little and gave a tiny shiver, then she looked up at Stoker. 'Mebbe she were scared? I used ter think as she knew one or two things as she'd sooner not a' knowed about the mister an' missus, like. Then I thought as it were just talk. But mebbe it weren't? D'yer think?'

'I think that's very possible,' he agreed, trying not to make too much of it and twist what she was going to say. 'Any idea what she knew?'

She shook her head. 'There are things as I don't want ter know. Me ma always said that, told me not to see things or 'ear things as I shouldn't. An' if I did, ter forget it like it never 'appened.'

'Very wise indeed,' Stoker said gravely. 'I am telling you exactly the same thing, and I mean it just as much as she did. Now tell me more about Harry Dobson. We've asked the regular police, but nobody seems able to find him. Did he do any special kind of carpentry work? Windows, doors, floors? Any particular builder he worked with?' He reached for the teapot. 'And have some more tea. If you'd like more cakes, we'll ask for them.'

She took a deep breath, scooped up all her courage, and asked for another chocolate cake.

'Kitty said as 'e were goin' ter get a place ter work on 'is own, like,' she answered. ''E were good at doors. Wanted ter make fancy ones, carved, an' all that. But 'e could 'a gone anywhere for that.'

'Where did he come from?' Stoker persisted. This looked more hopeful.

'Dunno,' Maisie admitted. 'North o' the river, I think.'

'Thank you. That'll narrow the search quite a bit.'

She frowned. 'Should I 'a said that before? Nobody asked. It were only wot 'e wanted. I dunno as 'e ever did it.'

He smiled at her. 'Maybe he didn't, but it's worth a try.'

She sighed with relief and ate the cake.

★ ★ ★

Stoker had naturally been assigned to other cases since the failure to identify the body in the gravel pit, and then the assumption that it was indeed that of Kitty Ryder. Those cases could not be ignored; they genuinely affected the security of the country. Therefore it was wiser that he continue to look for Harry Dobson in his own time. He did not relish trudging around the streets, in and out of public houses, music halls, taverns, but it was very possibly a task that he would gain little from doing at midday. He had learned a lot from Maisie that would narrow the search. He must forget the local area and go north of the river and at least try to find someone who specialised in good doors, even ones with carving on.

It took him four evenings walking in the late February rain, his sodden trouser legs flapping around his ankles, his boots letting in the water from puddles and overflowing gutters. He spoke to local builders from Stepney, Poplar, east to

Canning Town, then to north of Woolwich before he finally found Harry Dobson.

Stoker stood in the sawdust of the carpenter's workroom and faced a fair-haired young man with heavily muscled arms and mild eyes.

'You Harry Dobson?' Stoker asked. Could this be the young man Kitty Ryder had run off with, abandoning her position, and her warm, safe home on Shooters Hill? Stoker had expected to dislike him, to see in his face some evidence of the nature that would abuse a young woman who trusted him. He saw instead only a young man who was slow, careful. At the moment, he seemed a little sad, as if he had lost something, and had no idea where to look to find it again.

'Yeah,' the carpenter said quietly. 'You the feller with the warped doors?'

'No, actually I'm not.' Stoker felt like apologising. He stood blocking the doorway, but there was another entrance behind Dobson, leading into a timber yard. 'Sorry. I'm looking for the Harry Dobson who courted Kitty Ryder, who worked up on Shooters Hill.'

The colour leached out of Dobson's skin, leaving him almost white, his eyes dark hollows in his head.

Stoker tensed, expected him to turn and bolt out of the other door.

For seconds the two stood staring at each other.

Finally Dobson spoke. 'You . . . you police?'

'Yes . . . ' Stoker was rigid, all his muscles tight, expecting to have to chase this man, try to

231

bring him down before he escaped. He was sick with misery at the thought, and also physically very aware of the other man's strength. He was solidly built, muscular, and with powerful arms. Stoker was as tall, and wiry, but he had nothing like the sheer strength of Dobson. He would have to rely on speed, and years of experience in hard and dirty fighting.

Dobson took a deep breath. 'You come to tell me they got 'er after all?'

Stoker was stunned. 'Got who?'

'Kitty!' Dobson said desperately. ''Ave you come to tell me they killed 'er? I begged 'er not to go, but she wouldn't listen to me.' He gasped as if someone were preventing him from breathing. 'I promised I'd look after 'er, but she wouldn't listen.' He shook his head. There were tears in his eyes and he did not even seem to be aware of them.

'No!' Stoker said quickly. 'No . . . I haven't come to say that at all! I don't know where she is. I'm looking for her.'

The colour and the light came back into Dobson's face. 'You mean she could be all right?' He took a step forward eagerly. 'She's still alive?'

Stoker held up a hand. 'I don't know! The last I heard about her for sure was the night she ran away from Shooters Hill, way back in January.'

'She was with me then,' Dobson responded. 'I promised to look after 'er, an' I did. Then all of a sudden, about a week ago, she said she gotter go again, and there weren't nothing I could do to stop 'er. I begged 'er, told 'er I didn't want nothing except to keep 'er safe.' He shook his head. 'But she wouldn't listen . . . ' A look of helplessness washed over him again and Stoker was suddenly moved to an intense pity for him.

'She's probably all right,' he said gently. 'And she maybe was right to go. If I could find you, so could others. I don't suppose you have any idea where she went?'

'No . . . '

'Perhaps that's wise too,' Stoker conceded, difficult as it was. 'I'm a policeman, and I haven't heard of anyone finding her, dead or alive, so she's probably fine for now. You did the right thing.'

'What about 'er?' Dobson pressed. 'What if they find 'er, then?'

'We'll do all we can to see that we catch them before they do.' Stoker made a wild promise. He knew perfectly well that he was being unprofessional about this. Pitt's influence was rubbing off on him!

Dobson nodded slowly. He believed him. 'Thank you, sir,' he said solemnly.

'But you have to help me,' Stoker resumed a more serious manner. 'I can't catch him without your help . . . '

'Anything!' Dobson agreed eagerly.

'Why was she afraid of them? I know, but I want you to tell me what she believed.'

'She saw things and heard them,' Dobson answered straight away. 'She knew as there were something really bad going on in that house. I mean worse than just people pinching the odd thing 'ere and there, or messing around with other people's wives, an' such.'

'Not an affair?' Stoker was surprised, immediately wondering if Kitty had told Dobson the truth. 'What, then?'

Dobson shook his head. 'She didn't say. I asked her, told her to go to the police, but she said the police wouldn't be no good. For a start, she didn't think they'd believe 'er, considering who Mr Kynaston is, but also she said the police could be in on it anyway. And there in't no use getting angry with me! Don't you think I'd tell you, if I knew?'

'Yes,' Stoker said frankly. 'I think you would. Thank you, Mr Dobson. If we find Kitty we'll keep her safe . . .'

'You can't,' Dobson said instantly. 'You don't know who's after 'er.' That was a challenge, not a question.

'No,' Stoker admitted. There was a chill inside him as if a gust of cold rain had drenched his clothes, touching his skin with an icy hand. He drew breath to promise that he would find out, then he realised he had made enough extravagant promises for today. That one he would make silently, and to himself.

★   ★   ★

That same evening, Pitt was sitting by the fire in his home on Keppel Street. The long curtains across the French windows on to the garden were closed, but he could hear the wind and rain beating against the glass. The children were in bed. He and Charlotte were sitting quietly by the fire.

It was Charlotte who raised the subject of the unidentified woman in the gravel pit again.

'Do you think it's over?' she asked, putting her embroidery aside.

Pitt liked watching her sew. The light flashed on the needle as it moved in her hands, weaving in and out, and the faint click of it against the thimble on her finger was rhythmic and comforting.

'What's over?' He had not been paying attention. To be honest he was nearly asleep in the warmth of his home, with Charlotte so close he could have leaned forward and touched her.

'The Dudley Kynaston case,' she answered. 'I keep waiting every day for Somerset Carlisle to raise it again in the House. You know the hat wasn't Kitty's, but you don't know that the body wasn't — do you?'

He sighed, forcing his attention back to the issue. 'No, and there's no further evidence, so there's nothing to pursue. We have to let it go.'

'But you do know there's something wrong!' she protested. 'Didn't Kynaston admit to you that he had a mistress?'

'Yes, but it wasn't Kitty Ryder.'

'You believe him?' Her brow was puckered.

'Yes, I do.' He sat up a little straighter. 'From everything the other servants say, Kitty was a handsome girl, ambitious to better herself, not to have an affair that could cost her her job. Or worse than that, get her with child, and then out on the street with no money, no position and no future. I believe Kynaston. I really don't think a quick fumble with his wife's maid would be worth killing her to keep secret. I don't know why Kitty went, but I can't see her succeeding in blackmailing him or — from what the other servants say of her — even trying it. It looks as if she ran off with Dobson and then perhaps was too ashamed to come home again.'

'Maybe she was with child already, and she married him?' Charlotte suggested. 'I suppose you looked at all the marriage registers?'

Pitt smiled. 'Yes, my darling, we did.'

'Oh.' She was silent for several minutes. There was no sound but the flickering of the fire and the rain against the windows.

'Then what is Somerset Carlisle doing?' she said at last. 'Why did he raise the question in the House? He must have had a reason. For that matter, how did he even know so much about it?'

'I don't know,' Pitt confessed. 'He must be aware of something, or at least believe it. The information is not so difficult to get; he may have friends in the police, or in the newspapers.'

She frowned. 'What could he know that we don't? It has to be about Kynaston, doesn't it?'

'Or his mistress,' he said thoughtfully. 'He may have ways of finding out, on a personal level, that we don't.'

'Would it matter?' She was puzzled, her embroidery still ignored. 'I mean would it matter to Somerset? If it were someone he knew, or cared about, surely it would be the last thing he would want exposed publicly, wouldn't it?'

Pitt considered the possibility of the woman being someone Carlisle disliked, but as soon as the thought formed in his mind he discarded it. Carlisle was unpredictable in many ways — eccentric at times, to say the least — but he would not have descended to using his privilege of parliamentary questions for the purpose of conducting a private vendetta.

Charlotte was watching him. 'What is it?' she asked.

'I don't know. Talbot's involvement troubles me, but I can't put my finger on it. Carlisle dislikes him profoundly. It's there in his manners and his voice, polite and perfectly controlled so there's nothing to get hold of. I don't like Talbot either, and I'm perfectly sure he doesn't like me. But as far as I know, it's just because I'm not the sort of gentleman he thinks should hold this position.' He felt suddenly self-conscious saying this. Charlotte was the daughter of a family of both very comfortable means and long accepted social position — not high society like Vespasia, but far beyond the servant status of his own family. A generation earlier he would have been her footman, not her husband. He was more conscious of it than she. Talbot's attitude had brought it back again to the forefront of his mind.

'Then he's a fool,' Charlotte said angrily. 'It is too important a position to appoint people because of who their fathers were. We can't afford anything but the best. To try to undermine that is disloyal to the country. Of which I shall remind him, should he be rash enough to make such a remark in my presence.'

He laughed, but it was a little lopsided. He

knew that she was perfectly capable of doing exactly that.

'Are you going back to Carlisle?' she asked.

'Not until I have something specific to ask him,' he answered. 'We know each other too well for me to fool him for an instant. I wish I were as good a judge of him!'

'I'm glad you're not much like him,' she said gently.

★ ★ ★

Pitt was in his office in the morning, reading through reports from various officers around the country, when, after a brisk knock on the door, Stoker came in. Today there was nothing stoic about him. His usually bleak, rather bony face was alight with satisfaction. His eyes shone.

Pitt was in no mood for preamble. 'What is it?' he demanded.

'I found Harry Dobson,' Stoker said immediately. 'He's set up in his own workshop now, that's why we couldn't find him. Ordinary sort of bloke, but decent. I checked on him. No record with the police. Pays all his debts. Nothing bad known about him — '

'Get to the point, Stoker. Where is Kitty Ryder?' Pitt interrupted.

'That's it. She ran off from Shooters Hill with Dobson because she knew something that scared her so badly she thought she'd be killed if she stayed. Wouldn't tell Dobson what it was, but it was bad enough that when the hat with the red feather in it was found, she thought someone was after her again and she moved off. Wouldn't tell him where she was going. Maybe she hadn't decided.' His face tightened. 'Or she meant to keep on moving, too scared to stay in one place.'

'That's what Dobson told you?' Pitt asked.

'I believe him,' Stoker insisted. There was absolute certainty in his voice, in his face and in the way he stood square in front of Pitt's desk. 'I think he cares about her, and to be honest I don't think he's got the wits to lie anyway. It fits in with everything else we know.'

'Still leaves a lot unanswered,' Pitt said unhappily. What was she frightened of? Who did she think was pursuing her? Like Stoker, he wanted to believe that she was alive. He also wanted to believe that Kynaston had not harmed her, and the body in the gravel pit was someone they did not know — and, of course, if he were honest with himself, something that the local police could deal with.

'Sir?' Stoker said a little sharply.

Pitt brought his attention back to the moment. 'I suppose you checked with the locals that at least some of them had seen her with Dobson after the night she disappeared?'

'Yes, sir. Only got one, but I didn't find Dobson till yesterday late afternoon. I was lucky he was still working.'

'Late?' Pitt said curiously.

'Yes, sir. About seven o'clock.' There was a very faint colour in Stoker's lean cheeks.

'Your own time,' Pitt remarked.

Now the colour was deeper. 'I thought it mattered, sir,' he said a little defensively.

Pitt leaned back in his chair and regarded Stoker with interest and a growing sense of sympathy. This need to follow up a missing person, even in his own time, was a side of Stoker he had not seen before. It was interesting that Stoker was embarrassed about it, too. Far from feeling irritation or contempt for him, Pitt liked him the better for it. It showed a gentleness, a vulnerability he had not thought Stoker possessed.

'It probably does,' he agreed. 'Then the question is, what did she learn that was so terrible, or she thought was so terrible, that she fled without taking anything with her, or giving notice to anyone? And why has she not got in touch with the Kynaston house, or the police, to say that she's alive and well?'

'I've been thinking about that,' Stoker said, regaining a little of his composure. 'It's pretty plain from what she said to Dobson that she thought someone had come after her, and she wouldn't tell Dobson who. But nobody does that about an affair, whoever it's with.'

'No,' Pitt conceded. 'In fact I wonder now if Kynaston confessed to one at all only in order to satisfy our curiosity and get us to stop looking for anything further.'

Stoker bit his lip. 'Can't get away from that one, sir.'

'For heaven's sake, sit down!' Pitt told him. 'We've got to go back to the beginning on this. Did Dobson say if the blood and hair on the areaway steps were hers? If they were, how did they get there? I assume he didn't fight with her?

240

Were they put there to mislead? Did someone try to stop her? Who? It's hard to believe it was any kind of coincidence.'

Stoker coloured again. 'I didn't ask him. I'll go back and do that. Most likely seems to me that it was some kind of accident. Maybe she tripped.'

'One accident I can believe in,' Pitt answered. 'Two I can't. Whose body was it in the gravel pit? The local police can't find anyone missing, and they've checked for several miles around. Whoever it is, poor woman, she died violently, then was kept somewhere for several days between the time of her death and the time she was found in the gravel pit. And she was appallingly mutilated. There's no accident whatever in that.'

'No, sir. Someone's playing a very funny game with us. The stakes must be high.'

'Very high,' Pitt said gravely. 'And I'm not sure we even know who the players are.'

'Is Mr Carlisle a player, or a pawn?' Stoker asked.

'That's another thing I don't know,' Pitt replied. 'I've known him a long time. I think it will be wise to assume he's a player.'

'On whose side?'

'Ours — I hope.'

'And Mr Kynaston?'

'I think that is where we begin. Delegate everything else for the time being.'

'Yes, sir.'

11

Pitt had sat up very late the previous evening, rereading all the papers he had on the Kynaston case. He thought of it in those terms because the root of it lay in Kynaston's house. He had finally gone to bed at about half-past one, when the pages were swimming before his eyes and he was only wasting time looking at them.

He was jerked out of sleep by Charlotte's hand on his shoulder, gentle but quite firm, shaking him. He opened his eyes and saw pale grey daylight in the room. It was the first of March. The sun was rising earlier every day. The equinox was less than three weeks away, the first day of spring.

'Sorry. I slept in,' he mumbled, sitting up reluctantly. His head felt thick and there was a dull ache at the back of his neck.

'It isn't all that late,' she said quietly. Her voice was soft, but he had known her too long and too well to miss the strain in it.

Suddenly he was truly awake. 'What's happened?' His mind raced over thoughts first of his children, then of Vespasia, or even Charlotte's mother. Now he was cold, clenched up.

'They've found another body in one of the gravel pits up on Shooters Hill,' she answered. Her face was anxious, her brow furrowed.

All he felt was a wave of relief, as if the warm blood had started to flow in his body again. He threw off the covers and stood up.

'I'd better get dressed and go. Who called you? I didn't hear the telephone.'

'Stoker's here waiting for you, with a hansom. I'll make him a cup of tea and a slice of toast while you're dressing, and there'll be some for you when you come down.'

He drew in his breath to argue, but she was already at the door.

'And don't tell me you haven't time!' she called. 'The tea will be ready to drink, and you can carry the toast with you.'

Fifteen minutes later he was washed, dressed, hastily shaved, and sitting beside Stoker in the cab. They were going as fast as possible through the broadening daylight, rattling over the cobbles heading south.

'Local police called me,' Stoker told him. 'Haven't been there yet, came straight for you. They said this one's worse. A lot worse.'

'Another woman?' Pitt asked.

'Yes. But with fair hair.' Stoker did not look at Pitt as he said it. Perhaps he was ashamed of it, but there was relief in his voice.

'Does anyone know who she is? Any of the local police recognise her?' Pitt asked.

Stoker shook his head. 'Not at the time they called. Maybe they've got further now.'

Neither of them spoke for the rest of the journey as the hansom slowed a little going up the incline through Blackheath and then beyond on to Shooters Hill. Here the countryside was bare, the wind raking the grass between the few clumps of trees, which were none of them yet in leaf. Some of the gravel pits were filled with water after the winter rains.

Pitt prepared himself for the blast of the wind, which would be heavy and damp when he got out. He tried to imagine the sight that was waiting for them, as if foreknowledge could blunt the edge of the impact.

'I ain't waitin' for yer,' the cabby said gravely, his face wind-burned, half hidden by the muffler around his neck and chin. 'I'nt fair ter me 'orse.'

'Wouldn't think of asking you.' Pitt climbed out a little stiffly and paid the man generously more than he had asked for.

The driver found a sudden change of manner. 'Thank you,' he said with surprise. 'Good o' yer . . . sir.' Then, before Pitt could have the chance to change his mind, he urged his horse on, turned in a circle, and headed back down towards Greenwich to find another fare.

Pitt and Stoker walked into the wind towards the group of men they could see huddled about a hundred yards away. The tussock grass was rough and the ground between littered with small stones and weeds. In moments their boots were covered with pale, sandy mud.

Some movement must have caught the eye of one of the men because he turned, and then started to walk towards them, the loose ends of his scarf flapping. Before he reached them he stopped, nodding to Stoker, then speaking to Pitt.

'Sorry, sir. Looks too much like the last one not to let you know. Over this way.' He started to walk back, head bent, feet making no sound on the spongy earth.

Pitt and Stoker followed, each consumed in their own thoughts.

The sergeant in charge was the same man as before. He looked tired and cold. 'Mind those tracks there,' he directed, pointing at what there was of a pathway. 'Looks like a pony and trap, or something of the sort. Might have nothing to do with the body, but more than likely it was what the swine brought her here in.'

'So she didn't die here?' Pitt asked.

The man bit his lip. 'No, sir. Looks just like the other one back a few weeks ago. Even got the same kind of hair, same sort of build. From what you can tell, she must a' bin real 'andsome when she were alive. We'll need the doc to tell us for sure, but I reckon that wasn't all that lately. Week or two, at any rate.'

'Hidden from view?' Pitt asked.

'That's it,' the sergeant replied, 'she wasn't. She was right out there for anyone passing to see. Couldn't hardly miss her, poor creature.'

'So she was put there very recently?'

'Last night. That's why the wheel tracks are worth something, or might be.'

'Who found her?' Pitt asked.

'Young couple.' The sergeant pulled a grim face. 'Bin out all night. Walking the girl home so she could pretend as she'd been in 'er own bed, like. Not fooling anyone now!' He gave a bark of laughter.

'At least they reported it,' Pitt observed, keeping pace with him. 'They could have just kept going. Then it might have been a lot longer before we found her. Could have been more wind and rain, and we wouldn't have found the cart tracks. How far do they go?'

'Far as the main track over there.' He pointed. 'Then they get lost in all the gravel ruts. But then it's reasonable that's the way he came. Isn't really any other way.'

'Which means she was deliberately brought here,' Pitt pointed out just as they reached the group. They were all standing close together giving the illusion of sheltering each other, although the wind managed to pick them out, whip everyone's scarves and coat tails, and bend the grasses around their feet.

They parted slightly to allow Pitt to walk through and look down at the corpse that lay in the shallow dip in the ground. Her clothes were spread out around her, dark and lacking any distinguishing shape or colour in the wet early light. Her hair was immediately noticeable because it was thick and fair, a little longer than average. Pitt thought that in life it would have been beautiful.

Her face was harder to appreciate because it was already distorted by death and, like the earlier corpse, it had been obscenely lacerated by a razor-sharp blade. The eyes, nose and lips were missing. It was worse, because decomposition had begun, and small night animals had already reached her. As the sergeant had told him, she had been dead some time before she was placed here.

'What killed her?' Pitt straightened up, trying to control the horror and pity that welled up inside him. His whole body was shaking, and he could not control it. He looked from one to another of the men. 'I can't see anything obvious.'

The sergeant spoke quietly, his voice hoarse. 'We'll need the police surgeon to tell us for sure, but 'er inside is broken up pretty bad, and both her legs are broke, high up, across the . . . ' He drew his own hand across his upper thighs. 'God knows what did that to 'er.'

'But no blood,' Pitt said with surprise. He looked at the ground near her and saw nothing to mark the proximity except the claw marks of small animals. 'And she wasn't here last night?' he went on.

'She'd 'ave bin seen, this close to the main paths,' the sergeant answered. 'And 'er clothes are damp but not soaked. There's the cart tracks as well. No, she was put here after dark yesterday. God alone knows what for! But if we catch the swine what did it, you won't need the hangman . . . '

One of the young men cleared his throat. 'Commander Pitt, sir?'

Pitt looked at him.

'Sir, she's lying kind of odd, like her spine's bent, or something. But I were 'ere when we found the first one, sir, an' she were lying exactly the same way — I mean absolute exactly. Like it's the same thing all over again.'

Pitt had a flash in his mind's eye of the woman they had thought was Kitty. It was exactly the same, as if she had the same internal pain twisting her back.

The wind was rising, whining a little in the branches above them and rattling as it knocked the dead weed heads together.

'You're right. Well observed,' Pitt said. 'I presume the police surgeon in on his way?'

'Yes, sir.'

'Then I'll talk to the couple who found her, until he comes. Might as well let them be on their way. Anything else about her? I suppose no one has any idea who she is?'

'No idea at all, sir. Except the quality of her dress an' jacket suggest she could be another maid. Looked at 'er 'ands, an' she's got little burns and scars on them too, like she did a lot of ironing or cooking, or that kind of thing. And . . . there's a handkerchief in her coat pocket, an embroidered one with lace and an 'R' stitched on it. Far as I can recall it's a pretty exact match for the one we found on the other body. An' worse than that, sir, we found this on her.'

He took an envelope out of his own pocket and opened it. Inside was a gold chain with a very beautiful fob on it, also gold, about an inch in diameter, but of an irregular shape. It was slightly indented around the circumference, like a five-petalled rose. On the reverse were the initials 'BK' in an ornamental script. Bennett Kynaston? It had to be the missing chain and fob from Dudley Kynaston's watch that he claimed was taken from his pocket.

'I can just imagine what, the papers will make of this,' he said grimly. 'Let me see the handkerchief too, please?'

The man bent and picked it out of the dead

248

woman's pocket. He passed it to Pitt. It was a small square of white lawn, lace-edged and embroidered with an 'R' in one corner, with tiny flowers. It was an exact match for the earlier one.

'I'll go and speak with Kynaston,' Pitt said to the sergeant, then he turned to Stoker. 'Stay here. Speak to the couple who found her. Learn all you can. I'll catch up with you at the police station, or the morgue. Make damn sure this gets priority.'

'Yes, sir,' Stoker and the sergeant replied as one.

★ ★ ★

Pitt was cold and hungry when he knocked on the front door of Kynaston's house on Shooters Hill. This time he had no interest in the area steps, or the servants except as they might corroborate anyone else's story.

The door was opened by Norton, the butler, who regarded Pitt with unhappy misgiving. No one with any manners called at this hour. It could only mean bad news.

'Good morning, sir. May I help you?' he said very coolly.

'Thank you.' Pitt stepped inside, forcing Norton either to let him in, or deliberately to bar the way. 'I apologise for my boots. They are unfortunately filthy. I have been to the gravel pit . . . again.' He knew his voice was shaking. His body was tense, muscles looked tight across the shoulders and in his belly, as if he were as cold as the mutilated body up on the wind-combed

249

grass a thousand yards away. He had tried, really tried, to get it out of his imagination, to concentrate on his job, to watch and listen to the present, but he could not.

Norton was pale. He swallowed hard. 'I'm sure the bootboy would be able to do something for you, sir. Perhaps you would care for a pair of slippers in the meantime? And a cup of tea?'

Pitt was bitterly cold, and he realised his throat was dry. He was also on duty regarding a particularly vile crime. To accept cleaner footwear was a necessary courtesy to the housemaids who would have to try to clean the carpets after him. Tea and toast was a luxury, and therefore an indulgence.

'That is very kind of you,' he replied. 'Slippers would be a practical courtesy; the tea is unnecessary. I require to speak to Mr Kynaston before he leaves the house. You will doubtless hear about it very soon. I'm afraid there has been another body found in the gravel pits.' He saw Norton's look of horror. 'It is not Kitty Ryder,' he added quickly. 'In fact, it is quite possible that Kitty is still alive and well.' Instantly he knew he should not have said so much. Certainly Norton would tell his master. Pitt had given away his opportunity to catch Kynaston unaware. 'I'm sorry, but it cannot wait,' he added.

'Yes, sir.' Norton bowed his head very slightly in acknowledgement. 'I shall inform him immediately. If you would like to wait in the morning room, it is agreeably warm. See if these slippers will fit you.'

Pitt obeyed, taking off his prized boots, then

following Norton to the morning room, slippers in his hand.

Kynaston came only moments later, his face grave and anxious. He closed the door behind him and remained standing.

'Norton tells me you have found another woman's body in the gravel pits,' he said without preamble.

'Yes, sir, I'm afraid so. This one also has been mutilated, and appears to have been dead some time, but placed there only last night.'

The last dregs of colour drained out of Kynaston's face. He swallowed hard, as if something constricted his throat.

'For God's sake, man, why are you telling me this?' he demanded huskily. 'Do you imagine that it is Kitty at last?'

So Norton had not told him! Interesting. Had he not had the opportunity, or was his loyalty more divided than one might suspect?

'No, sir, I think that is not possible,' he replied. 'This woman has fair hair, very little like the description of Kitty Ryder. Also we have found Harry Dobson, and he says Kitty ran away with him, but has since left him. We checked, and neighbours and local shopkeepers saw her, alive and well, since she left here.'

'And you couldn't have told us this before?' Kynaston said in a sudden explosion of fury. His eyes were blazing, the colour dark in his cheeks. 'What the devil is the matter with you, man? Whatever you think of me, what about my wife's feelings? Or those of the other servants? She was part of our household! We cared about her!'

251

Pitt felt the lash of his words, but curiously it pleased him. The man was showing some sign of ordinary decency.

'We have only just found out, sir,' he answered levelly. 'Yesterday. Sergeant Stoker worked in his own time. This morning I was woken with the news of this second body, which also has a handkerchief identical to the one we found on the first body, and to several your wife possesses.' He took the gold watch fob out of his pocket and laid it on the table between them. 'And she also had this . . . '

Now Kynaston did sit down, hard, as if he were uncertain his legs would support him much longer. His face was ash pale. 'That is my watch fob. It used to be my brother's. That's why I was so upset when it was stolen.'

'Where did the theft happen, sir? Even approximately?'

'Oxford Street. It was crowded. I only realised when I went to check the time later. Someone is trying to make it appear that I am involved in this,' he said desperately. 'God knows why! I have no idea who this woman is, what happened to her or how she got there. Any more than I had for the first one, poor creature.' He looked up. 'If she is not Kitty, for which I am profoundly grateful, who is she? She's still someone, violently dead and her body discarded. Why aren't you doing everything you can to find out who she is, and who did this to her?'

Pitt controlled his own feelings with some difficulty. He had seen this body, and the first one.

'That's a regular police job, Mr Kynaston. I'm Special Branch, and my job is the security of the country. And in this case, to safeguard you and your reputation so you can continue with the work you do for the navy.'

Kynaston buried his head in his hands. 'Yes . . . I know that. I'm sorry. Tell me when this latest body was put there, if you know, and I'll account for wherever I was.'

'Some time after dark yesterday evening,' Pitt told him, 'and before light this morning, probably at least an hour before. I can't tell you closer than that at the moment. I might be able to after I've seen the police surgeon, and he has had time to look at her more closely. She's been dead quite a while.'

'How . . . how did she die?'

'I don't know that either. But perhaps we can exclude you before we've learned that. Where were you from sundown yesterday until, let's say, six o'clock this morning?'

Kynaston looked vaguely surprised. 'I was in bed most of the night, like anybody else!'

'From sundown yesterday evening, sir?'

'I dined out . . . at my club. I'd been working late in the City. I didn't want to come all the way home here to eat. I was tired, and hungry.' There was a sharp edge to his voice, but Pitt could not tell if it was from irritation or fear.

'Did you dine alone?' Pitt asked. 'Would one of the stewards remember you?'

'I had things to consider for a meeting. I was in no mood for idle conversation, however agreeable. But certainly the steward will remember me. Ask him.'

'Yes, sir, I will. If you will give me the name of the club, and the address. And if you recall which steward it was who served you, I'll speak to him personally. What time did you leave?'

'I didn't look at the clock. Half-past nine, roughly.'

'And you got home at what time?'

'The traffic was bad. Some stupid accident; man not in control of his horses. I was late. Ask Norton, he'll tell you. I think it was about eleven.'

'Did you speak to Mrs Kynaston?' Pitt and Charlotte shared a bed, but he knew that many people with large houses did not necessarily do so, especially when they had been married for some time. Kynaston's sons were at boarding school or university and both his daughters were married.

'It was unnecessary to disturb her at that time of night,' Kynaston replied. His mouth twisted in a bitter smile. 'But if you think I crept out of the house unseen, found some wretched woman's body and somehow or other carried it up to the gravel pits and left it there, then returned home to my bed again, you might ponder how I managed to do it without disturbing anyone and getting my clothes sodden. Or how I even carried her! It wasn't in my carriage. The groom would know if I'd disturbed the horses, and I certainly didn't do it in a hansom cab!'

Pitt smiled back at him. 'Frankly, sir, I don't think you did it at all. But someone did. All I have to do is be satisfied that it could not have been you, or anyone in this house . . . '

'Norton? Have you lost your wits?' Kynaston said incredulously. 'The coachman? The boot-boy?'

'No, sir. I never considered Norton a possibility. But your observation about the horses, and the idea of anyone doing such a thing in a hansom very nicely rules him out as well. Actually, we think it was probably a pony and trap.'

'I don't have one.'

'Yes, sir, I know that.'

Kynaston sighed. 'I suppose it's your job. I'm damned glad it isn't mine! I imagine someone has to do it.'

Pitt was stung. 'Yes, sir. And sometimes it is extremely unpleasant, full of darkness and tragedy. But if it were your wife or daughter lying out there you would wish me to do everything in my power to learn the truth, whoever it inconvenienced.' He took a breath. 'I shall speak to all the servants, with your permission, in case they are able to help.'

He expected Kynaston to lose his temper, but instead he began to tremble and went so ashen that had he not been sitting already he might well have fallen.

'I'm sorry,' he said very quietly. 'I spoke without thinking. This whole business is deeply distressing.'

Pitt wished he had not been so harsh. And yet he had meant what he said, even if he knew instantly that he should not have said it. Perhaps it would be wiser now to leave the matter of his affair until he was more composed. 'I'll keep you informed, sir, should we actually find Kitty Ryder. But it was certainly not her body in the gravel pit, either the first time or now.'

'Thank you. Norton will see you out.'

Pitt went into the hall where Norton handed him his clean and polished boots, and retrieved the slippers. Pitt thanked him.

★ ★ ★

Pitt spent the rest of the morning checking what Kynaston had said. He did not disbelieve him, but he wanted to have the proof so he could rebut any accusations made by journalists. More importantly he must be able to answer questions firmly, even tartly, that Somerset Carlisle might raise in the House, under the privilege afforded him as a Member of Parliament.

By two o'clock in the afternoon he was tired and miserable. His stomach was gnawing at him with hunger, so much so that he felt light-headed as he sat at one of the tables in a pub. Eating a big steak and kidney pudding with a glass of cider helped little.

Kynaston had been at his club, but he had left at least an hour earlier than he had said, and arrived home an hour later than he had told Pitt. Neither had there been any recorded incidents of traffic accidents or other delays. He had had Stoker speak to a number of hansom drivers, as they were the most reliable source of information as to the traffic conditions on the streets. It was part of their livelihood to know. Word of delays, accidents, and mischance of any sort spread like fire among them. There was hardly a street in London they did not frequent, let alone the way from Kynaston's club in central London to his home on Shooters Hill.

The barmaid passed by, checking that he was satisfied with his meal. He smiled his thanks and took another mouthful.

Why had Kynaston lied? Clearly he was afraid, but of whom? Of what? Where had he been for nearly two hours that he had not accounted for?

Perhaps the matter came back to his mistress again? The issue of Kitty Ryder's disappearance had all but died from the public mind. The newspapers' attention had been taken by other things. The police wished to identify the first body, but had already pursued it as far as they could. Kynaston might reasonably have believed that life was back to normal. Only the discovery of this new body in the gravel pit brought the whole thing flooding back to mind.

Pitt kept on eating, warmer at last.

No doubt the newspapers would have banner headlines on this second wretched discovery. They would sell thousands of extra copies on the sheer horror of it. They would go after Kynaston again because he was a public figure. It was a temptation they would not even try to resist.

Why in heaven's name had he lied? He must surely have foreseen that?

Pitt knew he must weigh how he would answer Talbot, when he sent for him, as he assuredly would.

Then another thought occurred to him. Was it

conceivable that Kynaston knew who had killed those women? Was he protecting him willingly? Or was he afraid of him? Was someone he loved in jeopardy of far deeper involvement than Kynaston could protect them from?

Pitt finished his meal without the enjoyment such cooking deserved, emptied his glass of cider. He went out to find a hansom to take him to Downing Street to report this latest event to Edom Talbot — although no doubt Talbot would have heard of it already, at least the facts.

Pitt was correct on that. He was ushered in immediately, and Talbot saw him within ten minutes. Only an interview with the Prime Minister himself could take precedence over this.

Talbot came into the room stiff with fury. His hands fumbled with the doorknob and he ended up slamming it in spite of himself. This was the residence and the office of the Prime Minister of Great Britain, and he could not afford such a loss of self-control. He blamed Pitt for it.

'What in heaven's name are you doing, Pitt?' he demanded in a low, angry voice. 'I thought you had this thing under control!'

Pitt knew that he could not afford to lose his own self-mastery. Narraway would not have, whatever he felt. He had a temper — Pitt knew that very well — but Narraway just had too much dignity to allow someone else to manipulate him. That thought was helpful. He clung on to it.

'We did have, sir,' he replied stiffly, 'until this new body was found. We have no idea yet who she is. I'm waiting for the police surgeon to tell

258

me what he has found, or can deduce. My first priority was to see if Mr Kynaston could provide proof that it has nothing to do with him, or anyone in his house.'

'And did you?' Talbot could not conceal his fear. His face was strained, muscles of his neck so tight he could barely turn his head without a wince of pain. His high, stiff collar must be biting into him.

'To my own satisfaction,' Pitt answered. 'But it won't satisfy the police, or the newspapers, if they get hold of it. It certainly wouldn't satisfy a jury.'

Talbot seemed not to be breathing, yet a nerve jumped in his temple.

'Be precise, man,' he snapped. 'What are you talking about? The Prime Minister can't deal in 'whats' and 'ifs' and 'maybes'. Is Kynaston implicated or not? If that damn fool Carlisle asks questions in the House again, the Prime Minister has to have a decent and absolute answer! And I have to be able to assure him that it is accurate. And in spite of appearance to the contrary, that Special Branch knows what the devil it's doing!'

Pitt kept his voice level with a considerable effort.

'This woman had a gold watch chain with a very unusual fob. The first one had the actual watch, you will remember . . .'

'Half the well-to-do men in London have gold watches,' Talbot snapped. 'Probably most of them have a chain and fob of some sort.'

'The watch was Kynaston's,' Pitt said levelly. 'He admitted it. The fob he owned to as well. It has the initials 'BK' on it. He said it had belonged to his brother, Bennett, and was of sentimental value to him. He said it had been stolen from him by a pickpocket, in Oxford Street, or near it.'

Talbot was silent for a moment.

Pitt waited.

'And do you believe him?' Talbot said at last.

'I don't know. There was a handkerchief like the first one as well.'

'It means nothing!' Talbot said sharply.

'And the watch and fob, on two different women, both dead and mutilated, and left in the gravel pits?' Pitt asked. 'On the other hand, we have evidence that the Kynaston's maid was seen alive and well sometime after the first body was found, and the second one does not resemble her.'

Something almost palpable eased inside Talbot. 'Seen alive after the first body was found? Then for God's sake leave Kynaston alone! You can't prove anything! Maybe this pickpocket is your homicidal lunatic!'

'Perhaps. But when I asked Mr Kynaston to account for his whereabouts at the time the body was left in the gravel pit, he lied about it.'

'So he's got some business, or pastime, he doesn't want to discuss with the public!' Talbot raised his eyebrows very high. 'Haven't we all? He was gambling, drinking, or whoring, for all I know, or care. He wasn't murdering some wretched woman and dumping her body in the gravel pits right outside his own damn doorway!'

'I was hoping for something definitive for the

newspapers,' Pitt explained. 'They might consider any of the pastimes you mentioned worthy of public attention, and I'm sure we would rather they didn't.' He kept the smile from his face with difficulty. It might well have been more of a sneer.

Talbot started to make a remark, then thought better of it. 'Keep me apprised,' he ordered instead. 'Do try to get this thing solved and out of the newspapers.'

'Yes, sir.'

★　★　★

The evening darkness had closed in and it was dripping sporadic rain when Pitt reached the police surgeon at the morgue. He knew the woman from the gravel pit would have been given priority. Surely Whistler would have all the information he needed by now?

He found Whistler in his office looking tired and a little gaunt. His clothes were rumpled and his tie had come undone. A kettle was steaming gently on the top of a wood-burning stove in the corner and altogether the room was very pleasant, apart from its proximity to the morgue itself. All real ease was torn away by the knowledge that within thirty feet of them there were cold rooms with corpses in, and tables on which those same corpses would duly be cut open and the pieces of them examined.

When Pitt went in Whistler was in the act of taking his work jacket off and replacing it with a more casual one. His hands were pink, the skin a

261

little raw, as if he had just scrubbed himself as hard as he could with an abrasive brush.

'I was expecting you,' he said wearily. 'In fact I thought you'd be here waiting, like a dog for its dinner.' He sat down behind his desk, which was covered with papers in no apparent order.

'Would it have been worth the wait?' Pitt asked, closing the door. He was grateful that he did not have Whistler's job, even if his clients were beyond pain, and Pitt's were not. They were also beyond help.

Whistler sighed. 'Tea?' he offered. 'It's colder than a witch's heart in that damn morgue.' Without waiting for Pitt's reply he moved the kettle into the middle of the stove and watched while it boiled. He talked as he made the tea in a battered pewter pot, which must once have been quite handsome.

'Cause of death is fairly obviously a very bad fall,' he said. 'From the look of the poor creature, might have been out of a window. Two storeys up, at least, maybe higher. Lot of broken bones, some of them downright splintered. Only good thing about it is that she probably didn't know much about it.'

Pitt winced without being able to help it. 'How long ago?'

'Ah!' Whistler poured the boiling water into the teapot and inhaled the fragrant steam. 'That's the more difficult part. At least two weeks ago, but I'd bet my money on more like three. But just like the other one from the gravel pit, she'd been kept in a cold place. Couldn't have made a better job of it if I'd had her here.

262

And I assure you, I didn't! No apparent marks of depredation, except a little bit from insects. Hadn't been out there more than a night. But I expect you know that. Do you take milk?'

'Yes, please.' Pitt was losing his taste for eating or drinking anything, even as chilled as he was.

'Sugar?'

'No . . . thank you.'

'Got no cake. Need to stop eating so much. Cut up too many fat people and seen what's inside 'em to want to become one.' He passed Pitt one of the mugs. 'Here.'

'Thank you. So she was kept for a couple of weeks at least? You're certain?' he asked.

Whistler looked at him sharply. 'Of course I'm certain! You've got a bloody lunatic here! The sooner you, or someone else, gets hold of him and locks him up, the better.'

Pitt asked the question he had been dreading. 'Are you certain she was murdered?'

Whistler's eyebrows shot up almost to his hairline. 'What? Man, half the bones in her body were smashed. She didn't walk herself up to the gravel pit in the middle of the night!'

'I'm not suggesting she put herself there,' Pitt said patiently. 'But could she have died from an accidental fall, and someone else put her there?'

'Two or three weeks after she died? And for God's sake — the mutilations! That's not done by animals or nature — it's grotesque, man: moral obscenity!' Whistler took a deep breath, then let it out slowly. 'But I suppose it's not impossible her death itself was accidental — if you can look at it in isolation,' he conceded. 'But why? Why would any sane man keep the victim of an appalling accident for weeks, mutilate her, and then dump her up at the gravel pit — and right where she'd be sure to be found? If he wanted to get rid of the body, why not bury her? Or even drop her, with a few stones around her waist, in one of the shallow lakes around there? By the time the summer dried them out, she'd be unrecognisable. There wouldn't be a cat in hell's chance of finding out who she was, or who put her there. If she was ever found at all!'

Pitt thought about it. 'Well, he doesn't appear to have been interrupted, so he had time to do whatever he wanted. He must have wanted her to be found.'

Whistler stared at him. 'We've got a lunatic on our hands.'

'Perhaps . . . '

'If this one isn't, I pray to the Good Lord we never get one that fits your idea of what is!' he said disgustedly.

'Anything else you can tell me?' Absent-mindedly Pitt drank the tea. For all the makeshift preparation of it, it was actually very good. After the subject of the conversation, and the fear that was forming in his mind, he was glad of its warmth.

'I'll write up a full report for you,' Whistler promised. 'But I doubt it'll help you much. As far as I can tell, she was a well-nourished woman in her late twenties. From the state of her it's hard to tell a lot. A few odd scars on her hands, just like the other one. Could have been a maid or laundress, or a young woman with her own house, but no one else to do the chores. But if she was poor, she still ate well. Her hair must have been beautiful, and she was tall and nicely curved in all the right places. Does that help?' He put his cup down and added more hot water to it.

'Not that I can see,' Pitt admitted. 'We'll get the local police this side of the river to find out if anyone's missing that it could be. Thank you, anyway.'

'Sorry I can't tell you when she died, closer than by a week or so. Can't very well rule anyone out over that.'

'Can't even tell who put her there,' Pitt replied. 'For whatever that might be worth!'

Pitt thanked him and left, glad to get outside into the wind, away from the heaviness and the closed air of Whistler's office where he could smell the morgue in his imagination.

He walked for a little distance, deep in thought. He was not ready yet to decide his next actions, although it was too late to do much this evening. When he got home he would have dinner, then help Jemima with her homework, or at least make suggestions. He would have a quick game of dominoes with Daniel, who was getting pretty good at it. Another year or two and he would have lost the chance. Daniel and Jemima would be bound up in their own futures. Jemima would probably be in love.

Charlotte would understand if Pitt continued working, but that was not an excuse to do so. Regardless of her wishes that he solve the case, he wanted to spend time with her for himself, time that had nothing to do with Kynaston, or dead women, or possible treason and threats to the state.

Walking home alone in the dark, the wind blustery around him, he would think.

Was someone trying to make Kynaston appear guilty of killing these women? It was an outlandish idea! Worse than eccentric, it was absurd. Since Kitty was alive, at least until a few days ago, the first body could not have been hers. Yet the suggestion that it was had been deliberately created by leaving the distinctive gold watch there. By whom? But more than that, why? Had there been a pickpocket at all? It was totally believable, and impossible to disprove.

He crossed a main thoroughfare and had to wait for a couple of carriages to pass.

Was Somerset Carlisle behind it? This was bizarre and macabre enough for him! It took Pitt back all those years to the case in Resurrection Row, and the corpses then. He remembered with a shiver and a strange, twisted amusement the resolution of that case. Perhaps he should have had Carlisle prosecuted then? But he had not. It was one of the very few occasions when he had bent the rules. His own sense of justice forced him to. Had Carlisle always known that? Yes, he probably had.

And now that Pitt knew Vespasia so much better, cared for her as much as he cared for anyone outside his own immediate family, it was still impossible! Carlisle had been his friend in times of disappointment, or need. He had never found any request for help too dangerous or too troublesome to fulfil.

He increased his pace a little, walking along the pavement.

And he also owed Carlisle for the rescue from his embarrassment, possibly even a major disgrace in front of Talbot. Not that Carlisle would ever attempt to collect the debt! And that made it heavier to carry.

Damn the man, and his charm, his courage and his outrageous behaviour!

In the morning Pitt resolved to have Stoker, and whatever other men he needed, dig more deeply into every aspect of Kynaston's life, his relationships past and present, personal and professional. Had he rivals for office? What exactly was his financial position? What were his debts, or expectations? And, of course, who was the mistress he guarded so carefully? And lied about? Had he rivals there, other than the woman's husband, of course? He could not now afford to ignore any of these things, distasteful as they were to pursue. The watch and the fob made them impossible to overlook.

12

Victor Narraway awoke early the following morning and was not in the least surprised to find Pitt at the door as he was about to begin breakfast. Last evening's newspapers had been full of the discovery of another mutilated body in the Shooters Hill gravel pits. Narraway had already lain awake for some of the night, thinking it over and over. He had fallen asleep at almost three in the morning, exhausted and without any further useful thoughts.

He welcomed Pitt in and asked his manservant to bring him breakfast. Pitt declined it and Narraway ignored him.

'You're going to sit here and talk to me. You might as well eat,' he pointed out. 'I don't think well on an empty stomach, and neither do you. Has this new body got anything to do with Kynaston?'

The manservant appeared with an additional cup and saucer. Narraway thanked him and poured tea for Pitt without asking him.

'Appears to have,' Pitt replied, taking the tea and thanking him for it. He realised he was actually grateful. After the first sip, he appreciated that he was hungry as well. 'She had a gold watch chain and a highly unusual gold fob, which Kynaston admitted was his, from the watch he claims was stolen from his pocket in Oxford Street. He made no insurance claim because its sentimental value was irreplaceable. It used to belong to his late brother, Bennett.'

Narraway stopped eating for a moment and looked at Pitt closely, trying to read whether he was thinking the same as he was himself. There was no time to waste. The whole matter was escalating.

'Do you believe Kynaston about the robbery?' he asked, not taking his eyes from Pitt's.

'I have no idea,' Pitt admitted. 'It seems extremely fortuitous, and yet he does not seem to me to be lying. Somebody could have stolen it, and left it on the body — like the watch left on the first body. The question is why. Is this personal or professional?'

'Any reason why it should be personal?' Narraway asked the question without hope that Pitt would have found any such reason. They were both working towards the answer they did not want, perhaps even for the same cause.

It was Pitt's job to find this truth, whatever it turned out to be. It was not Narraway's; the Government had dismissed him. He owed no more loyalty towards them than the average citizen did. No — that was not true, not completely. Old loyalties could not be disregarded.

'Carlisle.' Narraway said what they were both thinking.

Pitt nodded. 'It is he who is drawing attention to Kynaston in Parliament. What is the disappearance of Kynaston's wife's maid to Carlisle unless he has some deeper motive for raising the subject? Why would he do that?'

'Have you spoken to him?'

The manservant came in silently with Pitt's breakfast: eggs, bacon, fried bread, and fresh toast.

Pitt thanked him and began to eat with relish.

'No,' he answered after a few minutes. 'I've been putting it off . . . '

'You don't want to know,' Narraway said drily. 'Neither do I, but I think you have to.' He smiled very slightly. 'I don't . . . '

Pitt looked at him steadily. The amusement died out of Narraway's eyes and he coloured very faintly, just a flush across the bones of his cheeks.

It told Pitt all he was seeking to know. Narraway loved Vespasia enough to blind himself deliberately so he could protect Carlisle, because he was her friend. Pitt felt a sudden wave of emotion, a happiness that surprised him. But he would say nothing of that now, even though he was aware of a strange aloneness where he had counted on an ally. And yet it also pleased him. It was something he had not thought Narraway to be capable of, and from the awareness of it now, neither had Narraway himself.

'But I will have to do it soon,' Pitt continued aloud. 'I will be happy if he has some believable story to explain it.'

'Very subtle,' Narraway said sarcastically. 'Really, Pitt, you could do better than that!'

Pitt raised his eyebrows. 'Do I need to?'

'No — no, you don't. And I dare say I would have criticised you if you had. I would have seen it a mile off. Have some toast.'

Pitt accepted.

'I think Kynaston is the key,' he said after he swallowed the first bite. 'He seems to be prepared to lie, even if it brings him into suspicion of having dumped this second body in the gravel pit.'

'You had better be careful about it,' Narraway warned. 'Have all your reasons ready to explain why you're digging into the very private life of a man whose skills at invention are extremely important to the country.'

'If it's really just an affair, why won't he tell me and clear himself from suspicion of murder?' Pitt argued. 'I don't approve of him being in bed with another man's wife, but it isn't my concern, unless he's endangering the security of the country. I'm not going to expose it. Good heavens, I've spent all my adult life in the police! Does he imagine I haven't seen every kind of affair you can think of, and a few you wouldn't have?'

Narraway smiled. 'I know. You can't leave the job half done. I'm just warning you to be careful. Talbot already dislikes you . . .'

'I hardly know him!' Pitt protested.

Narraway shook his head very slightly. 'You are naïve sometimes, Pitt. Talbot doesn't need to know you to resent your rise to a position usually occupied by someone of considerable social standing, and frequently military or naval background as well. The fact that you're the best man for the job is irrelevant to him.'

'Why on earth — ' Pitt began.

'Because he's from the same sort of

background, you fool!' Narraway said with exasperation. 'And he knows Society's closed to him. You don't care, and that gives you a kind of grace, God help me, that allows you to be accepted. Added to which — and believe me I understand it — you know too many people's secrets for anyone to risk offending you.'

'And you?' Pitt asked.

'Or me either,' Narraway admitted. 'And neither do I care.' He stopped suddenly.

'And I have never minded that I married above me,' Pitt added wryly. 'Or hardly ever . . .'

Narraway drew in his breath, then let it out again soundlessly.

'It's not an insult,' Pitt said gently. 'I don't think there are any royal princes left for Vespasia to marry upwards, nor would she want to.'

'I hope not,' Narraway said with emotion. Then he changed the subject abruptly, a slight pinkness colouring his cheeks. 'Be careful of Talbot. Carlisle will not be there the next time to risk his neck rescuing you. You owe him a debt on that — which I suppose you are acutely aware of?'

'Yes . . . but . . . ' He had been going to say that it would have no effect upon his actions in confronting Carlisle over the bodies in the gravel pits; then he wondered if that were true. He had evaded it partly because disgracing him, possibly prosecuting him, would carry other dangers as well. But he had not forgotten his own debt to Carlisle either.

'I suppose I shouldn't have — ' he began.

'Don't be a fool, Pitt,' Narraway snapped. 'You

can't go through life without owing anybody. The real debts are hardly ever a matter of money: it's friendship, trust, help when you desperately needed it, a hand out in the darkness to take yours, when you're alone. You give it when you can, and don't look for thanks, never mind payment. You grasp on to it when you're drowning, and you never forget whose hand it was.'

Pitt said nothing.

'Carlisle won't call you on it,' Narraway said with conviction. 'You've turned a blind eye to his misdemeanours a few times.'

'And he's helped me more than once,' Pitt answered. 'Of course he won't call me on it! But I'll be aware of it myself.'

'It's more than that.' Narraway reached for the teapot and refilled both of their cups. 'It will be impossible to hide the fact that you're digging into Kynaston's private life. Are you certain you are prepared to deal with whatever you find? Ignorance is sometimes a kind of safety. And with the reactions of other people whose personal habits wouldn't bear being made public, you could lose some valuable allies. That sort of knowledge will earn you more enemies than any value it is likely to be to you. You'll find out enough you don't want to know in this job, without adding any more gratuitously. It's a balancing act: know, but pretend that you don't. You need to be a better actor than you are, Pitt, and less of a moralist, at least on the surface. Your job is to know, not to judge.'

'You make me sound like a provincial clergyman with more self-righteousness than compassion,' Pitt said with disgust.

'No.' Narraway shook his head. 'I'm just remembering how I used to be — at your age.'

Pitt laughed outright. 'When you were my age, you were twenty years older than I am!'

'In some things,' Narraway agreed. 'I'm twenty years behind you in others. It will be far better that I find out, and tell you just what you need, no more.'

Pitt did not argue. 'Thank you,' he said quietly.

★ ★ ★

The following day Pitt received a rather stiff request to meet his brother-in-law, Jack Radley. Since it was apparently about the Kynaston case, Pitt could hardly refuse. He saw Jack alone, if hardly privately, on the Embankment not far from the House of Commons. It was a fresh, windy day with the usual chill of early March. The air was cold off the river, salt-smelling, and too brisk for one to enjoy lingering so they walked along quite quickly together.

Jack came straight to the point.

'I hear you've been asking a lot of rather pointed questions about Dudley Kynaston, Thomas. What business is it of Special Branch if he has a mistress, let alone who she might be?'

Pitt could hear the sharp edge of criticism in Jack's voice, something he was unused to. They had many differences of view, but they had usually been amicable. The tone of this took Pitt by surprise.

'If it wasn't my business I wouldn't ask,' he replied. 'Although I hadn't realised I was so obvious.'

'Oh, really!' Jack was impatient. 'You're asking about where he was, who he was with, attendance at different theatres or dinners — then crosschecking. Everybody can work out what you're looking for.' He hunched his shoulders against the chill and pulled his white silk scarf a little higher. 'You don't suspect him of theft, or embezzling naval petty cash, or cheating at cards, do you? Or even being a little drunk and talking too much. Anyone can tell you Dudley Kynaston is a decent man from a good family who behaves like a gentleman and is intensely loyal to his country and all it means.'

He turned to look at Pitt. 'If he has a mistress, what of it? Maybe his wife is a crashing bore, or one of those chilly women who would break something if they laughed, or loved!'

Pitt caught him by the arm and swung him round so he was obliged to stop. They stood face to face in the wind.

'You say that with a lot of feeling, Jack.' Pitt allowed it to sound like an accusation. He had not entirely forgotten Jack's reputation before his marriage.

Jack coloured; his eyes under his amazing eyelashes were dark with temper. 'You're a self-righteous idiot sometimes, Thomas. You may have been promoted to be the guardian of the nation's secrets, but no one appointed you arbiter of our morals. Leave the poor man alone, before you ruin him with your suspicions.'

'I don't give a damn about his morals,' Pitt said between his teeth. 'I'm trying to prove he didn't murder two women and leave their corpses in the local gravel pit! But I can't do that if he keeps on lying to me about where he was at the relevant times.'

'I thought you didn't know when the second woman was killed,' Jack retaliated instantly.

'I don't!' Pitt was raising his voice now too. 'But I know within a few hours when she was dumped at the gravel pit, and I'm pretty certain how she was carried there. If Kynaston would tell me where he was, and I could confirm it, I'd be certain it was not he who did it.'

'Why the hell would you even suspect him?'

'You know better than to ask that,' Pitt replied. 'You know perfectly well I can't tell you.'

The anger drained out of Jack's voice. 'It must be intensely private . . . '

'I need to know for myself!' Pitt said exasperatedly. 'I'm not going to tell the world. If he isn't guilty he's wasting my time, but I'll let go of it and allow the regular police to do their job. If this case is no threat to Kynaston, it's nothing to do with Special Branch.'

Jack looked at him with disbelief. 'You really think Kynaston's desperation to hide who his mistress is could be a threat to the security of the state? Come on, Thomas. That looks a hell of a lot like an upstart officer wielding his new powers to embarrass his social superiors, because he can. You're better than that.'

Pitt was stunned. He stood in the bright light and the cold wind off the water chilled him right through his coat as if it were made of cotton.

'Kynaston's maid ran away the night before the first body was found, Jack,' he replied, his voice shaking not only with anger but with a degree of hurt. 'Because she saw or heard something that made her fear for her life. And that's not a supposition! She's been seen and spoken to since. Not by us — we can't find her — but by others with no interest in this affair. Now there's a second woman dead and mutilated and dumped in the same gravel pit. Physical evidence, which he doesn't deny, links him to both dead women. Kynaston lies about where he was, and won't tell us anything except that he's having an affair. But he must prove it, or allow his mistress, even discreetly to Special Branch, to say where they were. She could just confirm that he was actually with her. He works on highly sensitive state secrets for the navy. Wouldn't you want something better than an evasive answer?'

Jack looked as if the wind drove through his coat too. The last of the anger drained out of him and his face was pale and tight. 'Do you think he lulled her?' he asked very quietly.

'I don't want to,' Pitt replied. 'But he's hiding something a lot more than the name of a woman he's having an affair with.'

Jack said nothing.

'Would you sooner be publicly accused of murder rather than privately of infidelity?' Pitt demanded.

'It doesn't make sense,' Jack agreed unhappily, his face filled with concern, his shoulders hunched. 'Is he protecting someone, do you think? He counts family loyalty terribly highly.'

'Of course he does,' Pitt agreed sarcastically. 'That's why he has a mistress!'

Jack winced as if Pitt had slapped him. 'Perhaps that is more loyal than leaving a wife and publicly humiliating her,' he said so softly that the whine of the wind almost took his words away.

Pitt stared at him. It was a possibility that had not occurred to him. Then the worse thought followed hard on its heels. Was Jack speaking of Kynaston, or of himself? Charlotte had told him of Emily's unhappiness, but he had also seen it. She was without colour, all the fine lines on her face drawn downwards. It was not absurd that Ailsa Kynaston had taken her for Charlotte's elder sister, not younger. Was that at the heart of it why Jack so resented Pitt's pursuit of Kynaston's affair? Sometimes Pitt wished he did not have to know so much. This kind of knowledge could isolate you from all human closeness. He could not tell Charlotte. Her love of Emily, and her own candour, would betray it instantly.

'I know you've been offered a position close to Kynaston,' he said aloud. 'Be careful, Jack. Think hard before you accept it. You have a lot to lose.'

'You said there is physical evidence linking Kynaston to the murdered women?' Jack asked. 'Are you certain?'

'Absolutely. Don't ask me about it because I

278

can't tell you. It doesn't prove guilt, but it's highly suggestive. If you have any influence with him, Jack, tell him to explain himself. I can't let it go!'

Jack stared at him long and steadily, then gave a very slight nod, and turned and walked away, back towards the Houses of Parliament and the tower housing Big Ben rising up into the cloud-strewn sky.

* * *

Pitt could not tell Charlotte about his conversation with Jack. She knew him far too well: even if she did not ask, she would deduce from his discomfort that there was something he would not discuss. Her imagination would make the worst of it, probably that the rift between Jack and Emily was deeper than she had thought. She and Emily might quarrel at times over all sorts of little things, but underneath it she was intensely loyal. Entwined through all her life's memories were the images of Emily as the younger sister, the one two years behind whom it was Charlotte's nature and trust to protect. It had nothing to do with duty, or with need, for that matter. Emily had been supremely able to look after herself — until now.

That evening Pitt sat in his big chair by the fire watching Daniel and Jemima working on a large jigsaw puzzle. After some time he became aware of a pattern, not only in the picture beginning to take form on the card table, but in their behaviour also. There were three years

279

between their ages. Jemima was always those few steps ahead. It would be like that through life, until age began to be a disadvantage. Now it was all in Jemima's favour, but he saw her mind leap to a recognition, her hand reach for the piece, then fall back again, and she smiled as Daniel saw it and put it in the right space.

He felt a sudden rush of emotion, almost overpowering. He could see something of himself in her, but so very much more of her mother. That moment's discreet gentleness was exactly what he had observed Charlotte do, the quiet selflessness. Jemima was not yet sixteen, and there it was, the instinct to nurture, to protect.

How could he protect Jack, or Emily, in this wretched business, without crossing the boundaries of his own morality?

Jack had made a bad error of judgement with his loyalties once before. There would be those very happy to remind his superior of it, and throw his wisdom into doubt. The safety of the state was Pitt's duty, above and beyond that to those he loved. No one in the public trust could favour their own family. It was, perhaps, the ultimate betrayal of the oath he had taken, and the faith in him he had accepted.

And yet he learned secrets he did not want to know, vulnerabilities he could not protect. He had his own network of debts and loyalties; it was what made life precious: the honour, and the caring. Without such things it was empty, a long march to nowhere.

Carlisle had done favours for all of them, in

one case or another, especially for Vespasia. Could Pitt ever trust Vespasia in this, if Carlisle were involved, and he was becoming increasingly afraid that he was? She needed innocence of what he was doing, complete innocence, not an excuse for it.

Perhaps Victor Narraway was the only one he could trust without placing an intolerable burden on him.

But thinking back on their last meeting, perhaps he too was now compromised? He cared for Vespasia far more deeply than mere friendship. After all the fancies and hungers of his youth, and adventures since then, even his care for Charlotte, was this to be the love of his life, the one that touched him too deeply to heal over, or pass by?

What were Vespasia's feelings for him, more than friendship, interest, affection? No man, especially one so sensitive under the shell as Victor Narraway, could settle happily for that! If you love you want it all.

None of that should affect Pitt. Why should he interfere, except to make the decision not to place Narraway into such temptation again regarding the Kynaston case?

Pitt was alone in whatever action he took, or refrained from. He was more truly alone than he could ever recall. Whatever he did about Somerset Carlisle, it was solely his judgement to make. Was he really the right man for this job? He had the intelligence and the experience to detect. He had pursued and found the truth on many occasions where others had failed. On that his promotion was deserved. But had he the wisdom? Did he understand people with money and power, ancient privilege of history and title, pride and loyalty stretching intricate webs into all the great families in the land, and in some cases beyond into Europe?

Was he himself free from all debt and loyalty, all emotional pity that could corrupt? He looked at his family around him in the twilight. And it reached much further than that: to Vespasia, Narraway, Jack and Emily; further still to Charlotte's mother and her husband. To Somerset Carlisle, even. To all the people who had shared the moments of his life, helped or hurt, to whom he owed if not compassion, then at least honesty.

He did not want to know if Carlisle had placed those dead women in the gravel pit, but he knew he could no longer evade the issue.

If Carlisle had placed the bodies, then where had he obtained them? Pitt refused even to imagine that he had killed them himself, or for that matter paid someone else to. That meant they were already dead. Where would he find corpses that he could take? Not a hospital. He could hardly claim to be a relative because that was unbelievable. Nor, for that matter, could he prove he was an employer or other benefactor.

Therefore he had done it secretly, but certainly with some help. Possibly he had a manservant of some sort that he trusted, or even more likely, someone much closer to the edge of the law whom he had helped in the past, and who was now willing to return the favour.

There were always unclaimed bodies in a morgue, people who had no close relative willing to bury them. It would not be difficult to claim some past association, or previous servant, or relative of a servant, and offer to provide a decent burial, out of pity. Then what? Bury a coffin full of bags of sand, or anything else of the appropriate weight.

That would answer the question of where the bodies had been kept so chilled and clean. It would also explain the timing of discovery of them — only when Carlisle could find one that was suitable. They needed to be young women of the servant class, unclaimed by anyone else, and who had died violently. He must have combed all London for them!

If, of course, he had done it at all!

There was no evidence, only Pitt's previous knowledge of Carlisle and his belief about his character.

What proof could he find? He could have his men look through all the records of recent deaths of women in the London area, those that were violent and resulted in the kind of injuries the gravel pit corpses had sustained. Then see which were unclaimed by family, and if some benefactor had offered to pay for a funeral.

Then what? Exhume them to see if the corpses were there, or bags of sand instead? Perhaps, but only as a last resort, and he would need far more to justify it than a desperate imagination.

He would have the enquiries made, discreetly. No exhumations until he had evidence.

He must learn more about Carlisle, the

opinions of people who had encountered him in other contexts than those Pitt knew for himself. What were the man's private interests apart from politics and social reform, the numerous battles against injustice. Who were his friends, other than Vespasia? Was there anyone in particular he might have turned to for help in this extraordinary undertaking? Did he know Kynaston personally? Were there any other connections that were worth exploring?

He must do it with great care, and disguise his reasons for asking. If he spoke to more than a very few, Carlisle would undoubtedly hear of it and know exactly what he was doing.

One friend of Carlisle's whom Pitt spoke to was a highly respected architect by the name of Rawlins. Pitt took him to luncheon at a discreet and expensive restaurant. He gave the pretext of making a check on Carlisle in order to trust him with Special Branch information in order to engage his help in Parliament. Asking about Carlisle's friends in the past came quite naturally.

'Erratic,' Rawlins agreed. 'I wanted to build towers and spires that reached to the sky,' he said with a wry smile. 'Somerset wanted to climb them! I liked him enormously; still do, although I don't see him so often. But I never understood him. Never knew what he was thinking.' He sipped the very good red wine they were having with their roast beef.

Pitt waited. He knew from the look of inner concentration on Rawlins' face that he was searching memory, struggling to understand something that had long eluded him.

'Then he went off to Italy without finishing his degree,' Rawlins spoke slowly. 'Couldn't understand why at the time. He was in line for a first; he could have been an academic.'

'A woman?' Pitt suggested. So far there had been no mention of any love affair, only dalliances, nothing to capture the heart.

'I thought so at the time,' Rawlins conceded. He gave a slight shrug and sipped at the wine again. 'I learned long after that it was to fight with some partisans who were struggling for Italian unification. He never spoke of it himself. I only heard it from a woman I met in Rome, years later. She spoke of him as if his exploits were woven through the best and most fulfilling part of his life. I think she might have been in love with him.'

He smiled ruefully. 'I remember I was jealous. In her words, he sounded funny, impossibly brave, absolutely harebrained — but not unrecognisable as the man I had known.'

He sighed and took another mouthful of the excellent meal. 'He ended up in an Italian prison somewhere in the north, with both his shoulders dislocated. Must have hurt like hell. He never spoke of it. If you need to know, I'm afraid I can't help you. I haven't any idea what happened, or who did it. I could give half a dozen guesses as to why.'

Pitt avoided Rawlins' eyes, looking instead down at his own plate. 'Did you ever know him to commit violence against anyone?' he asked. 'Perhaps in the conviction that the end justified the means?' He did not want the answer, and he almost denied the question in the next breath. He could feel his muscles tense, as though he were waiting for a blow.

'I can't tell you,' Rawlins said quietly. 'Not in a way that would be of any value. I never knew him choose violence, in fact as a student I saw him go to some lengths to avoid it. He was argumentative, but never quarrelsome. But I do know that he was a man of intense passions. I don't believe anything would stop him doing something he believed to be necessary in a cause he cared about. He had too much imagination, and not enough sense of fear. He was an all-or-nothing sort of man. Judging by his speeches in Parliament, and the little I know of him now, he still is. Actually, I don't think that kind of thing changes. I'm sorry I can't be of more help.'

'Any friends I should worry about?' Pitt asked casually.

'Worry?'

'Fringes of the communal underworld, that sort of thing?'

Rawlins smiled. 'Carlisle? Quite possibly. He's a man of eclectic tastes and peculiar loyalties. But if he makes a promise, he won't break it.'

'That's rather what I thought,' Pitt agreed.

They finished the meal speaking of other things. Rawlins was a pleasant man, intelligent and courteous. Pitt found him not only easy to like, but easier to believe than he would have wished.

Nothing he had heard in the course of the

whole two days had painted a picture of Somerset Carlisle that was in any way different from the man he already knew, the man who had played such a grotesque and dangerous game with the corpses in Resurrection Row.

If anything, he was worse off, because it drew a picture of a man he not only liked, and was now compelled to admire, but one very capable of doing precisely what Pitt had feared.

13

Pitt arrived late at his office on the following morning, having been held up by a traffic accident on Euston Road. The whole thing had turned into chaos as everyone tried to find a way around it, and ended by getting jammed in a total impasse where no one had room to turn and extricate themselves.

Stoker was waiting for him, looking grave. 'Don't bother taking your coat off,' he said as soon as Pitt was in through the door.

Pitt stopped. 'Not another body!'

'No, sir, still the same one. Whistler wants to see you. And if you don't mind, sir, I'd like to come along too.'

Pitt had no objection to Stoker coming, but he was curious, and desperate for a little hope. 'Why?' he asked.

Stoker stared back at him, his dark grey eyes clear. 'I want to know more about what kind of a man does this to a woman. I want to know who it is that Kitty Ryder thinks she's running away from.'

'You still think it has something to do with Kynaston?' Pitt felt the knot tighten in his stomach.

'I don't know, sir, but it appears she thinks it has. If I could find her, I'd ask her why.'

'No more progress with that?' Pitt asked.

'Not much.' Stoker stopped, took a deep

breath, and went on, 'But I'm not giving up.' There was a faint colour in his bony face, just a smudge of pink across his cheeks. He looked at Pitt defiantly, offering no explanations.

'Well, if you succeed, you can ask her.' Pitt jammed his hat on again. 'But we can't wait for that. We'd better go and see Whistler. Just what I feel like first thing on a cold wet morning, get stuck in a traffic jam, then a visit to the morgue. Come on!' He led the way back out into the rain.

Pitt and Stoker had to wait several minutes to find a hansom. It was always like this on wet days. No one was willing to walk.

Finally they found a cab and splashed through the puddles to scramble inside, their sodden trouser legs flapping, coats flying open in the wind.

It was a long way from Lisson Grove to Blackheath, on the other side of the river and considerably further east.

'If someone's trying to make Kynaston look guilty of this, even if he isn't, then it's someone with a pretty good knowledge of his household,' Stoker said after a few minutes. 'And he knows Kynaston himself too. Either he knows why Kynaston keeps on lying, or he's got some kind of a hold over him so he doesn't tell us the truth.' He sat huddled in his damp coat, looking sideways at Pitt in the grey daylight.

'I'm afraid that's unarguable,' Pitt agreed. 'What I need to know is, why? To what end? I wish I could think it was personal vengeance of some sort, but we haven't found any kind of reason for it.'

They turned from Seymour Place right into Edgware Road then left and right again into Park Lane.

'Well, I dare say Rosalind Kynaston would be pretty angry if she knew about the mistress,' Stoker pointed out. 'And she could have taken the watch and fob easily enough.'

'She might hate him,' Pitt replied reasonably, 'but she wouldn't ruin him. If she did, she'd be ruining herself at the same time. His disgrace would be hers as well. And if he lost his income, that's also hers! You told me she comes from a respectable background, but she has no independent wealth. Unless you think she's got a lover too! One who would marry her, in spite of whatever this does to her reputation? I suppose it's possible, but I can't see it as likely, can you?'

Stoker thought for a moment. 'I don't know women that well, sir. Not as you must, with a wife and a daughter . . . '

'I'm not sure any man knows women,' Pitt said drily. 'Let us agree that perhaps my ignorance is not as total as yours. What about it?'

'Mrs Kynaston doesn't look to me like a woman who's got a secret lover, sir.' Stoker assiduously avoided his eyes. 'I remember when my sister Gwen was first in love with her husband, didn't know that much about him, but by heck, I knew she had something going on. Little things, like the way she did her hair, the way she took care with what she wore, not just some of the time, but all of it. That little secret smile, like the cat that got the cream. And even the way she walked with a little swish of her skirts, as if she knew she was going somewhere special.'

Pitt couldn't help laughing, in spite of the cold and the discomfort inside the rattling hansom squashing them together. He had seen exactly what Stoker was describing in Charlotte, years ago when he had been courting her. He hadn't understood it then: the happiness one moment, despair the next, but always the vitality. She had seemed to glow with life.

He had seen it in Emily too, when she was beginning to think seriously about Jack Radley. But that was another subject, and at the moment one of more pain than pleasure.

And, of course, now it was also beginning in Jemima. How quickly she was growing up. Pitt knew which young men she liked, and which held no interest for her. She was so pretty, brave and vulnerable, like her mother, imagining she was sophisticated, and as easy to read as an open book. Or was that only so to him, because he loved her, and would have protected her from every pain, if that were possible?

Charlotte's father would have protected her from the social disasters, not to mention financial, of marrying a policeman! The only fate worse would have been not to marry at all, and that judgement call was a fine thing! Thank heaven her mother had more emotional sense!

Would he have sense, when it came to Jemima marrying someone?

Not necessary to think of now. It was years away! Years and years!

They were moving steadily south towards the river. No doubt the driver would take them along the Embankment, then over one of the bridges on to the south bank.

Pitt regarded Stoker with a new respect. He had not thought him capable of such human observation. It came to him in a rush of clarity that he did not know Stoker very much at all. Outside his skill and intelligence in the job, and his well-proven loyalty, he was almost unknown!

'So you think Rosalind Kynaston is not having an affair?' he asked.

'That's right, sir. She looks like a woman who has very little to be happy about,' Stoker agreed.

'Do you think she knows of Kynaston's affair?'

'Probably. In my experience people do know, especially women, even if they can't afford to admit to themselves that they do. Of course, when they're not in Society, and there's not much money or a nice house to lose, there's not the same need to fix a smile on your face and pretend you've seen nothing. And I'll bet you anything you like,' he added, 'she's not the one who killed anyone and laid them out in the gravel pits — or slashed their faces to bits!'

Pitt shivered. 'Quite. But you agree that whoever is doing it, the whole thing is connected to the Kynaston house?'

'No question,' Stoker agreed. 'I just don't know how! I've been turning it over and over, but nothing makes complete sense. For a start, why these mutilations? What kind of a person cuts the flesh on the face of someone who's already dead? The only reason I can think of is to disguise who it is. But we've got no idea, anyway.'

'Or to draw our attention to it,' Pitt said, thinking aloud.

'You mean two dead women dumped in a gravel pit isn't going to make us stop and think?' Stoker asked with heavy disbelief.

'Doesn't make as big a headline as two that are mutilated in exactly the same way,' Pitt pointed out.

'What's the point of that?' Stoker was now looking at Pitt curiously, as if he expected an answer. He stared more intently. 'You mean it's to draw our attention even more to Kynaston? Like the handkerchiefs?'

'Maybe.'

'Why?' Stoker repeated.

'That's what I am struggling with,' Pitt told him, trying to find words that were honest, and yet did not tell him about Somerset Carlisle. Not naming him would be easy, but Stoker would know the answer was being evaded, and that was an insult he did not deserve. It would also damage the trust between them, which was one of Pitt's greatest assets. Without the trust of his men he was alone. He was increasingly aware of the lack of confidence from people like Talbot, and possibly others in the Government. Even in Lisson Grove he had yet to earn the kind of respect they had had for Victor Narraway.

'One thought that came to me,' Pitt went on as they crossed over the river and turned east, 'is that if Kynaston is suspected and the net seems to be closing around him, he would be extremely grateful to anyone who could prove his innocence . . . '

'He won't thank us for long, sir,' Stoker said with an odd gentleness, as if he were protecting a younger man from disillusion.

Pitt avoided looking at him, suddenly both moved and amused by his desire to prevent a pain that afflicted everyone from time to time. It was reality, bitter and as sharp as the icy edge of the spring winds that so often take the early flowers.

Pitt had to speak quickly, dispel the mistake before it had taken shape.

'I know that, Stoker. I was considering the possibility of someone else offering him rescue, at a price — someone who owes him nothing, but to whom he might then owe a very great deal.'

Stoker's eyes widened, sharp and bright. 'I see! At a price he would then go on paying indefinitely! That would be very clever indeed. And we would look stupid. We might find ourselves listened to rather less the next time we suspect someone!'

Pitt had not even thought of that. He wished that he had. It was a powerful and dangerous possibility.

'Indeed,' he said softly, barely heard above the noise of the traffic along Rotherhithe Street. 'It grows uglier, doesn't it? At least the possibilities do. The question arises again — who?'

'There seem to be conflicting lines of evidence, sir,' Stoker answered. 'One of them regarding Kynaston having a mistress and being guilty of murdering the maid who found out about it, but that doesn't make a lot of sense — unless there's a major piece missing. And then why four different women?'

Pitt was puzzled for a moment.

'Kitty Ryder, the first woman in the gravel pit, the second woman in the gravel pit, and the mistress,' Stoker counted. 'There's no way any two of those could be the same person.'

'I can't think of anything that makes sense of that,' Pitt admitted. 'And yet the two women in the gravel pit are linked by several circumstances: the place they were found, but not necessarily where they were killed, the fact they had been kept somewhere before being put in the gravel; the mutilations, which were hideous and seem to serve no purpose at all, because they were inflicted after death, but were not effective in hiding their identity, because we don't know them anyway. They both appear to have been maids, but no one has come forward to claim them. Not to mention Kynaston's watch on one and his fob on the other.'

Stoker nodded. 'So what about it all being nothing to do with who the women are, but to do with Kynaston — to try to blackmail or coerce him into doing something? Or not doing something? Perhaps he's behaving so stupidly about this whole thing because he had some evidence that would ruin someone, and he's being blackmailed into silence?'

'Possible,' Pitt agreed. It was possible indeed — and Somerset Carlisle did not fit into that story at all. That was why, much as he longed to believe it, Pitt did not.

'You got another idea, sir?' Stoker asked.

'Only a possibility,' Pitt answered. He could not shut it out any longer. He was lying to Stoker, and to himself. Somerset Carlisle was as sharp as an open razor in his brain. But Carlisle would not kill — surely? What would he care about enough to do all this: the bodies stolen from somewhere, the mutilation, which must have been hideous, almost unbearable to him, and yet he had performed this — if indeed it was him?

The only answer that fitted it all was something as serious as treason.

'Sir?' Stoker's voice broke through his thoughts.

'To force us to dig until we find the greater crime,' Pitt answered.

'Greater than murder?' Stoker's tone was hard with anger and disbelief.

'Yes, worse than murder,' Pitt answered levelly. 'Treason.'

Stoker sat rigid. He gulped. 'Yes, sir. I never thought of that — not — not in all this . . . '

'Please God, you have no need to,' Pitt said, staring straight ahead of him. 'It's only an idea . . . '

'No, sir,' Stoker turned to face the front also. 'It's our job.'

Whistler met them in his office in the morgue, a place that had become unpleasantly familiar to Pitt in the last few weeks. This time Whistler was busy and in no mood to offer the hospitality of tea.

296

'Newspapers got it,' he said curtly. 'Just want you to know it wasn't me.' He glared at Pitt as if already Pitt had doubted him. 'Like bloody dogs sniffing out the smell of death!' he said bitterly. 'Don't know what the hell they'll make of this one — probably anything and everything.' He started to shake his head, and ended up with his whole body shuddering, as if he had been dropped in cold water. 'The mutilations were all after death. Told you that before. When I looked at them closely, so were the broken bones. Only a few made when she was alive, most importantly, the fracture of the skull. Bruises were made at the same time. Can't bruise after you're dead. No blood flow.'

Pitt stared at him. 'Was it the blow to the head that killed her?' He did not know what he wanted Whistler to say. It was a nightmare. All that would make it any better was to wake up.

'Blow,' Whistler repeated the word, turning it over in his mind, examining it.

'Was it?' Pitt snapped.

'Large, flat object,' Whistler said slowly. 'Lot of bruises, can't define them exactly. Too long dead now. My opinion? She fell downstairs and cracked her head on the floor at the bottom. Nothing to think it wasn't accidental.'

Pitt felt relief wash over him with an intensity that was close to the sort of pain you get when a frozen limb comes back to life. 'So she wasn't murdered?'

'No reason to think she was,' Whistler agreed. 'But what bloody, God-awful lunatic then cut half her face off — that's another question

297

— yours, not mine!'

Pitt thanked him with a nod, and they left.

★ ★ ★

First Pitt would go and speak with Somerset Carlisle. If he had continued all this horror in order to force Pitt into investigating Kynaston, then it was time to face him and demand what crime he believed him guilty of.

He was undecided at first whether to warn Carlisle of his coming. Surprise had many advantages, and if he were to make it a formal appointment then he would have to state his reason for it. But if he did not, the chances were high of finding that Carlisle was not at home. And perhaps it would be a deceit that would only make him look absurd if he attempted deviousness. He picked up the telephone and made the appointment. Carlisle made no argument at all; in fact he had sounded as if Pitt were welcome.

As it was, a soberly dressed manservant welcomed Pitt at the door and ushered him into a pleasant and very individual sitting room where Carlisle spent the few evenings he had at home, in the winter by the fire now warming the whole room. For the summer there was a well-curtained French door.

'This must be important,' Carlisle said with a wry smile. 'It's a filthy night. What price spring, eh? Still, I suppose it will be the more welcome when it comes. Sit down.' He indicated a whisky glass on a table beside the chair from which he had risen. 'Whisky? Sherry?' He winced very slightly. 'Tea?'

'Later, thank you,' Pitt replied. 'If you still feel like offering it.' He found his throat tight and his mouth dry with the prospect of the unpleasantness to come, and a good whisky would have warmed him. Since he rose in rank, and income, he had learned the difference between good whisky and average. But he needed a clear head tonight. He could not afford to give Carlisle any advantage at all.

'That bad?' Carlisle indicated an armchair, then sat back down in the chair opposite. His keen face showed a similar tension to that that Pitt felt knotting inside him.

There was no point in being evasive. 'I think so,' he replied.

Carlisle smiled, as if they were playing some desperate parlour game. 'And what is it that you think I can do? I know no one who murders women and leaves them in gravel pits. Believe me, if I did, I would already have told you.'

'Actually, it is not so much that they died that concerns me at the moment,' Pitt smiled back. 'It is what appears to be their connection with Dudley Kynaston.' He glanced around the room with sharpening interest. He took time to notice the naval memorabilia more closely. The beauty of one of the paintings suggested a very fine artist, and perhaps worth a great deal of money. If not, then it had been chosen with some diligence. Perhaps it was inherited from someone who had long loved the sea.

Carlisle was waiting for him to continue. How

direct should he be?

'Kynaston's gold watch was found on the first body,' he said, watching Carlisle's expression and seeing only the slightest change. 'And the fob on the second woman. Among other things perhaps less tangible.'

Carlisle hesitated. Quite clearly he was debating within himself whether to banter or to face the real battle. He must have decided on the latter because the amusement died out of his eyes and suddenly in the firelight and the softer glow of the gas brackets above him, the lines in his face seemed deeper. He was older than Pitt, perhaps into his fifties. It was his energy that occasionally made one forget that. Now the sun and windburn from his years of climbing, the lines around his eyes where he had peered into far distances, marked his features.

'A very marked connection. How did he explain it?' Carlisle asked.

'That his watch was stolen by a pickpocket,' Pitt replied.

'And you believe him?'

'I'm inclined to. It is not beyond your abilities to have had someone take it for you.'

'Good heavens! Rather a back-handed compliment to my abilities. A dangerous undertaking, don't you think?'

'Extremely,' Pitt agreed. 'Therefore you had a very good reason. I cannot imagine any love affair he could have which would stir your anger or passion to the degree where you would use these women like this in order to draw me in.'

'He has at times allowed his heart to rule his

300

head,' Carlisle answered sharply, weighing his words. 'Not to love is to die by inches. Or perhaps it is worse than that. Maybe it is to hesitate on the shore of life and never step into its waters. But take it too far, and one can not only drown oneself, but take others with you.'

'True,' Pitt agreed. 'But I believe you have something very specific in mind.'

Carlisle's eyebrows rose in a sharp double V shape. 'Verbally, perhaps. But you are calling upon me, not I on you.'

'Really?' Pitt said softly. 'I had the idea that perhaps you were calling upon me, and that it was time I answered.'

Carlisle hesitated barely a second. 'Indeed? What gave you that idea, or are we past that particular point?'

'We are past it.'

'I see. And your answer is?' Carlisle sat motionless, his whisky forgotten. In fact, he had not drunk more than a couple of sips. Its colour reflected gold in the firelight, in the cut crystal it looked like a jewel itself.

'You have my attention,' Pitt replied. 'I am listening.'

Carlisle did not answer.

'Come on!' Pitt said more sharply than he had intended. Carlisle was stretching his nerves. He could not afford to lose this game. Nothing in all of his experience with Carlisle suggested he had ever acted lightly or taken crazy risks that could cost him his freedom, even his life, unless the stakes were high enough to warrant it.

'I investigated Kynaston, and found nothing,'

Pitt continued. 'Kitty Ryder is still alive, but she left at night, and without taking her belongings. She must have been very afraid of something. I can't see it as being the fact that apparently Kynaston has a mistress, unless she were an extraordinarily powerful man's wife?' Even as he said it, he did not believe it himself.

'That's not worthy of you, Pitt,' Carlisle sounded disappointed. 'Why the hell should I care who Kynaston's in bed with?'

'You don't,' Pitt agreed. 'So I wonder what it is you do care about — sufficiently to step into this macabre farce. And it is a farce, isn't it?'

Carlisle's eyes did not leave Pitt's face. 'Is it?' he whispered.

'If I don't find the truth of it, yes it is!' Pitt responded sharply, his own nerves taut.

He saw a flicker of fear in Carlisle's eyes, just for a moment, so brief he was not even certain he had seen it at all.

'I don't believe you killed either one of them,' he added. 'In fact you probably never saw them alive.'

Carlisle breathed out slowly. Something within him eased, but only a fraction.

'And put the pieces of the watch there as well,' Pitt continued. He did not mention the mutilations; that was a hideous lacuna between them. 'And probably the cupboard key. You must have been damn sure I wouldn't connect it up, and charge you!'

'You're the best detective I know,' Carlisle replied, his voice a little hoarse, as if his lungs were starved, his throat tight.

'So what is it you want me to find?' Pitt leaned forward. 'You left those women up there for the animals to eat! What matters that much to you, Carlisle? Murder? Multiple murder?' He said the last word very carefully. 'Still not enough! It has to be treason!'

Carlisle took a long, deep breath. 'Do you know Sir John Ransom?'

'Not personally. I know who he is.'

'Precisely,' Carlisle agreed. 'It was a rhetorical question. If the head of Special Branch did not know the name of the man who leads scientific inventions regarding the navy, and naval warfare, then we have very deep problems indeed.'

'What about Ransom?' Pitt asked.

'He is a friend of mine. A couple of years ahead of me at Cambridge,' Carlisle replied.

Pitt allowed him to continue, knowing that this much preamble must be necessary. A log of wood collapsed in the fire, sending up a shower of bright sparks, but Carlisle apparently did not notice it.

'He came to me two or three months ago,' Carlisle resumed. 'He had no proof at all, but he believed that certain highly sensitive facts regarding a new step forward in submarine warfare were being offered to another naval power. He did not say which because I believe he did not know.'

'From the department where Kynaston works,' Pitt concluded.

'Precisely. Ransom was very worried because he had little doubt in his own mind that it was occurring, but no idea who was responsible. But it rested between three men. The other two have since been exonerated . . . '

'Leaving Kynaston . . . ' Pitt said unhappily. 'But there is no proof, or you would not be discussing it. You would simply have handed over the evidence to us.'

'Yes. Without proof, allowing Kynaston to know that we are aware of what he is doing would only alert him, and perhaps make the matter worse,' Carlisle agreed.

'So you make it appear that he murdered his wife's maid, over some real or imagined love affair, and hope that I will pull your chestnuts out of the fire!'

'That's about right,' Carlisle admitted. 'But you're damn slow about it!' He gave a harsh, twisted smile. 'You like the man . . . '

'Yes, I do. But that has nothing to do with it,' Pitt said angrily. 'Whatever I think of him, I can't charge him with anything at all until I have evidence to prove it. And since Kitty Ryder was seen alive and well after the first body was found, and the second body doesn't even resemble her, I have no reason to accuse Kynaston!'

'I slipped up there,' Carlisle admitted, wincing at his own failure. 'But I didn't know Kitty had been seen. Are you sure?'

'Yes. I have a highly diligent assistant . . . '

'Ah! The redoubtable Stoker. Yes. An excellent man.' Carlisle smiled very slightly. 'If he could actually find the woman, then she would testify as to what it was she saw, or heard, and why she ran away. Although it would be better to have something rather weightier than the word of a runaway lady's maid.'

'I'll widen the search for her,' Pitt promised. 'Who else is involved? He must be passing the information to someone. And why, for God's sake?' Even giving words to the question and speaking it aloud was painful. He had not thought Kynaston more than perhaps self-indulgent with his mistress, certainly not a man to betray his own country. He had become used to disillusion but this still hurt.

Carlisle pulled his mouth into a gesture of apology. 'I have no idea. But I have no doubt he will have plenty of defenders simply because no one will wish to believe that he could have betrayed them, or that they could have let him! The Prime Minister will be displeased, to say the least of it!'

'I'm getting rather accustomed to displeasing the Prime Minister,' Pitt said tartly. 'It seems to be a function of the job. But catching Kynaston, even proving what he has done, is far from the end of the task . . . '

'Oh, I know that!' Carlisle agreed. 'You need to know all of it! More than anything else, you need to know exactly how much information he has given, and to whom. Preferably, you also need to know how he came into such a position, and everyone else who is involved. And then, naturally, you need to deal with him so that as few people are aware of it as possible, in the circumstances. To have a trial and exposure would be almost as damaging as the act itself.'

'Thank you, Carlisle! I am aware of that!' Pitt snapped. 'I also would prefer not to be obliged to

305

prosecute you! I accept that you did not kill either of the women, but you took their bodies from wherever they were kept — a morgue of some sort, I imagine — and you laid them out in the gravel pits. I prefer not to know that you also mutilated them in identical ways so we would be forced to conclude they were killed by the same person, and the link to Kynaston was too clear to ignore. Well, I have your message, and I understand it. You have succeeded.'

Carlisle was pale, even in the firelight. 'I am not proud of it,' he said very quietly. 'But Kynaston is betraying my country. He must be stopped.'

'I will do all I can to stop him,' Pitt promised. 'And you will help me, if I can think of a way. And from now on you will do exactly what I tell you to . . . so I can find a reason not to charge you with body-snatching, mutilating the dead, and generally being a damn nuisance!'

'Would you — ' Carlisle began.

Pitt glared at him. 'Yes I would! And if you involve Lady Vespasia in this I'll see you pay for it with your seat in Parliament!'

'I believe you,' Carlisle said very quietly indeed. 'I give you my word I have not done so, and I will not.'

'Thank you.' Pitt stood up. 'I thank you for at least this much truth. Now I wish I'd had the whisky!'

'It's still available . . . '

'No, thank you. I must go home. It's late, and I need to think how the hell I'm going to clear this up, starting tomorrow morning. By the way, where did you get the bodies? I assume you took them from some morgue?'

'Yes. But I'll see they are decently buried, when you've finished with them. As I promised in the first place,' Carlisle replied.

Pitt stared at him for a moment, trying to find words for what lay between them, and failing. He turned and left.

Outside the rain had stopped but the wind was even colder. Pitt thought, seeing the hard, brittle glitter of the stars, that there could be a frost.

Walking briskly along the pavement he thought again of Carlisle. The man infuriated him, but he could not dislike him. This time he had seen beyond the wit and the imagination to someone who dared to believe in things further than he could see himself, and who reached, however crazily, for the sublime. A lonely man.

He could not believe that Carlisle had had any part in the deaths of either of the women, he had merely seized an opportunity. Pitt could imagine him carefully cutting the dead faces, women beyond indignity or pain, and apologising for using them for what he believed was a greater and more desperate good. The man he had known in the past would never have killed anyone, even to expose treason.

But people can change. Unknown pressures can fall on them, old debts can need to be paid. Was that why Carlisle had rescued Pitt from the fury of Edom Talbot so fortuitously? And was it he who had created the situation in the first place, so Pitt would owe him a debt?

Did Carlisle owe someone this terrible thing?

Or was it Kynaston who owed an unpayable debt?

And perhaps the treason was far more than Pitt had yet guessed.

He looked up at the thin starlight, sharp-edged in the wind, and increased his pace.

14

Charlotte had deliberately chosen to spend more time with Emily, so when Emily invited her to go with Jack and herself to a reception for a visiting Norwegian explorer, and to listen to his lecture, she accepted. She did it for Emily's sake, not because she was particularly interested in islands in the North Atlantic, and whatever manner of birds might inhabit them. The thought of so much floating ice made her cold, even before she set out.

Had Pitt been at home it would have been a greater sacrifice, but he was out many evenings recently, pursuing one aspect or another of the case of Kitty Ryder. He had said she was alive, but they still could not find her.

As she sat while Minnie Maude dressed her hair up, a skill she was rapidly developing, Charlotte thought more about the whole issue. She had not questioned Pitt any more, because she knew from watching his face that he was deeply worried about the case, and that it now concerned some other issue, which he could not tell her. That did not mean she was not free to try to discern it for herself.

She knew more of the personal lives of people like Dudley Kynaston than Pitt or Stoker could do, because the Kynastons belonged to the level of Society in which she had grown up, and to which Emily had belonged all her life. She and

Pitt were now on the fringes of it, but to him it would always be alien, at least in some of its values, no matter how skilled he became at appearing to be comfortable.

★ ★ ★

When Emily arrived Charlotte saw that she was dressed in pale green, the colour that became her most. The gown itself was exquisite, and perfectly suited to the occasion. Charlotte recognised it as 'battle dress' from the way it fitted, and the beauty of the subtle emerald and diamond earrings that Emily wore with it. When she kissed her quickly on the cheek, the opinion was confirmed by the perfume she detected, so subtle she wanted to come closer again in order to catch it more definitely. It was nothing she could name, and no doubt very expensive. It was the sort of thing a woman buys herself, if she does not have to count the cost of it.

As soon as they were seated in the carriage and had moved off from the kerb into the roadway, Charlotte asked the question.

'Why are we going to a lecture on arctic exploration?'

Emily smiled. Even in the gathering dusk and the first glow of streetlamps, her satisfaction was visible. 'Because Ailsa and Rosalind Kynaston are going to it,' she replied. 'I have been getting to know Rosalind a little better recently. It isn't difficult or odd in the circumstances. If Jack is going to be offered this position with Dudley Kynaston, then we shall possibly become friends.'

'And is he?' Suddenly Charlotte forgot all concern with the Kynastons, or Kitty Ryder's plight. She could only think of Jack, because of how another disappointment would affect Emily.

'You don't want him to, do you!' There was a sudden edge of challenge in Emily's voice. 'He's brilliant, you know. Or perhaps you don't know? It would be very interesting for Jack to work with him, and a promotion, of course. But you must know that, if you've thought about it at all!'

Charlotte forgot her resolve to be patient, and gentle. 'I want him to take it, as long as Kynaston's not guilty of anything,' she said tartly. 'If he was having an affair with his wife's maid I suppose that isn't very important, except to his wife, and perhaps to the maid. But if he killed her, then I would very much rather Jack did not work with him. Until he is accused, of course, then I dare say he will be in gaol, and there will be no possibility of anybody working with him. But even if he did kill her, or threaten to kill her, and we never prove it, I would still rather that Jack had nothing to do with it.' She took a deep breath. 'Or even if it was his wife who killed her, unlikely as that seems, I would prefer no one I loved was involved with them.'

'Jack will be pleased to know that you love him,' Emily said icily. 'Even if it does appear to infect your imagination with grotesque fantasies. If every woman in London were to murder their maids because their husbands slept with them, we would be up to our knees in blood!'

'Not likely.' Charlotte was equally icy. 'She

311

wasn't stabbed. She was beaten, her face mutilated, and her body left up in the gravel pit to be scavenged by animals. Not much blood at all.'

'You are disgusting!' Emily spat out the words.

'Don't be so stupid!' Charlotte snapped. 'It's you I love, and I like Jack, very much, but that will cease instantly if he hurts you.'

'He isn't — ' Emily began, but stopped equally quickly. When Charlotte turned to look at her she saw the tears brim over her eyes and down her cheeks. At another time she would have said something, even hugged her. Now the emotion between them was too brittle. She sat in silence for several moments, allowing Emily time to regain her composure. When she thought it was long enough, she began another conversation. 'What is Rosalind like?' she asked. She did not have to feign interest.

'Actually, I like her,' Emily replied, her voice almost level again. 'She is much more individual than she appears at first. She reads quite a lot, and she knows about all sorts of unusual things: adventures, explorers, the people who go to Mesopotamia, and Greece, and dig up tombs and find amazing things — artefacts and writings. And she has great knowledge of plants. I went to Kew Gardens with her, and she could tell me where dozens of the different trees and flowers came from, and who found them. I started paying attention to her out of courtesy, but quite quickly found I was genuinely interested. And she is nothing like as bland or easily misled as I used to suppose.'

312

'Is that why she is going to this lecture?' Charlotte asked, surprised. Pitt had said little about Rosalind, and Charlotte had assumed her to be rather colourless. Perhaps she was guilty of supposing that because her husband had a mistress, then she must be dull. Did all married women suppose that? If a man seeks another woman, then his wife must be cold, tedious, plain — something one could avoid being oneself, so it would never happen to you?

'I look forward to getting to know her better,' she said.

* * *

Emily might be unhappy but she had lost none of the social skills. She could still make careful planning look like complete chance. She and Charlotte found themselves standing close to Rosalind and Ailsa Kynaston. They were related by marriage, and clearly knew each other well, but no one would have taken them for sisters. Rosalind was soberly dressed in a deep plum colour, which looked gracious and expensive, and yet it lacked the flair that Emily could have achieved with far less.

Ailsa, on the other hand, had the advantage of height, and the grace it gave her movement. There was a vitality in her face and a silver-pale gleam to her hair that attracted the eye, willingly or not. The sombre blues of her gown were of no importance; if anything they were a contrast that heightened her own energy.

They greeted each other with pleasure, as if it

313

were good fortune that had placed them so closely. Both Ailsa and Rosalind remembered Charlotte and affected to be happy to see her again. If they connected her immediately with Pitt and the wretched business that had brought him into Rosalind's house, they were too polite to say so.

Conversation was easy and touched only on trivial things. Emily was at her best, being both interesting and amusing. Particularly she made Rosalind laugh, leaving Charlotte free merely to listen, and to watch the language of look and gesture between Rosalind and Ailsa. Perhaps that was what Emily had intended. If she had, she could not have contrived it better.

'I am pleased so many people have come,' Rosalind said, glancing around at the steadily increasing crowd. 'I admit, I had feared there would be embarrassingly little support.'

'We will all leave grateful that our spring, if chilly, is not nearly as harsh as it could be,' Emily agreed.

Ailsa lifted her graceful shoulders a little. 'The north has a clean beauty that many people admire,' she said. She was not exactly contradicting Emily, but there was a coolness in her voice.

'Do you know the north well?' Emily asked with enthusiasm.

For a moment Ailsa hesitated, as though she were unprepared for the question.

'I have travelled north,' she conceded. 'It has great beauty, and one becomes acclimatised to the cold. Of course, summer is not cold at all, and brighter than here . . . quite often.'

'So you will be familiar with places like the ones Dr Arbuthnott will be mentioning,' Emily concluded. She turned to Rosalind. 'Have you been there also?'

Rosalind smiled. 'Oh, no. I'm afraid I have never been further north than Paris, which I find a marvellous city.'

'Paris is south from here, my dear,' Ailsa said gently.

Charlotte looked at her face. She was smiling but there was no warmth in it, in spite of her tone. If she had liked Rosalind, Charlotte knew that she would not have made the observation at all.

Rosalind coloured very slightly. 'I know that. Perhaps I would have been clearer if I had said "in Europe".'

Several appropriate remarks occurred to Charlotte, which would have put Ailsa in her place, but she refrained from making them.

'I would love to travel,' she said instead. 'Perhaps one day I will. But I still find people more interesting than even the most marvellous cities. And I am grateful that there are men like Dr Arbuthnott who will bring us photographs and magic lantern images to show the beauty of the places I will never visit.'

'A lifetime's worth of them,' Ailsa observed.

Charlotte pretended to misunderstand her. She was irritated at having her own life dismissed in such a way, but more offended for Rosalind, because to judge from her face, she felt the cut more keenly.

'Really? He did not look more than forty-five

in the photographs. But perhaps they are not recent?'

Ailsa stared at her, then quite suddenly a flash of amusement lit her face, almost appreciation. Charlotte realised she respected someone who would fight back. She smiled at Ailsa with all the considerable charm she could call on when she wished, and saw the recognition of it, and a quick acknowledgement.

They took their seats and an expectant hush settled over the room. Dr Arbuthnott appeared, to applause, and the lecture began.

Certainly what he had to say was interesting, and to Charlotte completely unfamiliar, but she could not afford to turn her attention to it fully. She and Emily had finally decided to take seats on the aisle immediately behind those of Ailsa and Rosalind. This gave her the opportunity to watch them both, while still appearing to be fully intent upon the lecturer.

Of course it would be ill-mannered to whisper to each other during the time when Dr Arbuthnott was actually speaking, but it seemed to Charlotte completely natural, and even expected, that at suitable moments one would speak to one's companion to remark on something of particular beauty or surprise. She did so to Emily without giving it thought.

Then she faced forward again, and began to study the two women in front of her. Both sat straight up, as governesses would have taught them. Beauty was a gift; deportment was acquired, as was graceful speech both in timbre and pronunciation. Having something of interest

316

to say was, of course, quite another matter.

Rosalind inclined very slightly towards Ailsa, and murmured to her, but so quietly Charlotte did not hear any of it.

Ailsa nodded, but did not reply. She did not lean her body towards Rosalind. A moment later she looked around the audience as discreetly as was possible, as if searching for someone she knew. Apparently she did not find them, because she did so again at the next opportunity, without being obvious about it. Charlotte was very curious as to who it might be.

She learned who, later in the evening after the lecture itself was finished and refreshments were offered. Many people congratulated Dr Arbuthnott and asked him further questions about the power and beauty of the far northern oceans.

Emily was in close conversation with Rosalind, and Charlotte had decided to follow behind Ailsa as closely as she could without being obvious. She made herself appear to be looking for an acquaintance, and felt as if she were behaving like a complete eccentric. She hoped she would never have to meet any of those people again socially. Possibly if they thought she was peculiar enough, they would take trouble to avoid her?

She was abundantly rewarded. She followed where she had seen Ailsa disappear, presumably seeking a little respite from the stuffiness and intense conversation of the room. She had walked quite casually under an elaborate archway leading to a side room, a minor gallery. It was beautifully proportioned but leading nowhere except to a large window.

Charlotte did not want a confrontation. It would be far too clumsy, and unmistakable that she had seen Ailsa go in and chosen to follow her. She dared not even go too close, because there were several very fine mirrors, and her passing in front of one would catch anybody's eye.

Then she stopped abruptly. Inadvertently she had placed herself exactly where she could see Ailsa reflected in a mirror to her side, giving a clear profile angled in a further mirror beyond Charlotte's line of sight. She could not take her eyes from it! Ailsa was standing quite still beside Edom Talbot. From their closeness to each other, and the look on Talbot's face, there was no one else in the room. He moved a little behind her so Charlotte could see only his arms as they gently curved around Ailsa's waist, and his shoulders above hers. She was tall, but he was several inches taller again. He was not a handsome man, but he was in a way distinguished, and quite unmistakable.

Ailsa did not move. She was smiling slightly, as though not only pleased but faintly amused.

Talbot's hands moved up a little from her waist, gradually inch by inch until he caressed her breasts. He did it with some confidence, as if he did not expect to be denied.

Charlotte studied Ailsa's face and saw her expression freeze. The gesture had not surprised her, but she found it distasteful. Charlotte could feel it as if it were her own body being touched. She saw the muscles in Ailsa's neck and throat

318

clench as if she almost stopped breathing.

Charlotte's mind raced. Why did she endure it? She did not believe for an instant that Ailsa did not know how to deal completely effectively with such a thing. She had only to turn around sharply and confront him, or — even more simply than that — take a very carefully judged step back and put her heel on the instep of his foot, and then her weight. She was a handsomely built woman. The pain would be excruciating. She could pretend it was accidental, and they would both know it was entirely on purpose. And yet she did not.

Talbot bent his head and began to kiss her gently along the back of her neck and shoulder. She seemed to struggle to master her feelings. He could not see her face, only Charlotte could, and she read the revulsion in it as if it had been her own.

Then Ailsa turned and kissed him back quickly and pulled away. She said something, and Talbot smiled back. They began to move.

Charlotte dared stay no longer. There were too many mirrors. She could not afford to be caught staring. One meeting of the eyes and she would never be able to deny it.

★　★　★

Charlotte had no opportunity to tell Emily until they were in the carriage again on the way home, moving swiftly through the brightly lit traffic.

'What?' Emily said incredulously. 'You must be mistaken! Are you sure it was Ailsa?'

'Yes, of course I am. Apart from her gown, which was quite individual, I could see her face!'

'Then maybe it wasn't Talbot! Could Dudley Kynaston have arrived, and we didn't see him?' Emily persisted.

'Dudley? She's the widow of the brother he adored!' Charlotte protested.

'Don't be naïve!' Emily said, more with disbelief than criticism. 'Bennett is dead! What greater compliment could the devoted Dudley give him than to step into his shoes?'

'That's disgusting!' Charlotte retorted. 'Would you be as quick into my shoes?'

Emily smiled. 'Oh, I don't know. I think Thomas is rather sweet! And he'd never be boring! Would he?'

Charlotte realised she was being teased just in time to avoid making a fool of herself, and perhaps making a remark whose sting would linger far more than she intended.

'He snores,' she said.

Emily looked crushed. 'Does he?'

'No!'

Emily sighed. 'Jack does. He looks quite beautiful asleep, with those eyelashes. But he does snore — sometimes.'

Charlotte swivelled around. 'Emily, were you serious that Ailsa could be the mistress that Dudley is so desperate to keep quiet about?'

Emily was immediately sober again. 'Well, it would make sense, wouldn't it? It isn't that it's so terribly scandalous, so much as it is a desecration of his adored dead brother.' She stopped. 'Except that Rosalind told me Ailsa

320

never really got over Bennett. She's still in love with him.'

'Perhaps Dudley reminds her of him?' Charlotte thought aloud. 'And in a weak moment, a lonely one, she slipped up?'

'What? And now she can't say no?' Emily asked incredulously. 'Yes, she could. I'll wager Ailsa could say no to anyone — and mean it. If she's playing along, then there's something she wants.'

'Except that this wasn't Dudley, it really wasn't,' Charlotte insisted. 'He was a similar height, but it was very definitely Edom Talbot. I saw his face. It was a reflection, but it was perfectly plain. She allowed him to touch her in a very intimate way, but she had to force herself to.'

'With Talbot,' Emily said thoughtfully. For a little while she was silent. 'There are so many possibilities,' she said at last. 'We need to discuss this. Come home with me and we'll talk. It's still early. I'll have the carriage take you home after. Please?'

'Of course,' Charlotte said instantly. It did not matter whether it was really to discuss whatever they might have observed this evening, or simply because Emily did not want to go home alone — or even worse, to Jack being silent and withdrawn. Possibly he would even be tense about the situation with Kynaston, and therefore perhaps irritable. The very fact that he was not sharing his anxiety with Emily was the cause of hurt, whatever it was about. He probably thought he was protecting her. Men could be incredibly stupid sometimes, trip over the obvious, and still not see it.

But then Emily ought to know that by now, and not make an issue out of something that was not meant to be one.

Or on the other hand, perhaps Jack was drifting out of love, and a far bigger change was needed. And Charlotte was certainly not wise enough to answer that question. But she would go home with Emily and stay at least an hour, if Emily wished it.

'Do you think it really could be all about Bennett?' Charlotte asked when they were sitting beside the fire in Emily's drawing room, which perfectly reflected her tastes and character in its rich golds and pinks, the flashes of red, and the paintings on the walls.

'Why not?' Emily asked. 'He seems to have been reasonable, from what Rosalind says. And actually very nice. He was the handsomer of the two brothers and, at the time he died, he was considered the one with the greatest promise.'

Charlotte thought for a minute, knowing Emily was watching her. 'That sounds a little difficult to live with,' she said at last. 'I wouldn't entirely blame Dudley if his feelings about Bennett were a trifle mixed. Although Thomas did say he still keeps a portrait of Bennett in his study. He seemed to be devoted. He admired him enormously and in a way strove to be like him, even to finish some of the work Bennett began . . . '

Charlotte shivered. 'Are you saying that now

he wants to complete it by having an affair with Bennett's widow?'

'Well, it's not impossible, is it?'

'No . . . '

'In fact it's not completely impossible that he started the affair before Bennett was dead!' Emily continued.

'But if Bennett were all that marvellous, why was Ailsa willing to betray him, and with his own brother?' Charlotte argued.

Emily pulled her mouth into a grimace. 'Not all men who seem handsome and clever and charming are all that interesting when you get to know them . . . well . . . '

'You mean in bed?'

'Of course I do.' Then Emily laughed. 'Oh dear! I'm not talking about Jack. That did sound a bit clumsy, didn't it?'

Charlotte was too relieved to argue. 'Yes,' she agreed. 'It definitely did! But I accept your denial. Do you really think it could go that far back? That's . . . years! Poor Rosalind. No wonder she looks a bit . . . crumpled.'

The shadow passed over Emily's face again. 'She does, doesn't she?' She hesitated. 'Do I?'

Charlotte had walked straight into a trap — perhaps not an intentional one, but very complete none the less. And Emily would see a lie, or an evasion instantly. She always had done.

'Compared with the way you usually are, yes, you do,' she said, hating each word as it came from her mouth. Had Emily wanted her to lie, even if neither of them believed it? It was too late now. She had to add something, retrieve hope

323

from it. 'Because you believe Jack has fallen out of love with you,' she added. 'That doesn't make it true! There are people who believe the world is flat! They even burned people for it, once.'

'Actually several times,' Emily said with an attempt at a smile.

'What's the point in burning anyone several times?' Charlotte asked without taking a breath. 'Seems a little excessive, doesn't it?'

Emily laughed in spite of herself. 'Are you trying to make me feel better?'

'I'm trying to make you see sense.' Charlotte poured some tea for each of them. It was Earl Grey, subtle and very fragrant, the exact opposite of the conversation.

'I've had another thought,' Emily went on. 'It's pretty awful! But what if Dudley and Ailsa really fell in love with each other, away back when she was married to Bennett? And what if it's far worse than that? Are we absolutely certain that Bennett's death was natural? He was awfully young to die, when he wasn't fragile before.'

Charlotte was stunned. 'You mean that Dudley killed him? That was the secret that Kitty found out? How on earth would she?'

'I don't know! Ladies' maids find out all kinds of things. I'd hate even to imagine what mine knows about me. In some ways, more than Jack does. Even more than you do!'

Charlotte followed the thought. 'Then why is Rosalind still alive and well? Or does she know, and has some kind of way of keeping herself safe? For heaven's sake, why bother? What on earth is a husband worth if he would so much rather be somewhere else?'

'Revenge? I don't know.' Emily leaned forward. 'Maybe they didn't kill Bennett. Maybe he found out and was so broken-hearted he committed suicide, and they covered it up? I'm sure a decent doctor could be persuaded to be discreet.'

'And that's the scandal?' Charlotte thought about it for several moments. 'That would be pretty awful, wouldn't it? What a betrayal! What a rotten tragedy. Dudley couldn't afford to let that be known. It's so . . . ugly!' She shut her eyes as if she could make the thought disappear. 'I wonder if you go on loving someone after that, or if you end up hating them because every time you think of them, even see their face, you are reminded of what you have become because of your feeling for them. Don't you think a really good love should make you strive to be the very best you can? The noblest, the bravest, the gentlest?'

Emily stared at her. 'Yes,' she said very quietly. Slowly her shoulders eased as the tension slipped away from her. 'Yes. I do.' She smiled. 'I'm glad you came this evening, and that you said what you did. I want to think about myself, for a little while, and what I need to do. We'll go on with the wretched Kynastons tomorrow, or the next day.' She reached for the bell to ask the footman to fetch the carriage round to take Charlotte home.

15

Pitt had debated the issue briefly with himself as to whether he should repeat to Stoker the information he had received from Carlisle, with the obvious necessity that he must also tell him all that he knew about Carlisle. That included the history between them, or as much of it as was required to have Stoker understand why Pitt trusted him, and the nature of the debt he felt towards him.

He realised the following morning that in fact the conflict in his mind was only as to how he would do it, what words he would use, and how much he could avoid discussing it all. It had begun with Carlisle owing a debt to Pitt for his silence in the Resurrection Row affair. Then, over the years, the balance had shifted the other way. Now, with the rescue from Talbot, the weight was on the other side: Pitt owed the greater debt.

Was that so Carlisle could collect the payment now? That was unlike the man Pitt had known. He would have abhorred such manipulation. Then what for? It surely had to do with debt — and honour.

There was a sharp tap on the door. He had barely answered it when it opened and Stoker came in, closing it behind him. He looked scrubbed and eager, but there were dark lines of tiredness in his face, hollows around the eyes. He had pursued this case as if something he had learned about the missing woman had made her particularly real to him.

But then Stoker was a man who did not do anything in half-measure. If he would have denied caring about the woman and said it was simply the best way to do the job, he would have been wrong: it was both.

'Sir?' Stoker interrupted Pitt's thoughts, impatient to know why he had been sent for.

'Sit down,' Pitt told him.

Stoker obeyed, not taking his eyes from Pitt's face.

Very briefly Pitt told him the history of events in Resurrection Row, the spectacular disinterment of corpses to expose murder and corruption, over a decade ago, and his first encounter with Somerset Carlisle.

Stoker stared at him with disbelief, laughter, and then amazement.

'Sorry, sir,' he apologised, regaining a more sober expression. 'You're not saying Carlisle's behind these bodies, are you? I could see why the other, but . . . ' His eyes widened. 'You are! Why? This is . . . grotesque . . . '

'So was the other, believe me,' Pitt answered him. 'And yes, I am sorry but I think he is behind these bodies too. He has the ingenuity and the means — '

'Not without help, sir!' Stoker interrupted.

'I dare say his manservant is involved, and would probably die before admitting it. He's been with Carlisle for thirty years. I looked into that.'

'But why?' Stoker demanded. Then he stopped abruptly, understanding flooding his face. 'To force you to investigate Kynaston! But what for? He didn't kill Kitty Ryder, because no one did. What could she know about him that would be worth that much? And how would Carlisle hear about it anyway? She wouldn't know someone like that . . . would she?'

'I doubt it. Carlisle knows about it from Sir John Ransom.'

'Oh!' Stoker let out his breath in a sigh. 'Are we talking treason, sir?'

'Yes, we are.'

'That's . . . very ugly. Then we have to get him, whatever it costs. I'd like to meet this fellow, Carlisle. Shake his hand.'

Pitt felt oddly elated. He had been afraid Stoker would resent Carlisle's interference and deplore his bizarre behaviour. Stoker went up not only in his professional estimation but also in his personal regard. For all his outwardly dour demeanour and his lack of relationships or ordinary pastimes, his loyalties were unbreakable, and now it seemed that beneath the rigid exterior he had a powerful imagination.

'I'll see that it is arranged,' Pitt promised. 'If it doesn't occur anyway in the natural course of events.'

'Thank you, sir,' There was barely a flicker in Stoker's eyes, but for an instant his mouth twitched as if he were going to smile, perhaps within himself, even to laugh.

'Now we have to find Kitty Ryder,' Pitt continued. 'You may take two other men to help you, if you wish. It is no longer a matter of solving a murder already committed, it is preventing a continuing betrayal of our naval weaponry secrets. Do not repeat that. As far as anyone else is concerned, she is a witness in danger.'

'Yes, sir. If Kynaston knows that, then won't he be looking for her as well?' Stoker's face was bleak with anxiety.

'That is the next thing I am going to do,' Pitt replied. 'Find out exactly what steps Kynaston has taken to find her.'

Stoker stood up. 'Who's he passing secrets through? We need to know that, sir. And make damn sure no one else does.'

'I realise that, Stoker! He won't be in it all by himself.'

Stoker frowned. 'What the hell makes a man like Kynaston betray his country? It has to be for something more than money. No one in the world has enough money to buy your life, your decency, your home, your friends! Your sleep at night . . . '

'I don't know,' Pitt admitted. 'Perhaps love?'

'Infatuation!' Stoker said with disgust. 'What kind of love can you offer anyone if you've sold your honour? And they certainly don't love you if they ask it!'

'I wasn't thinking of the love of men for women.' Pitt was framing the thought as he spoke. 'But perhaps your child's life? If we care about anything at all, we have hostages to fortune.'

'Kynaston's children?' Stoker was clearly

turning it over in his mind. 'They're all adult, or almost. But I will put someone into checking up on them, if you think it's worth it?'

'Yes, do that, before you start off to look for Kitty again.'

As Stoker left, Pitt turned his own attention to Kynaston. If Kitty had stumbled across information dangerous to him, and fled in fear for her life, then surely Kynaston would have attempted to find her himself? However frightened she was, there was always the possibility of her confiding in someone else, even if only for her own safety, or relief from the burden of carrying such knowledge alone.

Except that if she told anyone that Dudley Kynaston was a traitor to his country, who would believe her? It would inevitably create a stir and give away her whereabouts. If she were truly terrified, it would be far wiser to disappear and become as close to invisible as possible.

Would Kynaston then look for her? Or trust that she would be too frightened, and too wise, to repeat anything?

He would hardly go around the pubs and backstreets himself. A certain degree of enquiry for her would be natural. She was in his care and had disappeared from his house. A decent man would not need to explain why he had done such a thing. Perhaps it would be interesting to see his reaction to the question.

Pitt realised, as he set out to begin his own discreet enquiries as to whether it was Kynaston who was pursuing Kitty Ryder, that he still found it difficult to believe that Kynaston was a traitor and — given the right motive and opportunity — would also murder one of his servants, in order to protect himself.

Pitt could have given the job to one of his juniors. It was sufficiently important to move someone from one of the multitude of tasks that fell to Special Branch. But he did not wish any further men involved. He was not prepared to explain the reason to Talbot, or anyone else, should Kynaston hear of it and complain.

He spent most of the day doing the same kind of police work he had done in the past when investigating a murder. He went from place to place, asking openly about Kitty Ryder, obliquely about other enquiries for her.

In many accounts he was told of he recognised Stoker, but there were others in which the enquirer was fairly plainly Norton, Kynaston's butler.

'Yes, sir,' the barman at the Pig and Whistle replied, shaking his head sadly. 'Nice gent, Mr Norton. All very proper, like wot you'd expect a butler to be, but right concerned 'e were, for sure.' He wiped his hands on his apron. 'Reckoned as she were sort of 'is family, like. I told 'im all I know'd, which weren't much. 'E thanked me nicely, good tip, but no matter 'ow much I'd 'a liked to, I couldn't 'elp 'im. I ain't got no idea where she went, nor why, for that matter.'

'Did you ever ask?' Pitt pressed.

The man shook his head. 'Well, there were Mrs Kynaston's coachman too. 'E pressed kind of 'ard, but like I told 'im, I can't tell you wot I don't know. 'E asked after young Dobson, an' I told 'im all I know about 'im too.'

Interesting, Pitt thought. So Rosalind had sent someone herself, apparently someone who took the issue a little further.

Pitt thanked the barman and went to look for other traces of Harry Dobson, to see if the coachman had followed up on the information. He was not surprised to find that he had, although it took him the rest of the afternoon, and all the following day to be certain of it. It seemed as if the coachman had been given the time and had used it with diligence and imagination, but no success. It spoke much for Stoker's skill that he had at least found Dobson, if not before Kitty had moved on.

Perhaps he should not have been surprised. Kitty had been Rosalind's maid. It appeared that the loyalty had run in both ways. Charlotte would have combed London to find Minnie Maude if she had disappeared, regardless of her own danger, never mind cost or inconvenience.

Pitt decided that, before speaking to Kynaston himself, he would find the coachman and ask him at what point he had given up. It was unlikely he had anything to add that would be helpful in finding Kitty now, but he should not overlook the chance.

* * *

'No, sir.' The coachman looked puzzled. He stood in the stable just outside the looseboxes where the horses were peering curiously at Pitt.

The groom was coming and going with hay.

Pitt enjoyed the familiar sensations that took him back to his childhood: hay and straw; clean leather; linseed oil; the sounds of horses themselves shifting from foot to foot, munching now and then, blowing air out through their nostrils.

'It's not something to apologise for,' he told the man. 'It's to your credit.'

'I wish I 'ad, sir,' the coachman assured him. 'But I didn't. Ask Mr Kynaston, sir. I were busy on 'is errands, or else taking the mistress to where she went.'

'Wasn't it Mrs Kynaston who asked you to look for Kitty?'

'No, sir. She were upset she'd gone, like, but she never asked me ter go lookin' for 'er. Reckon as she ran off with that carpenter fellow she were courtin'. Only Mr Norton thought she might not 'ave. An' young Maisie.' He smiled and tipped his head. 'Too smart by 'alf for a scullery maid, that one. Either she'll make 'er fortune, or she'll come ter no good.'

Pitt was puzzled. The barman had been sure of himself, and the information he had given Pitt had been correct. He had followed it and found the coachman's trail, until he too had given up.

'You were seen and identified,' Pitt told him. 'Why on earth deny it? It's a perfectly decent thing to do. I know exactly where you went.'

''Ceptin' I didn't,' the man insisted. 'Whoever said it were me were lyin'. You ask Mr and Mrs Kynaston. They'll tell you.'

Pitt stared at the man, who looked back at him

without a shadow of guile. Then suddenly a completely different thought occurred to him. Ailsa was also 'Mrs Kynaston'. Was it possible she had offered her footman for the task, and this man was telling the truth?

Why would Ailsa do such a thing? As a favour to Rosalind, so her husband did not know? That answer was laden with several possibilities, the first to his mind was that Rosalind suspected her husband of some involvement in Kitty's disappearance and dared not have him know she was still pursuing it.

'It seems they were mistaken,' Pitt conceded. 'Perhaps they said what they thought I wanted to hear. Thank you.' He turned and left, his mind racing through other scenes and ideas.

For example, was Ailsa looking for Kitty for Rosalind's sake, or for Kynaston's? Was she trying to prove him innocent, for all their sakes? If Kitty were alive, then there was no murder connected to the Kynaston house.

He walked to the areaway, weaving his path through the ash cans and coke scuttles, and went up the step to the scullery door.

He was still too early to see Kynaston himself, so he waited in the morning room. He would have preferred the kitchen, but Norton saw to it that he did not linger there. It was in the guise of hospitality, but Pitt had a strong feeling that it was actually to keep him from overhearing the servants' gossip.

By the time Kynaston appeared Pitt had made up his mind. He would dislike forcing him to answer, but it would not be the first time a man he had personally liked had been guilty of appalling crimes.

Kynaston came in looking tired and cold, but his manner was as charming as ever.

'Good evening, Commander Pitt. How are you?' He held out his hand.

Pitt took it, something he would not normally do when interviewing someone he suspected. 'Well, thank you,' he replied. 'I'm sorry to disturb you yet again, but this time I have happier news.'

'Good. I'm delighted.' Kynaston smiled and offered Pitt a seat beside the fire, and whisky if he wished it. Again Pitt declined. One did not accept hospitality in such circumstances.

Before he gave the news he mentioned his conversation with the coachman. Kynaston was bound to hear of it, and one did not speak to a man's servants without saying so to him, even if it was rather asking for permission after the event.

'I spoke to your coachman,' he said casually. 'We are still looking for Kitty Ryder, and in our search we've come across what seems to be evidence that he had looked for her also — possibly in his own hours, but more likely at your request . . . '

Kynaston looked baffled. 'Hopgood? Are you certain? It was not at my request, I assure you. I'm surprised he had the time. Perhaps he had . . . an affection for her? She was a very handsome girl. I admit, that had not occurred to me.'

'So it was not at your request?' Pitt asked.

Kynaston's look did not waver. 'No. I had Norton make a few enquiries, but that was some time ago. He was happy to do it, but he had no success. I began to accept that she ran off with her young man, in what I regret to say was a very callous manner. I would have expected her to have the courtesy to give notice, as one would normally do. My wife was distressed, as we all were. It was an uncharacteristically thoughtless thing to do.'

'Hopgood assured me that he had not looked for her, either on his own or at your instruction,' Pitt agreed. 'I mention it only because no doubt you will come to hear of it, and possibly Mrs Kynaston will also.'

'Thank you.' Kynaston still looked puzzled. He had taken whisky for himself and sat with the glass in his hand, its rich colour made even warmer by the gaslamp now lit, and the reflection of the fire.

'Possibly it was Mrs Ailsa Kynaston's coachman?' Pitt suggested.

Kynaston's hand tightened on his glass so hard that the liquid spilled a drop with the change of position.

'Ailsa? I think that's . . . unlikely.' He thought for a moment. 'Unless Rosalind asked her to? Or she imagined she could help . . . ' He left the idea unfinished.

'Perhaps the informants told us what they thought we wished to hear,' Pitt said smoothly. 'It happens sometimes. Anyway, it is of far less importance now, since we are sure beyond any question whatever that neither of the bodies in the gravel pits was that of Kitty Ryder. The second one did not resemble her closely enough, and she has been seen alive and well sometime after the first body was found. I don't know where she is, but you and your household are relieved of all suspicion in her disappearance. And — perhaps more relevantly — you no longer need to grieve at the thought of her being dead. I'm sorry it had to touch you at all.' He stared at Kynaston, watching every muscle in his face, his neck, his shoulders, one hand on his glass and the other on the arm of the chair. He saw the tension like a bowstring. Kynaston all but stopped breathing.

Pitt smiled blandly, as if he had not noticed, but he did not speak. The whole art was to leave Kynaston floundering, offer him nothing to reply to.

Finally Kynaston moved, with just an easing of his shoulders as he drew in a deep breath. He set the whisky glass down.

'That is a great relief. My wife will be delighted. It was a very poor way to behave, but thank God Kitty was not . . . killed.' He pulled his face into an expression of revulsion. 'Presumably you will no longer be wasting your time looking for her. A very good result all round, even if it was hard to reach. I cannot imagine what the stupid girl was thinking of! Still, it hardly matters now.'

'Indeed,' Pitt nodded. 'Of course we still have to discover the identity of the two women who were found, but that will be a job for the local police.'

Kynaston let out a long, slow breath and his body slumped a little in the chair. 'Thank you. It is most considerate of you to come and inform me personally, Commander.' He stood up slowly, as if he were a little stiff. 'I hope we shall meet again soon, in pleasanter circumstances.'

'I hope so,' Pitt agreed. 'Good night, sir.'

★　★　★

Pitt arrived home earlier than he had done for several evenings and was able to have dinner with Charlotte and both his children. He put Kynaston out of his mind and listened to their conversation, their news and their ideas. Daniel was full of his plan to play cricket in the coming summer and could think of little else. He talked about different strokes, catches, styles of bowling and batting, but to Pitt's pleasure and carefully concealed amusement, he also spoke of strategy. He explained it at some length over the first course and well into pudding, his face alight with enthusiasm. Various condiments were moved around the table to represent different ways of placing his fielders.

Jemima rolled her eyes, but listened patiently. Then, just to keep up her own position in showing off abilities that no one else understood, she spoke at length about French Medieval history, smiling to herself as they pretended to be interested.

It was well into the evening before Charlotte and Pitt sat alone before the fire and she was able to tell him about her evening with Emily,

338

which she was clearly eager to do.

Pitt had difficulty keeping his eyes open. The room was warm and extremely comfortable. The light was soft, only one gaslamp was lit. The fire whickered gently in the hearth and every so often settled lower as the wood collapsed. It was Charlotte who leaned forward and put more fuel on: old apple wood, sweet-smelling.

Pitt made an effort to be interested.

'How is Emily?'

'Involved,' she said immediately. 'As I am. I think that's half her real problem — she's bored stiff!'

He tried to pay attention. 'Involved in what? Didn't you say it was a lecture on Arctic exploring, or something? I can't imagine Emily caring even remotely about that.'

'North Atlantic and North Sea,' she corrected him. 'And no, I don't think she cares about that any more than I do. Although some of his photographs were dazzlingly beautiful.'

'You said involved . . . didn't you?' He must be half asleep. He was losing the thread.

She was smiling, leaning forward a little, her eyes bright.

'Fascinated. I saw Ailsa, almost accidentally — although I did follow her, in a most extraordinary affair.'

'Affair?' She was speaking in stops and starts and he had lost the drift of it.

'Love affair, Thomas! Or perhaps it was more lust than love. Or maybe it was lust on his part, and something quite different on hers. I don't know what, not yet. But I mean to find out.'

He sat up a little further. 'Why? What are you talking about? And how is it your concern? It isn't Jack . . . is it?'

'No! Of course it isn't Jack!' She was completely upright, her back like a ramrod. 'Do you really think I'd be sitting here comfortably spinning it out if it were? I'd have brought you in here and told you before dinner!' she said indignantly.

'Oh. Yes, of course. Then why are you bothering with it?'

'Because it's Ailsa Kynaston and Edom Talbot!'

Now he sat upright, instantly wide awake. 'What? Who did you say?'

'You heard me, Thomas. I was following her, and I saw her, reflected through two mirrors. He stood behind her and put his arms around her . . . intimately. I'd have broken the foot of anyone who did that to me, unless it were you.'

'And she didn't mind?' he asked.

'Yes, she did mind, but she pretended not to. It took her a few seconds to master herself . . . '

'Are you sure? How do you know?'

'Because I could see her!' she said fiercely. 'Then she turned round and kissed him. But she had to make herself do it! Doesn't that send a hundred questions racing around in your head?'

'A couple of dozen anyway,' he agreed. 'I'd begun to wonder if she were Kynaston's mistress. This makes it look very different.'

'Not necessarily,' she argued. 'Maybe she's both?'

'Both?' he said incredulously. Why would she

340

allow Talbot to touch her, if she doesn't like him? Is that to mislead people that she's having an affair with him, and not with Kynaston?'

'Maybe,' Charlotte conceded. 'But it seems like a lot of trouble when no one seems to suspect it anyway. Unless, of course, Rosalind does?'

He was about to say something, but she rushed on. 'But there are a whole lot of other possibilities, Thomas. What if they have been in love for a long time? Even when she was married to Bennett Kynaston?'

'With Talbot?' he said incredulously.

'No, of course not! With Dudley! Maybe that's why Bennett died so young?'

'Of what? People can't die of being betrayed, even by a wife and a brother. Or are you saying they killed him? Isn't that a bit — ' He stopped. It was appalling, but then so was treason. Was it possible that the whole tragedy was domestic rather than political?

'They might have,' she answered. 'That would be a terrible enough thing if Kitty Ryder found out. She'd run from that house, middle of the night or not! I would. And of course,' she added, 'the other possibility is that Rosalind found out, and she meant to kill them in revenge, or to expose them. That would be more effective — '

'You're letting your imagination run away with you,' he told her sharply.

'No, I'm not!' she insisted. 'You think just because Rosalind looks as if she hasn't the fire to break the skin on a rice pudding, doesn't mean she wouldn't hold that over their heads!'

'You don't break the skin on a rice pudding with fire, darling!'

'Don't be pedantic!' she said exasperatedly. 'The flame inside her. There's something all twisted up going on there, Thomas. I'm only giving you a few possibilities. It's your job to find out which one is true.'

He looked at her perched on the edge of the chair, her eyes bright, the firelight catching red and gold in her hair, her cheeks flushed. It was the last thing she would have thought about herself, but to him she was utterly beautiful.

'You have enough flame inside you to cook me rice pudding for the rest of my life,' he said, keeping his tone light, for fear emotion swallowed him up.

'I didn't think you liked rice pudding!' she protested.

'I don't! But I like the flame!'

She laughed and moved forward off the seat and into his arms.

★ ★ ★

When Jack Radley telephoned Vespasia and asked if he might visit her in the afternoon, she was surprised, but she caught the edge of urgency in his voice.

'Of course,' she said, as if it would cause no inconvenience at all. She had intended to visit an old friend and spend a leisurely time looking at an exhibition of art. They had not met recently, except at such functions as allowed no serious conversation. She had been looking forward to it.

342

She would have her maid send a note, with profuse apologies. Perhaps she should send Mildred flowers tomorrow? A family crisis Mildred would understand. She had daughters herself, and now granddaughters as well.

Vespasia hesitated over offering tea. It was not a meal she imagined Jack to take, but it was an excuse to sit down and have an uninterrupted conversation. One never stopped until the full ritual had been observed. She believed that was what Jack wished for, even if a good stiff brandy would have been more to his taste.

He arrived punctually. For a man as busy as he was, it was a nice compliment to her that he had taken such care. But then, he had always had perfect manners. It dated from his years when he had lived on his charm. He had been the sort of handsome young man who had wit, poise, grace, and the intelligence never to overstay his welcome in any one place. He dressed perfectly, was graceful on the dance floor, had seen most of the latest plays, and above all never gossiped or carried tales from one household to the next, or spoke afterwards of the ladies he had accompanied to one function or another. He never drew comparisons, or made promises he did not keep. His ability to charm was deeper than a surface ease. There was a quality to his nature that was worthy of respect.

He came in now and greeted her warmly. The maid took his hat and coat, and he kissed Vespasia lightly on the cheek. He accepted her invitation to sit and assured her that he would be delighted to take tea with her.

The years had been kind to him. The touch of grey at the temples lent him a maturity, the few fine lines in his face deepened the sense of character, even gravity rather than mere handsomeness. But in spite of his smile, she could see that he was worried.

'Please, my dear, don't waste time leading up gracefully to whatever it is that concerns you,' she requested.

He smiled, relief easing out the worst of the tension in his body.

'Thank you. I dare say Emily has told you that I have the offer of a position working with Dudley Kynaston. It is something I would enjoy. He is an interesting man with a fine mind, and — more than that — I would be working on something specific rather than chasing many general subjects.' He hesitated. 'However, I know that Thomas has been investigating Kynaston because of the maid that went missing from his house, and then the body in the gravel pit nearby, which so resembled her. Somerset Carlisle was asking questions in the House, with the unspoken implication that there was a scandal about to break. That has not happened, but neither has the maid been found, or the body identified.' He stopped, waiting for Vespasia to offer some reaction.

'Yes, I am aware of these things,' she agreed. 'You are concerned to make the right judgement?'

He looked embarrassed. 'I can't afford to accept the position, and then find it has disappeared. I know Emily has private means, but I have always refused to live on her first husband's estate, which is in trust for Edward, anyway. It is not pride, it is . . . '

'Honour,' she said for him. 'It is not pompous to say so. I understand, and respect you for it. Not only can you not afford to lose the income from an excellent additional position to that of Member of Parliament, but you cannot afford the question of your judgement, should it transpire that Kynaston is involved in something uglier than unfaithfulness to his wife . . . '

Jack winced. 'You say that easily, as if I might think it acceptable . . . '

She smiled at him. 'You are too sensitive, my dear. I was not thinking anything of the sort. Whom you knew, or how well you knew them before you married Emily is not of interest to me, nor do I believe is it to her. It is completely unacceptable to me to betray trust, but I am perfectly aware that it happens far more often than one would wish. You cannot afford to judge other men on that, when considering whether you wish to work with them or not. It is a luxury beyond most of us, so we all pretend we do not know. On the whole, it works very well.'

'Not if you murder the maid and dump her body in a nearby gravel pit,' Jack said unhappily and with a hint of bitterness.

'Have you asked Emily's opinion about it?' Vespasia asked, almost as if the idea had been an afterthought.

Jack shook his head. 'I don't want to worry her

with it. She shouldn't be asked to make this decision for me, nor carry the burden of it if I'm wrong.'

'She may wish to,' Vespasia replied.

'Emily doesn't like anxiety,' he told her. 'Especially when there is nothing she can do.'

Vespasia smiled. 'Do you mean there is nothing she can do, or that you would really rather that she did not attempt anything, and you are worried that if you tell her, she will try to help you?' It was a question so direct as to be blunt, but she knew how many misunderstandings were created by the use of euphemisms. One ended up being so oblique nobody knew what on earth you were talking about.

He looked at her earnestly. 'I'm trying to look after her! I want to make the right decision, and then present her with it. She's been unhappy lately. I don't know why, and she won't tell me. I think she's either bored with me, or she wants me to make a decision without having to be guided, but of course if she said that to me, it would be guidance in itself.'

Vespasia sighed. 'For all your charm, you don't know women very well, do you! Would you try that protective manner with Charlotte?'

He was startled.

'No . . . she'd hate it. But I'm not married to Charlotte. We would disagree about everything, and it wouldn't matter — ' He stopped abruptly.

'My dear, you could disagree with Emily and it wouldn't matter,' she assured him. 'What you must not do is ignore her. If you continue with it much longer she will begin to think you are interested in someone else . . . '

'She knows better than that.' Now his voice was filled with emotion. 'I adore her. In fact I dare not tell her so, because she hates growing older, but I think maturity suits her. She seems more . . . more earthy, more reachable. I don't feel as if she's infallible any more, too confident, too ethereal to need my support, or protection . . . ' He faltered to a stop, looking as if he had said more than he meant to. He bit his lip and looked away from Vespasia, down at the table. 'I'm afraid she will resent being helped with anything, she is so sufficient . . . '

Vespasia reached across and touched his arm very lightly. 'My dear Jack, one of the advantages of growing older is that we begin to accept that none of us can manage without friends, people to love and people who love us, even now and then a little help and a little criticism, if it is gently given. You may find that even Emily has learned some wisdom.'

He looked at her with a flash of hope.

'My advice regarding Dudley Kynaston is not to commit yourself just yet,' she continued. 'Find some excuse to wait a week or so. Think of some other matters you wish to deal with, some other commitment you must conclude. And ask Emily's opinion, whether you actually take her advice or not.'

He flashed her a bright, utterly charming smile. 'I will do. May I have another jam tart? Suddenly I am hungry, and they are delicious.'

'They are there for you,' she replied. 'You may have them all.'

Vespasia had dinner with Victor Narraway. She had hesitated whether to accept his invitation or not. She could see Emily's situation so clearly, yet she was confused as to her own. She enjoyed Narraway's company more than that of anyone else she could recall. He had always been easy for her to talk to, to agree or disagree. Yet lately she had felt a peculiar vulnerability in his company, as if somewhere during their friendship she had lost the emotional armour she had kept safely in place for so many years. She found herself caring if he called again, even allowing her imagination to wonder what he thought of her, and if their friendship were as valuable to him as it was to her.

She was older than he, a knowledge which came with a degree of pain. It had never been of the slightest importance before. Now, absurdly, it mattered. He seemed completely unaware of it, but then he was far too well-mannered to allow such an ungallant thing to show. And it was clearly irrelevant. Of course it was. What was she allowing herself to think?

Because she could come up with no graceful way of declining, she accepted and found herself enjoying a late supper at one of her favourite restaurants.

However, they had barely finished their first course and were waiting for the second to arrive when he became very serious.

'There has been a development in Pitt's case,' he said quietly, leaning a little forward across the table so as to be able to keep his voice very low, and yet be certain she could hear him. 'It seems that the maid, Ryder, who left Dudley Kynaston's house in the middle of the night, has been seen alive and well since then, proving that it was not her body in the gravel pit.'

She heard the urgency in his voice and did not interrupt. It was irrelevant that she knew this much already from Charlotte.

'The second body was not hers either,' he continued. 'It seems unavoidable now to conclude that they were both placed where they would be discovered, in order to draw Pitt's attention to the Kynaston house.' He was watching her closely, judging her reaction.

'And do you know the purpose for this?' she asked, her stomach knotting as she feared he was going to ask her the same question. Her loyalties were torn. She was not certain, but she believed that Somerset Carlisle had done this, and then deliberately raised the matter in Parliament when no one seemed to be taking it seriously enough. It had not required her to draw her own conclusion as to why.

Narraway was staring at her intently.

'Please don't play games with me, Vespasia,' he said softly. 'I am not asking you to betray anyone's confidence, even if it is no more than trust in a long friendship. I think you know who placed the bodies where they were, and why they did so.'

'I can guess,' she admitted. 'But I have very carefully avoided asking.' This was horribly difficult. She would not willingly refuse him anything, but she could not betray a trust — for anyone. 'I . . . I will not ask him, Victor. I think he would tell me the truth, and then I would have to lie to you . . . '

He smiled, as if her answer had genuinely amused him, but there was also a look of pain in his eyes. She had hurt him, and the knowledge of it twisted inside her with a pain she could scarcely believe.

'Vespasia . . . ' He reached across the white tablecloth and put his hand over hers, very gently, but with too much strength for her to pull away. 'Did you really believe I was going to ask you? Please, give me credit for more sensitivity, and for caring for you more than that!'

She looked at him, and was furious with herself for the tightness in her throat, which made speech impossible. She would embarrass both of them.

'I do not know who it was,' he continued. 'But I am certain in my own mind. And such a man would not do so macabre a thing unless he had a profound reason for it. My conclusion is that he did it to force Pitt to investigate Kynaston, because he believes that Kynaston is committing treason against his country. What I do not know is to whom, or why. I do not think it likely to be anything so grubby as mere money. There is something far deeper, far more precious to him than that. Do you agree?'

She felt a tear slide down her cheek, and an overwhelming wave of relief.

'Yes, I agree,' she answered. 'It is very terrible to betray your country. I can hardly imagine

anything worse, except perhaps betraying yourself.'

The waiter arrived with the next course. They
were silent until he was gone.

'Then we have something of a test before we
decide what it is that Dudley Kynaston cares
about even more than his country,' Narraway
said. 'But perhaps not this evening. Thank you
for listening. I very much wished to share my
thoughts with you. You always make things seem
clearer. Would you like some wine?'

Silently she held out her glass. 'A debt that
honour demands he must pay,' she said quietly.

'What debt of honour could he owe greater
than that to his country?' he asked.

'I don't know. We must find out.'

16

Stoker drew in the help of two colleagues to help him rule out several of the places where Kitty Ryder might have been. But he was beginning to feel a flicker of desperation at how few possibilities there were left. Who was she so afraid of that she had run from Shooters Hill at night, and without taking any of her belongings? What had she seen or heard in the Kynaston house?

He had asked so many questions about her, heard so many bits of stories, that he felt as if he knew her. He knew the songs she liked, the jokes that made her laugh, that she loved roasted chestnuts, green apples, flaky pastry, although she wouldn't eat much because she did not want to lose her figure. She liked walking in the rain in the summer but hated it in the winter. She wanted to learn about the stars, and one day, if she ever had a house of her own, she would have a dog. He could imagine liking that too. It reminded him of the dreams he had once had about Mary. It seemed like ages ago, and yet the emotion returned with a sharpness that took him aback. He realised how much he missed the friendship of a woman. There was a tenderness to it that was different from that of men.

Kitty loved the sea, not the beach or the cliffs, but the endless horizon and the great ships that sailed as if they had white wings spread in the wind. If he ever met her he would be able to tell her about some of the voyages he had taken, and the places he'd seen. She loved to watch the sea birds flying at sunset with the light on their wings, and dream about how it would feel. He had never been able to tell Mary, because she hated the sea. To her it meant loneliness, separation, an exclusion of all that she cared about. The sea's endless horizons were full of dreams, and Mary was practical.

Where had Kitty gone to? Was she still alive, or had someone else already found her and . . . ?

He refused to follow that thought.

Where could she go to hide, and yet still be able to see the things she loved? Water, ships. He needed to stop chasing every clue and use his intelligence. From what he knew of her, if she were frightened and lonely, where would she go for comfort, to gather her courage or make a decision?

Somewhere where she could see water, smell the salt tide, watch sea birds in the fading light. Let her dreams take wing also, just for a while.

Greenwich, down by the Royal Naval College? Except that was too close to Shooters Hill. What about the other side of the river, near the railway station, where she could stand on the shore and look across at where the sailing ships were riding at anchor? Somewhere like that. That is where he would go.

He had no better idea. It was close to dusk as he got off the train and walked down towards the river to watch the light die over the water in limpid silvers and greys. One brilliant bar blazed like a banner across the west, reflecting in the ripples of a barge's wake, as if each crest were burning with it. He stood in silence, pleasure touching him, warming him with its untarnished beauty. Nothing could mar it; it was safe beyond the reach of human hands.

He waited until the very last of it faded and his skin was cold. Then he turned and saw a woman a few yards away, her face still towards it as if she could see some essence of it left behind. She was tall, maybe only two or three inches shorter than he, and what he could see of her face in the fast gathering dusk had a beauty that held him from speech. He simply stared at her. She seemed as if she belonged here, in the evening and the wide, darkening sky where the only colour left was an echo of the smouldering sun now slid below the west.

Then she became aware of him and her eyes widened in fear.

'Don't be frightened!' he said quickly, taking a step towards her. Then he realised that only made it worse and he stopped. 'I'm not going to hurt you. I'm only watching the . . . ' He nearly said 'sunset' but it was not the colour that held him, it was the quality of the light, the softness, the gentleness of the shadows. Did that sound ridiculous for a man to say?

She was staring at him. What had he to lose? She was a stranger he would never see again. ' . . . the way the light changes,' he finished. 'The darkness comes so softly . . . '

'Most people don't see that,' she said with surprise. 'They think it's all a kind of . . . dying. Are you an artist?'

354

He wanted to laugh; the idea was so absurd, so far from the truth, but actually it was also beautiful. A wave of longing washed over him. 'No,' he said quietly. 'I wish I were. I'm just a kind of policeman . . . '

The fear was back in her face. He should not have said that.

'Not an ordinary policeman,' he said quickly. 'Just for spies and anarchists, people who want to change the whole country . . . '

'What are you doing down here?' she asked.

'Just taking time for myself,' he said honestly. 'I've been looking for someone for weeks and I haven't found her yet. I'm not giving up, I'm just . . . taking a little . . . peace. Maybe I'll get a new idea where to look.'

'Is she a spy?' she asked curiously.

He laughed very slightly. 'No! She's a witness, I think. But I know she's in danger. I want to protect her.' He should be more honest. The twilight, the shared perception of the beauty of the sky over the river demanded it. 'And I want to know what she saw or heard that made her run. She left everything behind her, all her possessions, her friends, everything.'

She stood without moving, not even to change her balance. 'Then what?'

'Then we'll know much better exactly what the treason is, and be able to stop it going on.'

'What about her? Will you put her in prison, because she didn't tell you?'

'Of course not! We'll make sure she is safe . . . '

'How are you going to do that? Won't they know you've found her? Why would anyone believe her, not them?'

He stared at her. In the delicate, grey half-light her face was beautiful, not just pretty but really beautiful. Her hair looked dark, but not black. In the sunlight it could have been any colour, even auburn. And she was frightened, wanting to believe him but not able to.

'Kitty . . . ' The moment the name was on his lips he felt ridiculous. He was letting this get to him, send his brain soft!

She froze, like an animal ready to run but knowing it was useless. She was caught by a predator far stronger and far swifter than she was. But she would fight, he could see that in her face too.

He let out a sigh. 'I've been looking for you for weeks! We know Kynaston's betraying secrets, but we don't know why! Or how he's doing it. There's no point in just catching him, we need the people he's passing them on to as well.'

She had not said anything — certainly not that she was Kitty Ryder, but he knew it as surely as if she had. It was there in her silence, and her fear. He understood that he should not take a step towards her.

'My name's Davey Stoker. I work for Special Branch. You don't need to run any more. I'll take you somewhere you'll be safe . . . '

'Prison?' She shook her head sharply. Now she was shivering. 'I won't be safe there! The people after me are bigger than you! You don't even know who all of them are!'

'No! Not prison. Why would I put you in prison? You haven't done anything.' He knew exactly what he was going to do. 'I'll take you on the train, now, to my sister's house. She'll look after you. No one else will know, then they can't tell anyone. You won't be locked in. You can run, if you want to . . . '

'Your sister? She in the police as well?'

He smiled. 'No. She's married with four kids. She doesn't really know anything about Special Branch, except that I work there.'

'You haven't got a wife? They'd know to look there?' she asked.

'I haven't got a wife. And I suppose they might. They wouldn't know about Gwen. And it won't be for long.'

'Why would she do that? Take me in?'

'Because I asked her to,' he said simply. 'We're . . . close.'

She stood silent for a moment, then she made the decision. 'I'll come. But I haven't got money for a train . . . not more than a few stops.'

'I have. How about supper first? I'm starving. Do you like fish and chips?'

'Yes . . . but . . . '

He understood. 'It's not on me, it's on Special Branch.' It was a lie, but he knew why she needed to believe it. She was probably hungry too.

She nodded and started to walk very slowly back towards the street. He caught up with her quickly and they walked side by side, close, but not touching, keeping step with each other.

★ ★ ★

357

Gwen did not hesitate to welcome Kitty. She took one look at Stoker's face, and then at the fear and consciousness of obligation in the whole manner of the young woman with him, and opened the door wide.

'Come in,' she said, looking directly at Kitty. 'We'll have a cup of tea, then we'll sort out a room for you. It'll need a bit of juggling around, but it'll work. Don't stand on the doorstep, Davey! Come on inside!'

The warmth of the house wrapped around him immediately and as he watched Kitty's face he saw her smile. Gwen took her up the stairs, calling back instructions to Stoker to put the kettle on.

An hour later, extra beds were made up for children to move in with each other, and told strictly not to sit up all night chattering. Gwen and her husband were sitting talking to each other in the kitchen, and Stoker sat with Kitty in the parlour, although it was chilly because the fire had only just been lit. It was a room used on special occasions, and it felt like it.

It was time for explanations.

'What did you learn that made you leave in the night, without any of your clothes, or even a hairbrush?' Stoker asked quietly, but with no allowance for evasion in his voice.

Kitty took a deep breath, stared down at her hands locked tightly in her lap, and began.

'I worked it out that Mr Kynaston had a mistress. Once you think of it, it in't that hard to see. Just little things, you know?' She looked up quickly, then down again. 'The way he explained where he was going, answering questions nobody asked, but not the ones they did, and you only realise it afterwards.'

'You heard that?' he interrupted.

'Some of it,' she replied. 'Most gentry forget that servants have ears. They get so used to seeing us around, and mostly not speaking, they don't reckon we can put anything together and understand. Or maybe they don't care. If we want to stay in service we aren't going to tell anyone. And it doesn't matter what we think of them. I don't think that's part of anything . . . '

He was puzzled. 'So what did you learn that was so bad?'

'That his mistress was Mrs Kynaston . . . not his wife, but Mrs Kynaston as was the widow of his brother, the one whose picture hangs in the study, and he looks the way he does.'

'Are you sure it wasn't that he was just taking care of her, because of his brother?'

She gave him the sort of glance Gwen did when he said something completely stupid.

'If anybody took it on themselves to 'take care of' me like that, I'd slap 'is face as hard as I could,' she retorted. 'Then I'd kick him as high up as my skirts'd let me.'

'Oh . . . ' For a moment he could not think of anything suitable to say. He felt foolishly embarrassed. 'Did he know you saw, and think you would tell his wife?'

She gave a slight shrug. 'Don't think so. I reckon as she pretty well knew for herself. An' either way, she wouldn't want to think I'd seen. Sometimes you've got to live with things, an' the

359

only way to bear it hurting you so much is to pretend that no one else knows.'

He studied her face in the firelight. He could see that she was frightened. She had told him only what she knew he would almost certainly have worked out for himself. It might be painful, immoral, but it was a common tragedy. Not even poets and dreamers imagined all marriages were happy, or faithful.

'Miss Ryder . . . I need to know,' he insisted. 'Who are you afraid of? Knowing that Mr Kynaston was having an affair with his brother's widow was unfortunate but — as you said before — servants know all kinds of things. Did you say something to him?'

Her eyes widened. 'No! Wot do you think I am? A blackmailer?' She was angry, but she was also hurt.

He could have bitten his tongue. 'No, that's not what I meant! I'm trying to get you to tell me why you ran away. Nothing you've said so far is more than a domestic unhappiness: deep, maybe, but nothing for Special Branch to care about, still less to threaten your life. What is it that makes that matter, Kitty?'

'She were Mr Bennett's wife,' she answered, staring at him almost without blinking. 'But before that, she were someone else's wife . . . in Sweden.'

He blinked. 'Does that matter? Or are you saying she was still married to him? Then her marriage to Bennett would be bigamous. Is there money involved? Did she inherit from Bennett?'

360

She shook her head. 'I don't know. She seems sort of . . . comfortable, but not rich.'

'And Mr Kynaston knew that you'd found that out? How did you find it out anyway?'

'She were staying a day or two with Mrs Rosalind, like she did quite often. I had some cream for her, special made to keep ladies' hands white and soft. I'd made enough for both ladies, an' I took some to her.' She was watching Stoker carefully, her eyes never leaving his face.

'She has this ring she always wears, sort of wide and a bit flat, with stones set in it, but not like usual. Just little stones, and she never takes it off. But she had to for this, 'cos the cream would get in it, maybe even not be good for it.'

'Go on,' he urged.

'I went in to turn the bed down, an' she was sitting there using the cream on her hands. The rings were on the table by the bedside. I moved them in case the bedcover flipped over them and knocked them off. I saw what was inside the special one.'

'What was it?' His mind raced.

''Anders and Ailsa, July 1881 — and forever',' she answered. 'I must have froze, because I looked at the mirror on the dressing table where she was sitting, and I saw her staring back at me. I wanted to say something but my tongue was stuck in my mouth and I felt the room was swaying round me like I was at sea. The look in her eyes, she would have killed me. Then I heard Mr Kynaston coming up the top o' the stairs and along the landing. She changed all of a sudden like butter wouldn't melt in her mouth, and she were all sweet an' gentle with him. I went out past him and down the stairs into the kitchen.'

'How was she next time you saw her?' Stoker asked.

Kitty's face was pale. 'I only saw her once, going across the hall. I heard her tell Mr Kynaston that there was something missing from the room, something valuable. I knew she was going to say as I took it.' She closed her eyes, then opened them again suddenly, staring at him. 'I did something stupid. I couldn't afford to lose my place, or my character either. Nobody's going to take on a maid who steals!' she gulped. 'I stopped and I said to Mrs Kynaston that I'd be happy to come with her and help her look for it. I looked straight at her when I said it, too. If what were written on that ring mattered that much, then let him see it too! She knew exactly what I meant, and she changed her mind. Said to him that she probably hadn't brought it with her, and she was sorry for making a mistake. Then she looked daggers at me, and went on up to bed.'

He admired her courage, if not her sense.

'Did you tell Mr and Mrs Kynaston about the ring?' he asked.

'No. I went to the kitchen and waited till everyone had gone to bed, then I just left.' She hesitated for a moment. 'I went out the back door and just kept walking. It wasn't that far to the pub, and I knew they'd put me up for the night, till I could get as far as Harry's the next day. I knew he'd look after me. But it weren't long before someone came asking questions, and

I couldn't stay. Not fair to him neither, because I didn't want to marry him. I like him well enough, but not that much.'

'And how did the blood and hair get onto the steps from the areaway to the street? And the broken glass?'

She looked down, clearly embarrassed.

'It doesn't make sense,' he said quietly. 'I have to know.'

She raised her eyes. 'I'm not lying! Everything I told you was true.' She swallowed hard. 'Mrs Ailsa came after me into the kitchen. I knew she was 'oping to get me. She had a glass in her hand and she was smiling. I ran for the back door and she came after me. We fought on the steps. It was my hair she pulled out, but her blood . . . Just from her finger where she broke the glass. I didn't hurt her, I swear! I didn't even try — '

'I know,' he said quickly. 'Thank you. I don't know why it matters enough to come after you, but it must have something to do with what we suspect about treason. You stay here with Gwen. Don't tell anybody else about this — in fact don't talk to anyone at all until I tell you it's all right.'

She looked at him. 'What happens if you don't catch them?'

'I will catch them,' he said a little rashly. 'I always catch them. But I'm not alone. There are lots of us. Just stay safe here.' He stood up. 'Gwen'll look after you until I come back again. I may not do that for a little while. I'll be busy, and . . . and you'll be safe if no one knows you are here. Gwen's name's different from mine. No one around'll connect her with me. Please . . . do as I say!'

She nodded, her eyes suddenly filling with tears as she realised that for a little while, at least, she was safe.

He said good night to Gwen and her husband in the kitchen, and thanked her again. Then he went out into the night smiling to himself, his step light, the ground easy under his feet.

★ ★ ★

Pitt telephoned Narraway at home and was told that he had gone to the House of Lords. An hour later he had received a message from Narraway, in answer to his request. They met on the Embankment. It was still only a little past ten in the morning and the March wind had a new softness to it. It was easy to believe that spring would begin in a day or two.

Briefly Pitt told Narraway what Stoker had told him when he had arrived at Keppel Street a minute or two after seven. Narraway listened as they walked, without interrupting.

'Then it seems inescapable that Ailsa Kynaston is the force behind Dudley's betrayal of his country,' Narraway said when Pitt had finished. 'The questions are why, and to whom is he giving the secrets of our naval submarine plans, which possibly cover the whole area of weapons, on which our survival might depend! We need to know a hell of a lot more about her!'

'And Bennett,' Pitt added. 'Perhaps about his

death. It may be irrelevant, but it more likely has something to do with it. And we need to do it very quickly.'

Narraway gave a brief, tight smile. 'I hadn't thought you were telling me simply to satisfy my curiosity. That would have done over dinner, when you had the solution.'

Pitt made no excuses. 'You have connections I don't, people you know who won't trust me yet. I'm going to speak to Sir John Ransom and find out exactly what Kynaston has knowledge of, and see what I can learn from him. I've got to discover where the information is going, and through whom. What a mess!'

'Be careful how you tell Ransom,' Narraway warned. 'He may find it very hard to believe. The whole Kynaston family has been highly respected for several generations.' His face pinched as he said it, imagining the grief, the refusal to accept what would in the end prove to be unavoidable.

'He already has a good idea of it,' Pitt replied, remembering Carlisle's account, and his sadness for a friend betrayed. He turned and smiled at Narraway, a mirthless means of communicating that he had no intention of telling him how he knew. It was not that he did not trust Narraway, but that he did not want to place on him the burden of keeping it from Vespasia. Neither of them yet knew where this was going to lead.

Narraway did not press him.

'I'll let you know immediately,' Pitt added, coming to a stop along the path. The wind off the river was still cool, the bright sun on the water deceptive. 'Tell me if you learn anything new that would help.'

Pitt recalled Kynaston's study and the paintings he had said were of Sweden, several of them clearly attached to memories. He mentioned them, then thanked Narraway and turned to walk back to Westminster Bridge. He was not looking forward to having to tell Ransom what he now knew, but since it was unavoidable, the sooner it was done, the better. This was his job, one of the darkest sides of it.

★   ★   ★

Ransom received him immediately. He was a quiet man, tall and thin with grey hair receding from a high brow.

'I hoped you would not come,' he said, shaking his head a little. They were in his office, a large space, which he had managed to fill with books and papers. They were jammed in together on the shelves that lined three of the walls, and still they spilled over into piles on odd chairs, and even on to the floor. Pitt wondered how much he lost, or if actually he knew what every pile contained. From the steady eyes of the man and his gentle, precise voice, he imagined the latter.

'I hoped so too,' Pitt replied. They were both still standing. Somehow it did not seem the occasion to sit. 'I'm afraid it is now necessary.'

'Kynaston?' Ransom asked. 'Or am I preempting what you have to say?'

'No, you are actually making it easier,' Pitt

said truthfully. 'It is not yet proved, but I can see no alternative explanation for what I know.'

Ransom was pale. 'It appears I was denying what, if I were honest, I had already accepted was true. But I thank you for coming. Are you arresting him?'

Pitt shook his head. 'Not yet. I need proof before I blacken a man's name. I don't need to tell you that you do not allow him access to any further new material. And I need to have you tell the Government of the information he could have passed to our enemies — or even our friends, for that matter.'

Ransom smiled sadly. 'When it comes to weapons of war, it is not always so easy to tell the difference. I have not had such a thing happen since I have been in charge here. Of course I have thought of it — one has to — but somehow the reality hurts more than I had foreseen. I like the man. What in God's name can have made him do it?'

'I don't know yet,' Pitt answered. 'We may never know.'

Ransom looked at him, frowning, his face filled with misery. 'I suppose you find this sort of thing again and again, in your profession. How do you go on trusting anyone? Or don't you?' He stopped, searching to defend his idea in words. 'Do you learn whom to trust? Is there some sense, some formula that you use? How do you know when a man you have liked and believed in for years is actually heart and mind serving someone else, something else, different sorts of ideals and beliefs altogether? Do you then doubt everyone else as well?'

'No,' Pitt answered before he allowed himself to think of it. 'Then you are allowing them to destroy you, as well as themselves. Over time and experience you make enemies, for lots of reasons, but you also make friends. People who will disagree with you openly, but never betray you to another, even when you are wrong.'

Ransom said nothing.

'Actually I like Kynaston too,' Pitt added. 'You might be pleased to know that Kitty Ryder, the maid who disappeared, is alive and well. I would prefer it that you did not make that public, for her safety.'

Ransom sighed and rubbed the heel of his hand over his forehead. 'That's something. Although some poor woman is dead, whoever she is.'

'We'll give her a decent burial,' Pitt promised. 'Both of them. Thank you for your time, sir.'

Ransom shook his hand and Pitt left to begin the next step.

★ ★ ★

Narraway thought long and hard about whom he should approach regarding the death of Bennett Kynaston, and the relationship he had had with his brother. Certain records were easy enough to find: birth, schooling and university. He checked them, but it only confirmed what he already knew. The Kynaston brothers were wealthy, privileged in Society, extremely well educated and both of them well above average intellect.

368

Dudley was slightly the more serious of them: Bennett had the charm and was the one of whom all had expected great success. Nothing suggested tragedy to come.

Nobody was going to be willing to give away secrets. Narraway knew from the beginning that he would have to find someone who owed him a debt the payment of which they could not afford to refuse. Narraway found it distasteful to collect on a debt of help that had been freely given. Yet the only alternative was worse. The choice between good and bad was simple; anyone could make it without a moment's hesitation. It was the choice between bad and what might or might not be worse that tested the judgement.

And yet Narraway barely hesitated. He debated with himself all the way to see Pardoe, the man whose debt he was about to call in, but he did not digress from the path. A long time ago he and Pardoe had been in the army together. Pardoe had made a bad error. It was an honest mistake, but it would have looked like cowardice, and that would have ruined not only his army career, which he had not cared about so much, but his social career as well. 'Coward' was a word that closed all doors irrevocably. Narraway had covered for him, at some risk to himself, although in the end he had not suffered any consequences. But since he had put himself at risk, the debt existed.

He went to the offices in Whitehall where Pardoe worked and left him a brief, sealed message. Two hours later he and Pardoe sat down to dinner at Narraway's club.

Narraway approached the subject immediately. There was too little time to waste, and to begin with pleasantries would be almost insulting.

'I need a little help from you,' Narraway began. 'I wouldn't ask if it were not of the utmost importance.'

'Of course,' Pardoe responded, but already the shadow was across his face. He knew Narraway too well to imagine he was going to be given an alternative. Narraway had never asked anything of him before, and now the debt was due. Pardoe cleared his throat. 'What can I do to help?'

'Tell me about Bennett Kynaston, Ailsa, and Dudley,' Narraway replied.

'What about them?' Pardoe was confused. 'Bennett's been dead for years. I think Dudley looks after her to some extent, for Bennett's sake. He was devoted to him. But I'm sure you know that. It's hardly a secret.'

'Let's start with how Ailsa and Bennett met. Was it through Dudley?'

'Good heavens, no!' Pardoe was clearly surprised. 'It was by chance, in Stafford, I think. Ailsa was over on holiday.'

'Over? From where?'

Pardoe was slightly surprised. 'Sweden. Ailsa is Swedish. I think originally her name was Ilsa, and she changed it to the more Scottish-sounding name. I think she did not wish him to know she was Swedish.'

'Why not?' Narraway was puzzled. 'I thought both Bennett and Dudley loved Sweden?'

'They did, until . . . ' Pardoe was obviously embarrassed.

Narraway could not afford to ignore anything. 'Until what, Pardoe? I haven't time for delicate answers.'

Pardoe clenched his jaw and there was a small muscle beating in his temple. He looked wretched.

'Look, Narraway, this is all a long time ago, and a private tragedy. It happened when Bennett was on a trip to Sweden, and it can't have anything to do with whatever you're looking for. It wasn't his fault. It could happen to anybody. You of all people should know that!'

Narraway was surprised. 'I should! Why?'

'You've sown a few wild oats, and certainly used your charm to extricate yourself a few times.' There was an edge of bitterness in Pardoe's voice.

'Pardoe!' Narraway said sharply. He hated having to do this, but he was too good at it to find it difficult. 'Stop mincing around and tell me the story.'

Pardoe gave in. The weight of his obligation was something he could never have denied. He might have told any other man to go to hell, but not Narraway. Their relationship was old and deep, going back to their time together in the army in India.

'Bennett was very charming,' Pardoe said quietly. 'It was perfectly natural, not an act or something he turned on and off. He went for a long break, several months, to Sweden. He stayed with a family called Halversen. They all got along well, except that their younger daughter, Ingrid, was about fifteen. Lovely young girl, but a bit of a dreamer, very intense. I dare say we all are, at that age.' His face grew tighter, the muscles in his back strained.

'Go on,' Narraway prompted.

Pardoe resumed reluctantly. 'Ingrid fell in love with Bennett, and wrote him love letters that she never sent. He had no idea. When he finally found out, he was horrified. He had no intention of having anything but the occasional friendly conversation with a girl that age. He was about thirty at the time. Perhaps he wasn't as gentle as he could have been, or maybe he was! Regardless, the result was that she felt rejected, humiliated, even deceived. She took her own life, rather dramatically. Drowned in a stream near the house, but it was definitely suicide. The family blamed Bennett and read her letters to mean that he had seduced and deflowered her, and she died of misery and shame.'

'What a wretched tragedy,' Narraway said quietly, trying to imagine the pain of it, the misunderstanding, the hysteria of youth. 'Is that why Bennett couldn't go back to Sweden?' He was disappointed. It didn't seem to be relevant to Dudley's treason, but he could not tell Pardoe that.

'Good God, no!' Pardoe gave a grating laugh. 'The . . . family regarded him as a rapist and had him charged. The whole town was up in arms and he was arrested pretty much for his own safety. The father was a man of some influence. Gradually he prevailed on the local authorities to make the charge stick, and bring Bennett to trial. He was painted as an arrogant foreigner who went around seducing young girls too decent and too innocent not to be taken in. Abuse of hospitality is one of the most morally repellent of crimes in a lot of cultures. It's a betrayal of all that's basically good. It's practically a denial of God to some people — '

'I know that!' Narraway cut across him. 'What happened? Bennett died in England, didn't he?'

'Yes . . . yes. When Dudley heard of it he was frantic. He went to Sweden to do anything and everything he could to rescue the brother he adored.'

'And succeeded?'

'Yes. But at some cost. It turned into a very ugly battle, and Dudley finally found the help of a man called Harold Sundstrom, who had a great deal of influence. He used all his power to get Bennett out on bail, and then to escape out of the country altogether, and home to England. From England he persuaded the Swedish authorities to let the matter drop. He pointed out how much better it would be for the family's reputation, especially that of poor Ingrid. He paid the local coroner, or whatever they're called in Sweden, to say the death was accidental, and let the girl be buried in peace, without the stain of suicide, whatever the cause, or of having been virtually raped.'

'I see,' Narraway responded. What he saw was that Dudley Kynaston had saved the reputation, and possibly the life, of the brother he loved, and incurred a debt towards Harold Sundstrom that he would never be able to pay for the rest of his life — except by instalments of treason, an inch at a time.

Pardoe said nothing, but the answering emotion was in his face.

17

Early next morning, Pitt was sitting in his own kitchen with a cup of hot tea and fresh toast, butter and marmalade. With him were Stoker, Narraway, Vespasia, and of course Charlotte. Minnie Maude was busy making more toast, holding the slices of bread on the toasting fork as close as she could to the open door of the stove where the coals were hottest.

Narraway had already told them what he had learned about Ingrid's death and the accusation against Bennett Kynaston, and how Dudley gained such a debt of honour by having Harold Sundstrom rescue him, possibly from death.

'And Ailsa was his daughter-in-law, Anders Sundstrom's wife, and then widow?' Charlotte said as it became clear to her. 'So she is collecting Harold's debt from Dudley?' She frowned. 'Is Harold dead?'

'No,' Narraway replied. 'I've been up half the night checking various details with people I know. Harold Sundstrom is quite an important man. He was certainly alive and well a few days ago. He has a position in naval research . . . ' He let that last sentence hang in the air, its implication clear.

Pitt sat silent for a few minutes, turning over the pieces in his mind. 'And Ailsa manipulated her dead husband's brother into betraying his own country because she is a loyal Swede?' he asked thoughtfully. 'Or to help her first husband's father? That seems an odd division of loyalties.'

'And a betrayal of Bennett as well,' Charlotte added. 'Rosalind said that Ailsa was still so in love with him that she can't consider marrying anyone else . . . but she is still having a sort of an affair with Edom Talbot.'

Vespasia's eyebrows shot up. 'Edom Talbot? For heaven's sake why? She's a beautiful woman, certainly very striking. She could easily find someone of her own social class. And I think that would matter to her.'

'Perhaps she loves him?' Narraway suggested.

'No . . . she doesn't!' Charlotte said quickly. 'She finds him . . . ' She struggled for a word that was exactly right.

'Distasteful,' Pitt supplied it for her, remembering her description of the scene she had observed.

Stoker looked puzzled, and with some embarrassment Charlotte told him what she had seen reflected in the mirrors.

Instead of disapproval, which Pitt knew she had expected, Stoker's face reflected a degree of admiration. 'So she is still in love with Bennett Kynaston, her late husband, she is daughter-in-law of this Swedish chap in their naval department, and is using Edom Talbot, who is close to our Prime Minister, and sometimes to Dudley Kynaston, who is giving away our naval secrets to the Swedes,' he observed with incredulity. 'It doesn't make sense. Especially added to the fact that she was the one who was trying to hunt down Kitty Ryder. We've missed something.'

'Rather a lot,' Narraway said bleakly.

'Did Ailsa know anything about Bennett and Ingrid's death?' Vespasia asked.

'She had to,' Pitt replied. 'It was her father-in-law at the time who rescued him, at some considerable labour and cost to himself.'

Vespasia looked at him, her brow puckered in thought. 'What was Ailsa's surname before she married Anders Sundstrom?'

Narraway pushed his chair back and stood up. 'I shall find out. She is still a Swedish national, living here in Britain. It will be a matter of record. May I use your telephone, Pitt?'

'Of course,' Pitt replied quickly. 'It's in the hall.'

Narraway nodded and went out immediately. They heard his footsteps along the linoleum in the passage.

No one spoke until he returned. Minnie Maude silently made another piece of toast and refilled the teapot with boiling water, the patter of Uffie's claws on the floor behind her the only sound.

When Narraway returned, the tension in his body and the look in his face gave him away.

'Revenge,' he said simply. 'Ingrid Halvarsen was her sister. She probably married Bennett Kynaston for the purpose of revenge, only before she could ruin him he died of what seems to have been natural causes. She carried her vengeance on to Dudley. After all, he was the one who rescued Bennett from what she saw as justice the first time.'

No one argued, in fact no one said anything. It all made perfect sense now.

Charlotte was the first to speak. 'So she wanted to have an exquisite revenge, the disgrace as well as the ruin,' she said slowly. 'I suppose she meant to get Dudley in beyond any way of extricating himself, and then she would have exposed him?'

'Would have?' Vespasia said quickly. 'Surely she still will do?'

'We must prevent that!' Pitt responded. 'It would do immeasurable damage to us. We would lose all respect, or credibility. Even our own navy would have no belief in us. Our allies, enemies — '

'We understand,' Narraway cut him off. 'She is having an affair with Talbot, but does not like him. Therefore she has another reason for it. Does it have anything to do with the information going from Kynaston to Sundstrom?'

'What do we know about Talbot?' Pitt asked, speaking to himself as much as anyone else. He tried to put his personal dislike of the man out of his mind; his feelings were irrelevant, as was the fact that Talbot disliked him. He was surprised that it was Vespasia who answered.

'An ambitious man, who desires to belong to Society, which will always see him as an outsider. Unfortunately he has allowed it to make him bitter . . . '

Stoker looked at her quickly, but was too aware of his own status to make any remark. Pitt knew he was seeing her as someone exquisitely privileged who had never known exclusion from anything, let alone Society itself.

She caught his glance. 'I am not approving of it, Mr Stoker, merely observing it as possibly relevant to Mr Talbot's behaviour. It may not be something you have thought of, but most women understand Society's exclusions. Some of us even wish to have a vote as to which Government we live under, but that possibility does not seem to lie in the near future, regardless of our means, or intelligence.'

She had spoken quite gently, but Stoker blushed scarlet. Clearly he had never given the matter any thought; it was simply a part of life, and had always been so. He lifted his chin a little higher and swallowed hard.

'I'm sorry,' he said, looking directly at her. 'You are right. I never thought of that.'

She smiled back at him. 'At least since the Married Women's Property Act, I may own my own clothes.'

He stared at her in amazement.

She gave a wry, slight laugh. 'You are too young to remember. I mention it only to persuade you that I do understand the anger at what one perceives to be totally unfair. I have some sympathy with Mr Talbot. He is probably more intelligent and more able than many who will always be his superiors, not because of ability, or honour, but the circumstances of birth. The tragedy is that he may have allowed that resentment to rob him of the positions within his reach. No matter how understandable it is, anger is still a poison, albeit one that works

379

slowly, eating away at the judgement, at mercy and eventually at life.' She suddenly became aware that everyone was looking at her, and coloured very faintly.

Pitt was the first to speak, in order to fill in the silence. He saw Vespasia in a new light, perhaps more vulnerable than she had ever allowed herself to appear before. He had taken it for granted that all doors were open to her. Now that he considered it, clearly they were not. She was well-born and wealthy, perhaps. More importantly, she was still truly beautiful even now; but she was still a woman. His admiration for her, even love, had allowed him to forget that. But it would be tactless to say so now.

'Then it seems extremely likely that Talbot is the one also seeking a kind of revenge by selling the secrets of the establishment that has denied him, on a prejudice he finds intolerable,' he observed.

Charlotte drew in her breath as if to speak, then let it out again in silence.

'Do you disagree?' Pitt asked.

They all looked at her, waiting.

Now she had no choice. 'I agree that it is almost certainly Talbot,' she answered. 'But I think revenge could have waited, and it will satisfy him little. To succeed would have been far better. I think his more urgent motive may have been money.'

'Money?' Narraway repeated. 'Do you know something of his affairs?'

She smiled at him. 'I've seen how he dresses,

and I know what such suits cost Thomas. And shirts! Talbot has gold cuff links. I've noticed several different pairs. And shoes. And I've seen where he dines. I could feed my family for a week on the cost of one of his cigars. And I dare say some of the nice little trinkets that Ailsa wears were gifts from him. Whatever other arrangements lie between them, he desires her physically, and to court a woman like her, one needs to give gifts, flowers, to ride in carriages, dine at the nicest and most fashionable places. Possibly he has to compete with Dudley Kynaston, who has wealth, position and considerable good looks. He is also charming, and socially at ease. In fact his only disadvantage is that he is already married. And, since she does not love him — in fact she hates him — that is no disadvantage at all to her.'

Stoker stared at her, then at Pitt, then lowered his eyes.

'I think you are perfectly right,' Vespasia agreed. 'The question is, what are we going to do about it? And I believe we may not have an unlimited amount of time in which to decide.'

'We need proof, sir.' Stoker looked at Pitt. 'If he did it for revenge, I don't know what proof there would be of that. But if Mrs Pitt is right, and it was at least partly for money, then there will be proof. Once you know what you're looking for, there are always tracks of money changing hands, especially if it comes from another country. And if he's spent anything above what he earns, we can find it.'

'He implied he'd inherited money.' Pitt

recalled conversations with Talbot in Downing Street.

'We can check that too, sir,' Stoker said quickly. 'I'll do it straight away, if you wish.'

'Yes,' Pitt agreed, looking around the table, first to Narraway, then to Vespasia. A flicker of amusement crossed his mind that she held no office at all, official or otherwise, and yet he quite naturally sought her opinion, even in front of Narraway, who was his most trusted adviser.

He thought he saw an answering flash in her silver-grey eyes, but it was so quick he was not sure.

Narraway nodded and stood up. 'I will look more closely at Ailsa Kynaston and her past, and other possible connections, consulting the friend I spoke to earlier. Pitt, I don't doubt you will follow up on Dudley Kynaston and his associates, on the small possibility that we are wrong. Mr Stoker . . . '

'Yes, sir?'

'I would rather you did not give us details, but I trust you have Miss Ryder somewhere very safe indeed?'

Stoker blushed. 'Yes, sir!'

'And her statement in writing, and signed?'

'Yes, sir.'

'Witnessed?'

There was a short hesitation, less than a second. 'Yes, sir.'

Narraway caught it. 'But you are not sure if the witness is . . . unbiased?'

Stoker gulped. 'Yes . . . sir.' He had forgotten how quick Narraway was. He had worked with him for years, but had adapted his thoughts now to working with Pitt. Already Narraway belonged to the past.

Pitt felt vaguely uncomfortable for it, but there was no time to indulge emotions. Stoker had hesitated because no doubt the witness was one of his own family, his sister or her husband. He found himself smiling, but at how much care Stoker had taken, and at his rigid honesty, not any lapse of judgement.

Narraway must have seen Pitt's face, because he did not pursue it. They parted company, each to set about their own task.

★　★　★

Vespasia arrived home with her mind in turmoil. This complete lack of emotional discipline was ridiculous. She was not eighteen, or anywhere near it. She could do a great deal better. As soon as she was through the door into the hallway where the long window at the top of the stairs shed sunlight like a pathway upward, she was met by her maid.

'M'lady, Mr Carlisle called to see you. He seemed to feel it was urgent.' She took a breath, uncertainty in her eyes. 'I told him I didn't know when you'd be back. It could be hours, or even all day, but he was determined to wait. So I asked him to make himself comfortable in the sitting room. I hope I didn't overstep myself . . . '

Vespasia glanced at the long-case clock to her right. 'You did exactly the right thing, thank you,' she said. 'It is rather too early for tea;

perhaps he would like something else. If so I shall ring for you. Otherwise I would prefer not to be disturbed.'

'Yes, m'lady.' Relieved not to have been told she was mistaken, she hurried away.

Vespasia went into the sitting room, her mind racing as to what she should say to Carlisle.

Carlisle stood up. He was immaculately dressed as usual, but he looked anxious, even distressed, and as if he had not slept.

'I apologise for troubling you,' he began, 'especially at this hour in the morning, but I think the matter is urgent.'

'Then you are probably right,' she agreed, reasserting the composure for which she was so much respected, sometimes even held in awe. 'In all the years we have known each other, I have not seen you panic.' She sat down, so that he might also. 'What has happened?'

His quirky face still held its usual humour, but also a shadow of pain.

'I have had time to think very hard about what I have done in my outrage at Kynaston's treason,' he replied. 'And I realise that part of my reaction was fear. We have not so very long to go before the turn of the century. Much will change. The Queen is old and, I believe, very tired.' His own voice sounded weary as he said it. 'She has been alone for too many years. Because it has been so long in coming, I think the new reign will be very different.'

She did not interrupt him. She had had these thoughts herself.

'Powers are shifting,' he went on. 'I see

shadows in many directions. Perhaps it is just they that are frightening me, but I don't think so. We cannot afford treason now. The world political situation is growing more tense. Nevertheless, I acted . . . ' he looked for the right word, ' . . . I acted without foreseeing some of the results of what I was doing, or how they might affect others. Pitt did not charge me, and he easily could have.' He looked very directly at her, his eyes deeply troubled. 'I owe him a debt that I need to repay.'

She wished very much to help him, but there were bounds she could not cross. 'If you are looking for information, my dear, I cannot help you,' she told him. Her voice was gentle, but there was steel in it. She could not allow him to think that she would relent.

Humour flickered across his face and vanished. 'If you did, I would hate it more than you can imagine,' he replied. 'You are a fixed part in a constantly eroding universe. We have to have a Pole Star, one true north.'

She blinked rapidly to hide the tears that sprang suddenly to her eyes. 'That is quite the oddest compliment I have ever received,' she said a little huskily. 'But unquestionably one of the best. What is it that I can help you with, if not information?'

'Tell me of something I can do to help?' he replied.

'What could you do that they are not already doing?' She was puzzled. Did he have something in mind, or was he searching as discreetly as it seemed?

'Many things,' he said with a gesture of his hands as if to encompass a vast space. 'I am not restricted by the law. I know it quite well, but there are areas of it for which I have little regard. And if I can take risks when it suits me, I can make it suit me now.'

She looked at his face, the desperation in his eyes, and believed him. 'Please do not steal any more corpses and put them in dramatic and important places,' she said wryly. 'There are other ways of attracting people's attention.'

He gave a very little smile. 'You must admit, there are very few that work as well!'

'I do admit it, but I doubt any judge would dare to, whatever he actually thought. Not many of them have a lively sense of the absurd. How could they? But regardless of that,' she continued before he could answer. 'It will not work again for some time!'

'Please?' he begged. 'Something . . . '

What could she tell him, without breaking Pitt's trust?

Carlisle leaned forward a little in his chair, his face grave. 'Kynaston is selling our country's secrets to the Swedes, and God knows to whom they will then sell them on. Lady Vespasia, it matters too much to indulge in emotional self-protection. I don't know why he is doing it! But I do know he is, and I imagine his sister-in-law is involved, and possibly that rather rough lover of hers, Talbot. Although I have no idea whose side he is on. Possibly his banker's. And I apologise if I malign the man.'

'Do you think so?' she asked quickly. 'That he

lives beyond his means? A judgement, not merely an impression.'

He looked at her very steadily, unblinking. 'Would you like to know? More than just out of . . . curiosity?'

She knew what he was asking. She hesitated only an instant. It was like jumping off a cliff into an ice-cold sea, far below you. If you hesitated, actually looked down, you would never do it.

'Yes. I think I might like to know that very much,' she replied. 'I do mean know, not suppose. I suppose it already.'

He leaned forward and kissed her gently on the cheek. It was a touch of the lips, an impression of warmth, no more. Then he stood up and left. She heard his voice saying goodbye to the maid in the hallway, and thanking her for allowing him to wait for Vespasia, then the sound of the front door closing.

She sat quite still for half an hour. She watched it on the mantel clock. Then she rose and went to the telephone to call Pitt. She did not panic until she found that she could not reach him.

What danger had she pushed Carlisle into? This was not some game, it was treason. If not yet murder, it could be any day. They hanged people for murder, piracy — and treason. If he were guilty then Talbot had nothing to lose by killing him.

She must steady herself. She had prompted Carlisle to go after proof of Talbot's involvement. It was her responsibility to take care of him now. If she could not reach Pitt, then she must call

Narraway. What he thought of her was irrelevant, however much it might hurt. And it would. Now, when she might be about to lose it, she realised his good opinion of her mattered more than that of anyone else, and in a different kind of way. She understood with an amazing degree of pain that she loved him.

One did not fall in love at her age. It was undignified and absurd! And yet it was also as real as the passions of youth, and deeper. There was all the past hunger and laughter and experience to add to it, and experience of pain, and the infinite sweetness of life.

She picked up the telephone and asked for Narraway's number, her hands shaking. It seemed like minutes before she heard his voice at the other end, but it was actually barely a few seconds.

She began immediately. 'Victor, when I arrived home I found Somerset Carlisle waiting for me, in a state of some distress . . . '

'What has happened?' he interrupted. 'Are you all right?'

She sounded panicky. She must control it. 'Yes, thank you, I am perfectly all right. It is not myself I am concerned for. Please listen to me.' She could not allow him to think of her comfort now, and then find it impossible to tell him about Carlisle's danger.

'His distress was regarding his actions with the corpses, and the general . . . horror of it all,' she continued more levelly. 'He cares desperately about the treason. He sees a darkness coming, more than just a change. He is afraid for the future for all of us. The turn of the century will bring much that is new, shifts of power in Europe . . . ' Her voice was rising and beginning to sound panicky again.

She took a breath and resumed, more calmly. 'He is afraid that time is short to stop Kynaston, and that if we delay he may escape, or whoever he is giving the secrets to may find other ways to continue. They are selling our secrets to the Swedes, who could then sell them on to . . . anyone — '

'I know that, my dear,' Narraway cut across her. 'Time is very short. But if we do not find proof of Talbot's involvement, there is nothing we can do. And to arrest Kynaston and not Talbot, if he is our go-between, is only half a result . . . '

'Victor! Please . . . Carlisle seems to know that Talbot is involved. It all fits together too well for him not to. He has gone to try to find proof that Talbot has money he has not earned. He is continuously living beyond his means . . . '

'Gone where?' Narraway said with surprising calm; there was barely an edge to his voice.

'I don't know. I imagine to Talbot's house, or wherever he might hope to find proof of his income . . . '

'Have you told Pitt?'

'I can't reach him. He doesn't answer his telephone.'

'You said Carlisle has gone to find proof of Talbot being paid fairly large sums of money that he can't account for?' he repeated carefully.

'Yes.' She sounded steadier. 'He knew Talbot

was involved. I told him nothing.' She hesitated. She must explain before he asked. It was acutely painful that she had behaved with such little discretion, even more so since she knew she might well do so again. Her pity for Carlisle, and her understanding of exactly what he felt, were too powerful to ignore.

'Vespasia?' Narraway prompted urgently.

'Yes. I . . . Carlisle felt a terrible guilt over the way in which he drew Pitt into the investigation. He wants to redeem that debt, regardless of the cost to himself.'

'We'll deal with that later,' he told her. 'Right now we must consider where he may have gone. As you fear, if he is caught by Talbot himself, he will suffer nothing as simple as being arrested in the act of burglary. And worse than that, Talbot will know that we are after him. At best he will disappear, possibly to Sweden where we will not be able to reach him, and taking with him whatever else he knows. At worst, he may kill Carlisle . . . '

Vespasia felt herself freeze inside. She could have stopped him. She should have, however much it hurt or seemed a rebuff.

Narraway was silent on the other end of the telephone line.

She seemed to wait for ages. The ticking of the long-case clock was counting into eternity.

'There's less likely to be anything damning in the house,' Narraway said at last. 'Far more likely to be in his bank. I wonder if Carlisle will have thought of that.'

'But we can't gain access to anything in his

bank,' she said reluctantly. 'I don't even know if Thomas could . . . ?'

'Not easily,' he replied. 'Probably not at all, unless he thought of a really imaginative lie . . . but then that seems to be what Carlisle is rather gifted at.' There was a slight trace of amusement in his voice, not just anger. 'We must find out where Talbot banks. That may take a little while, but it will have for Carlisle as well. Please stay — '

She cut across him, something she would never ordinarily do. 'Victor, he is a social climber. It is intensely important to him to belong. He will be at the most exclusive bank there is.' She named her own bank.

She heard his sigh of relief. 'Yes, of course he will. Thank you. Do you think Carlisle will have thought of that?'

'Yes.' She had no doubt at all. It was a deep instinctive knowledge Carlisle would share. 'I'll meet you there,' she added.

'No! Vespasia!' His voice was sharp. 'It could be unpleasant . . . '

'I don't doubt it,' she agreed. 'But Carlisle will listen to me more than to you.' And, before he could argue any further, she replaced the earpiece on its hook, cutting the connection.

* * *

Nearly an hour later she and Narraway stood in the manager's office of the most prestigious bank in London — and, of course where she was known and respected. Narraway was not, but because of his previous position as head of Special Branch, and now a member of the House of Lords, he was known by repute.

The manager was an exquisitely dressed, aquiline-faced man in his early sixties. He concealed his nervousness behind a mask of propriety, but Vespasia could see that he was trying desperately to salvage the bank's reputation out of a disaster he could barely comprehend.

'But he was a Member of Parliament!' he said yet again. 'He said it was state business of the utmost importance. A constituent of his was involved in a financial transaction that could start a war, if it were not dealt with immediately. He proved his identity to me, beyond any doubt. And, apart from that, I know him by sight anyway. He banks with us! Has done for years. You must be . . . mistaken, my lady.'

Narraway glanced at the manager, then at Vespasia, but did not interrupt.

'Permit me to guess, Sir William,' she said with a very faint smile. 'Mr Carlisle wished to know if Mr Edom Talbot had received regular and very substantial payments from Sweden over the last year or so.'

His eyebrows shot up.

'Yes! Yes, indeed. He said they were fraudulent and could involve Mr Talbot, and even the Prime Minister himself, in an appalling scandal, if his fears were well-founded. I assured him they were perfectly legitimate, and the funds were all accounted for.'

'But spent,' she said drily.

'Of course.' His face was bleak. 'It was his

money, quite legally obtained. All the paperwork was in order, I assure you. The money was transferred in the usual way . . . '

'From a Mr Harold Sundstrom?' she asked.

Sir William paled. 'Yes, although perhaps I should not disclose that, except that Mr Sundstrom is a reputable gentleman in the Swedish naval establishment. We checked. There was nothing questionable about any part of the transactions. Were it anyone other than a man of Mr Carlisle's position I should have discounted his fear entirely.'

'But you didn't,' Narraway spoke at last. 'Did you show him the proof he asked for?'

'I did not. I merely gave him my word that all the papers were in order, and that the amounts were roughly what he estimated,' Sir William said stiffly. 'He wished to see them, but he accepted my assurance.'

Narraway's face was grim, his jaw tight. 'And you informed Mr Talbot that the enquiry had been made?'

'Of course. I telephoned him at Downing Street. He was extremely distressed. Which made me conclude that he was afraid Mr Carlisle's fears were well-grounded. Mr Talbot has somehow been the victim of an international fraud. I have no idea what it is, but — '

'I have,' Narraway said instantly. 'If you do not wish to have the bank complicit in treason, Sir William, you will keep all these papers in your safe and allow no one else whatever to see or touch them. And I mean anyone! Including Mr Talbot. Special Branch will come for them as soon as they can obtain the appropriate warrants. Do you understand me?'

'Yes, sir, of course I do!' Sir William said stiffly.

Narraway smiled. 'Thank you. The Nation will be obliged to you, although very possibly they will never know it. But I will make it my business to see that the Prime Minister does.' He took Vespasia by the arm. 'Good day, sir.'

Outside on the pavement in the wind and the sun, Vespasia let out a sigh of relief, and turned to Narraway.

He was smiling. 'Thank you,' he said quietly. 'Thank God for Talbot's social aspirations, poor devil.' Then his face shadowed again. 'But I wish Sir William had not told him. I suppose it was inevitable. We had better try Pitt again. Talbot may well run, and I have no means to stop him.' He took her by the arm and began to walk quickly. 'We had better find a telephone.'

She hated to say it, but honesty prevailed. 'You will move faster without me, Victor. Please go . . . Talbot will not only escape, he may take Ailsa with him, and leave Kynaston to take all the blame.'

'Which would be a hell of a mess,' he agreed without slackening his pace at all. 'Or worse than that, he could stop them himself, even kill them if necessary, and emerge as the hero.'

'How on earth could he do that, with the money in his name?' she asked. She had to run a step or two to keep up, although he still had her by the arm and it was more than a trifle undignified.

'Say that it was part of a plan to stop

Kynaston,' he answered.

'What about Ailsa? She doesn't love him!' she protested.

'Then he might very well have to get rid of her too,' he agreed. 'Perhaps that is what he has gone to do, rather than to the bank, whether he now knows we are on to Ailsa. It is only his word against Kynaston's, and it is Kynaston who stole the secrets.'

She was too out of breath to argue, even if she had had something useful to say.

They swung round a corner and, after glancing in both directions, he started across the street, still holding her arm. They had reached the discreet entrance to a gentleman's club, and he stopped abruptly, forcing her to halt.

'They won't let me in,' she told him. 'Don't waste time arguing with them, use the telephone and call Thomas. If you can't get him then try Stoker.'

He hesitated.

'For heaven's sake, Victor, get on with it!' she ordered him.

Without any warning at all he put both arms around her and kissed her firmly on the lips, with intense gentleness, as if he would have made it longer and deeper had time allowed. Then he turned and strode up the steps and in through the door, allowing it to slam after him.

Vespasia stood on the steps, stunned and burning with a sudden and completely over-whelming warmth, her imagination soaring.

He returned ten minutes later, his step light, his face shining with relief.

'You spoke to Thomas?' she said, moving towards him. 'He will go after Talbot?'

'Yes, with Stoker.' He put his hands on her arms, holding her so that she faced him. 'It was very good advice — 'get on with it!'' He repeated his words in exactly the tone that she had used earlier. 'One should have the courage of one's convictions, win or lose. Vespasia, will you marry me?'

She was speechless. They were standing in the middle of the street. It was as unromantic as it was possible to be. And yet she had no doubts at all. They should be thinking of Talbot, and whether he would kill Ailsa or not, of Kynaston's treason and the appalling damage a trial would do. Yet she knew without hesitation that the most important thing in her life was that Narraway loved her, not only as a friend, but in the same intense and passionate way that she loved him.

'Yes, I will,' she replied. 'But quietly, if you please. Not in the middle of the street.'

Such an intense happiness filled his face that two men passing by hesitated and looked at him, then at each other, but Narraway was completely unaware of it.

'I shall live the rest of my life so that you never regret it,' he said earnestly.

'I had not considered the possibility,' she replied with a smile. 'Time is sweet enough not to waste any of it in less than the very best way.' She touched the side of his cheek with her fingers, a tender and intimate gesture. 'Now may we please get out of the public thoroughfare, where we are causing something of a spectacle?'

18

Pitt hung up the telephone and turned to Stoker. He had requested the police to go to both Talbot's house and his office at Downing Street, but it was merely a precaution. He did not think for a moment that he would return to either place. He agreed with Narraway that Talbot would make an attempt to silence Ailsa, the only witness who knew exactly what he had done. Without her he could still twist the truth until he emerged the hero who had discovered Kynaston's treason and deliberately trapped him. Since he had worked so close with the Government, the Prime Minister in particular, there would be many happy to accept that answer. It would be the perfect way to avoid a scandal, which Talbot would know.

Pitt had now just telephoned the Kynastons' home. The butler had told him that Mrs Ailsa Kynaston was on her way to luncheon. He could not say with whom, but it was in a restaurant just across Tower Bridge. Apparently the walkway across the great span from the height of one tower to that of the other was a marvellous experience. Pitt had thanked him.

'Tower Bridge,' he told Stoker. 'Restaurant's just below. We'll get a hansom. Come on!'

'How long ago did she leave?' Stoker asked, following Pitt out on to the street and striding along towards the nearest corner to find a cab.

'Half an hour,' Pitt replied, charging out into the roadway and waving his arms as a hansom approached.

The horse drew to a startled halt, steering the cab sideways.

'Tower Bridge!' Pitt called out as he swung up into the cab. Stoker charged round the other side to climb in beside him. 'Fast as you can!' Pitt shouted. 'Double the fare if you make it in time!'

'Time for what?' the cabby demanded. 'Damn lunatic.'

'To save a woman's life,' Pitt replied. 'Get on with it!'

The cab lurched forward and rapidly picked up speed until they were driving as if their own lives depended on it. They swerved round corners on two wheels and thundered along straight roads, the driver cracking his whip in the air and other traffic scattering before them.

Pitt and Stoker clung on to their seat and by now Stoker had his eyes shut. Pitt lost track of where they were. They avoided the main thoroughfare, very wisely.

Pitt had two main anxieties ahead of all the others, ahead even of being too late to stop Talbot from possibly killing Ailsa. The lesser thing he feared was that they would succeed in getting there on time, and he would owe the driver far more than he could afford to pay. The greater was that he had misjudged the whole affair, and they would arrive to find neither Talbot nor Ailsa anywhere near Tower Bridge.

He sat with hands clenched, not only to keep himself from being hurled from side to side and cracking his head against the interior walls of the cab, but to try to stop his imagination from building in his mind a sense of total humiliation. He had abandoned the rules he had lived by all his life, taken decisions he had no right to. His initial instinct had been right — he was not fit for this job. He had not the wisdom nor the steel in his soul. He was guessing frantically and he was going to let everyone down.

They were now careering along the Embankment. If it were possible to look outside without risking breaking his neck, he might see the magnificent outline of Tower Bridge like twin battlements black against the sky.

Stoker was sitting rigid in his seat, eyes still closed. He would have nightmares about this. It was a pity; he was a good man and deserved better! Pitt wondered idly if Kitty Ryder had lived up to Stoker's vision of her. Everything in Stoker's smile, and his silence on the subject, made him think that perhaps she had. He was pleased. If this turned out to be a complete fiasco, it would not be Stoker's fault. He should escape the blame.

They came to a shuddering halt. Stoker all but fell out on to the pavement. Pitt climbed out more stiffly, straightening up as if he had been cramped for hours instead of less than one.

'There y'are, sir,' the driver said in triumph. He strained his neck up at the towers soaring into the air. 'She's a fine-looking bridge, in't she? Won't see the like o' that nowhere else. That's London, that is.' He gave Pitt a gap-toothed smile of pride. 'That'll be nine shillings and sixpence, sir.'

Expensive. Practically half a constable's weekly pay, and — since he had promised to double it — it was pretty well the whole of it. He fished in his pocket: thirty shillings altogether. He offered the man twenty. 'Thank you,' he said sincerely.

The man looked at the twenty shillings, then heaved a deep sigh. 'Ten'll do it, sir. Enjoyed myself. Old Bessie 'ere in't had a gallop like that in years. Put the fear o' God into some o' them along the way, didn't we, eh?' He grinned.

'Take the twenty,' Pitt said graciously. 'Give Bessie a treat. She's more than earned it!'

'Thank you, sir. I'll do that.' He picked all the shillings out of Pitt's hand and put it into his pocket. 'Good day, sir.' And he urged the horse on in a slow, steady walk.

It took them ten minutes to find the restaurant. It was now very late for luncheon and there were few diners left.

Suddenly Stoker gripped Pitt's arm so hard his fingers bit into the flesh.

Pitt froze, then turned slowly to follow the line of Stoker's gaze. Ailsa Kynaston and Edom Talbot were walking, arm in arm, towards the way out that led towards the steps up to the north tower of the bridge. They were close to each other, as if lovers. She walked with her head up, gracefully, proud of her height. He seemed protective, as though he would guard her, even though he was actually taking her out into the first heavy spots of rain.

Stoker shot a questioning glance at Pitt.

It was too late to back out now. He had made this decision. He must live with it.

Together they followed, at a distance just great enough to make it look like chance, but careful not to lose sight of them.

They were going to walk across the top, the already famous path between the two towers that spanned the entire river, so that they would have one of the most spectacular views in London. Perhaps getting wet was a very small price to pay. Considering the now torrential rain, they might even have the place to themselves.

To themselves! Suddenly the significance of that shot through Pitt as if he had been physically struck. He started to race up the steps two at a time, Stoker behind him. They burst through the doors on to the walkway high above the river. The first drops had now turned into a blinding deluge and they could hardly see it. They could just make out two figures standing near the rail looking over.

They started to run towards them, but slipping in the streaming rain, half blinded by it, hearing nothing but the beat of water and the splashing of their feet.

Talbot was extraordinarily strong. He caught her from behind and threw his weight into lifting her. She went over the edge, hesitated for a moment, struggling, then plunged into the void. In the thunder of the rain they did not even hear her strike the river below, but he knew that within moments the swift and icy current would drown her.

Talbot stared for a moment, then turned to see

Pitt only feet away from him, Stoker almost level with him.

Pitt smiled, or perhaps it was more a baring of the teeth.

Talbot smiled back. 'Terrible accident,' he said a little hoarsely. 'Or perhaps it was suicide. I was pursuing her. Not really my job, more yours, but you seem a little slow.' His voice was raised above the noise, but perfectly steady. 'She was passing secret information on to a foreign power, or maybe you hadn't worked that out yet. Better this way, perhaps? We can't afford a public trial. Make us look like fools. Make our enemies rejoice and our allies despair of us. Do more harm than the information itself.'

'Quite,' Pitt agreed, taking a deep breath to try to stop himself from shaking. 'Treason trials are extremely embarrassing. I always do what I can to avoid them. Trials for murder, on the other hand, are a completely different thing.'

Talbot froze as a terrible realisation struck him.

Pitt smiled again. 'Edom Talbot, I am arresting you on a charge of murdering Ailsa Kynaston. Lover's quarrel, I imagine. That's what it looked like, don't you think, Stoker? Citizen's arrest, of course, but it'll stand. As you say, nobody wants trials for treason. Makes us look incompetent.'

'Definitely, sir,' Stoker agreed. 'Seems the lady rebuffed him. Very hard thing to take, sir, women laughing at you, scorning you like that. Saw it myself. Damn silly place to tell a short-tempered man that you're finished with him.'

Talbot gave him a shrivelling look. Stoker

smiled back at him, as calm as the sun, which was reappearing through the wind-torn clouds.

★ ★ ★

Pitt went back up the river straight to the House of Commons and sent a message inside that he required to speak with Jack Radley immediately, on a matter of state.

He waited twenty minutes before Jack came out of the Chamber into the hall, treading softly in the echoing vault of it. He looked very pale.

'What is it?' he said in hushed silence of murmur and the soft shuffling of feet as others met and parted, or entered the Chamber he had just left. 'What's happened?'

Very briefly Pitt told him.

'I called you out to ask you to accept the position to work with Kynaston — ' he began.

'But you've just said he's guilty of treason!' Jack all but snarled the words.

'Exactly,' Pitt agreed, grasping Jack's arm. He held it so hard Jack pulled back, using all his weight, but it made no difference. 'He has sent real and important information to the Swedes, and thus God knows who else, in order to settle a debt of honour owed by his dead brother. I am going to have him now send them false information to settle his own debt — to us. If you agree, you will work for him, and oversee it . . . '

Jack's eyes widened and he stopped pulling away so completely Pitt had to adjust his balance rather quickly.

'Will you?' Pitt asked.

Jack gripped his hand so hard Pitt winced. 'I will!' he said fiercely. 'You'll never regret it, Thomas!'

'I know,' Pitt answered, returning the grip. 'Now I'd better go and inform Kynaston!'

★ ★ ★

Pitt went to see Dudley Kynaston that evening. He found him alone in his study, sitting beneath the portrait of Bennett. He looked pale but composed.

'I know Ailsa is dead,' he said quietly as Pitt closed the door. 'Did she speak to you?'

'No,' Pitt replied. 'But it wasn't necessary. I know why Talbot killed her. I tried to save her, but I was too late. But probably it is better this way.' He remained standing with Kynaston looking up at him, his face white, eyes hollow.

'You know . . . ' Kynaston said huskily.

'Yes. Probably more than you do,' Pitt replied. 'I know that she was Ingrid's sister and she never forgave Bennett for her death . . . '

Kynaston stood up from the chair. 'It wasn't Bennett's fault, for God's sake! She was infatuated with him! He never gave her . . . Ingrid's sister? Are you . . . sure?'

'Yes, of course I am! And it doesn't matter now what the truth of it was,' Pitt said gently. 'It probably was no more than a tragedy, but Ailsa blamed Bennett for it. She could not accept that the sister she adored was mentally fragile, obsessed with a man who did not love her. It was

Harold Sundstrom who rescued Bennett for you, so you owed him a debt you could never repay: Bennett's debt. I understand that. But it is still treason.'

'I know,' Kynaston admitted quietly. 'I suppose if I had been thinking clearly I would always have known. It began in such a small way! Just a simple question answered. It seemed almost harmless, just interest.'

'And you were in love with Ailsa . . . '

'Infatuated,' Kynaston amended. 'Ingrid was fifteen, you know! God! How could I blame her when I have no more sense myself? Then it was too late . . . I was terrified when they found that body in the gravel pit. I was so afraid it was poor Kitty. I thought they'd killed her to warn me!'

'Kitty is alive and well,' Pitt assured him. It was absurd to feel sorry for him, and yet he did.

'I'm glad. Whatever will happen to Rosalind? She doesn't deserve this either . . . '

Pitt's decision was already complete and he intended to carry it through. Once committed to, it would be impossible to reverse without acute embarrassment to the Government.

'Nothing will happen to her,' he said firmly. 'I have no intention of arresting you. That's not what I've come here for. I know you have been passing secret information to Ailsa, which she then passed on to Edom Talbot, who sold it to Sundstrom, incidentally the father of Ailsa's first husband. Perhaps you don't know that?'

Kynaston stared at him, eyes hollow. He gave a minute shake of his head.

'You are going to go on passing naval

information to Sundstrom,' Pitt continued. 'We will find a way for you to do it. Clearly he will know that Ailsa has died, and that Edom Talbot killed her in a lovers' quarrel. Seems she rejected him, and he couldn't cope with it. He will be tried for murder and found guilty.'

'But . . . ' Kynaston stammered.

Pitt smiled at him. 'Sir John Ransom will give you the information we wish passed on, and you will be given a new contact, now that Ailsa is no longer available. It will come through Jack Radley. I know that he shall accept the position you offered him after all, because I have seen to it.'

'But he's totally loyal!' Kynaston protested. 'He wouldn't — '

'Yes, he will, if instructed to,' Pitt told him. 'I know him very well. He's my brother-in-law, remember. He'll make a very good job of sending all kinds of information to Sundstrom.'

Kynaston blinked. 'You mean misinformation . . . ?'

'Precisely. You have done much damage. You will now do much good. That is how you will repay your debt.'

Kynaston sat back in his chair, tears filling his eyes. 'Thank you,' he said so hoarsely the words were hardly distinguishable. 'Thank you, Pitt.'

Books by Anne Perry
Published by Ulverscroft:

THE ONE THING MORE
A CHRISTMAS VISITOR
A CHRISTMAS GUEST
A CHRISTMAS BEGINNING
A CHRISTMAS GRACE
A CHRISTMAS ODYSSEY
A CHRISTMAS GARLAND
A CHRISTMAS HOMECOMING
A CHRISTMAS HOPE

THE INSPECTOR PITT SERIES:
CALLANDER SQUARE
SILENCE IN HANOVER CLOSE
CARDINGTON CRESCENT
BETHLEHEM ROAD
HIGHGATE RISE
BELGRAVE SQUARE
BEDFORD SQUARE
HALF MOON STREET
LONG SPOON LANE
BUCKINGHAM PALACE GARDENS
BETRAYAL AT LISSON GROVE
DORCHESTER TERRACE
MIDNIGHT AT MARBLE ARCH

THE REAVLEY FAMILY SERIES:
NO GRAVES AS YET
SHOULDER THE SKY
ANGELS IN THE GLOOM

AT SOME DISPUTED BARRICADE
WE SHALL NOT SLEEP

THE WILLIAM MONK SERIES:
A SUDDEN FEARFUL DEATH
THE FACE OF A STRANGER
SINS OF THE WOLF
WHITED SEPULCHRES
THE TWISTED ROOT
DEATH OF A STRANGER
THE SHIFTING TIDE
DARK ASSASSIN
EXECUTION DOCK
ACCEPTABLE LOSS
A SUNLESS SEA